Please return on or before the latest date above.
You can renew online at *www.kent.gov.uk/libs*
or by telephone 08458 247 200

CUSTOMER SERVICE EXCELLENCE

Libraries & Archives

00884\DTP\RN\07.07   LIB 7

Margaret James was born and educated in Hereford, and later at Queen Mary College, London. While working as a library assistant in Oxford she met her husband, a research scientist. Subsequently she went to work for local government but after the birth of her second daughter she decided that she would like to write. As well as novels, she has also written short stories for women's magazines, and at present she and her family live in Berkshire.

A SPECIAL INHERITANCE

A story of three very different women, inextricably bound together by their relationship with one man . . . In 1945, country girl Shirley Bell falls passionately in love with Peter, a German prisoner of war, but then he is repatriated. When Shirley finds she is expecting his child, she is glad to accept an offer of marriage from kind, sensible Gareth . . . Delia Shenstone, Shirley's best friend, becomes a brilliant example of what a determined career woman can achieve in a man's world. But privately Delia has her own share of heartache . . . Growing up in a small Midlands town, Shirley's daughter, Jenny, determines to make a success of her life while seeking out her natural father . . .

MARGARET JAMES

A SPECIAL INHERITANCE

Complete and Unabridged

ULVERSCROFT
Leicester

First published in Great Britain in 1994

First Large Print Edition
published 2004

The moral right of the author has been asserted

British Library CIP Data

James, Margaret, *1949* –
  A special inheritance.—Large print ed.—
  Ulverscroft large print series: family saga
  1. Domestic fiction
  2. Large type books
  I. Title
  823.9′14 [F]

  ISBN 1–84395–189–4

Published by
F. A. Thorpe (Publishing)
Anstey, Leicestershire

Set by Words & Graphics Ltd.
Anstey, Leicestershire
Printed and bound in Great Britain by
T. J. International Ltd., Padstow, Cornwall

Author's Note

Evesbridge is an imaginary town, which has no factual counterpart. Anyone who knows the West Midlands well, however, will have no difficulty in recognising in my Evesbridge some features of the city of Hereford. The town centre of Evesbridge in particular is very similar to Hereford's own.

All the same, Evesbridge is not Hereford, but rather a distillation of several small Midland towns, all remembered from my childhood in that most beautiful part of England.

Cologne, of course, is a real place, but here I have created streets, shops, hotels and factories which are not there and never were. The city is not a centre of the coffee industry and it goes without saying that the firm of Eisenstadt GmbH does not exist, nor is it based on any actual German company.

Prologue

Autumn, 1964.

'Mrs D. Berners, 93 Archway Street, W5.' Handing the letter to her mother, Jenny Hughes left the dining table and went to sit on the comfortable old sofa by the fire. 'It sounds really nice,' she went on. 'It'll be a proper home from home, I bet.'

'Maybe.' Mrs Hughes shrugged. 'I still don't know why you want to go and work for a coffee merchant,' she muttered. 'Goodness, Jenny — you don't even like coffee!'

'Oh, Mum!' Jenny laughed. 'As if that's got anything to do with it. Anyway,' she went on, as if this clinched the matter, 'Delia thinks it's a very good idea.'

'Well, of course. Delia would.' Taking a teaspoonful of sugar, Shirley Hughes stirred it into her after dinner coffee. 'Did Delia find Mrs . . . ?'

'Berners. Mrs Berners.' Yawning, Jenny stretched. She rested her stockinged feet on the warm fender. 'Yes, as it happens, she did.'

'I see.'

Shirley's friend of many years, Delia Shenstone was a successful journalist on a weekly magazine, and Delia was all for Jenny leaving home. Delia was the one who'd told the girl to stay on at the local grammar school, who'd encouraged her to take her A levels — but who had then dissuaded her from going to university.

It was Delia who'd seen this particular job advertisement, and she who had pushed it under Jenny's nose. 'You'd use your languages here,' she'd said, brightly. 'There'll be opportunities for travel, too. You never know, you might end up at head office itself! Cologne's a beautiful city. There's the cathedral, the shops, the art galleries. Plenty of Roman remains too, if you're interested in them.

'That part of Germany is lovely. Just think of all those deep, dark forests, and castles on the Rhine. You can't let this go, Jen. You really can't.'

Her eyes shining, Jenny had agreed that this opportunity was too good to miss. She'd written to Eisenstadt UK at once.

But as soon as Shirley had heard that strange, foreign name, as soon as her daughter had come back from her first interview in London triumphant and full of herself, Shirley had thought, it must be something to do with *him*. Eisenstadt UK, a firm of tea and coffee merchants, was a West German company now established in England. Looking at the headed notepaper, Shirley had seen that Peter Eisenstadt was managing director of the London branch.

Shirley had summoned up her courage and confessed all. She explained to her daughter precisely why she should not go and work for this particular firm.

But, to her mother's great surprise, Jenny was apparently unmoved. The job was hers, she had said, and she was still going to take it.

★ ★ ★

2

The living room clock ticked reassuringly, the curtains were drawn against a dull, rainy evening, and Shirley's old tabby cat dozed peacefully by the fire. Shirley murmured now, as she toyed with her coffee spoon. 'You're curious about Peter, aren't you?'

'Sort of.' Folding her arms behind her head, Jenny continued to toast her toes. 'Yes, I admit I'm curious about Peter. But that's not why I want the job.'

'Isn't it?' Shirley had agonised for a whole, miserable week before finally making her confession. Now, she bit her lower lip. 'Have you considered that your Dad might be hurt? You obviously don't care tuppence about me. But have you thought about how your father might feel?'

'He won't be upset.' Secure in the unbounded confidence of her eighteen years, Jenny smiled. 'Look, Mum. He knows I think of him as my Dad. That he *is* my Dad. As for this other man — well, he might have given me blue eyes and brown hair or whatever, but he's nothing at all to me.'

'Then why are you so anxious to meet him?'

'I'm not anxious to meet him! I'm keen to have this job. Good heavens, Mum, when I first applied I had no idea at all that the managing director was — who you say he is.'

'So why — '

'Listen, Mum, it's not as if I've just discovered all this. I've known about it for years. You and Dad — well, I must have been about twelve when you told me my actual father was a German prisoner of war.' Jenny shrugged. 'It's no big deal. It never was. Your husband's my Dad.'

3

'Oh, Jenny!' Willing the girl to see just how foolish it would be to stir up this hornet's nest, Shirley tried reasoning again. 'Jenny love, don't you understand how silly you're being?'

'*Am* I being silly?'

'Yes! Besides, there are plenty of other jobs! You could — '

'I know, I know.' Coolly, Jenny met her mother's gaze. 'But this opportunity's too good to miss. That's all.'

'So if you see him?' Getting up from her chair, Shirley went to sit beside her daughter. 'Jenny, if you meet him? As you're almost bound to do?'

'He won't know who I am. As far as he's concerned, I shall be a perfectly ordinary English girl. A bilingual secretary, keen to make a career in international business.'

'All the same . . . '

'He never knew you were pregnant. You said so yourself. No one else knows anything about it. So why should there be any difficulty?' Jenny touched her mother's hand. 'Anyway, Mum — it might not even be the same man.'

'I suppose not.'

But now Shirley sat staring into the fire, remembering. In the course of that beautiful golden autumn, she had fallen in love. Deliriously and passionately in love. She had never known anything like it, before or since.

She could recall that time as if it were yesterday. She could see its colours sharp and clear, feel the cold autumnal winds tugging at her hair, and she could hear Peter's voice. In fact, she could remember almost every word he'd said . . .

She rose to her feet and began to collect the dirty china together, to take it through to the kitchen.

'It'll be okay, Mum.' Following her mother out of the living room, Jenny ran hot water into the washing-up bowl. She grinned. 'Don't worry. I shan't rush up to him and shout, 'Daddy!' I shan't have anything to do with him at all.'

Shirley said nothing more. She knew from experience that she would be wasting her breath.

★　★　★

Upstairs in her bedroom, Jenny looked at her letters again. The one from her prospective landlady was warm and friendly. The one from Eisenstadt UK, however, was cool, businesslike and to the point. The paper was expensive, and the name of the firm, together with those of the directors, stood out in bold relief.

Jenny traced the name. Peter Eisenstadt. How did she feel about him? Did she hate him, was she angry with him for leaving her mother, did she resent the fact that he didn't even know of her existence? Or was she simply curious about him? She honestly didn't know.

Again, her fingers traced the name. She was hoping desperately that she would meet him. Talk to him, maybe. Or at least see him, face to face.

Part 1

1945–1960

1

'Well, the Jerries asked for it. They started the bloody war.' Shaking their heads over all the stories of dreadful civilian hardship, of Russian brutality towards their defeated enemies, by June 1945 the farmers and tradesmen of the little Worcestershire town of Evesbridge were getting thoroughly fed up with the endless newspaper reports from our correspondent in Germany. Daily, they grew more calmly philosophical about the sufferings of their vanquished foes.

Now, as more details of the sickening cruelties of the Third Reich became common knowledge, as every cinema newsreel revealed yet further horrors, sympathy for destitute German women and their hungry children became a commodity in very short supply.

A couple of hundred German prisoners of war, all of them convalescent from either wounds or illness, happened to be locked up in Bradleigh Latimer Camp, a former RAF base near the town. Awaiting orders for their repatriation, the authorities didn't really know what to do with them. Most of the men weren't fit enough to undertake any heavy work.

But then, in the July of 1945, it was decided that at least some of them should be sent to work on the land, and local farmers were asked if they could use any help with the harvest.

Henry Bell had foreseen that, in order to get his crops in, he and his family were probably going to have to do without sleep for the rest of the summer. He agreed that he most certainly could do with some extra hands.

'I'll definitely take two of them. Maybe three,' he told the policeman who suggested the scheme to him. 'I'll speak to the wife about it, and let you know.'

'Go on, Harry.' The policeman laughed. 'Take three of 'em. Free forced labour. Can't be bad.'

'Huh.' The farmer scratched his head. 'I'd heard they was all a load of cripples,' he muttered. 'Amputees an' that, only fit for light work. They won't be much use in the fields.'

'They ain't all shot up. Some of 'em's had typhus or something, but they're better now.' The policeman grinned. 'Big strong Huns these are, Harry. They'll have all that baling of yours done in no time. Look, I'll put you down for three.'

'Well, so long as they can put in a good day's work.' The farmer frowned. 'I ain't feedin' Jerries for nothing.'

★ ★ ★

The internment camp was only five miles away from Blackstone Farm, a small mixed holding deep in the rich pastureland of the English Midlands. During the war years the farmer and his family, assisted by a couple of day labourers well past the age for conscription, had kept things going. Just about. Working all the hours of daylight and half those of

10

darkness too, Henry and Agnes Bell and their teenaged daughter Shirley, together with John Tidyman and Mike Deaver, had sown grain and potatoes, preserved a small dairy herd, and even coaxed reasonable returns of carrots, swedes and turnips from the stiff, clay soil.

But Agnes was not looking forward to another harvest, and she lost no time in telling her husband so. 'For goodness' sake, Harry!' she cried, when he brought up the subject, 'for crying out loud, take them! What with Mike's rheumatism and John moanin' and complainin' about his old feet, I dunno how we'll get them spuds in otherwise.'

'Nor do I.' Reflectively, the farmer rubbed his chin. 'You won't mind having Huns about the place?'

'No. You can hire Chinamen for all I care.' Agnes put Henry's dinner in front of him. 'If these chaps can lift 'taters, I don't give a damn what nationality they are.'

So the prisoners arrived the next day, and Henry Bell was pleased to see that at least two of the young men were tall and robust. Strong and broad-shouldered, evidently taken prisoner in the fullness of youth and beauty, these two blond giants were obviously completely recovered from whatever wounds they'd sustained, and would be plenty of use in the harvest fields. But the third German, a slight, pale-faced boy of about nineteen, looked hardly capable of lifting a spade.

Seeing Henry Bell frown, their guard glanced towards this third specimen of Teutonic manhood. 'Will you want the runt?' he asked. 'He's useful for

11

peeling spuds, an' all that. If you don't, I'll take him back.'

'Hang on a minute.' Henry Bell thought about it. He eyed the German boy suspiciously. 'He ain't got TB, has he?'

'Nah, course he ain't. Been checked over all proper, he has — same as the rest of 'em. Don't you worry 'bout none of that.' The guard was growing impatient now. 'Well, then? Do you want 'im, or not?'

The farmer grimaced. 'Oh, leave him here,' he said, at last. 'He can help the wife and Shirley with the cows, and there's all sorts of odd jobs to be done.'

So the runt stayed.

Delivered at six each morning and collected at nine in the evening, the prisoners were worked hard. Hans and Fritz, as the farmer dubbed the two blond men, were set to work in the fields, and soon acquired calloused hands, aching backs and magnificent golden sun tans.

The farmer's daughter, a slim, fair-haired girl of seventeen, had been detailed to deliver their lunch at twelve every day. This was a task which she came to hate. They'd been stiff and formal at first, but the two young men gradually lost their reserve and were soon greeting her with grins and gestures of welcome which embarrassed her a great deal.

'An' what are you smirkin' at?' she enquired one hot Wednesday afternoon, as John Tidyman unscrewed the stopper of the flask containing his midday cider. 'What's so funny, eh?'

'Them two 'andsome Krauts.' The old labourer

12

cackled. 'Fancies you, they does. Eh, Mike?'

'Not half.' Mike Deaver nodded. 'Old Fritz, he'd 'ave you behind them haystacks soon as look at you, give 'im half a chance.'

'Rubbish.' Now uncomfortably aware of Hans' — or was it Fritz's — bare shoulder a few inches away from her own, Shirley unpacked the basket. 'Lunch!' she snapped, to the blond Adonis on her left. 'You stop for half an hour. No more.'

Fritz — or was it Hans, for she really couldn't tell them apart — grinned back at her. 'Bacon today?' he enquired, politely. 'Or cheese?'

'Cheese.' Not in the least impressed by the fact that the man was trying to learn some English, she handed him a packet of sandwiches. She scowled at him. 'A few pickled onions, too.'

'Pickle onion, you say?' Taking the packet, the German sat down. Opening it he smiled, displaying strong, white teeth. 'Very good,' he said, biting into the fresh bread. 'Tell your mother very good indeed.'

Shirley placed the basket on a convenient bale of straw and looked at John Tidyman, who was notionally in charge. 'How's it going?' she asked, narrowing her eyes to stare across the wheat field.

'All right.' John always removed his false teeth in order to eat, and now he leered at her gummily. 'Should be finished by Friday.'

'Good. I'll tell Dad.' Shirley picked up the empty basket. All the way back across the field she could feel four pairs of eyes on her bare legs, and she heard muttering broken by gusts of coarse male laughter. When it came to making crude remarks about women, language differences were evidently

13

no barrier to understanding. Obviously Fritz, Hans, Mike and John were marking her out of ten. Tomorrow, she decided, she'd wear her corduroy breeches out in the fields.

★ ★ ★

The runt didn't look like a German, didn't fit the stereotype at all. Small, slight and dark-haired, his complexion was very pale and his eyes a translucent blue-grey. With his heartshaped face and regular, delicate features, Shirley thought he would have made a pretty girl. Her father evidently thought so too, for he'd christened this third German Daisy.

While feeling distinctly uneasy in the company of Hans and Fritz, Shirley didn't mind their friend at all. 'What's your name?' she asked one morning, as she and the young man cleaned out the milking parlour.

'Peter, Miss Bell.' Straightening up, the boy wiped his hands on his overalls. Reaching for the bottle of disinfectant, he poured some into a bucket and stirred it round.

He was so cool and formal that it was obvious he was an outsider, a foreigner. But, unlike the other soldiers, he didn't behave like a prisoner. When spoken to by Henry Bell, he did not stand to attention and stare straight ahead, nor click his heels and bark out his reply as if it were a curse. Now, passing Shirley the bucket, he met her eyes. 'My name's Peter Eisenstadt,' he said.

'Right.' Shirley smiled at him. 'Well, Peter

Eisenstadt, it's well past eleven. Shall we go and have some coffee?'

Although the young man had never spoken more than a couple of words to her, Shirley knew he understood English. The guard had said so. At the camp, apparently, he acted as interpreter and general go-between. So now, correctly assuming that unless she gave him permission to talk he'd remain mute for ever, Shirley decided that if he spoke her language he could jolly well speak it to her. 'Coffee,' she repeated. 'I know it's dreadful stuff nowadays. But it's hot and reviving, so will you have some?'

'Thank you.' Stiffly, Peter nodded acceptance. 'Thank you, Miss Bell. I will.'

However, despite Shirley's repeated efforts to draw him into conversation, Peter remained reserved. If asked a question, he replied. If Shirley remarked on the weather, he murmured something in response. But he never started a discussion himself, and in the end Shirley gave up. He evidently didn't want to talk to her, and it seemed unkind to force him. Especially as he needed all his energy for his work.

Peter was not strong enough for farm labour. He did not complain, but his cracked and bleeding hands, his weary air and the blue smudges of fatigue under his eyes all told their tale. The other soldiers teased him, making comments in German at which they laughed loudly, but which he ignored. Shirley wished she knew what they were saying.

In the evenings, when the truck came for the men, Fritz and Hans would clamber into the back, chaffing the driver in broken English and repeating

15

the jokes with which John Tidyman had entertained them that day. Three good blokes together, they grinned and guffawed, leading the driver to observe to anyone who would listen that some of these Jerries weren't half bad chaps. Once you got to know them.

But Peter Eisenstadt was a different proposition entirely, wasn't one of the lads at all. 'Come on, Daisy May!' shouted the driver one August evening. 'God, where's the bugger got to now?'

Henry Bell looked round the yard. Seeing Peter appear in the doorway of a barn, he gestured impatiently. 'Yes, you,' he cried. 'Come on! Pick your feet up.'

'Hurry yourself.' Hans — or it might have been Fritz — leaned out of the truck and shouted out something in German, making Peter frown. 'We don't have all the night!'

'I'm coming.' Pointedly addressing the driver only, Peter muttered an apology for being late. Then he hauled himself into the back of the vehicle, sinking wearily on to a pile of old sacks.

'You'll miss your own bloody funeral, you will.' The driver revved the engine. 'Well then, what was you doing? Making eyes at the farmer's daughter?'

'What do you say?' Turning round to stare at Peter, Fritz grinned. 'What is this making eyes?'

'Flirting.' The driver changed gear. 'I wondered if Daisy here's been trying it on with young Shirley.'

'Oh.' Laughing, Fritz slapped his knee. 'Well, Eisenstadt?' he demanded. 'Did you kiss the *Fräulein*?'

'Of course not.' Peter reddened. 'I have too much respect — '

'You mean, you wouldn't know how.' Elbowing the driver in the ribs, Hans bared his fine white teeth. 'Pretty girl, that Shirley Bell,' he said.

'Not half.' The driver nodded agreement. 'Bit of all right, she is.'

'Nice legs.'

'Yeah.' Slowing down to take a bend, the driver grinned back. 'Good pair of pins on her.'

'Nice — how do you say it — chest.'

'What?'

'She has a nice chest.' Unable to put his thoughts into English, Hans described an hourglass shape with his hands. 'Very nice, eh? Good to hug and kiss.'

'Oh . . . yeah.' The driver had known Shirley from babyhood. Now he decided that he did not much care to hear a Hun making even flattering personal remarks about her. 'You lay off young Shirley,' he advised. 'Don't you go gettin' no fancy ideas about her.'

'What do you say?'

'Leave her alone.' Glancing at the German, the driver scowled. 'You lay one finger on Shirley, an' Henry Bell, he'll have your balls for breakfast. Here, Daisy May?'

'Yes?' Peter rubbed his eyes. 'What is it?'

'Explain, will you? Tell this randy sod here to keep his dirty hands off Miss Bell.'

2

August became September, became October. The harvest was over and the ploughing began. By now indispensible to Mr Bell, Hans and Fritz had been given leave to live out of camp and were found lodgings in a nearby village, from which they could walk to the farm.

Soon there was even talk of Hans (whose actual name, it now transpired, was Wolfdietrich Kiesinger) applying for naturalisation, for he had struck up a very good friendship with his young, widowed landlady.

He repainted her kitchen and repaired the guttering on her roof. He dug over her garden and planted her winter greens. 'He'll be puttin' a bun in her oven before long,' muttered Mrs Friar's next door neighbour, in strict confidence to Mrs Bell. 'The carrying on I hears! Laughin' and shriekin' till all hours, they are. Dunno where he gets the energy, believe me.'

Found to be as trustworthy as the other two prisoners, from Monday to Friday Peter was provided with a room at the farmhouse itself. Every morning at half past five, as the raucous jangling of Mrs Bell's ancient alarm clock reverberated through the house, he would get out of bed and into his working clothes. Hacking and coughing, he clumped downstairs to fall gratefully on the large cup of ersatz coffee which Mrs Bell provided for him.

He wasn't at all well. Even the farmer thought so. 'Give old Daisy summat light today,' he told his daughter, as he got up to go out into a damp, chilly morning. 'Get Mike to do all that stacking and lifting for you, eh?'

'Right.' Shirley nodded. 'Stables and byres this morning, is it?'

'There's a good girl.' Henry Bell glanced at Peter, who was rubbing his eyes and whose face was now the colour of wet cement. 'Keep your eye on him, won't you? Poor little bleeder. He don't look to me as if he'll last the winter.'

★ ★ ★

'You know you're not supposed to do things like that!' Walking into the barn where Peter had been told to spend the morning cleaning tack, Shirley was alarmed to see him manhandling a half-hundredweight sack of potatoes across the brick-tiled floor. 'Peter!' she cried. 'Put that down!'

Peter took no notice of her. His back to her, he continued to lug the heavy sack across the barn floor.

'Peter!' Angry now, Shirley strode over to him. Hands on her hips, she glared at him in irritation. 'Peter, didn't you hear what I said?'

'Mrs Bell wants the potatoes.' Doggedly, Peter manoeuvred the sack through the doorway. Seeing how muddy the yard was, he made as if to hoist it on to his shoulder.

Shirley stared at him. So slim and so small, no taller than Shirley herself, he certainly weighed far less than she did. Now she was afraid that, if he tried to lift the sack, he'd collapse. 'Don't pick it up,' she said, quickly. 'Look — Dad wants us to muck out the stables this morning. If you do your back in, you won't be able to help me, will you?'

No reply.

Leaning forward, Shirley grabbed the end corners of the sack. 'Come on,' she said. 'Carry it this way. We'll keep it out of the dirt, then.'

The German did as he was told.

'Thank you, Peter.' Shirley let her ends of the sack go when they were inside the kitchen. 'Push it over there, please. Right into the corner. That's fine.'

The farmhouse kitchen was invitingly warm. A delicious smell of baking tempted them to linger. Looking over towards the range, Shirley saw that one of the big black kettles was just coming up to the boil. 'Would you like a cup of tea?' she asked.

'Excuse me?' Peter had turned and was already on his way back to the barn. 'I'm sorry, Miss Bell. What did you say?'

Shirley smiled at him. 'Would you like some tea?'

Peter looked at her for a moment. But then he nodded. 'Please,' he replied.

'Right. Two teas coming up. You a bit chilly?' she asked, seeing him shiver.

'A little.' He shrugged. 'But the days are much colder now.'

'Yes, they are.' Carefully, Shirley measured precious tea leaves into a pot. 'There's frost at night.'

'In the morning also.' Although his face was solemn, now Peter's blue-grey eyes were amused.

'The trees were white today.'

'Sorry?'

'The trees were covered all with the frost.'

'Yes. So they were. Why don't you sit down?'

'Thank you.' Peter sat. 'The English always like to speak of the weather,' he observed. 'They talk about it all the time. Perhaps they think of nothing else?'

'Don't be silly.' Shirley laughed. Reaching for two cups, she measured milk into each, then poured tea. 'Have your elevenses, then,' she invited. 'Would you like a piece of seed cake?'

'That would be very nice. Thank you.'

Sitting at the kitchen table, Peter flexed his fingers. He rubbed the joints. 'Some rheumatism, I think,' he said, examining the index finger on his right hand. 'I cannot make this one straight.'

'Let's see.' Shirley looked at his hand. 'That's rheumatism right enough,' she agreed. 'Look, I'll find you something to rub on it. Remind me this evening.'

'Thank you. You're very kind.' Peter actually smiled at her now. 'This cake is good. Did you make it?'

'No, my mother does all the baking.'

'But she teaches you, I suppose?'

'Not really.' Shirley grinned. 'I don't do much cooking or housework. I'd rather be outside.'

'For a woman, it's important she knows how to cook.' Peter drank the last of his tea. 'You don't think so?'

'Oh, maybe. I dare say I'll pick it up.' Indifferently, Shirley shrugged. 'Don't you worry about me.'

That was quite the wrong thing to say. Now, Peter reddened. Evidently, he considered himself rebuked.

The door opened. Mrs Bell came in from the yard. Seeing Peter seated at the table, she frowned. 'What are you doin' in here?' she demanded.

'He brought the spuds in. We were having a cup of tea.' Shirley got up. 'Come on, Peter. Time to get back.'

'He can go on his own. He knows the way.' Giving Peter a sour look, Mrs Bell opened the door for him. 'Right then, my lad. On your feet. Shirley, I'd like a few jobs done in here. If you don't mind.'

★ ★ ★

In spite of a strong German accent, Peter's English was very proficient, and Shirley wondered where he'd learned to speak it. At school? At university? Or had he just picked it up in the camp, from the guards?

Somehow, that didn't seem likely. She wondered then if he'd been trained as a spy. If he was one of those secret agents she'd read about in *Picture Post*, who'd been parachuted into England and told to pass himself off as an Englishman. If so, he wouldn't have deceived a five year old. It was no wonder he'd been caught.

After that first proper conversation, Shirley found Peter was rather more willing to talk to her. Winter was approaching and many of their routine chores were now done indoors. As they worked, they chatted. 'You can call me Shirley, if you like,' she said, one chilly afternoon. 'I call you Peter, so it seems only fair.'

'But your father would not like that.' Peter frowned. 'He would think it incorrect.'

'Go on with you.' Shirley grinned. 'He wouldn't mind at all. Try to say it,' she invited. 'Say Shirley.'

'Sch-schurlay?'

'No, that's all wrong. Shir-ley.'

Peter concentrated. 'Schirlee?' he hazarded.

'Near enough.' Shirley nodded her satisfaction. 'I don't suppose I say your name properly, either.'

★ ★ ★

'Did you enjoy being in the army?' she asked him one cold morning, as they sliced roots for the cattle. 'Did you like being a soldier?'

'No, I didn't. In fact, I hated it.' Peter scowled. 'If it hadn't been for this stupid war, I would never have thought of that at all.'

'Wouldn't you?'

'Of course not.' He hacked at a swede. 'I'm not — how do you say it — I'm not at all suited to the army. I'm not strong enough to be a good soldier. Also I hate to fight and kill — I hate to do things like that.'

'If it hadn't been for the war, what would you have done?'

'I was meant to go to the university. My father was wanting me to become a professor of languages there.'

'I see.' Reaching for another root, Shirley glanced up at him. 'Are your parents teachers, then?'

'My mother is. She teaches music. But my father is in trade.'

'What sort of trade?'

'He works for the family firm, in Cologne. Since many years, we Eisenstadts have been in the tea and coffee business.' Peter shrugged. 'The men in my family usually become merchants. If they don't become priests.'

'Priests? Like in the church, you mean?'

'That's right.' Peter tossed a handful of slices into a bucket. 'We're Catholics,' he explained. 'It's natural to want to go into the church. A couple of my cousins are already priests. One of my uncles is a cardinal. You can see, it's not a military background at all.'

'No.' Shirley looked up again. 'Why weren't you a conscientious objector?' she asked.

'A what?'

'A conscientious objector.'

'I don't know what you mean by that.'

'Yes, you do. Look, you needn't have got involved in the fighting at all. You could have driven ambulances, for example. Or worked on the land.'

'Oh, I see.' Peter sighed. 'No, I had to go into the army. Otherwise, I'd have been shot. There was my family to think about, too. If I had refused to serve, the disgrace would have killed my father. He was a hero in the first war, you see. A German patriot, who — '

'A patriot, eh?' Contemptuously, Shirley sniffed. 'So that's what you call it over there.'

'I'm sorry?'

'Patriot.' Shirley grimaced. 'A Nazi, more like. A

Nazi, that's what you are.'

'I'm not a Nazi!' Blue eyes blazing, Peter glared at her so fiercely that Shirley flinched. 'No one in my family is a Nazi! No one at all!'

'Then why are you in a Nazi army?' Recovering, Shirley glared back at him. 'In England, men and women who don't agree with fighting work on farms. In factories. In hospitals — '

'Oh Shirley, this *is* England!' Peter shook his head. 'This is the land of liberty! What does your song say? Mother of the free? Germany's quite different.'

'How's it different?'

'In every way! To conform is — oh, what's the word — one must do this. To resist, well, that takes more courage than I have. But all the same, I never agreed with anything Adolf Hitler said.'

'Then why did you join the army?'

'Because I did not wish to die in a concentration camp.' Now he looked at her, his blue eyes wide. 'Shirley, I do not make excuses. But you must try to understand that I could not decide for myself.'

'Couldn't you?' Shirley threw the last slice of turnip into a bucket. 'Come on,' she said, curtly. 'We've lots to do. There's still the cows to see to, and the sties to clear out.'

Snatching up two buckets, she marched off across the yard. 'Mike?' she shouted. She noticed Mike Deaver, sloping off for a quiet smoke. 'Mike! I want that slicing machine repaired this afternoon. Took us an hour to do the cattle feed this morning. We ain't got the time to spare.' She turned to Peter. 'Come

25

on, you. Shift yourself.'

Obediently, Peter followed her.

★　★　★

That Saturday, all the prisoners were taken on an outing. Packed in army lorries, they were driven into Evesbridge and marched into the local cinema. There, they were obliged to watch a special new film.

Some men were physically sick. Others sat silent and speechless, unable to believe their eyes. Yet more broke down and wept.

Peter himself was extremely upset — and he was prepared. He'd been repeatedly forewarned. Since May the English newspapers had been full of all that, and the guards at the camp had been only too pleased to let him read their well-thumbed copies of the *Daily Express*. They'd given him a rundown of each day's new revelations, and drawn his attention to anything they thought he might have missed. In fact, they had taken a positive pleasure in Peter's distress, and enjoyed rubbing it all in.

Flat, greyish photographs were one thing. Cinematic likenesses fifteen feet high were quite another. Peter thought those moving images, those blurred black and white newsreel pictures, would haunt him forever. Steeled though he'd been, those gaunt, accusing faces would stay with him for the rest of his life.

He tried to talk to Shirley about it, but found her coldly dismissive; sarcastic, even. 'Of course you didn't know,' she sneered. 'I expect some of *your* best friends were Jews.'

'They were!' Peter grabbed Shirley's sleeve. Urgently, he shook her arm. 'When I was in kindergarten, in Cologne, my most special friend was a Jew! He was called Leo Weissmann. Later, we were at school together . . .'

'Were you, now?' Shirley shrugged. 'What happened to him?'

'His father saw what was coming.' Peter let Shirley go. 'He sent Leo and his sister to America, in 1936.'

'What about the rest of the family?'

'I don't know.' Remembering a particularly horrible image from the film, Peter winced. 'They were taken to Poland. They died in a camp, I suppose.'

'Exactly. Because you and others like you let it happen. Look, I don't want to talk about this.'

'Please, Shirley!' Now, Peter looked close to tears. 'You don't understand how it was. When the Jews were first being deported, we didn't think it was right. But there wasn't much we could do about it. We — '

'You could have protested, couldn't you? You could at least have said — '

'My father and some other merchants did ask questions. They were told there was a scheme. All the Jews in Germany were to be resettled in Poland, in special areas set aside for them. They'd be happy there, the authorities said. They'd really prefer to live in the east, among others of their own kind.

'My father didn't believe a word of this. But, to be

27

honest, other people did. Jews as well. In fact, some Jewish families seemed relieved to go. The men had been dismissed from their jobs. Some people had been turned out of their homes. Perhaps they thought things *would* be better in the east. They were allowed to take luggage and other possessions. Sometimes even their furniture.

'Plenty of townspeople thought this was a good thing. 'Germany is for Germans,' they said. 'Let the Jews go to live in special places. All together and out of our way.' You see?'

'I see.' Shirley grimaced. 'How neat and tidy. So what happened to the ones who weren't deported?'

'Those who could afford to emigrate often did.'

'What about those who couldn't get out? Did anyone help them?'

'Yes, of course. My own father did. He found some ways of getting money out of Germany. He got hold of passports for those who wished to leave. Then this became too dangerous, so he and his friends made a new plan.

'They bribed an official at the Gestapo offices. When the police were to come for a certain family, my father and his friends would arrange to take one or two children away. They hid them in our warehouses down by the docks, while false papers were prepared.

'At least sixteen children were saved. They were taken by train to Aachen, or smuggled over the border into Switzerland. Shirley, do you understand what my parents did? They risked their own lives, you know.'

28

'But you kept your head down. *You* joined Hitler's army.'

'You blame me for that?'

'Don't you blame yourself?'

'If I'd tried to get out of army service, I and my parents would have been taken by the Gestapo. If I had been found fit to serve — and I *would* have been, there's no doubt about that — my father and mother would have been taken to a public square and shot.'

'But why?'

'As a warning to any other parents who wanted to keep their sons safe at home.'

'What about you?'

'I would have been sent to a camp. From there I would not have returned. My sisters would have been left alone in a city which was just rubble and ash. Perhaps in my situation you might have done the same.'

Scuffing the floor of the barn with his boot, Peter stared morosely at the sacks of vegetables ready for market. 'I'm not a hero,' he admitted.

'No, you're not,' Shirley agreed.

'But how about you?' Peter looked at her. 'Are you a heroine?'

Shirley thought about it. Now, she supposed he had a point. Threatened with torture and death, would she have dared to defy the government?

'I tell you what,' she said firmly, 'we won't talk about this any more. It's all over and done with. What's the use of going on and on about it?'

'What shall we talk about then?'

'I don't know. You suggest something.'

29

'Music? Books?'

'What?' Shirley laughed. 'I don't know anything about books.'

'In that case — '

'But if you do, talk on. I'll listen.'

So, Peter talked to her. He spoke of English classics, of which she had just about heard, but which she had never thought to read. Her indifference astonished him. 'You must read these books,' he cried. 'Shirley, you must! You have a library? In the town, there is a public library?'

'What? Oh — yes.' Hoiking another sackful of carrots on to the pile already bagged up, and realising that soon she and Peter would have to go out into the cold to open another earthen clamp, Shirley nodded absently. 'Yes, I suppose there is.'

'Then you must use it.'

'Must I?' Shirley counted the sacks yet to be filled. 'Well, perhaps I'll get a ticket.'

★ ★ ★

Shirley had liked school well enough. She'd enjoyed it, even. But, as in the case of all her friends, it had been a foregone conclusion that she would leave at fourteen. By then, she'd have learned all she needed to know, read all the books she had to read, and would work on the farm.

As the days went by, however, she found she was becoming curious about these neglected works of great literature and was increasingly interested by what Peter had to say about them. He knew so much, he made her feel ignorant and stupid.

30

So, filled with a spirit of intellectual enquiry, the following Wednesday she left her father at the cattle market in Evesbridge and took herself off to the country library. There, she looked for some of the titles which Peter had recommended. Not expecting to get anything out of them, she nevertheless lugged the books home.

They were not beyond her. In fact, they weren't obscure at all. Tucked up in bed at night, she found she enjoyed reading. So now, while packing carrots and greens or chopping swedes, Peter and Shirley discussed Jane Austen, argued about George Eliot, and agreed that Thomas Hardy was a bore.

'Trollope?' she repeated, late one afternoon. 'Is that what you said?' She'd never even heard of Trollope.

'Anthony Trollope. *Barchester Towers*.' Peter smiled at her. 'I'm sure you'd enjoy it.'

'I'll get it when I'm next in town.' Ruefully, Shirley smiled back. 'You'll be going home soon,' she said, regretfully. 'I doubt if I'll read anything after you leave.'

'Why do you say that?'

'While you're here, we can talk about it. It all seems worthwhile. But when you've gone . . . '

'But you must read.' Earnestly, Peter looked at her. 'Now you've started, you must carry on. Shirley, education's the key to everything. It's — it's mankind's only hope of salvation.'

'Learning is salvation, eh?' Shirley topped and tailed the last swede. She yawned. 'Well, I dunno about *that*. Didn't do you much good, did it?'

Peter picked up a bucket of turnip chips. 'Don't

31

mock learning,' he said. Dragging the heavy bucket, he left the barn and walked over to the byre, where the cows were waiting for their supper.

★ ★ ★

The runt was earning his keep. The farmer was delighted. Although he was not so strong, Peter worked at least as hard as either of the other two prisoners and Henry Bell was disposed to like the German lad. But the idea that this German might like his daughter never entered the farmer's head.

In common with many fathers of girls, he had hardly noticed that his little Shirley had grown up. He still thought of her as his good little lass, a hard and willing worker who could be trusted to get on with the job in hand. To Mr Bell, it seemed perfectly reasonable that Shirley and Peter should work together unchaperoned, for they co-operated so well.

'Shirley, you're so pretty.' Sitting on the low wall of a pigsty one sunny autumn morning, Peter watched Shirley walk towards him from across the yard. 'So very pretty.'

'What?' Shirley sat down beside him. She began to fold her headscarf. 'Sorry, what did you say?'

'You're pretty.'

'Am I?' Shirley blushed. 'Now, why do you think that?'

'Because it's so.' Now looking her full in the face, Peter's usually solemn features blossomed into a smile. 'You have the most beautiful eyes. Your hair has so many different colours in it that it changes with the light. In the evenings it's quite dark. In cloudy weather, it's like copper. But this morning, it's spun gold.'

'Oh.' Her usual admirers being the young farmers of the area, Shirley was not used to being so poetically commended. Now she was embarrassed. Her blush deepened. 'Come on,' she said, rather too sharply. 'Dad wants the stalls cleaned. Then there's a couple of tons of spuds to bag up.'

Jumping to her feet, she walked towards the byre. Somewhat chastened, Peter followed her inside. 'Don't hate me,' he pleaded, as he reached for a bottle of disinfectant. 'Shirley, please don't hate me!'

'I don't hate you!' Crossly, Shirley sloshed water into a bucket. 'Whatever gave you that idea?'

'When I said you were pretty, you were so annoyed. As if you think a German has no right to tell you such a thing.'

'Don't be silly.' Shirley stirred the disinfectant into the water. 'I didn't mean that at all. In fact . . . I think you're quite nice.'

'*Nice*. The Englishman's favourite word.' Moodily, Peter began to work. 'In England, everything is nice. It's a nice day, you've had a nice breakfast, this is a nice farm. You're a nice girl, and — '

'You're a nice boy!' Laughing now, Shirley put her hand on his sleeve. 'You are! I like you, Peter. Really I do.'

'If that's so . . . ' Hastily, Peter glanced towards the door. 'If that's so, may I kiss you?'

'What?' Taken completely by surprise, Shirley flushed a brilliant scarlet. 'I — '

'A nice boy. But not to kiss.' Bitterly, Peter sighed.

'A dirty Hun, that's what I am. Less than human. Now I suppose you'll go and tell your father I was insolent.'

'No.' Shirley had meant what she said. She liked Peter very much, and now she pitied him, too. 'You can kiss me,' she said, kindly. 'If you'd really like to, you kiss me.'

'It's all right.' Peter scowled. 'I don't want a favour.'

'It's not a favour. I'd *like* you to!'

'Yes?' His face brightening, Peter looked at her. 'Really?'

'Honestly.' Shirley held out her arms to him. 'Peter, come here.'

★   ★   ★

A week went by, then another. The days were much colder now, for autumn was well advanced. October gave way to a bright, crisp November. 'I'm allowed to go out on Sundays now,' Peter told her. 'I'm a — what's the word — a trusty. Shirley, could we go walking together?'

'That's a good idea,' she replied. As there was nobody about, Shirley kissed him. 'Let me think — where shall we go?'

The following Sunday afternoon was cold but sunny. Setting out after dinner, Shirley climbed the hill to the west of the farm, walked along the Ridgeway and met Peter near a stand of oaks on its southern side.

Taking her hands in his, he kissed her. Then, hand in hand, they walked through drifts of fallen beech

34

leaves towards another distant copse.

Halfway towards the copse they reached a barn. Stacked with bales of hay, it was a ruinous place with barely three quarters of a roof. Great ugly gaps pierced its walls, and ivy rampaged through the cracks in the brickwork. A few hundred yards down the path, the tumbledown farm buildings which belonged to the owner of this dilapidated property could be seen through some trees.

'The Draytons' place.' Shirley gave Peter's fingers a squeeze. 'They're ever so religious. They spend all Sunday in Evesbridge, in church. Dad's got no time for them at all. He says that if Mr Drayton stopped praying and started working, if he didn't take all that 'lilies of the field' stuff so literally — '

'Lilies of the field?'

'They toil not, neither do they spin. Oh, never mind. Come and sit down for a moment.' Shirley pulled Peter towards the barn. 'Come on,' she repeated. 'There's nobody here.'

The barn was warm and dry. Half-full of hay, it was a perfect shelter from the cold autumn wind, and in the sunshine a patch of hay had become almost hot to the touch. Shirley and Peter sat down on a bale.

Taking Shirley in his arms, Peter kissed her. For a minute or two, Shirley kissed him back. Then she pulled away, and looked at his face.

How pale he was! White as marble, his skin had no colour at all, except for the blue-grey smudges of fatigue beneath his eyes. Poor thing, she thought, we're working him to death. Poor Peter. Now, she felt such a terrible, heart-wrenching tenderness for him that she could have wept.

'What's the matter?' he asked, seeing her blink and frown.

'Nothing.' Shirley bit her lip hard. 'Peter,' she began, 'listen to me.'

'What is it?'

'You'll be going home soon.'

'I suppose so.' Peter shrugged. 'In fact, the commandant was talking about it yesterday. He told us — '

'You'll see your family again.' Shirley looked into his eyes. 'You'll see your parents, and your sisters. You'll like that, won't you? You've been so homesick here.'

'Yes, I have. Very much.' Peter took Shirley's hand. He played with her fingers. 'You're not at all like a German girl,' he observed. 'Not in the least.'

'They all have two heads, I suppose — and webbed feet.'

'Silly.' Peter laid his head on her shoulder. 'Don't joke,' he said. 'I mean you're — oh, I don't know the word in English — you're comfortable. You're like a feather pillow.'

'I'm fat and squashy, you mean. Thanks very much.'

Peter looked up. 'Don't be cross. I mean that I like you.' He hugged her. 'With you, I feel warm. Comforted.'

'That's good.' Shirley rested her chin on the hollow of his collar bone. Perhaps, although Peter was so thin, he was like a feather pillow too?

In spite of the wind, the day was mild for

November. On this bright blue afternoon, the large patch of sky visible through the barn's broken roof was a brilliant, deep azure. Looking into that wonderful blue, Shirley felt happy, contented and perfectly at peace. She stroked Peter's ear. 'Are you asleep?' she asked.

'No,' he replied. 'Just thinking.'

'What about?'

'It's not so important. You don't need to know. Shirley?'

'Yes?'

'I love you. I love you so much.'

'Do you?' Shirley smiled at him. 'That's nice,' she said. 'Because I love you, too.'

'Good.' He kissed her forehead. 'Are you a virgin?'

'Yes!' Now, Shirley frowned at him. 'Of course I am!'

'So am I.' Peter looked into her eyes. 'Shirley, shall we make love?'

A sudden surge of desire engulfed her. 'Yes,' she replied. 'Let's.'

★　★　★

As she unfastened her suspenders, rolled off her thick lisle stockings and tucked them into her shoes, Shirley knew she was being stupid. It wasn't as if he was forcing her, either. In fact, it was quite the reverse, for now Peter sat there silent, at a loss what to do next.

'Don't be scared.' She smiled at him. 'We're bound to make a mess of it the first time.'

37

'I suppose so.' Peter shrugged. He pulled his shirt from the waistband of his trousers. 'You won't laugh at me?'

'Of course I shan't.'

Shirley unbuttoned her cardigan and pushed it away. She took off her blouse. Releasing her hair from its clips, she shook it free. She stripped off her liberty bodice and vest.

Naked to the waist, she took Peter's hands in hers. 'Touch me,' she whispered. 'Touch me here.'

With goodwill and charity on both sides, with genuine affection as their guide, Peter and Shirley kissed, touched - and eventually lay together in the straw, locked in a lovers' embrace.

'Lovely girl,' said Peter. He held her in his arms. 'Beautiful girl, I do love you!'

'I love you, too.' But now, stroking Peter's thin back, tracing the outlines of his shoulder-blades, Shirley was near to tears. She looked up at the sky. She saw that clouds had scudded over, and the heavens were now a dull grey-blue. She shuddered. What on earth had possessed her? Here she lay, coupling with a German. With a German coward who had openly admitted he'd been too scared to defy the Gestapo. Here she was, literally rolling in the hay with a Hun. Surely, she thought, surely I'm nothing but a whore? In France, girls who'd slept with Germans had been tarred and feathered and had their heads shaved, or worse.

Still lying on her, Peter kissed her again. 'We'll be married,' he promised. 'When I get back to Germany I'll make a home for us, and I'll send for you. Oh, Shirley — will you like to be a *Hausfrau?*'

★ ★ ★

She saw him twice more. He appeared at the farm on Monday morning, and somehow they got through the day. Somehow, Shirley resisted the temptation to creep along to his bedroom that night. On Tuesday, they sneaked off to the Draytons' barn and there, risking discovery by Mr Drayton or one of his sons, they made love with a passion and intensity which left them both in tears.

On Tuesday evening, Peter and the other soldiers were collected by two military policemen in an army jeep. Henry Bell was informed that his three particular Germans were to be sent up to Hull that very night. There was room for them on a ship to Hamburg.

'So that's the end of them.' Standing at the kitchen sink, the farmer washed his hands. 'Well, now our boys are coming home, I'd sooner have them working for me. To be honest, I never really trusted them Jerries.'

It appeared that Hans had jilted Mrs Friar. He'd gone back to the Fatherland without making any promises to see her again. But she'd got her guttering fixed, and her Brussels sprouts were coming on nicely.

'She 'ad a letter from Tom Garbutt last Friday,' remarked Agnes Bell, tartly. 'He's bein' demobbed next week and he's keen to see 'er. Old Tom, he was always sweet on Gilly Friar.' Agnes laughed. 'I

39

reckon that Hans taught her a thing or two, eh? Tom'll be gettin' a warm welcome there.'

★ ★ ★

By the time Shirley noticed that her chest hurt, that she was feeling sick in the mornings and that her period was long overdue, Peter Eisenstadt had been processed and repatriated. He'd travelled with those who had chosen to leave, who were presumably glad to be going home — even to a Germany defeated and starving.

Shirley supposed Peter would be sent to the British sector. Was Cologne in the British sector? That or the American, surely. She tried to find some comfort in that. She tried to understand, too, that he'd had to go. An almost unbearable homesickness pulled him, giving him no peace. *Heimweh*. With tears in his eyes, he'd spoken of that.

He hadn't known she was pregnant. Poor Peter, she thought, it wasn't all his fault. She'd been willing, and encouraged him, after all.

But why didn't he write to her? Why hadn't he been in touch? She needed to know where he was — otherwise, how could she go to him? Or had he written, perhaps, and the letters gone astray?

Sometimes, Shirley was optimistic. Today, she felt, she would certainly hear from him, so she hung around the farmhouse, waiting for the postman to call. The next day, she despaired. Then, one winter morning, she made up her mind. If she did not hear from him today, she would know he was dead. Or at any rate, that he did not mean to contact her again.

So, that morning, she walked to meet the postman as he came up the track. 'Waiting for something special, are you?' he enquired kindly, as he checked through his bag.

'Not really.' Shirley's heart sank. If Peter had written, the postman would know — in fact, he'd have broadcast it all round the village. She could imagine the consternation at the local sub post office. Shirley Bell had received a letter with a German stamp! She'd been in correspondence with a Hun! Shirley wouldn't have put it past the local postmistress to have steamed the letter open — in the interests of national security, of course.

But now, Shirley finally despaired. Hope and anxiety gave way to a dull, wretched resignation. Peter wasn't even going to write, let alone send for her. Telling her mother she didn't feel well, she went back to bed, and cried for the rest of that day.

Afterwards, she gave herself a strict talking to. There was no point in weeping and wailing. She must forget all about Peter Eisenstadt.

If she could.

3

Evesbridge railway station could never have been a pleasant place, even when it was new. Situated in a particularly rundown area of the small cathedral city, it was close to the malodorous canal which carried chemical waste away from a paint-works, and abutted on the south side by an even more offensively foul-smelling tannery.

It had been neglected and unpainted since long before the war. In the spring of 1947, on the bright April day that Delia Shenstone's young eyes first saw it, the sunshine was lighting up even its darkest corners, and drawing the most unflattering attention to the thick overlay of smuts and soot which begrimed its Great Western livery of sickly cream and mud brown.

'Evesbridge! Evesbridge!' shouted a guard. 'Change here for all stations to Cardiff and the Birmingham line. Evesbridge!'

'The door's stuck,' Delia mouthed through the glass, at the indifferent porter who was standing there, staring at her. A vacant smile on his weatherbeaten face, he was evidently mildly entertained by her imitation of a goldfish, opening and closing her mouth soundlessly as she jerked at the leather strap which should have released the window, but wouldn't.

Panicking, assuming the train must be going to leave any second now, she rapped on the glass. But then, as the great engine gave a shudder and exhaled a gush of steam, the porter lunged forward, opened the door and released the prisoner. 'Tricky, them doors,' he remarked. 'Old rolling stock this is, see?'

'Is it?' Delia grimaced. 'Can you help me get my luggage out?' she asked sharply, pointing to three small shabby suitcases and a brown paper carrier bag behind her.

'Ah.' The porter grinned at her, displaying a set of greenish-grey teeth. 'You'll have to get out yourself first, Miss,' he replied.

He held out a grubby hand, which steadied her as she jumped on to the platform, but left a perfect set of black fingerprints on the sleeve of Delia's cream linen jacket. 'Full four minute wait here,' he muttered, as he tugged her luggage out of the compartment. 'For the Shrewsbury connection, see. It's over the footbridge now, Miss.'

On reaching the way out, Delia gave the porter a shilling. He pocketed it without comment. She gathered up her cases and, by now in a rather bad temper, struggled out into the sunlit station forecourt. Wondering if she'd find such a thing as a taxi there, she screwed up her eyes and stared around her. There wasn't a single car in sight. She decided that they probably still used horses and carts in this dozy little town.

★ ★ ★

It was only a month ago that Delia had received the letter offering her the post of library assistant at Evesbridge County Library. That same day, she had

43

also received the two cards which were all that marked her nineteenth birthday. Smiling to herself, she'd pushed the letter into her handbag and sighed happily. This was the best birthday present she could have had.

For now, she was on her way, and although this first stage of her journey was to lead to a badly-paid job in a small provincial city, that didn't much matter. Delia had it all worked out.

When she had applied for this particular job, however, Delia hadn't even known where Evesbridge was. So she'd been obliged to go to the local reference library and pore over the Ordnance Survey, searching for it.

Eventually she'd found it. A small country town smack in the middle of a flat, well-wooded plain, the Malvern Hills rose to the east of it and the Welsh Mountains to the west. She looked in the gazetteer then, and discovered that Evesbridge was famous for its white-faced cattle, its cider and its hops.

Cows and booze. Delia shook her head. A place like that could hardly be the centre of the universe. It certainly wouldn't have the spirit and vitality of her native Birmingham, for there'd be no concert halls or art galleries, and it probably didn't even have a cinema. But still, it would do. It was where she would begin . . .

★ ★ ★

'I'm leaving the factory.' Taking off her grubby turban, Delia picked up her comb and began to tease the day's tangles out of her hair. 'Did you hear me?' she added, more sharply. 'I'm going, I said. My notice expires on Friday.'

'Does it, now?' Aunt Bet, a half-sister of Delia's father and Delia's notional guardian, looked up from her *Daily Mirror*. Comfortable in the warm, untidy living room of her terraced home in the middle of Smethwick, she lit a Woodbine and inhaled. 'Just as well,' she murmured, indifferently. 'When all the men have come back from the Far East and the rest are out of the hospitals, you girls'll all be sacked anyway. So what you goin' to do now?'

'I've got a job in a library. In Evesbridge.'

'Oh?' Aunt Bet poured her niece a cup of tea. 'How did you come by that, then?'

'It was advertised in the *Recorder*.' Delia sat down at the table. 'There was a long list of local authority posts.'

'Local authority posts, eh?' Grinning, Aunt Bet shook her head. 'Well, well. You've gone and got yourself a post, have you? Fancy. So now I suppose all them certificates your Dad insisted on you gettin' will be put to good use?'

'Sorry?' Delia began to drink her tea. 'Oh, yes,' she agreed, absently. 'Maybe they will.'

'Or maybe they won't.' Aunt Bet grinned again. 'We'll see, my lady. We'll see.'

Bet Harris had no great opinion of learning, and little reverence for education, so, as the scholar of the family, Delia had always been the butt of her aunt's admittedly genial ridicule. She had endured the taunts of her cousins for more years than she cared to remember.

There were times when she was on the point of

giving up, of vowing never to read another book again. If she had, Ray, Gerry and Mick might have left her in peace and stopped calling her Lady Muck, and asking why she fancied herself as a know-all.

But four years in a light engineering factory had been more than enough. Delia was sick and tired of being in the company of women who thought of nothing but babies and matrimony. She was bored to tears by tours round troublesome wombs and trips up renegade Fallopian tubes. She didn't want to know that Mrs Delaney had got a nice bit of fish for her Alan's supper. She was tired of hearing that now the war was over, the government ought to do something about all them queues. Shocking it was up the market yesterday.

'You walkin' out with anyone, sort of thing?' Mrs Hobday had enquired only that morning, for what seemed like the millionth time. 'No? Well, don't you fret. Now the men are all comin' home, there'll be a feller among 'em for you.'

Delia had winced. The last thing she wanted was a feller. Men — or at any rate, all the men she knew — got on her nerves and bored her to tears.

Living in a household which consisted of herself, her aunt and three adolescent male cousins, Delia couldn't help but see the less attractive side of the opposite sex. Ray, Gerry and Mick all took a keen interest in girls, and frequently discussed the arts of seduction, usually over a glass of brown ale. Gerry, the eldest, took *his* girls to the pub, bought them port and lemon, and went on from there. By closing time, he expected to have his hand up a girl's skirt.

46

Down Brick Alley, he reckoned — if he was lucky — to get a bit further. Then —

'Where will you live, eh?' Aunt Bet's harsh Birmingham accent broke into Delia's idle reverie. 'I'm saying — '

'I'll find some lodgings, I suppose.' Delia finished doing her hair and looked up at her aunt. 'There must be plenty of people in Evesbridge with a spare room to let.'

'Where is it, this Evesbridge?'

'Near Worcester. Over towards the Welsh border.' Ready to go out again now, Delia drank down the last of her tea. 'A country town it is, right in the middle of nowhere.'

'Oh.' Thinking how much she'd miss Delia's ration coupons, Aunt Bet pursed her lips. 'Wouldn't suit me,' she said decisively. 'I like a bit of life, I do. I like to go round the shops. See a flick.'

'Yes, I know.' Feeling the need to be conciliatory, Delia smiled again. 'Talking of shops, I saw some nice skirts in Freeling's only yesterday.'

'Did you? New in, were they?'

'Yes, I think so.'

'What colours?'

'Black, grey and a sort of dark blue. Quite smart they looked.'

'Oh.' Interested, Aunt Bet nodded. 'I'll get down there,' she said. 'See what I think.'

'You do that.'

'Was you goin' to get one?'

'No. That style does nothing for me. But they'd suit you. You've the right figure for a straight skirt.'

'You want to put a bit of weight on, that's what

you want.' Complacently, Aunt Bet smoothed her jersey over her generous bosom, and stretched out her short, sturdy legs. 'You'll never get a man, else. Fellers worth havin' don't go for skinny girls. Told you that before.'

'Yes, you have. Lots of times.' Getting up from her chair, Delia went through into the kitchen.

★ ★ ★

Aunt Bet wasn't impressed by Delia's ambitions and schemes. She never had been. But although she disliked the airs and graces which Delia gave herself, she had a soft spot for her dead brother's child. She was fond of the orphan who had arrived on her doorstep in the September of 1943, the sole survivor of a firebombing raid which had demolished a row of houses in a posher area of the city, putting paid to Arthur Shenstone and his toffee-nosed wife, with whom Bet had never got on.

Bet had tried to be kind to Delia. Recently she had offered to treat the girl to a nice perm which, she said, would get the hair out of Delia's eyes and let people see her face. 'For your birthday, pet,' she'd wheedled. 'Have it done for your birthday.'

Delia had turned her aunt's offer down. The idea of a nice perm, which would involve spending a morning in Merle (originally Brenda) Carter's shabby little salon, and coming out of it with her blonde hair frizzed into a bush and smelling like a bucketful of babies' nappies, had made her shake her head in disgust. Although nice perms were all the rage, Delia kept her hair short, straight and

48

clean, bobbed to her chin with a neat fringe covering her forehead.

'It's very kind of you, Aunt Bet,' she'd said, seeing her aunt's face darken. 'But I can't afford to buy all the curlers I'd need afterwards, and — '

'You won't get nothin' else then.' Aunt Bet was not to be mollified. Ungrateful little hussy, she'd thought. 'You need something doin' to your hair,' she'd cried. 'Look at you! About fourteen years old, that's all anyone would think you are. I'm tellin' you, it don't suit you straight. It wants a bit of body.'

'Does it?'

'Yes!' Aunt Bet had patted her own corrugated haystack, then removed a lipstick-stained Woodbine from the corner of her mouth. 'You'll never get a nice man goin' round lookin' like little orphan Annie. Mark my words you won't. You ain't nothin' special, my girl.'

She sniffed. 'But if you don't want to go to Merle's, I suppose it's no good me draggin' you there. Just you remember though, I did offer.'

'Yes. You did.' Almost ashamed of her ingratitude, Delia had tried to look suitably contrite. 'But no thanks, all the same.'

★   ★   ★

As she put on her best coat, Delia glanced at her face in the kitchen mirror. Indeed, she wasn't very special. Her eyes were a typical English blue-grey; nondescript, she supposed. Her nose was small and straight, a bit snub at the end. Her mouth was her

49

best feature, sensual and full. Compared with Veronica Lake or Rita Hayworth, however, Delia Shenstone was nothing to write home about at all.

She pushed her hair back off her forehead, making a face of mock despair. She was certainly no Betty Grable; but then she wasn't Quasimodo either. She wasn't in desperate need of a nice perm. Patting her straight, shiny bob, she went through to the scullery, where she slipped on her shoes.

'Where're you going?' called her aunt, as she heard the back door open.

'Out,' Delia replied.

'Where to?'

'Cinema, I 'spect. With Dora Slater.'

'Who you goin' to see?'

'Leslie Howard.'

'Don't like him.' Bringing a trayful of dirty crockery into the scullery, Aunt Bet sniffed. 'Always looks a right pansy to me. Pity he died, though.'

'Yes. Pity, that.' Delia kissed her aunt's powdered cheek. 'See you about eleven.'

★   ★   ★

Delia walked down the road. Avoiding broken paving stones and potholes, she skirted piles of rubble which had been there for so long that willow herb and dandelions bloomed cheerfully upon them. At the end of the road she caught the bus into town.

'Nice to see a happy, smiling face,' remarked the conductress, as she took Delia's fare. 'What you got to be so pleased about, then?'

'Nothing in particular.' Delia took her ticket.

But she continued to smile. In three days' time she'd be away from these dusty, dirty streets. Being a library assistant wasn't the big time, but it would be better than pressing buttons all day and listening to Mrs Delaney and her friends.

4

There were no taxis, nor even any horses and carts. Except for several rusting lorries and two mongrels fighting over a disagreeable-looking bone, Evesbridge station forecourt was completely deserted.

Delia tapped her foot in irritation. She waited a few minutes but then, despairing of any wheeled transport making its appearance, she dumped her cases on the pavement and went back into the station.

She rapped on the window of the booking office, waking a somnolent clerk. She told him what she wanted.

'Taxi, eh?' The man scratched his head. 'No,' he muttered. 'You won't get no taxi here. Couldn't find you a taxi if you was to offer me a thousand pound.'

What about a coach and four then? wondered Delia, but only to herself. 'I see,' she said, out loud. 'In that case, could you tell me the way to the bus station?'

'Ah.' The clerk grinned. 'Well, you goes straight down the road, look. You takes the first right. Then you crosses into Maybury Street, an' it's there on your left.'

'Thanks.' For nothing. Going back out into the sunshine and gathering up her unwieldy luggage, Delia wondered how long it would take her to walk to the bus station. Her carrier bag was sagging. The locks on one of the suitcases were unreliable, and she now had a horrible vision of all her underclothes scattered across Maybury Street for the citizens of Evesbridge to admire.

She saw an old Austin Seven coming up the road, but since it was obviously a private car she took no notice of it. Just as it swept past her, however, an elderly man appeared at her side. He stepped on to the wide expanse of tarmac which led to the station entrance.

Evidently, the old man hadn't noticed the car. Possibly, the driver hadn't seen the old man. But now, reversing into a convenient parking space, the car missed the pedestrian by inches.

Witnessing this near collision, Delia cried out in alarm. Seeing the old man collapse in a heap on the tarmac, she abandoned her luggage yet again and ran over to him. 'Are you hurt?' Anxiously, she shook his arm. 'Did he hit you, or did you fall?'

The old man said nothing. Obviously in shock, he simply stared at her.

'Christ, fancy walking out like that. He didn't even look!' Now the driver of the car had joined them, and together he and Delia helped the elderly man sit up. 'Why didn't you stay on the pavement?' demanded the driver. 'Why didn't you wait for me to park?'

'He didn't see you, that's why,' said Delia, bluntly. 'It seems you didn't see him!'

'Of course I did.' A good-looking, dark-haired boy only a few years older than Delia herself, the driver shrugged. 'But it's usual to wait until a road is clear before crossing. You must admit that.'

Delia didn't think it worth arguing the point.

After all, the old man had stepped backwards smartly enough. So smartly that he'd lost his balance, fallen heavily against a concrete post, and possibly injured himself badly.

Delia looked at him again. Pale with shock, his face white and drawn, she guessed he must be at least eighty. 'Are you hurt?' she repeated, her voice soft with concern.

The old man blinked. He considered the question. Experimentally, he rubbed his shin. 'I reckon I've done me leg in,' he said. Then, seeming to recover all his faculties at once, he glowered at the driver of the car. 'Me leg's bust. That's it.'

'Broken?' asked Delia, gently. 'You think you've actually broken your leg?'

'Nah. But it's bruised bad enough, I'll bet. As for me ankle, I've twisted *that* summat shocking.' His face a normal colour now, the old man scowled at the motorist. 'What did you want to come at me like that for?' he demanded.

'I'm sorry.' The driver shrugged an apology. 'I thought you'd wait.'

'Did you, now?' The old man snorted in irritation. 'Oh, bugger it,' he muttered, in the direct way of the countryman. 'I'd come for them chicks specially.'

'Chicks?' repeated Delia, mystified.

'Day old chicks.' The man grimaced in annoyance and pain. 'Special delivery, they was. I won't be able to carry 'em home now. I'll have missed the bus . . .'

'I can take you home, you and your chicks.' Now, the motorist was smiling. Relieved the old man wasn't seriously hurt, his air was almost jaunty.

'Look — you let this lady help you into the car. I'll go and fetch your chicks, and the parcel I've come to collect. Then I'll drive you home. We'll be there in two shakes.'

'That we won't.' Foxily, the old man grinned. 'I lives at Barton Wells. Thirteen mile out that is, near enough. I reckon I ought to see a doctor, too. You can't be too careful, not at my age.'

'That's a very good point,' Delia agreed. 'I think we ought to take this gentleman to a doctor, straight away.'

'Right.' The driver nodded. 'There's a surgery just down the road. I'll take Mr — '

'Johnson,' said the old man. 'Albert Henry Johnson.'

'I'll take Mr Johnson right over.'

'I think I'd better come with you,' Delia said. Standing up, she brushed the dust from the hem of her skirt. She offered Mr Johnson her hand. He took it, and between them Delia and the driver got him on his feet and into the front seat of the little car.

'Gareth Hughes, by the way,' said the young man. He started the engine.

'Delia Shenstone,' said Delia.

'Very nice, too,' observed Mr Johnson. 'So, now we all knows one other, how about gettin' me to a quack?'

★　★　★

The surgery was only two minutes' drive away. By the time they arrived there, however, Mr Johnson was positively chirpy. In fact, he was recovered

55

enough to make some very rude remarks about Gareth's driving.

'Now, you watch out for them kids,' he advised tersely, as Gareth turned into a parking space. 'Wait till they're out of the way, before you tries any more of your fancy stuff.'

Helping Mr Johnson into the doctor's crowded waiting room, Delia stumbled against somebody's foot. The woman was wearing white summer sandals, and Delia was appalled to see that her own heel had left a big, black smudge on the pale leather. 'I'm so sorry,' she said. 'Did I hurt you?'

'Not really.' The woman, who had a small child on her lap, met Delia's anxious gaze. 'Don't worry about it,' she added, but rather frostily.

Delia bit her lip. Carefully, she helped Mr Johnson into a comfortable chair. Then she sat down herself, beside the woman with the infant.

The baby, whom Delia assumed must be a little girl, for pink bobbles decorated her knitted matinee jacket and matching bonnet, looked about six months old. Now, noticing Delia's wristwatch, she grabbed at it. When Delia held it up for her inspection she beamed, jigging up and down in delight. Hearing it tick, she grinned, revealing two little pearls of milk teeth.

Delia smiled back at her. 'What's the matter with your baby?' she enquired, for the child was now crowing and burbling with pleasure, and didn't seem in the least unwell.

'Nothing's the matter. She's here for a check-up, that's all.' As cool as her daughter was friendly, the child's mother shrugged. 'She had bad jaundice when she was born. So Dr Graham likes to keep an eye on her, see.'

'Oh.' Delia didn't know if infantile jaundice was a life-threatening disease, or a trivial childhood indisposition which soon passed. She tried to look both impressed and consoling. 'Is she better now?' she asked.

'Seems to be.' The baby's mother bounced her daughter on her knee. The infant blew bubbles, and giggled. 'There don't seem to be much ailing her these days.'

'That's good.'

Hoping it would not be long before the doctor called Mr Johnson, Delia tried to think of something else to say. But now the baby's mother was rooting around in her shopping bag. Soon, she found what she wanted. She handed the baby an old-fashioned coral teething ring. Then, looping the pink ribbon which dangled from the ring around her child's fat little wrist, she opened her own library book and began to read.

Seated on Mr Johnson's other side, Gareth Hughes was also reading. But now, hearing Delia sigh, he put down his battered copy of the *Tatler* and smiled at her. 'New to Evesbridge, are you?' he asked, conversationally.

'Yes.' Delia returned his smile. 'I've come to work here, actually. I start at the county library on Monday.'

'Ah.' Gareth Hughes nodded. 'Got some decent digs?'

'I don't know yet.' Delia shrugged. 'They're in Lyall Street.'

'Oh. Well, that's a good area. Big old houses, they are. Victorian.'

'Oh.' Glancing at Mr Johnson, Delia saw that he was nodding. Soon, he would be fast asleep. Indeed, the atmosphere in the waiting room was so stuffy that she was beginning to feel like a little doze herself.

'Mrs Bell? Mrs Shirley Bell?' Bustling into the waiting room, her uniform crackling almost indignantly under its coating of starch, the doctor's nurse glared fiercely at the young woman with the baby. 'Come along now, Mrs Bell,' she rapped. 'Doctor hasn't got all day.'

'I'm coming.' Shirley Bell pushed her book into her bag. Gathering up her baby and her shopping, she rose awkwardly to her feet.

Delia watched her walk into the surgery. Then she turned to Gareth Hughes. 'I'll go and get a bus, I think,' she said. 'Will you stay with Mr Johnson, and give him a lift home?'

'Sure.' Gareth grinned. 'You go and catch your bus. You'll want the number five. Ask the conductor to put you off on the corner of Mortimer Road.'

'Okay.' Delia stood up.

'I'll ring you, shall I?' Gareth Hughes' dark eyes twinkled. 'I'll give you a buzz, at the library. To see how you're getting on.'

'That would be nice.' Delia nodded. 'Yes, you do that.'

5

'Good afternoon, Miss Shenstone. How very nice to meet you! You had a pleasant journey, I hope?' A middle-aged widow living on an Indian Civil Service pension and therefore obliged to let lodgings, Mrs Newby ushered her new tenant indoors. A perfect lady, she waited until Delia had her back turned and was hanging up her jacket before giving her a good look up and down.

A pretty girl, thought Mrs Newby. Neatly if somewhat shabbily dressed, her hair was clean and her clothes well brushed. Later, she observed that the girl's smooth, clear complexion was all her own. Unlike so many young women these days, Delia wasn't painted like a circus clown.

'Would you like a cup of tea, Miss Shenstone?' she enquired, as she took Delia upstairs to see her room. 'Dinner's at six, but I'm sure you'd like a drink and a biscuit now?'

'Yes, I would. Thank you.' Looking round the large, sunny bedroom, Delia smiled her satisfaction. 'This is lovely,' she said.

'I'm so glad to you like it.' Mrs Newby smiled back. 'Well, I'll just go and put the kettle on. You make yourself comfortable here. Have a wash, if you like. The bathroom's just along the landing.'

'Thank you.' Delia's hands were filthy, and smuts from the railway lay stickily on her face. 'I'll be down in a few minutes,' she said.

As she patted her face with the clean towel provided, Delia eyed her reflection in the bathroom mirror. Refreshed, she felt human now.

Mrs Newby looked human, too. Fully prepared for some old dragon in a flowered crossover pinny, who'd demand a month's rent in advance before her lodger was even over her threshold, who'd bark out that there were to be no visitors, no music and no washing done on the premises, Mrs Newby and her faded, comfortable, chintzy home had come as a very pleasant surprise.

★ ★ ★

Monday morning, Delia was up early. Dressed as smartly as her limited wardrobe would allow, she applied lipstick, wiped it off, applied it a second time, removed it again.

Now, the butterflies in her stomach were doing cartwheels. Her hands shook like an old woman's. 'Pull yourself together, Shenstone,' she told herself, firmly. 'It's only a new job.'

She went downstairs. She put on her coat. 'No breakfast today, Miss Shenstone?' asked Mrs Newby, bustling out of the kitchen with a teapot and cups on a tin tray.

'I don't always bother,' replied Delia, who now felt really sick.

'Have some tea or coffee and a piece of toast.' Mrs Newby nodded towards the kitchen. 'Come along. You can't last until lunchtime on fresh air and exercise, can you?'

Mrs Newby was a paragon among landladies. But

Miss Deirdre Ryan, the senior librarian at Evesbridge County Library, was not a paragon at all. A tall, stout, red-nosed woman well past her fiftieth birthday, she had a mean, shrewish face which Delia was to find exactly matched her mean, shrewish nature.

Having coped on her own for the greater part of the war years, she had been obliged to mend torn pages, shelve returns and tidy the stock, as well as order and catalogue books. But now she had a minion again. Her status would be undermined no longer. As librarian, she would do the brainwork, while her assistant did the chores.

She showed Delia round the library, telling her all about the readers as they progressed. 'The largest borrowing group,' she began, 'consists of girls and older women. They read only romances. The schoolchildren take out story books, picture books and text books. Nine times out of ten these become overdue, and have to be recalled.

'Men come in here to read the newspapers. Now and again, one will take out a novel — but if a man reads a book, it's invariably a Western. Or a thriller. The classics,' concluded Miss Ryan sourly, 'stay on the shelves. No one in Evesbridge bothers with literature.'

The library was organised on traditional lines, the books being classified under the usual decimal system. The romantic fiction, however, was set apart, segregated from other novels in a special purdah all of its own. Each romantic novel had a big red R inked on its spine, and readers were rationed to one book at a time. This caused a great deal of moaning and groaning, especially from the country women who came into Evesbridge only on market day, and who resented having to make one little novel last a whole working week.

'Can't I 'ave another, Miss? For me friend?' Thinking the young, pretty assistant looked far more reasonable than the sour-faced old misery who'd been in sole charge of the library for so long, the country women grinned winningly at Delia. 'Go on, duck,' they wheedled. 'It's for me neighbour, really. She can't get out. It's her legs, see. Give us that there *Shadow of the Sheikh*, as well. Be a love.'

As Delia did so, she wondered if Miss Ryan had the power to get her sacked for insubordination.

★ ★ ★

A hideous building of Victorian yellow brick housed both the library and the council offices. Situated in Evesbridge's High Street, the place had been a target of abuse ever since it was built. But, although many citizens had hoped a stray German bomb might reduce it to rubble, it had survived the war years intact and still stood proudly, its nineteenth century ghastliness complete.

Adorned with unnecessary turrets and spikes, decorated with gargoyles and statues of civic worthies, and finished off with a frieze of mythical beasts prancing around its parapet, the building was a monstrosity, a blot on the otherwise attractive landscape of the pleasant little country town.

Inside the building, echoing corridors, slippery parquet floors and very high ceilings gave the place a thoroughly institutional air. The *eau de Nil* paintwork which was common to all the rooms cast a pale, sickly light on the readers at the great oak tables below.

It was no wonder, thought Delia, that those who had the price of a subscription preferred to go to Stanford's library, which was housed in a pretty Georgian mansion in a quiet no-thoroughfare close to the cathedral. There, one might browse unmolested, unobserved by Miss Ryan's suspicious eye.

As the librarian had said, no one borrowed the classics. This suited her new assistant. Let loose in a treasure house of ideas and information, Delia began to work her way through Dickens and Austen and Fielding, through Richardson and Trollope and Sterne.

Discovering the reserve stock, which had been packed into crates and left to moulder in the cellar throughout the duration of the war — for the local Home Guard had taken possession of half the library and had needed some shelf space for its documents and files — Delia opened the boxes and began to struggle through Maupassant, Victor Hugo and Flaubert.

'What a determined little scholar you are,' observed Miss Ryan frostily, astonished that a mere library assistant should actually want to read the books which she was merely required to sort, stamp and put away. 'Mark my words. If you carry on at this rate, you'll simply ruin your eyes.'

Delia said nothing. That lunchtime, she'd put her name down for shorthand and typing classes run by the local authority. Her days at Evesbridge Country Library would soon be numbered.

★ ★ ★

On her knees in the children's section of the library, one Wednesday morning Delia was busy tidying the lower shelves. From this lowly vantage point, she had a clear view of the reference section and the librarian's huge, mahogany desk.

Happening to glance up, she stared for a few moments, trying to remember where she'd seen the young woman standing there before. 'Please,' the woman was saying, as she balanced her pretty, dark-haired baby on one hip, 'please, could you find me a copy of *The Magic Mountain*? It's by Thomas Mann. I'd like Clarke's translation, if you have it.'

'What?' Finally deigning to look up from her cataloguing, the librarian eyed the girl warily. 'Thomas Mann, did you say?'

'Yes, that's right. I'd like *The Magic Mountain*, in translation. Do you have a copy?'

'Oh, we might have. In the reserve stock.' Taking an index card out of her box, Miss Ryan began to write. Perhaps she hoped this troublesome person would take the hint, and go away.

But the girl persisted. 'May I borrow it then?' she asked.

'Well, I'm not sure where it would be.' Miss Ryan sniffed. 'We're extremely busy,' she added, crossly. 'We really haven't time to go burrowing in the cellars today.'

'Could I call back later?'

'I don't think there'd be much point.' Now Miss Ryan was quite pink in the face. 'You see, I — '

'Are you telling me I *can't* borrow it?'

'I don't even know if we have a copy!' Miss Ryan smiled a perfectly ghastly smile. 'The catalogues aren't anywhere near up to date. We were short-staffed throughout the whole of the war, and the library's only just beginning to get properly organised again.'

She reached across to the returns trolley. 'Why don't you have a nice new novel?' she suggested. '*Love's Cruel Fury*, what about that? It would take your mind off your troubles, maybe.'

The girl flushed scarlet. She looked so angry that for a moment Delia wondered if she might actually hit Miss Ryan. She didn't — but her blue eyes blazed. 'If you don't have *The Magic Mountain*,' she retorted, fiercely, 'I don't want *anything*.' Turning on her heel, she marched out of the library. She let the door slam behind her.

Now Delia remembered where she'd seen the girl before. It had been in that doctor's surgery, months ago. Mrs Bell. That was her name. Mrs Shirley Bell.

Finishing her work in the children's section, Delia went over to the main desk and began to sort out the returns trolley. 'What did that lady want?' she asked, artlessly. She enjoyed irritating Miss Ryan.

'Which lady? Oh, you mean that girl. Something by Thomas somebody or other.' Miss Ryan grimaced. '*The Magic Mountain*. It's a foreign book, I believe.'

'Wouldn't that be in the reserve stock?' Sweetly, Delia smiled. 'Along with the other German books?'

Miss Ryan pursed her lips. 'Look, Miss Shenstone,' she began, 'there's something you should understand, and it's this. We don't want to lend the more expensive books to just anybody. Most certainly not to a person like that.'

Delia stared. 'Whatever do you mean?' she asked.

'Oh, dear.' Heavily, Miss Ryan sighed. 'Well, Miss Shenstone, I know that in theory we should obtain books for anyone who asks for them. Provided that person belongs to the library, of course. But in practice, we must use a little discretion. Country people — tenant farmers, labourers, their wives and daughters — do tend to be careless. As for that girl: well, she wasn't quite the thing. Was she?'

'How do you mean?'

Miss Ryan looked pained. 'A baby, but no wedding ring,' she hissed. 'You see, there were Polish airmen here during the war years and a certain sort of girl was notorious for — well — associating with them. Now, if we lent one of our more valuable books to someone like the woman you just saw, it would probably come back with the spine broken and the pages stuck together with baby sick. If it came back at all.'

* * *

A week or so later, during her mid-day break, Delia was walking down Howard Street when she saw Shirley Bell again. Rocking a pram piled high with bags and packets of groceries, she was gazing intently at the display of rather horrible dresses in a draper's shop window.

Delia crossed the road and stopped by the pram. 'Hello,' she said.

'What?' Startled, Shirley Bell jumped. Disturbed, the baby in the pram let out a loud wail. Her mother pacified her, then looked up at Delia. 'Oh,' she said. 'I know you, don't I?'

'Sort of. I was — '

'At the surgery that time. You trod on my foot.'

'Yes, I did. Sorry.'

'Now you work at the library. I've seen you there.'

'Yes.' Recalling Miss Ryan's rudeness, Delia blushed. But then she smiled. 'Actually,' she said, 'that's why I stopped to talk to you. I heard what you wanted that day. *The Magic Mountain*, wasn't it?'

'Yes.' The girl narrowed her eyes. 'So?'

'We were really busy that morning. But things are quieter now. So, if you still want the book, I'll see if I can dig it out for you, shall I? If we have it in stock, I'll send you a card. If Evesbridge doesn't have its own copy, I could try other libraries round about.'

'Well — that's ever so kind of you! Thank you.' The girl opened her handbag. Getting out an old pre-war diary, she tore out a leaf, then wrote her name and address in a large, childish hand. 'I'll be hearing from you, then?' she asked.

'Yes. In a week or so, I expect.' Taking the scrap of paper, Delia put it in her bag. 'I'll be seeing you, then.'

Back at the library, Delia found the book. A handsome, leather-bound edition which had been a gift to the library from the translator himself, it was a pleasure to handle and was certain to be a pleasure to read.

Delia sent off the card.

The following Wednesday, Shirley Bell came into the library. Reluctantly, Miss Ryan handed her the book. She'd seen Delia's handwriting on the reservation slip, so now she told her assistant off, for sending out correspondence without endorsement from the librarian herself.

Two weeks later, Shirley Bell returned the book. Delia put it on the trolley. 'Was it any good?' she enquired.

'Yes. A bit above my head, though.' Ruefully, Shirley Bell smiled. 'I reckon I'll stick to English authors in future. Could I make a reservation, do you think?'

'Yes, of course. What did you want?'

'Some of the Palliser novels. Trollope. You know?'

'Aren't there any on the shelves?'

'No. I looked.' Sitting her baby on the edge of the desk, Shirley rummaged in her handbag. Eventually she found a very dog-eared, tattered list. '*The Eustace Diamonds*,' she read. '*Phineas Finn*. Could you get those?'

'I expect so.'

'Great.' Shirley grinned. 'I'll call in next week, shall I? To save you sending out a card.'

'Right.' Glancing at the clock, Delia realised it was almost lunchtime. 'Are you busy just now?' she asked.

'Busy?' repeated Shirley.

'Yes.' Delia picked up her handbag. 'It's my lunch break,' she explained. 'I was wondering if you could

— if we might go and have a cup of coffee somewhere? I'm new to this area, you see. I don't know many people here.'

'Oh, I see,' Shirley said.

As it happened, Shirley had finished her mother's shopping. She had at least an hour to spare before she met her father at the cattle market. Her feet were killing her, and she had just been thinking how much she would like a cup of tea. But she hated going into cafés on her own. Now, here was the answer to her prayer.

'All right,' she agreed. 'We'll go to the Continental, shall we? Then Jenny can have an ice.'

So, five minutes later, Delia Shenstone, Shirley Bell and Shirley's daughter Jenny were sitting in the Continental Café, eating ices out of aluminium dishes and finding out about one another.

'You're a Brummy, aren't you?' asked Shirley, as she tied a soft white bib around Jenny's neck.

'Yes.' Delia grimaced. 'Is it that obvious?'

'I should say so.' Shirley began to spoon ice-cream into her baby. 'Were you there during the war?'

'Yes. I worked in a factory.'

'Poor you. Why have you come to Evesbridge?'

'I was offered a job.' Delia shrugged. 'But I'm only working at the library until I can get something better.'

'How do you mean, better?'

'Well, more interesting. I'm going to night school, I'm learning shorthand and typing there. In the end, I want to work on a newspaper.'

'So in the meantime, you're using the library to

69

get yourself all wised up.'

'You could say that.' Delia smiled. 'What about you? Do you live on a farm or something?'

'Yeah.' Shirley grinned. 'A country bumpkin, that's what I am. Open wide for Mummy, poppet,' she cooed. 'There's my good girl.'

'She *is* good, isn't she?' observed Delia.

'She's a little angel,' Shirley agreed. 'Most of the time, anyway. Ever so cold for June, isn't it?' she added, wiping the baby's chin.

For ten minutes or so, comments on the miserable summer weather, the everlasting rationing, and the awfulness of ready-made clothes these days helped the conversation to drift harmlessly along. Delia ate her fish-paste sandwiches and drank her ersatz coffee. Glancing at the clock, she saw that if she was to pick up the few bits of shopping she wanted, she'd have to go soon.

But then, as Delia reached for her bag, Shirley looked up. She met Delia's eyes. 'I expect you've noticed I don't wear a ring,' she said.

'I'm sorry?' Embarrassed, Delia blushed. But then she told herself not to be silly. 'Well,' she said, candidly, 'since you mention it, I have.'

'Shall I tell you about it?'

'If you want to.' Still surprised by this sudden burst of confidence, Delia shrugged. 'But don't feel you must. I mean — '

'I'd like to.'

'Oh. I see.' Understanding, Delia smiled. 'In that case, go ahead.'

'Got time to listen, have you?'

'Half an hour, at least,' Delia replied. The

shopping could wait. 'I'll get us another two coffees, shall I? Do you fancy a piece of that apple pie?'

★ ★ ★

'My father thought it was a local boy,' said Shirley. Slowly, reflectively, she stirred her coffee. 'Or a Polish airman.'

'But it wasn't.'

'No.' Shirley looked down at her hands. 'It was a farm labourer. A casual, hired for the harvest. Disgusting, isn't it? I expect you're shocked.'

'No, I'm not shocked.' In fact, Delia was very touched, and flattered to be confided in. 'What happened?' she asked.

'I had an affair, of course. For a few weeks, it was wonderful. But come November, I was up the spout.'

'Pregnant, you mean?'

'Yes.' Shirley grimaced. 'The chap had cleared off. By Christmas, I was knitting bootees, and wishing I was dead.'

'That's awful.' Delia's face was soft with sympathy. 'Did you like him a lot?'

'Like him?' Shirley sighed. 'I thought I loved him! But it wasn't love. I felt sorry for him, I suppose. Now, of course, I'm sorry for myself, and for Jenny here.'

'Yes.' Delia looked at the baby. 'What was he like?'

'Very nice.' Now, remembering, Shirley smiled. 'He was kind. Considerate. Well-educated, but not stuck up. He talked to me as if I was clever, too.'

'What did he look like?'

'He had dark hair. Blue eyes. A nice face — sort of open and friendly, like. Honest-looking, if you know what I mean.' Bitterly, Shirley sighed. 'He said he'd marry me, and I believed him. Fool that I was.'

'Do you still think about him?'

'No.' Vehemently, Shirley shook her head. 'I must forget all about him. When he left us, I don't know where he went. So I couldn't get in touch with him, even if I wanted to.'

'You must know his name.'

'I know his first name. But his surname was odd. I don't know how to spell it, and I don't know who to ask. He might have been lying about it, anyway.'

'That's true.' Glancing at her wristwatch, Delia realised she should have been back at work a quarter of an hour ago. She stood up. 'I must go,' she said, apologetically. 'But I've enjoyed talking to you. Shall I see you again?'

'I'm always in town on Wednesdays. I do the shopping for Mum while Dad's at the cattle market.'

'Shall we meet next week, then? Outside the library, at twelve? We could have lunch, maybe.'

'Okay.' Shirley smiled. 'I'll look forward to it.'

'I'll try to get those books for you.'

'Thanks.' Shirley put the baby back into her pram. 'I'd really appreciate that.'

6

As he'd promised, Gareth Hughes rang the library. Her lips pursed, Miss Ryan handed Delia the telephone receiver, listened to the conversation, and afterwards made herself unpleasant on the subject of receiving personal phone calls at work.

That same evening, Delia and Gareth met again. Sitting on a bench in the Cathedral Close, his long legs stretched out in front of him and his hands folded behind his head, he smiled when he saw her coming. 'Sit down,' he invited.

'Thanks.' Having been on her feet all day, Delia was tired. She flopped down beside him. 'How are you?' she asked.

'Fine, thanks. What about you?'

'I'm okay.' Delia yawned. 'I'm a bit tired, though. I've started an evening class in French, and I'm finding it hard to keep up. So I have to do a lot of homework.'

'Did you learn any French at school?'

'Yes, but I've forgotten most of it.'

'Why have you taken it up again?'

'It's something to do.' Delia wasn't going to confide her ambitions to Gareth. Not just yet, anyway. 'It's a good way to meet new people, too.'

'I suppose it must be.' Gareth got up. 'Well now — where would you like to go?'

'Where do you suggest?'

'Have you eaten?'

73

'Yes, thanks. Today, it was Mrs Newby's special.'

'Mrs Newby's your landlady?'

'That's right.'

'Is she nice?'

'She's lovely.'

'Good.' Gareth helped Delia to her feet. 'Well then, let's go for a ride. We'll drive out to Hampton Frome and have a drink at the Red Lion. Okay?'

'Fine.'

'Right. The car's in Stafford Street, by the castle gates.'

As they walked through the town centre, Delia noticed Gareth had a slight limp. She wondered if this were the result of a recent or childhood injury. But, since she hated hearing about other peoples' accidents, she didn't ask him. He might tell her something horrible. Any talk of fire or blood or destruction brought all the details of that dreadful evening flaring back to life, made her relive the night her parents had been killed. It was bad enough when such things came in dreams. It made Delia feel sick and ill when real people talked about what the war had done to them.

This squeamishness was something she had yet to learn to cope with. But she would *have* to cope with it, if her ambitions to become a journalist were to be fulfilled . . .

It appeared, however, that Gareth was not one for reminiscences. They spent the evening in a country pub, playing darts, drinking local cider and chatting to the landlord and his wife. At any rate, Gareth chatted. Delia was too tired to talk much.

When she did happen to remark on the beauty of

the evening, the landlord grinned. 'A Brummy, eh?' he grinned, winking at her. 'We don't get many of them round here. Now, let me see. Bournville? No — a bit too posh. Selly Oak? Edgbaston? I know — Handsworth.'

'Near enough.' Aware that this was just a guess, Delia was nettled all the same. She didn't want to be so easily pigeonholed. Now, she decided she would lose her accent completely. Or at least soften it a bit.

'Penny for them?' demanded Gareth.

'What? Oh — nothing.' Delia forced a smile. 'It's getting late, though. Do you think you could take me home?'

Gareth obliged. Stopping outside Mrs Newby's front door, he kissed Delia on the cheek, and asked if he could take her out again.

★ ★ ★

The summer faded into autumn. Delia had become something of an expert on the country pubs of Worcestershire. She'd grown very fond of Gareth, too.

He obviously liked her — but didn't assume that buying her drinks gave him the right to undress her. This alone made him a pleasant change from every other boy she'd ever known.

'Here's your young man.' Hearing the Austin Seven draw up outside the house, Mrs Newby backed away from the sitting room window. She didn't want to appear nosy. 'Do you think he'd like to come in and have a cup of tea? Then you won't have to rush your pudding.'

Mrs Newby approved of Gareth. He was clean, he was decent, and he was a man who liked a chat. In fact, he talked all the time. But then, one Sunday afternoon, he took a break from talking about his own plans and ambitions to ask Delia about *her* job. 'Do you enjoy working in the library?' he asked, casually.

'I don't mind it.' They were walking through a pretty black and white village, and Delia was hoping she might spot a teashop soon. Taking Gareth's hand, she led him up a promising byway. 'But Miss Ryan's a bit of a pain.'

'You don't say?' Gareth laughed. 'When I was a little lad, she scared me stiff. My Mum often left me in the library, you see. While she did her shopping, or met her friends in town.

'Miss Ryan used to stand over me, glaring. One day, I dropped a toffee paper on the floor. She threw me out!'

Delia could well imagine it. 'So you were sticking all the pages together with Bluebird Popular Mixture, were you?' she enquired.

'That's right. Juvenile delinquent, I was.'

'I see. When you became a big lad, what did you do then?'

'I joined the army.' Gareth shrugged. 'I was born in 1921, so I was involved right from the start.'

'Were you demobbed in '45?'

'No, long before that.' Gareth pushed his hands into his trouser pockets. 'I was wounded in 1941. Then I was out of it.'

'Were you overseas?' Now, thought Delia, this is it. She braced herself for what he might tell her.

'Were you in a battle, or what?'

'Nothing so glorious, I'm afraid,' Gareth replied. 'I was stationed in North Africa, with the Worcestershires. It had been nice and peaceful for a few weeks, the sun tans were coming on a treat. Then one of the brass hats decided it was time we had some exercise, so we were told to attack an Italian convoy.'

'What happened?'

'We mucked it up.' Gareth shrugged. 'It should have been a piece of cake, but somebody misunderstood their orders, and our company was cut off from the main advance. The Italians ambushed us. Left us all for dead. But when the rest of the battalion came back to look for us, they found a couple of us still alive.'

'Oh, God.' Delia shuddered. 'What happened to you?'

'I had half a dozen bullets in my back, and a broken leg.'

'But they got you to hospital?'

'Yes. That was paradise.' Gareth grinned. 'So anyway, they tidied me up. But then the army downgraded me to cripple, and I was out of it.

'I went to some ministry or other. They gave me essential war work, filling in little pink forms. When I met you, I'd just started at the local hospital, in the records department.'

'Do you like it there?'

'It's okay. But if something better turns up, I shall be off like a shot.' Again, Gareth shrugged. 'My mother died earlier this year, and my Dad took it rather badly. I couldn't leave him on his own just now. But in due course, I'll get a professional qualification, perhaps. Become an accountant, or something like that.'

By now, they'd reached the outskirts of the village. The teashop had failed to materialise. So, disappointed, they turned to go back to the car. Gareth was limping a little now, and Delia asked if he was tired.

'A bit,' he admitted.

'Do you want to sit down for a while?'

'That's a good idea. We'll find a nice mossy bank, shall we? Then I can ravish you.'

'We'll sit on that bench over there. The one by the church.'

'In full view of the vicarage.'

'Yes.'

'Spoilsport.'

'Aren't I just?'

Gareth drove her home at dusk. Stopping the car outside Mrs Newby's house, he took Delia in his arms. He kissed her. 'Shall I see you tomorrow?' he asked. 'We could go to the flicks, maybe.'

'That would be great.' Delia gave him a final kiss. 'I must go in,' she said. 'I've got some ironing to do.'

'All right. I'll let you.'

'Goodnight, then.' Delia smiled at him. 'See you tomorrow. Seven o'clock. Don't be late.'

★　★　★

Delia watched as the car drove away. Going up to her room, she sighed. Gareth had begun to get that look in his eyes. A look which told her as plainly as possible that he wasn't going to be satisfied with mere hugs and kisses much longer.

She didn't think he was in love with her. Not yet. If she broke it off with him now, he'd easily replace her. Wouldn't he? The problem was, she didn't want a lover. She hadn't time for an affair. But she hated the idea of losing a friend.

As she wondered what to do about it, she had an idea. Tomorrow, they were going to the cinema. Perhaps Shirley Bell would come, too? Mrs Newby wouldn't mind putting her up for the night, Delia was sure. The baby must be old enough to be left with her grandparents now.

Yes, that was perfect. She'd show Gareth that although she enjoyed his company, she didn't want him all to herself. She thought of him as a friend. Nothing more.

'Mrs Newby?' Delia tapped on her landlady's sitting room door. 'May I use the telephone? For a quick local call?'

'Certainly, dear,' Mrs Newby replied. 'Just leave your sixpence in the dish.'

★　★　★

'Oh, come on,' said Delia, persuasively. 'When did *you* last have an evening out?'

'I dunno, to tell you the truth.' Shirley laughed. 'About a year ago last Christmas, I think.'

'There you are, then. Look, it's the new Clark Gable. Surely you'd like to see that? You don't have to worry about getting home, because you can spend the night here. You can even have my bed.

I'll sleep on the floor.'

'But won't this man want you to himself?' Weakening, for she rather liked the idea of a trip to the cinema, Shirley frowned. 'I mean — if he's taking you out, won't he expect — '

'Oh, I don't think so, he's not that type.' Delia laughed. 'In any case, he's only a friend. His name's Gareth. I've mentioned him to you before, I'm sure I have.'

'Well, if you honestly don't think he'll mind.'

'He won't.'

'All right, then.'

'You'll come?'

'I'll get the bus in. I'll be in town by five. Shall I meet you at the library?'

'Yes. Then we'll go to Latchett's for our tea. I'll treat you.' Triumphantly, Delia grinned. 'See you, then.'

★ ★ ★

'This is Shirley.' Deliberately dowdy in an old navy coat which had belonged to Aunt Bet, Delia introduced Gareth to her friend. 'Gareth Hughes — Shirley Bell.'

'Hello, Shirley.' Gareth held out his hand. 'Did you two just bump into each other, then?'

'Actually, Gareth, I asked Shirley to come with us. That's okay, isn't it?'

'Well — yes. Of course it is.' Now Gareth managed a brave little smile. He cleared his throat. 'That's fine by me. Right then, ladies. Shall we go in?'

Gareth took it so well that Delia was proud of him. Shepherding the two girls into the cinema, he bought their tickets, led them upstairs to the balcony, then sat down between them.

Arms folded, he spent the first half of the programme staring fixedly at the screen. He listened to the soundtrack with such concentration that one would have imagined he was trying to memorise the script.

The lights came up again. Without saying a word, Gareth got up, went to the kiosk in the foyer, and came back with two ice creams. 'Here,' he said. 'One each.'

'Thanks very much.' Blushing, Shirley accepted hers. 'How much do I owe you?' she asked, reaching for her purse.

'That's okay.' Noticing her face was bright red, Gareth smiled at her. 'Go on, then. Eat it up, or it'll drip all over your dress.'

'Aren't you having one?' asked Delia.

'No. I don't like ice cream.' Gareth sat down again. 'I read somewhere what goes into those things. Lard. Gravy browning. Industrial dyes.'

'Go on with you.' Sensing that he wasn't quite so annoyed with her now, Delia relaxed. 'Try a lick of mine?'

Shirley relaxed, too. Relieved that Delia hadn't mentioned their first meeting — for of course she'd seen Gareth Hughes before, he was the young man who'd been with Delia that afternoon at the surgery — she felt happier now she had something to do, even if that something was only eating an ersatz ice cream.

Did Gareth remember her? Apparently, he didn't. She wouldn't mention it and prayed he wouldn't, either. 'What's the main film about?' she asked bravely, for as she spoke he turned to look at her.

'Gang warfare on the streets of Chicago.' Gareth grinned. 'There'll lots of blood, guts and gore. I hope you've a strong stomach?'

'Oh, yes.' Shirley nodded. 'We killed a pig yesterday,' she said, conversationally. 'Poor Jerry Trotter. Didn't he squeal!'

'He'll be so many hams and sausages by now, I suppose?'

'Mum's starting on him this evening.' Shirley finished her ice-cream. 'It'll be pig's fry for supper tomorrow night.'

★ ★ ★

When they reached Mrs Newby's, Shirley scuttled indoors, leaving Gareth and Delia on the step.

'Shall I see you tomorrow?' Half inclined to punish Delia, but also anxious to kiss her, Gareth looked into her eyes. 'What about driving out to the Red Lion? Just you and me, that is.'

'I've got French tomorrow evening. But I could meet you for lunch, maybe.'

'I can't make lunch.' Gareth put his hands on her shoulders. Manipulating the joints, he hurt her. Just a little. 'What if I pick you up from work at five, then we could — '

'I'm working till seven every evening, for the rest of this week.'

'Then going home to wash your hair, no doubt.'

Gareth pinched harder. 'Okay,' he said. 'I'll phone you sometime.'

'Not at work.'

'I'll phone you, I said.' He walked down the steps, got into the car and drove away.

Shirley was already in Delia's bed. 'Can I read while you get ready?' she asked.

'Yes, do.' Picking up her spongebag, Delia went off to the bathroom. As she washed her face, she felt how hot it was. She had made rather a mess of that . . .

She had refused Mrs Newby's offer of her late husband's charpoy, and now she suffered for it. All night, she dozed, woke, dozed fitfully again. At seven o'clock, stiff with backache, she sat up, yawned and sighed.

In Delia's comfortable bed Shirley slept on, breathing regularly, her hair disordered on Delia's comfortable feather pillow.

★ ★ ★

Gareth phoned Delia at work, on Wednesday morning when the library was always busiest. He was offhand with her, and it was only with some difficulty that she eventually managed to persuade him to meet her for lunch.

In the café, she looked at him. He was such a nice man! A nice, good, decent man — and a very ordinary one, too.

He wanted a wife. If it had been branded across his forehead in letters of fire, it couldn't have been more obvious. He wanted his own home, his own hearth, his own children, and a wife to look after the whole ménage.

Delia speared a chip. She sighed. Her plans had no room in them for a husband. No room at all.

7

It wasn't in Gareth's nature to sulk or bear grudges. Soon, he forgave Delia completely. After all, he knew she liked him, for the way she kissed and hugged him told him that. Encouraged, he began to drop hints about going on holiday together. He told her how pretty Devon always was in spring. He mentioned a country hotel by the sea.

Eventually, Delia could stand it no longer. On the day Gareth began to tell her about some new houses just going up on the outskirts of the city, adding that mortgages were readily available, she panicked and told him she couldn't see him regularly any more.

He took a great deal of convincing, and as she spoke Delia felt as if she were kicking a wounded kitten. 'We'll still be friends,' she assured him. 'We'll still see each other, to talk. I'd still like to go to the pictures with you now and then.'

'Right.' No promises had been made or broken, so at least Gareth's self-esteem remained intact. 'I'll see you around,' he said, bleakly. 'We'll have a drink, maybe. If you're free.'

'Of course we will.' Now, Delia hated herself. 'Gareth, you were thinking about getting up a darts team, weren't you? With Ben Davies, and that other man. You'll be busy practising for the next few weeks.'

'Sure.' Gareth shrugged. 'Right, then. I'll see you sometime.'

Gareth took his rejection very badly. He did not phone or write to her, and when Delia finally rang him at work, he told her rather sharply that he was in a meeting, and could not speak to her just then.

The indifference in his voice hurt Delia more than she cared to admit.

But Gareth was hurt, too. 'Women,' he muttered, as he and Ben Davies sat hunched over a lunchtime jar in their favourite city pub. 'I'll never understand women. Even if I live to be a hundred years old.'

'Did she give you the push, then?' asked Ben Davies, who was not the most tactful of men.

'We decided to call it a day,' Gareth replied, coldly for him. Remembering he had a great pile of work to get through that afternoon, he decided that perhaps he ought not to get drunk. He stood up. 'I'll be getting back,' he said.

'Right.' Ben ordered another half. 'Watch how you go.'

Turning into Maybury Street, Gareth practically fell over a pushchair. 'Sorry,' he began. Grabbing the woman's arm, he steadied her. 'Oh, hello,' he added, smiling now. 'I didn't recognise you at first.'

Shirley Bell blinked into the sunshine. Then, realisation dawned. 'Hello, Gareth,' she said, primly. 'How are you?'

'Fine, thanks. What about you?'

'I'm okay.'

'What are you doing in this part of town?'

'Shopping.' Now, Shirley smiled a tight, polite little smile. 'I wanted some dress material from

Harrison's, and I had to go to the surgery. Jenny was due for her jabs.'

She looked down at the child in the pushchair. 'This is Jenny,' she said.

'Hello, young lady.' Gareth grinned at the baby, who was blowing bubbles and talking to herself. Now, having completely forgotten that a horrible man had just been sticking needles into her bottom, she beamed at Gareth and burbled a reply.

'I couldn't agree more,' he said. He let the child grab at his shiny cufflinks. 'Are you her auntie or something?' he asked Shirley.

'No. I'm her mother.' Tensing herself for the inevitable questions, Shirley prepared to meet Gareth's eyes.

But now, Gareth was talking to the baby again.

Eventually, Shirley got fed up. 'Well, it was nice to see you again,' she began. 'I expect you — '

'Are you going back into town?' interrupted Gareth.

'No. To the bus station.' Kicking the brake off the pushchair wheels, Shirley walked on. But now, to her surprise, Gareth strolled beside her. 'I didn't realise you were married,' he said, casually.

'I'm not.' Shirley looked straight ahead. 'I'm a single mother, as they say.'

'Oh, I see.'

'I'm in a bit of a hurry, as well.'

'So am I.' Gareth smartened his pace. 'Where do you live?' he asked.

'With my parents. We have a farm, over towards Canon Lea.'

'Oh. Are you tenants there?'

'Yes.' Now the bus station was in sight, and Shirley could see the yellow Canon Lea bus waiting. As she hurried towards it, she saw the driver climb in. She heard him start the engine. 'I'll have to dash,' she said. 'Goodbye.'

'I'll see you on to the bus.' Running awkwardly, Gareth left Shirley behind. Reaching the bus shelter, he called to the driver that another passenger was coming.

A minute later, Shirley came panting up. With Gareth's help, she folded the pushchair and got herself and Jenny on to the bus. 'Thanks,' she gasped, flopping gratefully into the front seat. 'Thanks ever so much.'

'My pleasure.' Gareth smiled at her. 'Bye.'

Thoughtfully, Gareth watched the bus pull out. Then he walked back to the hospital.

He'd told Ben Davies the simple truth. He didn't understand women. Still smarting from Delia Shenstone's treatment of him, he had been mortified to find his most basic instincts had seriously misled him there.

As for her friend, she was a sour-faced little madam if ever there was one. But, as he sat down at his desk, he realised he would like to know the little madam better. He decided it wouldn't do any harm just to ask her out.

Bell. Towards teatime, he got out the telephone directory and ran his index finger down the column, looking for the entry. There it was. Bell H R, Blackstone Farm, Canon Lea. He'd ring her in a day or two, he decided, and ask if she'd like to go out that weekend.

As it happened, Shirley herself answered the phone. She seemed surprised to hear from Gareth Hughes, but she answered his polite enquiries after her health, and assured him that Jenny was very well.

Then, as she was saying it had been kind of him to call, he took a deep breath and asked her. 'Are you free on Sunday? Would you like to go out for a ride?'

'A ride?' Shirley sounded astonished. 'With you?'

'Yes.' Nervously, Gareth cleared his throat. 'The fact is, I'd like to take you out. We could drive over to Stokelea Castle, maybe. Or to Hanley Manor. The gardens are supposed to be lovely at this time of year. Or perhaps we could go to Worcester. Have tea somewhere . . . '

'That sounds nice.' Thinking about it, Shirley found she quite liked the idea of spending an afternoon with Gareth Hughes. 'Is Delia coming?' she enquired.

'No, she isn't,' Gareth replied. 'We don't often see each other these days. Didn't she tell you we'd more or less split up?'

'She did say something, but I haven't spoken to her for a month or more.' Shirley made a mental note, must ring Delia. 'Well, now — what time do you want to meet?'

'I'll pick you up about two, shall I?'

'That'll be fine. Jenny will have finished her nap by then. You don't mind if Jenny comes, do you?'

'Not at all,' said Gareth, nobly. In fact, he'd forgotten all about Jenny. 'Now, let me just make sure I know how to get to Blackstone. Out on the

Bradleigh Latimer road, aren't you?'

'That's right.'

'I'll find you.'

'I'm sure you will. Bye.'

Shirley looked at Jenny, who was chewing the corner of a rug. 'We're going out on Sunday,' she told her.

Jenny spat out a mouthful of fluff. 'Mum!' she cried, in triumphant reply.

★   ★   ★

Mr and Mrs Bell had never blamed their daughter for her mistake. When it became clear that Shirley was pregnant, Agnes Bell had taken the girl aside and, after confirming her suspicions, asked how Shirley could have been so silly.

But this was the beginning and end of her criticism. From then on, she had simply rearranged her own and her daughter's workloads, so Shirley would be spared any lifting or other strenuous toil.

Shirley's father had frowned and sucked his teeth. 'You daft, or what?' he'd demanded, but more in sorrow than in anger. 'Listen to me. Did 'e force you?'

'No.' Miserably, Shirley had shrugged. 'It was my own fault.'

'Was it, now.' While secretly vowing that if he ever discovered the identity of his daughter's seducer, he would qualify him to run in the Geldings' Hurdle, Mr Bell had been satisfied. He left the matter there.

He decided it was most likely that his poor child had been taken advantage of by some married neighbour. But, to his everlasting credit, he did not demand to know who the father of Shirley's baby was. Being a genuinely loving parent and seeing that his daughter was sorry enough for herself, he did not think it necessary to add to her distress.

He put up with comments and innuendoes from his friends and neighbours, and told his wife to do the same. Soon, realising that Mr and Mrs Bell were going to stand by their erring child, the local people eventually stopped making catty remarks.

Women began to knit. They'd all known Shirley from babyhood, they took her for a decent girl, and, as they plained and purled, they agreed among themselves that anyone could make a fool of herself on a Saturday night. As the piles of woolly leggings and matinée jackets grew, they sagely conceded it was only the innocent, trusting girls who ever got caught.

Jenny herself became the light of her grand-parents' lives. Coming into the world one warm summer night, she lay against her grandmother's shoulder and made soft baby noises into Mrs Bell's ear. She did not cry. Instead she gazed around Shirley's bedroom and, apparently satisfied with it, closed her eyes and dozed.

'What a little biddy.' Tears in her own eyes, Mrs Bell had turned to the midwife and beamed. 'Oh, bless her! What a little lamb.'

* * *

Watching Shirley and Gareth drive away, Mrs Bell gave Jenny a hug and took her back indoors. 'Come on, my pet,' she murmured. 'We'll go an' wake Grandad. He can get out your bricks and make you a castle. Then you can knock it all down again.'

For Jenny was not going for a ride. When Shirley had told her parents about the proposed outing to Worcester and said she would be taking Jenny along as a chaperone, Mrs Bell had laughed. 'Don't be so daft, girl,' she said. 'Poor little mite, why would she want to sit in the back of some old car, having her little insides shaken to glory? Go by yourself. Unless you'd prefer to ask this lad in to tea?'

'I fancy a drive. But I could maybe bring him back for something to eat. We could go for a ride, then come back here about five?'

'You do that.' Mrs Bell nodded. 'Now, you be careful,' she said. 'You know what I mean. You've only got to grin at some lads, an' they think it's an invitation to I don't know what malarky.'

'Gareth isn't like that.' Shirley smiled. 'I'll be safe enough with him.'

Putting Jenny into her playpen, Mrs Bell looked narrowly at her husband. 'You see him?' she demanded. 'You see him out the window, did you?'

'I did.'

'That him, you reckon? Jenny's Dad, I mean.'

'No.' Henry Bell sucked his pipe. 'No, I doubt it. Wrong sort of colourin'. Wrong build.' Glancing affectionately at his granddaughter, he shook his head. 'Looked a decent enough lad,' he observed, thoughtfully. 'Girl deserves a bit of pleasure, don't she? An' now she knows what's what?'

'I hope she does.' Mrs Bell ran water into the kitchen sink. 'Take her out of there,' she said, pointing to Jenny. 'Pile them bricks up for her, then let her push 'em over. You know she likes that.'

Henry Bell did as he was told.

★   ★   ★

Gareth reversed the car out of the farmyard. 'Where to then, madam?' he enquired.

'Stokelea Castle, I think.' Shirley smiled at him. 'I've never been there.'

'It's all in ruins, you know,' Gareth told her. 'There's not much to see.'

'That's okay.' Shirley shrugged. 'I like ruins,' she went on. 'I'm interested in antiques. For example, your little car here — '

'Now, don't be rude about Flora.' Gareth grinned. 'She's a game little thing, if you treat her right.'

They reached the castle, walked amid piles of broken masonry and climbed the one remaining tower. As they descended, Gareth took Shirley's hand. But when they reached ground level again, he kept it in his. 'We'll go for a walk, shall we?' he suggested now. 'There's a nice clear path through those beech woods, and it's certain to be dry underfoot.'

'All right,' said Shirley. 'You lead the way.'

For a while, they walked in silence. Then, as they came to a stream which ran chattering through the wood, Gareth spoke. 'You're ever so pretty, you know,' he told her. 'I thought that the first time we met.'

Shirley laughed. 'Go on with you,' she said. 'You

don't even remember the first time we met. Have you seen Delia since I spoke to you last?'

'No.' Gareth stiffened. 'These days, she's either at her evening classes, or she's working late. She's got no time for me.'

'Oh, dear.' Sympathetically, Shirley sighed. 'You really like her, don't you?'

'Yes. But she's not at all bothered about me. She was once, but not now. Dunno what I've done. But then, I don't understand women.'

'I don't understand men.'

'Oh, we're simple!' Now, Gareth smiled. 'Well, I am, anyway.'

'Are you?' Shirley looked into his eyes. 'Were you surprised when I told you Jenny was mine?'

'Yes, I was. Very surprised.'

'I look like a decent girl, then?'

'What's that supposed to mean?'

'In spite of being a tart, I don't look like one.'

'Oh, for God's sake! I didn't think that at all!' Gareth looked away. 'I was surprised because — well, you can't be more than eighteen — '

'I'm nearly twenty.'

'Well, there you are, then. You're too young to have a child.'

'Oh, rubbish. Plenty of girls of my age are married, with two or three kids.'

'Maybe.' Gareth looked right at her again. 'Look,' he said. 'Perhaps we ought to talk about this. Why do you think I asked you out?'

'*I don't know!*'

'You don't, do you? Doesn't stop you jumping to conclusions, though. You think I'm only after one thing. But you're wrong.'

'Oh?' Rather taken aback, Shirley stared at him. 'Well actually, Gareth,' she began, 'I didn't think that at all.'

'You didn't think what?'

'That you'd — well — '

'Go on. Say it.'

'That you'd try to grab me.' Shirley blushed. 'You don't look like a seducer, you know.'

'Don't I? Look, suppose for a moment that I tried to kiss you. What would you do?'

'Dunno, really.' Shirley shrugged. Then she grinned. 'Do you want to find out?'

'Should I risk it?'

'If you think it's worth it.'

'I see.' Gareth took her hands in his. 'I think it's worth it,' he said.

'In that case, what are you waiting for? Easter?'

'A cheeky little madam, aren't you?' Gareth took her in his arms. 'I thought you were such a meek little mouse.'

'I see.' Shirley shrugged. She smiled up at him. 'You can't trust anybody, can you?'

Five minutes later, Gareth reluctantly let her go. 'It's getting dark,' he said. 'I'd better take you home. Jenny will be wondering where you are.'

★ ★ ★

He stopped the car in the lane which led to the farmhouse. Then, he kissed her again.

Shirley kissed him back. Although she felt none of the passion, none of the urgency, none of the

95

electric excitement which had practically convulsed her while kissing Peter — but no, she mustn't think of Peter — she decided that kissing Gareth was nice. 'Will you come in for tea?' she asked.

'I don't think so. Not today.' Gareth looked into her eyes. 'Shirley, shall I see you again?'

'Do you want to?'

'Yes I do, very much.'

'When?'

'Next weekend? We could take Jenny to Stowerton, to the fair. She's too young for the rides, but she'd like the colours and the noise. She could have a balloon and some candyfloss, if there is any.'

'She'd love that.' Shirley opened the door of the car. 'You'll come for us then, will you?'

'Yes. On Saturday. About half two.'

'Great.' Leaning towards him, Shirley kissed him again. 'Thanks for a lovely afternoon.'

'You don't have to say that.'

'I mean it. I've enjoyed myself.'

'Get away with you.' Gareth started the car. 'See you next week. Watch how you go.'

★　★　★

He took her out every weekend. On Sundays, they drove into Evesbridge or Worcester, had tea in a café and took Jenny for walks on various playing fields and greens. Gareth pushed her high on the swings, making her squeal with delight. 'Garriff carry me!' she would insist. 'Garriff give me piggy-back.'

Soon, it became clear that Jenny adored Gareth. At the mere mention of his name, her eyes lit up.

The sight of him sent her into paroxysms of delight. She cried when he went away. Shirley herself became more attached to him than she'd meant to be.

She told him about her affair with Peter, and he said he understood. At any rate, he neither condemned nor reproached. Instead, he just shrugged and said, well, such things were common enough.

'I expect he did love you,' he added, gravely. 'After all, I do.'

So when Gareth asked Shirley to marry him, she wasn't really surprised, and she immediately replied that of course she would.

8

Delia kept herself busy. At work from half-past eight every morning until seven o'clock most nights, she dashed back to her digs for a hasty supper before rushing out again to her evening classes in shorthand, typing, basic book-keeping and French or German conversation.

'It's nice to have outside interests,' observed Mrs Newby one evening, as she watched Delia gobble up her dinner, then gulp down a cup of coffee which was still scalding hot. 'What is it tonight?'

'French, then dictation practice. I must go.' Jumping up, Delia pulled on her coat and grabbed her bag. 'I'll be late, so don't wait up for me.'

Mrs Newby sighed. That young woman was exhausting herself. She'd get brain fever and end up in the local sanatorium, if she didn't watch out.

⋆   ⋆   ⋆

'You're actually going to *marry* him? Good grief!' Sitting in Latchett's café, Delia gaped in absolute disbelief. 'But for heaven's sake, why?'

'Because I love him, of course!' Mortally offended, Shirley glared. 'So if you've changed your mind and want him for yourself, you're too late.'

Now, she displayed the neat engagement ring, in which a small solitaire diamond winked and sparkled. 'He's mine,' she added. 'See?'

'Good heavens, *I* don't want him!' Recovering from her surprise, Delia grinned. 'I can't imagine why you do.'

'He's nice, that's why,' said Shirley. 'He's generous, he's kind — '

'He's ignorant, he's dull — '

'Don't be so horrible!' Now, Shirley was angry. 'Right,' she snapped. 'I shan't tell you anything else.'

'I'm sorry.' Abashed, Delia hung her head. 'That was very mean of me. Please go on.'

'Where was I?' Shirley frowned. 'Oh, yes. Well, it's official now. When we told our parents, they were delighted. So we all had a special tea together, to celebrate. That was last week.'

Remembering, Shirley smiled again. 'Mr Hughes is just like Gareth. He looks the same, has the same sort of way with him — '

'No doubt he's just as good, kind, *et cetera* — '

'Yes, he is. Look, will you stop being so sarcastic? I know you're jealous. But honestly, there's no need to go on like this.'

'I'm *not* jealous at all. In fact, I'm very pleased for you both.' Thoughtfully, Delia stirred her coffee round and round. 'Is it going to be a white wedding?' she asked now. 'Complete with bridesmaids and bells and all the frills?'

'Good heavens, no.' Shirley blushed. 'I hardly think that would be the thing. Do you?'

'Well, perhaps not.'

'It'll be a register office job, round the back of the Shire Hall. Then, we'll have everyone to high tea at Blackstone. Mum's got it all worked out.'

'Where will you live?'

'Gareth's Dad is selling his house and going to live with his sister. He's giving us the deposit on one of those new semis they're building out at Martley, by the railway.'

'That'll be nice.' Delia smiled at her friend. 'I got through all my City and Guilds exams,' she remarked, carelessly.

'Did you? Congratulations!' Shirley beamed. 'I did mean to ask. Well? Did you get a distinction in every paper?'

'I only scraped a pass in book-keeping. But otherwise . . . '

'Jolly well done!' Genuinely impressed, Shirley's delight was obvious. 'So what will you do now?'

'Write to a few editors. I want to work on a newspaper.'

'So it's goodbye Miss Ryan.'

'Good riddance, more like.' Delia grimaced. 'Do you know what she said yesterday?'

'Surprise me.'

'She told me that if I carried on the way I was going, I'd never catch a man. It seems men don't care for women who are clever. I'd better watch my step.' Now, Delia stood up. 'What are you doing this afternoon?' she enquired.

'Going back to the farm with Dad.' Shirley glanced at her watch. 'I'll have to rush. The vet's coming over at two, and Dad will want to talk to him. He doesn't trust my Mum to understand what he says.'

★ ★ ★

Delia spent weeks searching the Situations Vacant columns in the trade press. Eventually, she found something which she thought might do. She applied for a job as a general trainee on the *Stourhampton Echo*.

The *Echo* was the oldest newspaper in the West Midlands. Founded in 1754 and never a week missed, Delia would have put money on the certainty that it had never employed a woman before.

She would have won her bet. Interviewing her, the editor told Delia straight away that he'd expected D G Shenstone to be a lad. But he'd liked the article she'd written for the *Library Gazette*. He thought her work showed definite promise.

If he did take her on, however, he couldn't risk paying her a man's wage. Two pounds a week was all he'd be prepared to offer a girl — and that only on the clear understanding that she would put in the same working hours as a man.

He'd expect her to turn up for work on the dot, and he wasn't going to tolerate being messed about. For example, he wouldn't put up with any nonsense like women's complaints keeping her off sick for days on end.

'I'm not payin' somebody who has to spend a week in bed every month,' he told her, darkly. 'So unless you're fit, and I mean fit — '

'I haven't been ill for years.'

'Get away with you. *My* wife — '

'Is nothing to do with me.' Coolly, Delia looked at him, this fat, florid man in greasy tweeds, whose nicotine-stained fingers were as fat as bursting sausages, whose flannel shirt was yellow-grey with perspiration. She disliked him already. 'I can work as hard as any man,' she insisted. 'Give me a trial, and if I don't suit — '

'If I take you on, my lass, you bloody well *will* suit.' Clenching his meaty fists, Mr Holliday glared. But then he relaxed. He even grinned. 'All right, then,' he said. 'I'll stick my neck out and give you a chance. Start Monday.'

'This Monday?' Delia frowned. 'That's far too soon. I have to give notice on my present job, I'll need to find some digs — there are all kinds of arrangements to be made.'

'Bloody well make them, then! Monday, eight-thirty sharp.' Mr Holliday picked up a pencil. 'Good afternoon, Miss Shenstone. Shut the door behind you on your way out.'

★   ★   ★

On Sunday afternoon, Gareth and Shirley took Delia to Evesbridge station. 'Got it all?' asked Gareth, as he pushed her last case into the third class compartment.

'I doubt it.' Delia tossed a brown paper parcel into the rack overhead. 'But Mrs Newby will send on anything I've left behind, bless her little cotton socks.'

'Write, won't you?' Shirley handed in a carrier bag full to overflowing with various odd and ends. 'Send me a postcard now and then.'

'Of course.' Leaning out of the carriage window, Delia hugged her friend around the neck, then kissed her cheek. 'You'll hear from me,' she promised. 'All about me, too!'

The train pulled out. Gareth and Shirley watched until it was out of sight. 'She's crazy,' said Gareth. He gave Shirley a loving hug. 'She's quite mad.'

'Why do you say that?'

'Well — she's packed in a secure job in local government to go and work on a pathetic little rag. Now, instead of training to become a librarian, she'll be making tea. Folding inky pages. Proof-reading the births, marriages and deaths. Deadly, or what?'

'She won't be doing that sort of thing for long. In five years' time, she hopes to be in Fleet Street.' Slipping her arm around Gareth's waist, Shirley smiled up at him. 'You still hanker after her, don't you?'

'No.'

'Liar.'

'I'm not a liar!'

'Fibber, then.' Shirley hugged him. 'I know I'm only second best.'

'You're not! Oh, sweetheart, don't ever think that.' Gareth hugged Shirley tight. 'I fancied Delia. I admit that. I liked her a lot. But she wouldn't have been happy with me. I wouldn't have been enough for her, and she saw that long before I did. Besides — I love *you*.'

9

'He's only taken you on because you're cheap.' Nastily, the chief reporter grinned. 'You know that, don't you?'

'He hates women,' put in the sub-editor, wisely. 'It's a well-known fact. You won't last long.'

'You'll never be able to lift them type cases.' Bill Lucas, the old man in charge of the equally ancient presses which lurked in the *Echo*'s rat-infested basement, snorted in derision at the very idea. 'Do yourself a mischief, you will.'

Such was Delia's initial reception from the staff at the *Stourhampton Echo*.

A little local paper, the *Echo* had a circulation of five thousand and a staff of six. Delia was the most junior member of the team. At first, she met with nothing but hostility, obstruction and suspicion. Teased and bullied from daybreak to sunset, she was a victim of the meanest practical jokes and the butt of the most insulting remarks.

In the office, she managed to keep her cool — just about. But most evenings she went home to her cheerless lodgings, flung herself on her sagging bed and burst into tears of frustration and despair.

She would never have believed ordinary working men, husbands and fathers all, could be so cruel. The chief reporter never had a good word to say either to her or for her, the sub-editor told her she was useless, and the editor himself never opened his mouth except to swear at her. She learned only by default.

But she stuck at it and gradually, very gradually, she began to prove her worth. Willing to work very hard and put in longer hours than any of the men, she would do anything from fold pages until two in the morning to trail all around Stourhampton and the surrounding district, often in the pouring rain, trying to sell advertising space to local businesses and shops.

Sam Holliday eventually realised that at a couple of pounds a week, Delia was the best bargain he'd made for a very long time. If he used Delia's copy, he wouldn't have to depend on unreliable local contacts for reports on clubs and societies — or for news shorts. He would not have to flash around half so many ten shilling notes, and he'd save a fortune on halves of bitter, if Delia could do it all.

'I'll keep you on a bit longer, Tiger Lily,' he told her, as he reviewed her position at the end of that first traumatic year. He grinned. 'You know what — I reckon we might eventually lick you into shape. Turn you into a reporter, even. But don't tell the lads I said that. They'll think I'm going soft in the head.'

★ ★ ★

Two, three, four years went by. As Delia learned her trade, she also earned a little — just a little — respect. The men became less obnoxious and their nicknames for her a little less insulting.

She earned her wages, too. More than earned

them. 'He exploits you, Squeak.' Treating Delia to a drink in the reporters' local one evening, the sports editor put his hand on her knee. 'Tell me, how long have you been here now? Two years, is it? Three?'

'Four. Nearly five, actually.' Delia put Dick Searle's nicotine-stained paw back on the table. 'Why?'

'I reckon it's high time you were moving on.' Dick grinned. 'Or settling down.'

'Meaning?'

'Well — you're a girl. You're young. Not bad looking, either. Want a fag?'

'No, thank you.'

'You ought to be married, is what I'm saying.' The sports editor lit up. 'You should be at home, with hubby and a couple of kiddies. That's where you ought to be.'

'I see.' Delia shook her head. 'That's what Sam Holliday thinks, too.'

'He's right.' The sports editor looked grave. 'You're a nice girl,' he added, meaningfully. 'One of the best. Look, if you ever fancy going to the pictures one evening, let me know.'

'Will your wife be coming, too?' Finishing her drink, Delia stood up. 'I must be going,' she said. 'I have to do something for the old man.'

'I'll see you home, shall I?'

'That won't be necessary, thanks all the same.' Delia picked up her handbag. 'You stay here. Get a few more pints in, eh?'

★ ★ ★

'Yes, that's fine.' Grinning, Mr Holliday looked Delia up and down. 'Just what we need, in fact. Well done.'

'Thanks.' Surprised and gratified that her special report on Stourhampton's annual summer carnival and its five hundred year history had been so warmly received, Delia herself smiled now. 'I'll give it to the subs, shall I?'

'Let me see the pictures first.' Mr Holliday's grin became wider and more vulpine. 'Well, now — where was I?'

'You said you liked my article.'

'So I did.' The editor sniffed. 'Of course, we'll have to shorten it.'

'Fred will have to trim it here and there, you mean? That's okay. I — '

'I mean, *you'll* have to cut it!' Reaching for his cigarettes, Mr Holliday lit a Craven A. 'Lose at least a thousand words. Bloody hell, woman — you can't have the whole of page four!'

'Why not?' demanded Delia. She glared at him. 'Listen, Mr Holliday! You promised I could have that space! You gave me a free hand, to do anything I — '

'Look here, Tiger Lily — who's the editor of this paper? You or me?'

'You said I could have that page. You told me you wanted to see what I could make of it.'

'You didn't do too badly, either.' Mr Holliday laughed his fat laugh. 'Now, dear girl — if you've finished having your attack of the vapours, could you go and find those pictures? Bring them back here in five minutes or so. When I've had my coffee.'

'As it happens, there *is* something else.'

'Oh? What?'

'I want a pay rise. I want at least another twenty five shillings a week.'

'Really? What makes you think you deserve that?'

'Well, for a start, I work very hard. A sight harder, let me tell you, than Dave Bennet or Brian Hopkins. They knock off at five, every single day. I work until six or seven. They're paid a lot more than I am. The Union rates — '

'Union rates be damned!' Now, the editor became angry. 'Delia, my love,' he muttered, 'anyone who talks to *me* about Union rates is just asking for the sack, and well you know it. As for Dave and Brian — they're blokes.'

'Well? What of it?'

'Bloody obvious, isn't it? Oh, Christ — damn this throat!' Mr Holiday coughed his revolting smoker's cough. 'They've families to support!'

'So what?' retorted Delia. 'So Dave has his ancient old mother to keep. Brian's got half a dozen kids. What's that to me? Just because they're men with dependents, it doesn't mean — '

'Oh, doesn't it?' From the glowing butt of his previous cigarette, Mr Holliday lit another. 'Women,' he muttered, sourly. 'Give one an inch! Look, you had a pay rise last April. What are we paying you now? Five guineas a week?'

'Four pounds, seventeen and six.'

'Right, I'll up that to a round fiver.'

'Six pounds ten.'

'Nothing doing.' Mr Holliday snorted. 'Six pounds ten, indeed. Bloody nerve. You're already paid as much as you deserve — and more!'

'You think so? I don't.'

'Oh, for crying out loud!' Mr Holliday banged his fist down on his desk, hurting his knuckles. 'If you don't like it here, sweetheart, you know what you can do!'

'I'll do it, then! I'll find another job.' Picking up her article, Delia turned to go. 'Cut by a thousand words, you said?'

'Twelve hundred.' Mr Holliday scowled. 'I don't think the good people of Stourhampton really need to know that back in fifteen sixty something or other there was a ducking stool on the village green. Nor that witches were burned there in the ruddy Middle Ages. If you cut out all that nonsense, there'll only be about a thousand words left.'

Delia let the editor's door slam behind her. Striding into the main office, she saw Dave Bennet grinning at her. 'Hello, sunshine,' he began. 'What — '

But Delia ignored this cheery greeting. Frowning, she sat down at her desk.

'Old man upset you again?' Dave leaned over her, patting her shoulder and trying to look down the front of her dress. 'Never mind, princess. Come over the pub and tell your Uncle Dave all about it.'

'Shut up, Dave.' Poring over her article, Delia sighed. She'd have to get another job now. She'd as good as given in her notice, after all.

★ ★ ★

The neat pile of cuttings was growing. Reading some of her articles and reports over again, Delia was bound to admit that as far as subject matter went they were terminally uninspiring. This wasn't exactly her fault. Nothing very exciting had ever happened in Stourhampton.

She read through another couple of snippets. In spite of their dreary content her articles were, she thought, fairly well written. She tipped out another load of stuff. Here was a photograph, a good one — here she was smiling at the mayor at a civic reception, and the caption mentioned our reporter Delia Shenstone. She'd send that off, too.

Taking out the address book in which she kept notes of all her important contacts, she copied down the name and address of one person in particular. Well, Don Jarrow had told her a dozen times that if she ever fancied a move down south, he was sure the *Wessex Reporter* would be keen to snap her up.

Don Jarrow. Remembering him, Delia grimaced. Don was an oily individual, as greasy as they come, who'd once worked as a news photographer on the *Stourhampton Echo* — but then landed himself a peach of a job in Dorchester. If Delia applied for a position on his paper, would he assume she was after him?

Oh, she'd deal with that later, she thought, as she composed her letter to the editor. If Don Jarrow did put in a good word for her, so much the better. She'd deal with his wandering hands if and when the time came.

★ ★ ★

'The *Wessex Reporter.*' Summoned to Mr Holliday's cluttered little office in order to explain herself, Delia repeated the name. 'Surely you've heard of it?'

'Don't be so bloody cheeky. Of course I've heard of it.' Mr Holliday frowned. 'Who does it belong to?'

'It's part of the Hornchurch group.'

'I see. What's so bloody marvellous about the Hornchurch group, eh? Or the flaming Wessex Whatsitsname, come to that?'

'It's a very good local paper,' Delia replied. Surely even Mr Holliday knew that the *Wessex Reporter,* based in Dorchester but covering most of Dorset, was an important link in a chain of provincial newspapers snaking all over the south of England? 'But it reports national as well as local news. It covered the Lessco scandal — do you remember that? When two crooks were trying to get old people to sell their homes at below cost, promising them investment dividends and purpose-built flats in return. Flats which didn't exist and weren't going to be built.'

'Can't say that rings any bells.' Derisively, Mr Holliday sniffed. 'So your mind's made up, is it?'

'I think so.' In fact, Delia *knew* so. She'd been so surprised and delighted to be offered a job on the *Reporter* that she'd accepted it there and then, before the editor had a chance to change his mind.

'Well, there's gratitude for you.' Deeply, Mr Holliday sighed. 'I've taught you all I know. Watched over you like a father. Turned you into a real professional — and this is how you repay me.'

Now, the editor stood up. 'I dunno how we'll

111

manage without you, and that's the honest truth.'

'You'll cope.' Sweetly, Delia smiled. 'After all, you only took me on as a favour in the first place.'

★   ★   ★

Don Jarrow had left a note for her. Sellotaped to a bottle of Coty *Emeraude*, he wished her well, said he was sorry he'd missed her and hoped she'd soon be chasing him again. He was now working as a freelance mainly for the *Daily Express*, and looked forward to the day when Delia herself arrived in Fleet Street.

From her very first day on the *Wessex Reporter*, Delia realised that everything was going to be quite different now. It was as if she'd come out from under a stone and was standing in the sunshine at last.

Quite literally, in fact. Whereas the *Echo* had occupied dark, frowsty little offices at the back of the market hall, the *Reporter's* staff worked in light, clean, airy premises, in a centrally-heated building which actually had carpets on its floors.

The editor of the paper was, so rumour had it, well in with the proprietor's wife. If that was indeed the case, Tom Freeman had put his association with Mrs Hornchurch to good use. Thanks to her, all her husband's newspaper offices were civilised places. The *Reporter* had its own canteen, and fresh black coffee was available all day long.

'Go out with Ted Allen at first,' said the editor. A ravaged-looking workaholic in his middle thirties, Tom Freeman welcomed his new reporter cordially, and shook her by the hand. 'Do your calls with Ted this week. Get to know the area. Do you drive?'

'No, not yet.'

'You'll have to learn.' Mr Freeman grinned. 'Ted will teach you, if you ask him nicely. But do bear in mind that he's a happily married man.'

'Yes. Of course.' Blankly, Delia stared. Was her new skirt too short? Her make-up too bright? Did she look like a husband-snatcher, or what? 'I'll be off, then,' she said.

'Right. Have fun.'

Delia went back to the reporters' room. Glancing at the big desk diary in which the chief reporter noted down the jobs for the day, with a reporter's name pencilled in against each assignment, Delia saw that her own first job was to do an interview with the manager of a small motor assembly plant. So, that bright spring morning Delia, Ted Allen and a photographer climbed into Ted's old Ford Popular and drove to the factory.

Directed to the administration block, they found the manager's office. Greeted by a smart secretary, they were ushered into an equally smart reception room and left alone with an unchaperoned drinks cabinet. 'Mr Jameson will be with you very shortly,' purred the secretary, as she walked towards the door. 'In the meantime, do make yourselves comfortable.'

'Tell Mr Jameson there's no hurry.' Ted Allen helped himself to Scotch.

'No hurry at all,' agreed the photographer, knocking back a large gin. 'Delia, do you want a sherry?'

The three journalists were covering the opening of a new section of the factory, which would make tractors and result in the creation of two hundred badly-needed new jobs. It had been agreed that Delia would interview the manager himself, while Ted and the photographer toured the works, chatting with the employees. The door of the reception room eventually opened, to admit a large, grey-haired, smartly-suited man, together with a younger but equally presentable companion.

'My deputy, Mr Kingston.' Having introduced his right hand man, Mr Jameson looked enquiringly at Ted Allen. 'You are?'

Ted Allen made the introductions.

'Miss Shenstone.' Taking Delia's hand, Jack Kingston shook it firmly. He smiled. To her extreme annoyance, Delia found she was blushing.

Ambitious, greedy, and determined to succeed in life, Jack Kingston was a high-flyer already earmarked for top management. Looking at him, however, Delia's first impressions were of a tall, fair-haired man who knew he was attractive to women. From the way he was smiling at her, she imagined that for any woman daft enough to encourage him, he was more than likely to be trouble.

Now Mr Jameson was talking to her. 'As I was saying to Mr Allen here,' he went on, 'I think it might be best if I took him over to the factory now. You could stay here and talk to Mr Kingston — he'll fill you in on the company's background, and bring you over to the works later. How about that?'

'That's fine by me.' Delia took out her notebook. 'We'll see you in about ten minutes, then.'

'There's no rush,' said Ted Allen, grinning. 'See you when we do.'

The others went away. 'Well, Mr Kingston,' began Delia, 'may I start by asking a few general questions about the company?

'Fire away.' Jack Kingston sat down. 'Ask anything you like.'

★   ★   ★

Delia wrote up the interview and gave it to one of the subs. An hour later, she was told the editor wanted a word with her. 'What have I done?' she asked the Chief Sub, a dour man in his fifties who hated everybody.

'How the devil should I know?' was the reply.

Knees knocking, Delia tapped on the editor's door.

'Ah, Delia. Come in, come in. Sit down for a moment.' Now, the editor looked down at Delia's article, which lay on his desk. 'This is a splendid piece of work,' he began. 'Clear and to the point. Well done.'

'Thank you.' Relieved, Delia smiled. 'I'm glad you like it.'

'So am I, believe you me. No, don't get up.' Tom Freeman reached for his cigarettes. 'Now, then — how are you getting on?'

'Well, it's early days yet, of course. But so far, everything seems to be fine.'

115

'Rub along with the lads, do you? Found somewhere decent to live?'

'Yes.' Delia felt her smile falter. 'Mr Freeman, have I done something wrong?'

'Far from it. I've confirmed your appointment.' Delia's boss grinned. 'From next month, you'll be getting an extra two guineas a week. So be a good girl, and don't ask me for another rise until next spring at the earliest. Eh?'

'A rise?' Delia was almost speechless. 'I thought I was on three months' trial,' she began. 'I thought — '

'Oh, nuts to all that probationary stuff.' Tom Freeman opened a folder. 'Carry on as you are now, and you'll be news editor this time next year. You can tell that idle sod Nick Harper I said so. Well, haven't you any work to do?'

★ ★ ★

Shrugging off her misgivings that all this was too good to be true, Delia told herself that after so many years of slogging for the *Stourhampton Echo* she richly deserved a decent break. She decided she would make the most of this one.

Her appointment was formally confirmed, and her editor remained pleased with her work. So pleased that she felt she could risk moving out of digs and into a place of her own. Although flats were in very short supply, she eventually found one she both liked and could afford. The landlord didn't want children in the place — ideally, he'd have preferred to let to a single man — but eventually he agreed to rent the flat to Delia. So now she took out a five year lease on this small apartment above a shoe shop.

The flat had its own front door at pavement level, a big bay window overlooking a picturesque little street, and it was only two minutes' walk away from the office. Letting herself in one evening, Delia heard a car draw up beside her. 'Hello?' The driver had wound down the window on the passenger side, and now he leaned across the front seat. 'It is Miss Shenstone, isn't it?'

'Oh — hello.' Delia turned and walked towards the car. 'I didn't recognise you at first.'

'But you know me now.' Jack Kingston grinned at her. 'I must say, you're looking very well.'

'Thank you.' Delia found herself smiling back. 'I've just finished work,' she told him. 'I — '

'You're just about to have your supper.' Jack Kingston grinned again, baring fine, white teeth. 'Look,' he said, 'I'm on my way to the Holly Tree. It's a nice little pub two miles this side of Winsfold. Do you fancy a drink?'

'I don't think so. I'm rather hungry. I skipped lunch, you see. So really — '

'A few shorts would give you an appetite.' Jack winked at her. 'Come on,' he said, persuasively. 'Think of it as a sort of thank you for that splendid write-up you gave the firm.'

Delia was tempted. She was tired, she was hungry, and — never fussy about what she ate — the idea of a couple of drinks, a packet or two of crisps and maybe even a block of chocolate, if she was lucky, was rather enticing. Or at any rate, it was just as attractive as the thought of a few rather ancient sausages and some fried spam, followed by tinned rice pudding, eaten alone in the flat. 'Okay,' she agreed. 'I'll come.'

'Splendid.' Jack pushed open the door of the car. 'Hop in.'

He revved the engine and shot away from the kerb, narrowly missing a bollard and frightening a pigeon, which rose squawking into the air. 'It's a nice pub,' he said. Turning off the main road, soon they were heading for open countryside. 'Good beer, comfortable bar. Horse brasses, pewter tankards — all that.'

'Roaring log fires?' asked Delia, hanging on to her seat.

'What?' He glanced at her. Then he laughed. 'Not in summer,' he admitted. 'But yes, in November there'd be roaring log fires as well.'

'It sounds wonderful.'

'It is.' Overtaking a pre-war Jaguar, Jack put his foot down hard. 'Now, let's get a few things straight,' he said. 'I've noticed you don't wear a ring, but — well, a beautiful girl like you, I couldn't help wondering. There must be some lucky man in your life?'

'Must there?' Cheek, thought Delia. Deciding to let him go on wondering for a little while longer, she laughed. 'Is it much further?' she enquired.

'No. In fact, we're nearly there.' He drew up outside a charming, ivy-clad inn. 'Here we are, then,' he said. 'Out you get.'

★ ★ ★

Jack bought two whiskies and put one in front of Delia. 'Drink up,' he invited.

'Er — well actually, I don't much like spirits.'

'Go on, drink it! Liquid cereal, that is. It'll do you good.'

'If you say so.' Delia drank up.

'Attagirl.' Jack drank his own whisky. 'Well,' he said, 'that's given you a bit more colour. Have another one?' Without waiting for Delia to reply, he went off to the bar.

By now, Delia was very hungry. As Jack sat down again, her stomach rumbled noisily. Jack laughed. 'What do you want to eat?' he asked.

'Nothing.' Now Delia was feeling distinctly light-headed. 'I'll eat when I get home.'

'That might not be for hours yet. Look, they do a very good supper here. Let me get you a pie and chips.'

Before Delia could stop him, he had summoned the barmaid and ordered. 'Tell me about yourself,' he said.

'What do you want to know?'

'Everything.' He grinned. 'I like a good story. Now — where were you born?'

'In Birmingham.'

'I thought I detected a trace of an accent somewhere. I'm from Dudley myself.' But now, seeing the barmaid hovering with two plates on a tray, Jack beckoned her over. 'Well, Polly,' he said, rubbing his hands, 'that looks good! What do you think, Delia?'

'Yes, it looks very nice.' Delia smiled her thanks. But, having winked at the barmaid, Jack now had his trotters in the trough and was bolting his pie.

'There's a pub on the White Marston road which does an excellent steak and kidney pudding,' he told her, as he wolfed down an excellent home-made chicken pie, accompanied by fresh vegetables and chips. 'I'll take you over there sometime.'

'Will you? Promise?' Delia took a gulp of her third whisky. Then she started her dinner. After a few mouthfuls, she grinned. 'This is delicious,' she said, as she speared a fat, golden chip.

'What?' Jack glanced up. He grinned back. 'I do like to see a girl who enjoys her food,' he said.

★ ★ ★

Delia had no intention of getting involved in a serious relationship. She was too busy, and far too ambitious to have any time for things like that. But, when Jack Kingston asked if he could drive her anywhere after work that coming Friday evening, she didn't imagine it was because he was anxious to spare her aching feet. Or that he meant to deposit her on her doorstep, then go straight home to his lonely bedsit, his landlady's cheerless sitting room, or his sock-strewn bachelor flat.

As she settled down in the passenger seat of his very comfortable company car, he grinned at her. 'Shall we try that pub in White Marston?' he suggested.

'Do I get to sample the steak and kidney pudding?'

'You do. You'll enjoy it, as well. Here, do you like claret?'

'I drink almost anything.'

'God! That's a terrible admission.' He pulled away smartly. 'I can see I'm going to have to educate you.'

He drove to the pub at White Marston, bought her the promised steak and kidney pudding, and tried to explain why the wine he'd ordered was vastly superior to the rotgut available in the reception room back at the factory. At about eleven o'clock, he drew up outside the door of her flat. As she was about to get out of the car, he caught her by the wrist. 'You've forgotten something,' he said.

'Oh. Sorry.' Delia sat down again and folded her hands in her lap. 'Thank you for a very pleasant evening,' she said, politely. 'Everything was most enjoyable.'

'My pleasure.' Jack was still holding her wrist. 'Now say goodnight.'

'Goodnight.' Looking at him, Delia laughed. 'My goodness, you're transparent,' she said. 'Look, how much was that meal? If I pay for my share and give you something towards your petrol, will we be quits?'

'Don't be like that.' Tightening his grip on her arm, Jack reached across to touch her face. 'Tell me some more about yourself,' he said.

'There's nothing much to say.' Delia shrugged. 'As you already know, I was born in Birmingham. I'm an only child, and both my parents were killed during the war. I'm a poor little orphan. Isn't that sad?'

'Yes, it is. Very sad.' Jack's fingers caressed her cheek. 'But you must have some relations? Some ties?'

'No. None.' Catching his hand, Delia held it. 'What about you? Where do you live? Who do you live with?' She grinned at him. 'No, we'll go back to the beginning, shall we? Tell me what you did in the war.'

Jack frowned. 'Why do you want to know that?'

'Everyone wants to know what people did in the war. Hadn't you noticed?' Delia laughed. 'All right, don't tell me — I'll guess. You were in a cookhouse in Darlington, for the duration. No, that's not it. I know. You were a conscientious objector. A hospital orderly in the Non-Combatant Corps. Right?'

'Wrong.' Jack leaned towards her. Very carefully, he kissed her on the mouth. 'I was in the Commandos,' he said.

'Were you?' Delia opened her eyes wide. 'I say!'

'Don't be too impressed. I was an NCO, not an officer. I wasn't involved in anything sensational. Although I did in fact manage something quite remarkable. I came out of it all without a single medal to my name.'

'Where were you?'

'In the Balkans with Tito's mob, trying to sabotage German transports. We cocked things up mostly. I was there for half the war.'

'What happened afterwards?'

'I came out in 1946, did a course in business studies, and got a job at the new Albion works.'

'So you started at the bottom. But you were keen and soon you got promotion. Great natural ability coupled with massive ambition propelled you to the top. Within five years, you — '

'Cut the journalese. It was just luck.' Jack himself

laughed now. 'The old man took a fancy to me and made me his general factotum, which is what I am today. I'm likely to remain that too, unless he gets a coronary. That's more than enough about me.'

'Is it?'

'I think so.' He kissed her again, very lightly touching her lips with his. 'Come on,' he whispered. His hand brushed her left breast. 'You know you want to.'

He was right. She did want to, very much. More than anything, she wanted to wrap her arms around him and kiss Jack Kingston back. But falling in love wasn't on Delia's agenda. She simply hadn't the time. She opened the car door. 'Goodnight, Jack,' she said.

10

'I have to work tomorrow morning,' said Jack, who had left it a week, just long enough for Delia to miss him a little. She had to admit his sense of timing was brilliant. Now, he paused. 'But I should be free by twelve, so if you fancy a pub lunch?'

'Lunch, you say?'

'Yes.' He laughed. 'You do eat lunch, don't you?'

'I suppose so.'

'You'll come, then?'

'Well, all right.'

'Don't sound so enthusiastic, you might strain something. I'll pick you up at home, shall I?'

'Yes, okay.' Delia replaced the receiver. She stared out of the window, thoughtful now.

In her handbag was a letter from Shirley, which had arrived that morning. As usual, Shirley was full of news. Jenny was doing very well at school. Gareth's back was playing him up — apparently, there were lots of bits of shrapnel still embedded in his spine, and the specialist thought he might have to have an operation. The garden was looking lovely this year, and there was going to be plenty of fruit, especially on the apple trees.

As for Shirley herself, she was well, but she was sorry to say that although she had thought another baby was at last on its way, this had turned out to be a false alarm. However the doctor had said not to give up hope. He was going to give Gareth some tablets, and Shirley herself was to have a D and C. Then they would see what happened next . . .

All this was so ordinary. So dull. But, Delia reflected, this was also real life. Wasn't it?

Just then, a secretary brought Delia a note from the Chief Sub, so she had to stop daydreaming and start work for the day.

★   ★   ★

'How on earth do you know about these places?' The Georgian splendour of the smart country hotel made Delia stare. 'Jack? However do you find hotels like this?'

'Easy. Mr Jameson entertains clients here.' Jack glanced at Delia's rapidly emptying plate. 'How's your dinner?' he enquired.

'Fine.' Delia smiled at him. 'It's absolutely delicious, in fact. I've never tasted anything quite like this steak.'

Jack was indeed something of a miracle worker. In the dreary Britain of the 1950s, in which hardly any pubs served even the simplest of meals, and some hotels still offered you spam and mash for dinner, such excellent restaurants as this were as rare as rubies, and people who knew about them tended to keep them a closely guarded secret. Now, Delia chased a last piece of meat around her plate. 'Do you bring your other girlfriends here?' she asked.

'*Other* girlfriends?'

'Yes.' Delia put down her knife and fork. 'You're not going to tell me this is the first time you've ever been here? Without Mr Jameson, that is?'

'I've brought one or two other girls here, I admit that.' Candidly, Jack met Delia's eyes. 'But I'll also tell you this. I've never enjoyed myself as much with anyone, as I do with you.'

He picked up the bottle of hock and, without asking if Delia wanted any more to drink, he poured.

* * *

It was six o'clock when they drew up outside Delia's flat. Leaning towards her, Jack kissed her. He did this tentatively at first. But then, surprised and gratified that she was responding, he kissed her more firmly.

Not a man to waste anything, he now took her in his arms. He pulled her close to him. 'You kiss me now,' he murmured, into her hair. 'Go on. Do it.'

She did, and he laughed. 'You're an enigma, you are,' he said. 'Look at you. The archetypal frozen virgin, the pattern of a strait-laced spinster — kissing a man in a public street. Enjoying it, too.'

'Who says I'm enjoying it?'

'It's obvious.' He grinned at her. 'You're good at kissing. A natural. People always enjoy doing what they know they do well.'

'I'm not sure how to take that.'

'It's a compliment, so accept it gracefully.' Now Jack's hand was on Delia's neck, stroking her collarbone. 'You must have someone, somewhere,' he said. 'Some man or other?'

'There's no one. I told you before. There's no one at all.'

'No?' Jack touched her face. 'Did somebody hurt you?' he asked. 'Love you and leave you, perhaps?'

'Oh, honestly.' Delia laughed at him. 'Why are men so conceited? If I'm alone, it can't be by choice. Oh, no! It's because somebody walked out on me, it's because no one wants me. It's because — '

'No.' Jack kissed her again. 'It's not because no one wants you. *I* want you.' He stroked her cheek. 'I've wanted you for weeks now. I'll want you for a long time to come. So what are we going to do about it?'

'Stop it.' Delia pushed his hand away. 'It's time you went home.'

'I don't want to go. You don't want me to leave, either.'

'Don't I?' Delia met his eyes. He was right. She was aching for him. Longing for him. Against her better judgement, she was falling in love.

'What shall we do?' he was asking now.

'We could go back to your place, maybe?' Delia looked at him. She was curious to see where he lived. 'We could go — '

'No.' Jack shook his head. 'Two rooms and a gas ring, that's all I've got. My landlady's a gorgon. No guests are allowed in the bedrooms, and visitors are discouraged at all times. I'd be out on my ear if I so much as let *you* into the front hall.'

'Why don't you get a place of your own, then? Surely you could afford it?'

'I suppose I could.' Jack shrugged. 'But I'm okay

127

at Tennyson Drive for now. Unlike you, I'm not a nest-builder. So anyway — may I come up for half an hour?'

'Well . . . ' Delia considered. 'Just half an hour?'

'No more.'

'Okay.' Delia got out of the car. While Jack locked up, she opened the door of the flat.

★   ★   ★

'Will you have a cup of coffee?' she asked, bringing in the tray and placing it on a low table between the sofa and the single armchair, on which she now sat down herself. 'I saw this in the grocer's, so I pounced on it.'

'Good for you.' Jack was prowling about the room. Looking out of the window, he gazed across the roofs into the soft summer twilight. He sat down on the sofa. 'Come over here,' he said.

'I'm quite comfortable where I am.'

'Oh, for God's sake! Stop messing me about.' Jack's eyes were beseeching now. 'Come and sit by me. Please?'

Delia did as he asked.

Jack drank his coffee, put his cup back on the tray, then began to stroke Delia's shoulder. 'Mean lady reporter,' he murmured. 'Heart of stone, will of iron, is everything about you hard? Does everything match?'

'More coffee?' suggested Delia.

'Don't move.' Now Jack's hand slid down to Delia's breast. 'Not quite everything,' he said, stroking it. Pulling her into his arms, he kissed her.

'That's better,' he whispered. 'Come on, Delia. Kiss me back.'

Five minutes later, Delia pulled away. 'You could still have that coffee,' she said.

'No, thanks. It'll keep me awake.' Jack yawned. 'God, I'm tired. I think I need an early night.'

'Oh.' Delia stood up. 'In that case, why don't you go home, take a nice relaxing bath, and have one?'

'Invite me to stay here.' He yawned again. 'You know you'd like me to.'

'Rubbish.' Delia looked away. But then, she couldn't help looking back. Jack's dark blue eyes were glittering brightly now. His mouth looked so kissable . . .

'You can stay here,' he prompted.

'Oh, very well. You can stay here.'

★　★　★

'I knew you'd be all right underneath,' he murmured, as he held her. He grinned at her. 'You liked it. Didn't you?'

'Yes, I did.' Delia wrapped her arms round his neck. Embarrassed, she hid her face against his chest.

'Good. So did I.' Now, he rolled on to his back. 'Sit on me,' he said.

'What?'

'Sit on me. Please. It's good this way.'

★　★　★

Going to bed with a man was one thing — but it was quite another to let him stay the night. Delia woke from a light doze to realise Jack was still there. She would have to get rid of him, and soon. For what if the milkman saw him? What if the landlord heard his tenant entertained men all night? It didn't bear thinking about.

'You must go home.' Shaking his shoulder, Delia made Jack open his eyes. 'Home, Jack! Now!'

Jack opened one eye. 'What time is it?' he muttered.

'Well after midnight.' Delia shook him harder. 'Jack! Please get up!'

'All right.' Drowsily, Jack levered himself into a sitting position. He rubbed his eyes. 'Make me some coffee, will you?'

'Then you'll go?'

Jack grinned. 'Then I'll go.'

As she heard his car drive off into the quiet summer night, Delia sighed. But then she smiled. Going back to bed, she took the pillow which still smelled of him, and hugged it. This delicious feeling of well-being, this pleasant light-headedness must be it. She must be in love.

11

Shirley Hughes opened her letter. Pouring herself more coffee, she settled down for a good long read. Delia's letters were always interesting — far more so, Shirley feared, than Shirley's own ever were.

This letter was no exception. Delia had plenty to say, telling Shirley all sorts of interesting things which she'd learned in the course of her work, including some fascinating gossip about the wives and mistresses of the local bigwigs, and corruption in local government.

'How is Jenny these days?' she asked. She really ought to get down to Evesbridge some time soon, and see them all again.

Jenny was fine, and growing up fast. Quick and clever, she did very well at junior school, and when the time came she passed her Eleven Plus with ease. She was offered a place at the local high school for girls.

So now, while most of the other children in her class put on new uniforms of dull forest green, and trekked off to the secondary modern school on the edge of the housing estate where the Hughes family lived, Jenny was resplendent in a distinctive velour hat, smart double-breasted navy coat and black patent shoes. Every morning, she went with Gareth into the town.

'Snob, snob,' the other children chanted, as she walked back down her road at four o'clock each day.

'Just look at her, in her posh coat and silly hat! Don't she think she's it?'

In her junior school days, Jenny would have belted anyone who teased or tried to bully her, but now she was at the grammar school she tried to ignore the catcalls and remarks. For one thing, there were too many of her tormentors to fight. So, often alone, but sometimes in the company of Pauline Ballard who was the only other grammar school child in the road, she ran the daily gauntlet of abuse apparently unconcerned, unwilling to let her former friends see how much their ridicule hurt her. All the same, she and Pauline made an odd little couple, whose common suffering rather than affection bound them together.

One Friday afternoon, Pauline's hat was snatched and tossed into the canal which ran alongside the road, so Jenny scrambled down the bank and helped her fish it out again. 'I wish I was at the secondary mod,' moaned Pauline, whose best friend from junior school nowadays cut her dead. 'I hate the grammar.'

'Why?' With a handful of grass, Jenny began to wipe the mud off her expensive Start Rite shoes. 'What's the matter with it?'

'All the teachers are snobs. All the girls are stuck up. I can't do the French comprehension and my Dad doesn't understand my maths homework.'

'If you come round to our house tonight, I'll help you with your maths.'

'Will you, Jen?' Pauline's wan little face brightened slightly. 'Promise?'

'Yes. Come round about seven.'

'Great.' Pauline almost managed a smile. 'Jenny, do you like the grammar school?'

'It's all right.' Jenny shrugged. 'We're going to be there for the next five years or more. We might as well make the best of it.'

'If you fail your first year exams, they chuck you out.' Pauline sighed. 'I think I might fail on purpose.'

'Don't do that!' cried Jenny. 'I won't have any friends at all if you leave!'

* * *

In the first year at Evesbridge Grammar School for Girls, there were several pupils who were absolutely mad on ponies. Their parents were rich enough to indulge this passion. Jenny was brainy, and generous enough to let anyone copy her homework — so, in return and as a special concession, these well-heeled pony lovers were prepared to allow Jenny Hughes from the Martley Estate to edge into their upper middle class milieu.

Desperate for any crumbs of friendship, Jenny tagged along with this horsey set and spent hours poring over library books, studying the points of the horse, dressage techniques and general stable management. Soon, she was as obsessed with ponies as the rest of the girls.

Nagged and badgered almost to death, Gareth eventually agreed to shell out for riding lessons. Each Saturday morning he drove his daughter over to Raylett's riding stables, there to be bored into a stupor as he watched several little girls, most of

133

them clad in ruinously expensive riding outfits and mounted upon extremely pretty little ponies, canter about the field showing off.

Less elegantly turned out than Annabel Morley, Jessica Hallet or Victoria Langdon-Greene, Jenny spent her hour on one of the riding stables' own docile hacks and then leaned on the fence watching the others for as long as Gareth would let her.

'Oh, Dad! Just another ten minutes,' she would plead, hanging on to his sleeve. Her eyes wistful, she would gaze at Jessica or stare at Annabel, willing one of them to canter over to where she stood and offer her five minutes on Rainbow, or suggest that she help rub Dulcie down. 'I wish I had my own pony,' she would murmur, as she watched her friends canter by. 'Oh, Dad! I do wish — '

'When I win the pools, honeybunch.' Gareth himself wished she wouldn't look so hungry, so anguished — so absolutely consumed with longing. 'You should have picked yourself a richer father, my love,' he would add, ruffling her hair.

'What? I don't want any Dad but you!' Then Jenny would grin up at him. 'You're the best Dad in the world.'

'I don't know about that.'

'Yes, you are. All right, if you're fed up, we'll go home. But can I ask Jessica Hallet round for tea?'

* * *

'Someone's had a busy weekend,' remarked Ted Allen, as he observed Delia yawning over her third cup of coffee and lighting her fourth or fifth cigarette. 'What have you been up to, then?'

'Nothing much.' Stretching contentedly, Delia smiled at him. 'In fact, I had a long lie in yesterday morning. I really don't know why I'm still tired.'

'Miss Shenstone, the old man wants to see you.' Julie Fisher, one of the editor's two highly efficient secretaries, looked into the main office now. 'Miss Shenstone? Mr Freeman says in five minutes' time.'

Going into his office, Delia found the editor sheafing through some photographs. Briefly, he glanced up. 'Sit down, Delia,' he murmured. 'I shan't keep you a minute.'

He continued to examine the photographs for a good thirty seconds more — but then, evidently satisfied, he pushed them to one side. 'Well, Delia,' he began, 'how would you like to start a women's page?'

'That sounds interesting,' Delia replied. 'What exactly did you have in mind?'

'Well, when I was glancing through last week's paper, it struck me that some parts of it are a bit of a rag bag. I wondered if we might pull all the female interest stuff together. Have a page of recipes, beauty hints, the odd book review — interviews with local ladies who've done anything remarkable, all that sort of thing. Maybe we could have an advice column, or your stars for this week. The kind of stuff only women seem to like, in fact. Would you be interested in editing that?'

'Perhaps.' Delia frowned. 'You aren't thinking of a page that's nearly *all* recipes and beauty hints, are you?' she asked. 'Because if you are, I should tell you now that I'm not qualified to advise people on how to make the best Christmas puddings. Or even to boil eggs. As for an advice column — well, to be quite honest, I reckon the editors of women's magazines make all those problems up.'

'Right then, no bleeding hearts. Some astrology, perhaps?'

'Supplied by an agency, or dreamed up by Julie and Frances at three o'clock on a Wednesday afternoon?'

'Okay, no astrology.' Mr Freeman grinned. 'What about looking into herbal remedies or folk medicine?' he suggested. 'Interview women who make their own cosmetics, and ask them how it's done. See if any of them have their own little businesses, flogging home-made scent and stuff like that. I know, you could talk to local women who go out to work. Ask them how they combine doing a paid job with bringing up a family and running a home.'

'If I can find any who do anything like that.' Delia sniffed. 'After the war, most of the working mothers were sent packing. 'Off you go, Mrs Smith. Mr Jackson is back from the Far East and needs your job, so please empty your locker by lunchtime.' So much for the appreciation of a grateful country.'

'Right, then — research that and do a piece on it. But don't make it too heavy.' Mr Freeman lit a cigarette. 'Look, my dear, there'll have to be *some* beauty stuff, fashion notes, cookery hints. After all, that's the sort of thing women like. Saving your presence,' he added quickly, seeing Delia frown.

'All right.' Delia agreed. 'We'll have some fashion notes and recipes, *et cetera*. But not just that.'

'No. But look, please don't appear to despise the nation's housewives, whatever you do. Cooking's a perfectly respectable activity. There's nothing demeaning or frivolous about feeding a family — and surely telling housewives how to stretch the housekeeping money and provide interesting new meals for their kids and husbands isn't really a waste of time?'

'Maybe not, but I wouldn't know where to begin.'

'Get on to the gas and electricity boards. They'll be only too glad to tell you all you need to know.' Mr Freeman smiled. 'Well, Delia? Will you do it?'

'Can I can have a whole page?'

'Half a page to begin with, to see how it goes. Get Frank to drum up a bit of appropriate advertising — at preferential rates, if need be. Then, if it proves popular with the readers, we'll see about a full page spread.'

'Right.' Delia stood up. 'When will you want to see something?'

'On Friday morning. Let me have a rough lay-out of your proposals for the first piece, and your plans for the next three. Borrow Julie, if you like. She's not very busy this week, so she could do all your phoning and typing. She's always saying she'd love to be a journalist, so now's her big chance.'

He looked at Delia. 'It's your big chance, too,' he added impressively. 'Don't throw it away.'

★ ★ ★

'My own page!' Delia crowed, the following Saturday morning. 'Mine, Jack. Mine! To do with as I please.'

'Good for you.' Having arrived at half past eight, before Delia was dressed, Jack had dragged her back to bed again. Lolling against her pillows, he grinned at her. 'So what did you have to do to get that?' he enquired.

'What's that supposed to mean?' Offended, Delia glared at him. Then she remembered. There was a new management trainee at the factory, a female graduate who was evidently very pretty as well as very brainy. She'd apparently upset quite a few apple carts, including Jack's. Just recently, he was making constant nasty cracks about women who slept around — who fornicated their way into good jobs which were the rightful property of men. 'Come on,' Delia insisted. 'What did you mean by that?'

'Nothing.' Sleepily, Jack smiled. 'Go down on me.'

'What? God, you're lazy.' Delia shook her head. 'What about giving me some fun?'

'I can't. I'm worn out. I've had a hard week.' Jack closed his eyes. 'Go on,' he yawned. 'Do your stuff.'

Instead, Delia stroked his nose. 'Is that all it is?' she whispered. 'Just general fatigue? You're not having problems, are you?'

'Problems?'

'Yes. Men of your age sometimes do, you know. Especially after a hard week. Or even after an easy one!'

'You cheeky little bitch. I'll take my belt to you, I will.'

'You'll have to catch me first.' Delia jumped out

138

of bed, and went to put the kettle on.

As she waited for the water to boil, she counted the years. Two, three — going on for four now, it must be. She sighed. This affair was going nowhere. Jack was fun, and she was very fond of him — sometimes, she thought she loved him — but he was so self-centred! Such a light-weight. Certainly, he was not a marrying man.

Soon, Delia realised, she would be thirty years old. Although she didn't want children — she didn't particularly want marriage, either — just recently she was beginning to crave some sort of commitment. Some security. Perhaps it was time to move on.

Glancing back into the bedroom, she saw Jack had fallen asleep. So she did a little cleaning up, then settled down to some work. At twelve, the door of her sitting room opened. Jack walked in. Scratching his chest, he grinned at her. 'Lunch?' he suggested.

'I don't want any,' she replied. 'I'm too busy.'

'Go on with you.' Jack inspected his finger nails. 'Let's go to the pub.'

'I haven't time.'

'Nonsense.' He walked over to her. Now, he ran his fingers through her hair. 'Come on,' he murmured. 'I can't take you out tonight, I have to finish some annual reports. But we could have lunch down at the Fleece. Then go for a little drive.'

'Go away.'

'Let's have ten minutes in bed, then.'

'Get off!' Crossly, Delia pushed him away. 'Jack, I'm *trying* to work, sod you!'

'Language.' Jack shrugged. 'What shall I do, then?'

'Go home to your annual reports?'

Eventually, Jack did just that.

As she heard the street door slam and the car drive away, Delia gnawed at her pen. Instead of delighting her, these days Jack was just as likely to make her cross. She had once wondered if he was the man she might marry. Now, when she thought about it, she was glad he'd never suggested anything of the sort. The idea of having him around all the time appalled her. When he went away on his ever more frequent business trips, sometimes she was almost relieved.

By September, the women's page was well established and Delia was enjoying the sweet pleasures of unqualified success. Then, one sunny Tuesday morning, she woke feeling not her usual energetic self, but instead rather ill. She made it to the bathroom just in time to be violently sick.

All that day she felt terrible. Julie remarked on how wan she looked, and even Mr Freeman asked if she thought she might be coming down with something. 'Shall I get Ted to drive you home?' he asked. 'You might have that 'flu thing that's going round.'

'I'll stay here, thanks all the same. Spread it about a bit.' Delia managed a weak smile. Julie brought her a mugful of coffee, but that almost made her throw up. 'All right,' she agreed, as Julie expressed her concern. 'If I'm no better by this evening, I'll take tomorrow off.'

She struggled through the rest of the week. But by

Friday she could no longer pretend she had a mild form of 'flu. It wasn't that at all.

★ ★ ★

Just recently, Delia had not seen much of Jack. She didn't particularly regret that — these days, they squabbled as often as they talked. Outings to quaint country pubs were infrequent now. Expensive restaurant meals were a thing of the past.

True, Jack still liked screwing Delia. Delia still liked going to bed with Jack. But the affair was doomed and until now Delia had been content to let it die a natural death.

That Friday, however, she rang Jack at work and asked him — ordered him, in fact — to call round at her flat. No, tomorrow morning would not do. It had to be this evening. She had some news, which she couldn't tell him over the phone.

Jack turned up a good hour later than arranged, by which time Delia was almost beside herself with anger, panic and dread. 'Whatever's the matter?' he asked, as she dragged him inside. 'Delia, what — '

'I'm pregnant!' she cried. 'Did you hear me, Jack? I'm expecting a baby!'

Jack stared at her. '*What* did you say?'

'You heard.' Delia collapsed on the sofa. 'It's your fault,' she wailed. 'It's all your fault!'

'Come on, sweetheart. It takes two to tango.'

'But you've always said *you* would deal with that side of things.' Delia was crying now. 'You told me I shouldn't worry. That you'd be careful. 'This brand's foolproof,' you said. You told me I didn't need to bother with creams and foams — '

'Are you sure you're expecting?'

'Sure! Positive, convinced — absolutely certain I am!'

'So what do you want me to do?' Now, at last, Jack had the grace to look concerned. 'What shall I — '

'It's obvious, isn't it?' Delia shrugged. 'We'll have to get married,' she said.

'Ah. Well, sweetheart — '

'We must!' Now, Delia's eyes were wild. 'Jack, I'm not prepared to give birth to an illegitimate baby. In fact, I won't!'

'You may have to.' Jack grimaced. 'You see, there's one problem.'

'What is it?'

'Can't you guess?'

Delia stared at him. She saw his face was ashen. 'My God — not that!' she cried. 'Tell me it's not that!'

He did not speak.

Now, Delia felt very cold. Icy fingers of dread crawled down her spine, and freezing tentacles of terror clutched at her heart. 'You're not, are you?' she whispered, beseechingly. 'How can you be?'

Still, Jack did not reply.

Delia forced herself to be calm. 'But how?' she demanded, shakily. 'Where? When?'

'Ten years ago,' he replied.

'But you are separated?

'No. I'm sorry.' Now, Jack began to talk. Rapidly, he attempted to explain. He was a happily married man. He had a huge mortgage on a pretty Victorian rectory, in a village twenty miles from Dorchester. To make ends meet, his wife worked as a nurse at the cottage hospital there.

'Have you children?' asked Delia, woodenly.

'Two. A boy and a girl.' Jack would not meet her eyes. 'I'm sorry,' he said, again.

'*You're* sorry!' For a moment, Delia thought she was dreaming. Then, she tried to make sense of what she'd just heard. She failed. 'But you live in digs,' she said, slowly, painfully. 'In Tennyson Drive. You have rooms — '

'I use them during the week.' Jack shrugged. 'It's convenient to stay in town, you see.'

'But what about weekends? You've often been here at weekends. You come over at Easter, at Christmas, you — '

'Rachel thinks I go to rugby matches, with the lads. Or on business trips.'

'I see.' Delia felt numb.

For a few moments, they were both silent. Then, Jack tried to take Delia in his arms. 'Come on,' he said, kindly. 'Cry if you want to. Have a good howl, then we'll talk about it and decide what to do.'

'I've already decided.' Breaking free of him, Delia turned away. 'I can't stay pregnant, so you'll have to do something.'

'*I'll* have to do something?'

'Yes.' Delia met his eyes. 'Tell me who to go to. To have it taken away.'

'What?' Now Jack grew pale again. 'My God, Delia! I don't know anyone who does that sort of thing. I don't — '

'Find someone, then! There must be hundreds of

143

crooked doctors in this country, and some of them must live here in Dorset.'

'Yes, but — '

'I'm sure that among your many and varied acquaintances there must be people who know — *those* people. That fat car salesman, for example, whose wife had been in some expensive private clinic. They were at that party we went to last Christmas Eve. I'm sure you remember. Ask him.'

'Fat salesman?' Jack racked his brains. 'Jim Harman?' he hazarded. 'Is that who you mean?'

'I don't know his name. But he was a big, florid man in a dinner jacket, and his wife was a withered-looking creature in a silver cocktail dress. She bored me rigid droning on about this place. Nice and private, it is. Very expensive. If they gave her a hysterectomy, they probably do — other things, as well.'

'You're serious about this, aren't you?' Jack had put Delia's initial outburst down to shock and panic — but now he wasn't so sure. 'You really want to get rid of the child.'

'Of course I do! I've no choice.'

'Nonsense.' Once again, he tried to take her in his arms. 'Look, darling,' he soothed, 'I'll stand by you. If you want the child, go ahead and have it. I'll find a place for us. I'll leave Rachel, and come and live with you. Maybe even get a divorce, if that's what you want.'

'Oh, do shut up.' Wearily, Delia pushed him away. 'I don't want you to divorce your wife,' she said. 'I don't want you to come and live with me. You're a liar, a cheat and a coward. I want nothing more to do with you.' She met his eyes. 'There. Have I made myself plain?'

'Perfectly. But you're forgetting something. Delia, it's my kid, too.'

'It's *my body*!' Delia glared at him. 'It's my life. My reputation. My career's at stake. *I won't* have an illegitimate baby, not for you or anybody. No, no, no!'

'Selfish bitch.' Jack glared back at her. 'Your career. Your life. You're selfish, that's what you are, selfish through and through.'

'Unlike some people, I've never pretended to be anything else.' Now, the tears were ready to flow in earnest. But Delia would not cry. Not yet. 'Phone Jim Harman,' she said. 'Get the name of that clinic. Make the arrangements.'

'It won't be that easy. God, Delia! Do you understand what you're asking me to do?'

'Yes. But do it all the same,' Delia replied.

'Okay, okay.' Jack picked up his overcoat. 'I'll be in touch.'

As she heard the street door slam, Delia began to sniff, then to sob, and soon she was weeping like a child. But then, she told herself to stop this. She must not give way. Heartbreak might come later. But, just now, heartbreak would have to wait.

★   ★   ★

The place to which Jack drove her turned out to be not, as Delia had feared, a back-street slum. Instead, it was a smart, private clinic housed in an elegant

Victorian mansion on the outskirts of a small seaside town, a couple of hours' drive from Dorchester itself.

Jack had tried very hard to change Delia's mind. He'd appealed to her good sense, her reason, her putative maternal instincts and, as a last resort, her finer feelings as a woman. He told her how happy motherhood had made Rachel. Finally, he informed her that in his opinion abortion was first degree murder, and that when she died she would go to hell.

Delia had let him talk. Then she'd asked if he had made the appointment at the clinic. 'Yes,' he replied. 'But, sweetheart — '

'Will you drive me there?' she demanded. 'Or shall I go on the train?'

'I'll drive you,' he replied.

★ ★ ★

'Go and walk on the sands or something,' Delia told him, as she got out of the car.

'I'll come in with you.'

'No, you won't.' Delia reached for her bag. Her heart thumping, she walked across the gravel sweep and went into the house.

The quiet corridors were painted a cool, soothing blue. Escorting her patient down a long, narrow passage, the nurse's tread was muffled by the deep pile of the carpet. Instead of the expected smell of carbolic, there was a pervasive fragrance of unseen flowers.

'Will you come this way, Mrs Shenstone?' The

nurse opened a door. 'Doctor will be with you in a moment. Would you like a cup of tea, while you wait?'

'No, thank you.' Feeling weak at the knees, Delia sat down. 'May I smoke?' she asked.

'Yes, of course.' The nurse drew up a pretty little occasional table, and placed a heavy glass ashtray upon it. Then she left, closing the door silently behind her.

'Mrs Shenstone?' A calm, middle-aged, grey-haired man, the doctor smiled a professional smile and ushered Delia into the examination room. Here, he told her there was nothing to worry about. The operation would be quite simple. Then he left her, to be replaced by a different nurse, who took Delia to a private room and asked her to undress, then get into bed.

'Would you like to settle your account now?' she enquired politely, as she tucked her patient in. 'That would save a little time later. Of course, it's entirely up to you.'

'I'll pay now.' Opening her handbag, Delia took out a thick bundle of banknotes. Without a word, the nurse accepted them. Too polite to count them in front of her patient, she then produced a form which she asked Delia to sign.

'Will it be a general anaesthetic?' asked Delia, who by now was rather frightened, and found all this professional detachment more unnerving that she cared to admit.

'That's for Doctor to decide.' Frostily, the nurse smiled. 'But in cases like yours, a local is all that's normally required.'

'Oh. I see.' Delia shivered. 'When will I be going to theatre?'

'In about two hours' time.' The nurse smoothed Delia's pillows. 'Try to relax,' she advised. 'If you want anything, the bell is by your bed.'

★ ★ ★

Delia closed her eyes and let her mind wander. Hearing the scrape, scrape, scrape of the curette, she tried to shut her ears to the sound. But she couldn't. It seemed to have got inside her head. She felt tears come into her eyes and, powerless to control them, she let them gather and spill over.

How much longer, she wondered, fixing her eyes on her left knee, determined not to let her gaze leave it. She wondered what had been in the rather nasty drink she'd been given by the theatre nurse. Some sort of sedative, she supposed, something to render her docile while the doctor did his work.

It didn't hurt. Not very much. Although now she decided that, on the whole, she'd have preferred to be unconscious while all this was going on.

But then she supposed that even if she'd offered to pay for it, the risks involved in general anaesthesia were too great to make it worth the bother of knocking her out. It would be a very sordid end, wouldn't it, to die on the operating table in the course of an illegal operation? Something like that wouldn't do the clinic's reputation any good at all.

Very much aware of cramp in her right leg, Delia tried to ease her foot out of one of the stirrups. But now the nurse held her ankle. 'It won't be long,' she soothed. 'Five minutes, no more.'

Delia closed her eyes, letting her mind wander again. Then, to her surprise, the nurse was bending over her. 'All finished, Mrs Shenstone,' she said, smiling her frosty smile. 'I'm going to clean you up now. Then, when you've had a rest, your husband can take you home.'

★ ★ ★

Jack was waiting in the car park, smoking. 'All right?' he asked, as Delia walked unsteadily towards the car.

'I'm still a bit dozy. They gave me something to knock me out.' Delia let him open the car door for her. Gingerly, she sat down. Carefully, she swung her legs inside. They drove back to Dorchester in complete silence.

'Shall I come in?' asked Jack, as he switched off the engine.

'No, I'll be okay.' Delia collected her bag and took her gloves from the compartment on the dashboard. 'Really, Jack. I'd rather be on my own.'

'I think we ought to talk.'

'About the money, you mean? Well, I can't pay you yet. But I shall. Every last penny. I have the number of your bank account, and I'll pay it in instalments, five pounds a month until it's cleared. If you want to charge interest, you can.'

'Delia!' Laying his hand on her arm, Jack shook her. 'Please stop all this. I don't want your money!'

'Then what do you want?'

'Look, you're upset. I think I ought to come up

with you and see you're all right. I'll make you some supper, scrambled eggs or something. Shall I do that?'

'No.' Delia opened the car door. 'Jack?'

'What?'

'Don't come here any more.' She was standing on the pavement now. 'Don't phone me, don't call round. I don't ever want to see you again.'

Delia made herself some tea and toast. She turned on the gas fire and sat by it shivering, her hands cupped around her comforting hot drink.

Alone, feeling vulnerable and weak, she let the tears roll down her cheeks. But as she wept, she made a vow. No man would ever hurt her like this again.

12

Chicken pox was going round the school, and Jenny caught it. 'I'm almost certain you had something like this when you were three or four,' observed Shirley crossly, eyeing her pock-marked child with distaste. 'Don't scratch!' she cried, as Jenny began to investigate a blister on her nose. 'It'll leave a scar. I'll find you some of that ointment the doctor gave us.'

Jenny watched her mother go. She scowled. How humiliating it was, to catch a baby's disease at her advanced age! Now, she wouldn't be able to go out with Delia, who was expected on a visit this weekend.

By the weekend, however, Jenny was feeling much better, and was anxious to get up. 'You look a lot brighter today,' agreed Shirley, as she handed her little invalid a cup of early morning tea. 'How does your throat feel now?'

'It's not so sore. But I still itch.' Jenny sipped her tea. 'How much longer do I have to stay in bed?' she enquired.

'Well, since you've been quite poorly, I think you should stop there today and get up tomorrow.' Shirley drew back the curtains to reveal the sunniest Friday morning for weeks. 'Delia will cheer you up,' she added. 'She's dying to see you, and hear all about your new school.'

'She'll probably faint with horror at the sight of

me,' muttered Jenny, diving back under the bedclothes to conceal her spotty face.

★ ★ ★

'Delia!' Sitting propped up against her pillows, tastefully arrayed in the bright pink nylon bedjacket which was her favourite garment of all time, and which set off her glowing complexion to perfection, Jenny beamed in welcome.

'Hello, Jenny.' Sitting down on the child's bed, Delia shook her head in dismay. 'Well,' she observed. 'What a sight.'

'Don't!' Jenny blushed. 'I know I look a mess,' she muttered. 'You'll just have to avert your eyes while you're talking to me. Oh, Delia — it's been ages since you were here last! What have you been doing? Where have you been? Tell me everything!'

Delia's visits were the high points of Jenny's year. Delia herself was Jenny's favourite person, there was no doubt at all about that — but there was just a tiny element of cupboard love in this affection, for, like King Wenceslas, Delia always came loaded down with presents, too.

Now, as the visitor sat on her bed drinking a welcome cup of tea, Jenny unwrapped her first gift. Since she was too old for toys, these days she always hoped for bath salts, lipsticks or costume jewellery. She opened a little velvet box. 'Oh, Delia!' she cried, delighted. She held the silver locket up to the light. 'I've wanted one of these for years. Thank you!'

'I've got you some books, too.' Delia handed her a square, heavy package. 'Go on, then. Open it.'

Jenny needed no second bidding. 'But it's all in French,' she cried. Frowning, she skimmed the pages. She glanced at a second book. 'So is this!'

'They're Perrault's fairy tales. The complete set.' Delia found the story of *Cinderella*, which was beautifully illustrated with the most delicate of watercolours. 'I'll translate for you, if you like.'

'Oh, you don't have to do that.' Affronted, Jenny grabbed the book back. 'I can read French myself. Well, I almost can.'

'I thought you could. That's why I bought these.' Delia handed Jenny a third book. 'This one's in German,' she said. 'Do you know any German?'

'I'm learning it at school. What about you?'

'I'm doing a course at the moment, as if happens. I go to evening classes twice a week.' Delia smiled. 'We're both beginners, then.'

'Yes.'

Opening the book at the first page, Jenny studied it. ''*The Ice Maiden*',' she read. ''Long ago, in the Black Forest, there lived a woodcutter and his three daughters. Two girls were *häßlich*' — ugly?'

'Yes, I think so.'

' 'But the third' — no, the youngest — 'was very beautiful'.'

'Cleversticks.' Delia poured herself a second cup of tea. 'Continue.'

' 'One day, when the woodcutter was crossing a stream, he saw a piece of gold under the water. How it' — what's this word?'

'Where? Oh, that's from *glänzen*. To shine. 'How it shone, with an almost unearthly radiance.' You know, Jen — you're quite good at this.'

'Oh, I like languages.' Jenny turned the page. 'Shall I go on?'

'Yes.' Delia nodded. 'Tell me a story while I finish this cup of tea.'

'Could you get me some more of these?' Finishing the last page, Jenny closed the book. She looked at her friend. 'I mean, could you post me some? I'll pay you out of my pocket money.'

'I'll send you the set.' Delia put her teacup on the tray. 'Oh, sweetheart,' she continued, 'you don't have to pay me! It's a pleasure to get things for people who appreciate them. My cousins' kids never read anything but the *Beano*.'

'I read that, too. I like Minnie the Minx.'

'But you read other things as well. Look, when I'm in Frankfurt, I'll get some books for you. Harder ones, not baby stuff like this.'

'Are you often in Frankfurt?' asked Jenny, impressed.

'No,' Delia replied. 'But I'll be going there next month to do a story for the *Reporter*. The town has just started an exchange scheme, you see. Schoolchildren from Dorchester are to go to Germany for holidays, and next August a whole crowd of German kids will come to England.

'The Mayor of Frankfurt has invited the editor of the local paper and a few other people to spend a weekend in Germany as his guests. Mr Freeman can't go, and the deputy editor's wife has just had twins. So he's sending me instead.'

'Lucky thing.' Jenny sighed. 'I'd like to go abroad,' she said. 'I'd love to travel.'

'You will,' said Delia. 'When you leave school, you

can do anything you want. So don't be too keen to tie yourself down to marriage and babies, will you? When you're eighteen, go off and do something exciting instead.'

'Still nattering?' A pile of freshly-ironed linen in her arms, Shirley stuck her head round the bedroom door. 'I'm going to start supper now,' she said. 'Delia, it's your favourite. Chicken pie, with mushrooms and ham.'

'Lovely,' said Delia. 'Shall I come and give you a hand?'

'If you like. Or you can stay and entertain little madam here — it's up to you.'

'Stay with me!' Jenny grabbed at Delia's hand. 'I'll read you another story if you stay here with me.'

Delia hesitated. More than anything, she wanted to talk to Shirley. To confess everything. To admit she'd been a fool. To let Shirley comfort her.

But, as she looked at Jenny, she realised this would have to wait. Perhaps she and Shirley could take a walk after lunch on Sunday, instead.

★ ★ ★

'Do you have boyfriends, Delia?' asked Jenny, closing another book. 'I mean, you're not married, I know — but do you have friends who are men?'

'What a funny question.' Delia shrugged. 'Yes, Jenny,' she replied, carefully. 'I have friends who are men.'

'Are they nice to you? Do they buy you flowers and chocolates? Do they take you to the pictures?'

'Well, some of them do.' Recalling that on her last

155

birthday Jack Kingston had turned up at the flat with half a florist's shop in his arms, Delia winced. 'Yes, I get my share of flowers and trips to the cinema,' she said.

'But what do you do about holidays? What happens at Christmas?' Jenny had been thinking about this for some time now. 'Where do you go then?'

'To my Aunt Bet's, in Birmingham.'

'Do you like it there?'

'Yes, it's fine.' If you like hordes of shrieking kids, Delia thought. If you like obnoxious, illiterate brats whose average IQ is about twenty-one and a half, whose mothers' idea of a good time is getting drunk on rum and blackcurrant and slagging each other off, whose fathers bump into parts of me they could easily avoid, and expect me to enjoy it.

She took Jenny's hands in hers. 'I was hoping we could go shopping in Worcester tomorrow,' she said, firmly changing the subject. 'Will you be up to it?'

'Oh, yes!' Jenny beamed. But then she grimaced. 'If you won't mind being seen with a spotty little kid?'

'I shan't mind.' Delia ruffled her hair. 'You can always put a paper bag over your head.'

'Delia?' Shirley's voice echoed up the stairs. 'Delia! Gareth's home. Come and say hello.'

'I'd better do as I'm told.' Getting up, Delia grinned. 'Your Mum doesn't stand any nonsense, does she? At any rate, not from me. Coming!' she cried.

Jenny pulled a face. It wasn't as if Delia was Gareth's special friend. In fact, they didn't seem very interested in each other at all, although Jenny had never been able to work out why.

13

A change of scene was exactly what Delia needed, but she hardly expected to get it. Indeed, when a chance to escape from Dorchester actually presented itself, she wondered if this was just another cruel trick of fate. But then, she thought, perhaps she *was* entitled to some good fortune in her career. After all, she was hardly lucky in love.

So now, notebook open and biro ready in her right hand, she sat in the easy chair she had bagged, and gazed all around the room. Jeremy Blackburn's penthouse suite was, she decided, where she belonged. Large and airy, it was situated at the top of a brand new, multi-storey office block. Its chrome and leather fittings spoke of power, fame and success.

The meeting of departmental editors took place every Thursday morning at ten o'clock sharp. Now, by five minutes to, everyone involved had arrived. They were closely followed by the editor himself.

Suave in a black shirt, white trousers and, today's sartorial sensation, some amazing green suède shoes, Jeremy Blackburn sat down at his enormous ebony desk. 'Delia, my love?' His accent was one nobody could ever quite place. 'Would you like to get us started?'

It was Jeremy's way to let his senior staff say their pieces, speak their minds — and then, as often as not, shoot them down in flames. 'Sorry, darling,' he would say. 'But that won't do at *all*.' Six months into publication of the new magazine, this autocratic behaviour had so far lost him two departmental editors and alienated several more.

But Jeremy knew exactly what he was doing. The wonder boy of Fleet Street, he had arranged the finance, cajoled the backers and finally launched *World Wide Magazine* almost single-handed. While his detractors had given the publication six weeks at the outside, a year later the circulation figures were still climbing.

A weekly digest of news, reviews and current affairs, the magazine was a new departure for the big publishing conglomerate which ultimately owned it. Designed to appeal to the widest possible spectrum of society — to be serious and responsible enough to attract the intelligentsia, but lively enough to beguile the stylish — *Paris Match* and the West German *Stern* were vague role models. But *World Wide Magazine* sought to be more wide-ranging than either of these, with no obvious political leanings either to the left or the right.

It was, its critics declared, casting its net far too wide. In trying to please everyone, it would end up pleasing nobody. Certainly, it had had its teething troubles. An incautiously candid article about a celebrated film actor had, although cleared by the paper's legal experts, resulted in a libel action which was still dragging on and looked likely to cost the magazine dear.

★　★　★

Delia had been head-hunted by Jeremy Blackburn himself. A friend of Tom Freeman — they'd both worked for the Press Association during the war — Jeremy had read some of Delia's work, and been impressed enough to offer her a job. When she resigned from the *Reporter*, however, Tom had been very sniffy, telling her she'd be out on her ear within the year.

'There's no market for that sort of stuff,' he declared. 'Not in England, anyway. Yes, I know your Hun and your Frog prefer their news in magazine form, but the English give up comics when they leave elementary school. There's no call in this country for tabloid hybrids between the *News of the World and the Spectator*.'

'Oh?' Delia went on clearing her desk. 'Isn't there?'

'Nope.' Tom grinned. 'But I know what it is. You've succumbed to the lure of Fleet Street. You've been seduced by the bright lights of the Big Smoke.'

'Perhaps I have.' Candidly, Delia met his eyes. 'It's a good offer, Tom. Even you must see that.'

'This time next year, you'll be knocking on my door. Cap in hand.'

In spite of Tom Freeman's gloomy forecasts, however, 1959 gave way to 1960 and Delia was still women's page editor of the new magazine. Not that she intended to remain so much longer. She had her eye on the features editor's job. The present incumbent of that particularly lucrative post was slipping a bit. Jeremy had noticed. If Mark Grady didn't watch his step, he'd be out in the corridor sorting the mail — while Delia slipped neatly into his shoes . . .

'Delia?' repeated Jeremy Blackburn, a trifle impatiently now. 'Come to life. There's a good girl.'

Delia shook herself. 'Well,' she began, as always very much aware that she was the token woman on the editorial committee, and that Tim Ryman, the sports editor, was as usual staring fixedly at her legs, 'I'm happy to say that the reader response to the article on new forms of birth control was immense. We've had twenty or thirty letters a day, and dozens of phone calls, so I shall definitely be doing a follow-up piece on that.

'Now, I don't know if you've all seen the rough of next month's spread on Irina Vassileyevna, but — '

'Irina who?' put in the features editor.

'Irina Vassileyevna, the Russian gymnast. Only twelve years old, but already third in the world. This should provoke a huge postbag — especially since we've made quite a thing of contrasting Soviet attitudes towards talented kids with the somewhat blinkered outlook prevalent in the UK.'

'You've trodden on *my* feet, too.' Tim Ryman scowled sourly at Delia, then glanced towards his editor. 'Jeremy, correct me if I'm mistaken, but I thought *I* was sports editor of this rag?'

'So you are, Tim — so you are. But Delia's article stresses the human, day to day aspect of being a gymnast. She talks about diet, the rigours of training, the need for family support, and all that stuff.' The editor grinned. 'Little girls from Land's End to the Western Isles will be just itching to get into their leotards and on to the parallel bars. Now,

161

Delia, what are you going to do for our Germany issue?'

'Germany issue?' Tim Ryman lit a Capstan Full Strength. 'Is this something else I don't know anything about?'

'It's what we're going to discuss today.' Jeremy looked round his team. 'I thought we'd devote twenty pages to it. Give it the works, in fact. The rebirth of the Fatherland from the ashes of defeat — the economic miracle — the contrasts between the democratic Federal Republic and the Communist DDR — all that kind of thing. Frank Thorn's already drummed up plenty of advertising, so the whole thing should be a great success. So now, Delia — if you haven't any ideas of your own — '

'You've hardly given me a chance to come up with any,' murmured Delia, but only to herself.

' — I'd suggest you take food and drink. Yes, I'm well aware that wines and spirits are really Gregory Tyler's territory — but the two of you can pool your resources there. Now look, I want two or three full page colour spreads, so have Tony Holland take some of those arty food shots of his. I know he's expensive, but he's good.

'Oh, and just to get you started, I know a bloke who's friendly with this chap in the coffee business. He's come over from Cologne, to set up a branch of his company here, so you could go and talk to him. Get some brand information, maybe a few recipes — perhaps we could even run an offer, or a competition.

'The chap's name is Eisenstadt, and the firm's head office is somewhere in Southampton Row. I believe this fellow speaks good English, so if your German's not up to much, it won't matter.'

'I'll send Janet Lucas over.' Scribbling furiously, Delia jotted down the coffee merchant's name. 'It's time she did some one to one interviews, and I don't suppose this Mr Eisenstadt will give her a rough ride.'

'Why should he? This'll be free publicity for him, after all. Now, Tim — I'll want something from you on West German athletes. How they compare with those supermen from the East, okay?'

* * *

Delia had arranged for her most junior reporter to go and interview Mr Eisenstadt. She was to get enough information to write a five hundred word article, rounded off with a recipe or two. But, on the morning in question, Janet's boyfriend phoned to say she had fallen down the stairs to her flat. She had broken her ankle, so would not be in that week. Nor the week after.

Delia reached for her diary. She saw that the other cub reporter was already out, interviewing a woman who made traditional German confectionery — gingerbread houses, *Stollen*, and so on. But Delia's own morning was more or less clear. So, rather than cancel at the last minute, she decided she would go and see this Mr Eisenstadt herself.

She soon wished she had stayed in her nice, warm office, dipping into the huge heap of unsolicited copy which always balanced precariously on her desk, or roughing out ideas for future spreads. For, as soon as she stepped out into the street, a flurry of dirty London sleet hit her full in the face. A bus splashed her with icy, filthy water, and a foraging pigeon tried to trip her up.

Not really looking where she was going, she then stepped into a puddle full of rubbish being swept along the pavement by the torrent from a blocked drain. Needless to say, there wasn't a single taxi to be seen.

Eventually, however, she managed to flag down a passing cab. 'Where to then, beautiful?' asked the driver cheerfully, eyeing the drowned rat in the back.

'Southampton Row.' Now, Delia realised she had forgotten her cigarettes. 'I'm in a hurry,' she added, tersely. 'Could you step on it a bit?'

'Right you are, sweetheart.' Grinning, the driver swung the vehicles across two streams of fast-moving traffic. Carving up Ford Populars, intimidating Austin Minors, and leaning on his horn at the mere sight of one of the new Minis which bounced cheekily along the highway like the little toy cars he'd obviously decided they were, at one junction he even took on a double decker bus. By the time he pulled up outside the address in Southampton Row, Delia felt extremely ill.

The offices of Eisenstadt UK were on the third floor of the block, and proved to be even more luxurious than those of *World Wide Magazine*, which Delia had previously thought the ultimate in corporate chic. A young, pretty receptionist took her along a thickly carpeted corridor, tapped on a door, then showed her into a warm, pleasant room.

Now, Delia observed that *this* office was as different from Jeremy Blackburn's neon-lit eyrie as it could possibly be. Here, there was rosewood furniture and deep-buttoned upholstery. Not a trace of chrome, ebony or leather was to be seen. All the same, its ambience spoke of power, of money, and of success.

Looking up from his desk near the window, a small, slim man of about Delia's own age rose to greet her. Taking her hand he shook it firmly and then, to her relief — for her own German was still rudimentary — welcomed her in almost perfect English in which there was only a trace of a foreign accent. Since he'd been in England for such a short time, Delia was impressed.

'Sit down, please.' Indicating an armchair opposite his desk, Peter Eisenstadt sat down again himself. 'Now, Miss Lucas — '

'Miss Shenstone, actually.' Delia got out her notebook. 'Delia Shenstone. Miss Lucas has had an accident, so I have come in her place.'

'I see. Well, Miss Shenstone, I can give you twenty minutes. So — what do you wish to know?'

'We'll start with some background, shall we?' Delia looked at him. 'You came here, I believe, to open a sales office for your family's firm?'

'That's correct.' Peter Eisenstadt smiled at her. 'I've been here in London for about six months.'

'I see. What are your impressions so far? Do you like England?'

'Yes, I do. Very much.' Glancing through the window at the sleet, Peter's smile became rueful. 'Of course, the weather is quite dreadful. But I

165

was prepared for that.'

There was a knock on the door. The receptionist came in, this time carrying a trayful of coffee things. So Peter poured strong black coffee into little cups, while the receptionist offered his guest a choice of sweet biscuits.

Sipping her coffee, Delia found it very hot, very strong and deliciously reviving. Just as she liked it, in fact. 'Well, now,' she continued, 'you came over here in — about the middle of last July, was it?'

'Yes, that's right.'

'Was it your first visit to England?'

'Oh, no. I was here in 1945. As a prisoner of war.'

'Were you?' Surprised, Delia stared at him. 'Honestly?'

'Yes, indeed.' Her host shrugged. 'Why are you so surprised?'

'You don't look old enough, that's all.' But then Delia recollected herself. 'I'm sorry,' she murmured, embarrassed. 'I didn't mean to be rude. It's just that — '

'One hardly minds being thought a few years younger than one actually is.' Peter didn't seem at all offended. Indeed, his expression was amused. 'I was a very juvenile prisoner,' he explained. 'Very much the baby of the camp.'

'I see. So — when you were captured, were you brought straight to England?'

'Yes. One moment I was a civilian in Cologne. The next, I was in the front line doing my best to be a gunner. Then I was on a transport bound for England. I was a prisoner for far longer than I was a soldier. But do you wish to know about this? It has nothing to do with coffee. Of course, if it's of any interest to you or the readers of your magazine — '

'Oh, it is!' Warmer and more comfortable now, Delia drank more coffee and accepted another biscuit. 'Please go on. How did you come to be in the army? Were you an officer cadet, or — '

'No. Just an ordinary private soldier. I went into the army when I was eighteen. In the January of 1945, I think.' Recollecting, Peter grimaced. 'Yes, it must have been January,' he said. 'It was so cold. I'd been very ill that winter, and I still had a terrible cough.'

'Well, you don't want to know so much about that. To cut a long story short, the Americans came to the village where we were dug in. We'd been given old rifles, and told to hold out for as long as we could. The Americans had machine guns and tanks, so of course it was hopeless. We did our best, but most of us were killed and the rest taken prisoner.'

'So then you were sent to England.'

'Yes. I believe that saved my life. In the camp, I was given proper medical treatment. Also, I was fed.' Peter laughed. 'You can't imagine how wonderful it was to eat potatoes again. To taste real bread and jam.'

'So you got better. What then?'

'I was sent to work on a farm. Eventually, I was repatriated.'

'I see.' Delia looked up from her notes. 'I believe that after the war some former prisoners asked to remain in England. Did you ever consider applying for naturalisation?'

'Oh, no!' Peter shook his head. 'I'm a German,' he

167

said, simply. 'I like England, certainly. I think the English are among the nicest, kindest people on earth. But my natural home is in the Rhineland, and that is where I shall always belong.'

'Yes. Of course.' Having made rough notes of all this, Delia was already sketching out a piece on former prisoners of war. 'What made your company decide to set up a branch in England?' she asked.

'We feel that our established brands could supply a demand at the more expensive end of the market. We also have a new product which is selling well in Germany, and which we hope will do likewise here.'

'What is this product?'

'Our own version of decaffeinated coffee. We've done some trials and customer surveys and these lead us to hope that this new line will be the one which establishes us firmly in the British market.'

'But decaffeinated coffee *isn't* new.' Delia was scribbling rapidly now. 'There's at least one brand already available here. Isn't that a German product, too?'

'Yes, it is. At present, though, that particular brand is seen as something of a gimmick. It's sold mainly in health-food shops and delicatessens, and it has a rather — what's your word — eccentric image. It's far too expensive to interest the mainstream retailers.

'But we have found a new way in which to manufacture our own version of this product. We can do this much more cheaply than was possible before. We have improved the process, for in our product the taste is enhanced rather than impaired. Now, we have one of the larger grocery chains interested, so with luck — '

'You'll break into a potentially huge British market.'

'Let's hope so.' Picking up a fountain pen, Peter began to doodle on the edge of his blotter. 'Anyway: as it happens, the managing director of this grocery chain tried our product, and was very impressed. He liked the taste well enough, but was also pleased to find that after drinking it in the evening he slept soundly at night.

'Of course, we don't make any medical claims. But if our product is appreciated by insomniacs, this won't do us any harm. We've also been told that people who suffer from headaches after drinking ordinary coffee can take our new brand without any ill effect.'

'A universal panacea, in fact.'

'I'm sorry?'

'Nothing.' Delia blushed. 'I was clearing my throat.'

'I see. Well, Miss Shenstone — you will try some, I hope? To see if you can tell the difference between this and ordinary coffee?'

Without waiting for Delia's reply, Peter pressed a buzzer on his desk. Almost immediately, a severely dressed, middle-aged woman entered the room. 'Ah, Miss Heligmann,' he began, 'a pot of coffee, please — the new variety. Also, two more clean cups. Miss Shenstone, you have five minutes left. What else did you wish to know?'

'Let me see.' Glancing up from her notes, Delia's eyes met Peter's. She noticed his were blue. Very large, clear, and of a deep, translucent cobalt-grey, they were eyes any woman would kill for. 'Your family name is well known in Germany,' she said. 'How long have you been in business there?'

'Oh, in one way and another for at least two hundred years.'

'Who actually owns the company now?'

'It's still a family concern. My cousin Josef is chairman. My mother has a controlling interest. My sisters are on the board.' Peter shrugged. 'I myself am a director and major shareholder.'

'I see.' Five minutes, he'd said. Now it was only three. Or even two. But now, to Delia's great delight, the secretary came in, bringing with her another trayful of coffee things and another plate of biscuits. Now she'd be able to spin the interview out for at least ten minutes more. 'What do you like, or not like, about London?' she asked.

'I don't know London well. But what I have seen of it is very impressive. St Paul's, Westminster Abbey, the Tower — these are all very fine. The National Gallery has some wonderful things, and the British Museum must be one of the greatest treasure houses in the world.'

'What about the people?'

'They are very nice indeed.' Peter smiled at her again, this time looking directly into Delia's eyes. 'Everyone is so pleasant, so friendly. Also helpful. I think I have nowhere else met women so charming. Nor so beautiful, as here.'

Accepting this only mildly chauvinistic compliment, Delia smiled back at him. She thought Peter Eisenstadt was charming, too. Having wondered if he would turn out to be a caricature of a German, the very model of a bombastic, red-faced Hun, she now decided he was one of the nicest men she had ever met.

But, as she glanced at her watch, she realised her time was almost up. In fact, he was now on his feet. Opening a desk drawer, he took out some keys.

Delia closed her notebook, then stood up herself. Should she ask him? Dared she?

She decided she had to. 'In London,' she began, 'there are all kinds of things the casual visitor doesn't see. Small art galleries, for example. Little theatres, pubs and restaurants, all hidden away. I know London very well.'

'I'm sure you do,' Peter Eisenstadt agreed.

'Perhaps you would like to know it better?'

'I beg your pardon?' Peter's eyes met hers. 'I'm sorry, what are you saying?'

Delia took a deep breath. 'I'm saying, would you like to come out one evening, and have a drink with me?'

Peter stared at her. Evidently, he was horrified. Well, perhaps not horrified, but certainly surprised. Or maybe he was trying not to laugh — was fighting to keep a straight face?

Too late, Delia realised she didn't even know if he was married. Now, she decided he must have a wife. They probably lived in Wimbledon, or somewhere like that, in a nice new house with their two or three children. She blushed, and wondered what on earth had possessed her.

Still, Peter stared. But then, he cleared his throat. 'Thank you, Miss Shenstone,' he said, but carefully.

'That's a very nice idea. May I telephone you?'

Of course, thought Delia. The classic evasion. Don't ring me, and I shan't ring you. She blushed again but, grateful that he'd let her down so graciously, she forced a smile. 'Certainly,' she said. Opening her handbag, she took out a card, on which she scribbled her address and home telephone number.

'Thank you.' Peter stuck the card into the corner of his blotter, where it lay on top of half a dozen other notes, memos and miscellaneous scraps of paper. Soon, Delia thought, it would get lost. Or be deliberately thrown away.

'I'm afraid I must leave you now,' Peter continued, politely. 'I have to go and see a customer. But it's been a very great pleasure to meet you.'

He held out his hand. Mechanically, Delia shook it. 'Do stay and finish your coffee,' he said, as he opened the office door. 'When you're ready to leave, tell Miss Heligmann. She'll call a taxi for you.'

★ ★ ★

At home that evening, Delia could not relax. She cooked a dinner she did not eat, then watched a television programme without actually seeing it at all.

Eventually she got out writing paper and then, forcing herself to concentrate, she wrote to Jenny Hughes, telling her about a recent trip to Italy, where she had been to report on the new fashions.

Next, she wrapped up some pretty earrings, set

with chips of lapis-lazuli, which she had bought in Milan. The moment she had seen them sparkling in the jeweller's shop, she had thought of Jenny Hughes. For these lovely stones would bring out the colour of Jenny's eyes.

★ ★ ★

'That's very kind of Delia,' said Shirley, as Jenny displayed her beautiful new earrings, then handed her mother the silk scarf which her friend has also enclosed, for Shirley herself. 'That's very thoughtful indeed. Remember to write and thank her, won't you?'

'Of course I shall. I always do.' Jenny turned from the mirror, in which she had been admiring herself. 'Mum?' she began.

'Yes?'

'We had a woman from the hospital come to talk to us today, about careers in nursing. Well, after what she said, I certainly don't want to be a nurse! But I've been wondering what I *should* do after I leave school.'

'Your Dad thinks you ought to go to college.' Shirley reached for her daughter's hand. 'Oh, love — he'd be so proud of you, if you got a degree.'

'But I don't really want to go to university.' Confidently, Jenny smiled. 'Nobody actually needs a degree. I'll do my O levels, of course. Perhaps even do some As. But then I'd like to go to London, and get a job.'

'Like Delia?' asked Shirley, smiling.

'Like Delia,' Jenny agreed. 'I'll write to her

tonight, I think. To thank her for the earrings and ask her if she's got any ideas. She knows all sorts of people, after all. She'll be aware of jobs and careers I've never even thought of.'

14

It was a week since Delia had met Peter Eisenstadt. Back home at the end of a particularly trying day, she gazed at the telephone, positively *willing* it to ring — but she knew perfectly well that it would not. Or, if it did, it would only be Jim Alexander, a reporter on a national daily, with whom Delia was having a very half-hearted affair.

This liaison was becoming increasingly tedious, for although Jim wasn't deceiving Delia, he *was* cheating on his wife, and he was terrified lest she should find out all about it and divorce him. This was something he didn't want at all, because she had money.

Certainly Delia liked Jim. He was an entertaining companion who was very inventive in bed. But these days she honestly didn't know why he was bothering to commit adultery, for fear of discovery was turning his hair grey. Perhaps, she thought, she ought to find herself a single man. The problem was, she never met any these days.

The Victorian conversion, in which Delia had a small, dormer-windowed flat on the top floor, was a big, solid building constructed as if to withstand a siege. Delia's own little flat was warm and comfortable, just like a womb. Now, foetus-like, she lay curled up on a pile of cushions, in front of the electric fire. She glared balefully at the phone. 'Stupid thing,' she muttered, hating it, and wanting to throw it against the wall.

For at least half an hour, she'd been toying with the idea of making herself some supper. Now, she decided that she would. After all, she had to eat. Leaving the sitting room door ajar, she went into the kitchen. 'Ring, damn you,' she muttered, as she passed the phone. 'Ring!'

Of course, there was no good reason why she should not call *him*. No reason, that was, except she was afraid of a rebuff — which she knew would wound her to the heart.

She spread butter on a roll. She made some coffee, and drank it. She looked at the kitchen clock. It was only five past nine. She'd been invited to a party that evening, and there was still time to doll herself up and go.

She decided she couldn't be bothered. She'd have a shower, then go to bed.

The running water splashed noisily against the sides of the bath. The spray buzzed in her ears, excluding the world. But then, suddenly, she heard it. Clear and unmistakeable, it was the insistent ringing of the telephone bell.

She leapt out of the bath. Naked and dripping, she charged into the sitting room and almost fell on top of the phone. 'Yes?' she gasped, out of breath and literally gasping for air. 'Hello?'

'Hello. Is that Miss Shenstone?'

'Peter!' she cried.

But now, she bit her tongue, cursing herself. Germans never used Christian names casually, and now he'd think she was mad. Or extremely rude. 'I mean, Mr Eisenstadt,' she faltered, abashed.

'That's right.' He sounded relaxed, calm — amused, even. 'Is anything the matter?' he asked.

'I was in the shower. I thought I heard the phone. I wondered if it might be important.' Delia found she could hardly breathe. Each intake of air was as hard to swallow as a lump of mashed potato. 'You know what I mean,' she went on, recklessly. 'You're not expecting a call, but then suddenly — '

'Oh, yes,' Peter agreed. 'It's a shock sometimes. I've been meaning to call you,' he continued, 'but I've been working every evening this week. By the time I arrived home, it seemed too late to trouble you. But tonight, I am making the time. So — have you eaten yet?'

'Well, actually — no.' Delia hadn't eaten properly for days. That evening, she had merely picked at her bread roll, then thrown it out for the birds. 'I only got in from work about twenty minutes ago,' she lied. 'I was going to make myself some scrambled eggs.'

'That doesn't sound very interesting.' Peter cleared his throat. 'I need to eat something. Will you come and have a meal with me?'

'Well, I — '

'There's an excellent French restaurant in the Finchley Road. I think that stays open till midnight. Or there's an Italian place in Fulham, which I believe is very good. Look, I could come and fetch you.'

'That would be great!' Now, huge waves of happiness were crashing over her, and Delia beamed in delight. 'When will you be here?'

'In about half an hour. The traffic's still quite bad,

so give me a good thirty minutes.'

'Fine.'

Returning to the bathroom, Delia was singing. She towelled her wet hair almost dry, showered herself with talc, then slipped on a robe. Going into her bedroom she found her hairdryer, then brushed her blonde hair into a glossy golden waterfall, turning the ends under and flicking back her fringe, so that her finely-arched eyebrows were clearly visible.

She made up her face, and then put on a favourite dress. Made of a clinging, black wool jersey, it always made her feel glamorous and seductive. She looked at herself in the mirror. Did she need a little more mascara? More eyeshadow? Perhaps not. There was no need to overdo things.

She went back into the bathroom, brushed her teeth, then reapplied her lipstick. She smiled at her reflection in the glass. 'Calm down,' she told herself. 'You're behaving like a fifteen year old on your first date.'

At last, the doorbell rang. Dashing down the three flights of stairs, she ran across the hall and flung the front door open wide.

'Good evening.' Car keys in his left hand, Peter stood waiting on the step. He smiled at her. 'Well, you look very nice,' he said.

'Thank you.' Delia beamed at him.

'I'm sorry I'm a bit late. I had to take a phone call. Right, then — where do you want to go?'

Anywhere, she thought. Anywhere at all. To a transport café. A milk bar. A tea and sandwiches stall in Covent Garden. 'I don't mind,' she replied.

'To that French restaurant, if you like.'

'Okay. The car's just along here.'

They walked towards Peter's dark red Mercedes. 'So how's business?' asked Delia, as he drove smoothly away.

'Fine,' he replied. 'This week, we have made an excellent deal with the Bestprice group. Their stores will stock all our products on six months' trial. They'll arrange special promotions, in-store tastings, free gifts and money-off coupons. Soon we shall start an advertising campaign, both on television and in the press.'

'Goodness. The big time.'

'Of course.' Peter changed gear, put his foot down and soon he was driving as if he were on a German *Autobahn* rather than in a quiet London suburb. 'This time next year,' he continued, 'our *Goldbrand* products will be found in every kitchen in England. But I'm sure you don't really want to hear about our promotion drive. What have you been doing?'

'Oh — all sorts of things,' Delia replied. Did this man know there were speed limits in England? Holding tight to the door handle, she tried to steady herself. 'I don't think I want to go all the way to the Finchley Road, after all,' she added. 'There's a very nice restaurant quite near here. Why don't we go there, instead?'

'Where exactly is it?'

'Second on your left.'

'Up here?'

'Yes.'

The Mercedes roared up a deserted street. Reaching an arcade of shops, Peter pulled in and

179

braked to a shuddering halt. 'Do you mean the place back there?' he asked. '*The Golden Lily?*'

'That's it.'

'What sort of restaurant is it?'

'Chinese. Do you like Chinese food?'

'I eat anything.' Peter took the keys out of the ignition. Glancing at Delia, he smiled — but then his expression became serious. Concerned. 'You look so tired,' he said, kindly. 'Exhausted, in fact.'

'I am.' Now, taken unawares, Delia tried to control the great wave of desire which suddenly threatened to engulf her. She looked down at her hands. 'I've been working hard,' she muttered.

'Poor thing. You should have had an early night.'

'Perhaps.' Delia glanced up again. 'Aren't you hungry?' she asked.

'Yes, a little.'

'Then let's go and eat something.' Delia reached for her handbag. 'Er — may I call you Peter?' she asked.

'Yes, of course.' Engagingly, Peter smiled. 'After all, it's the English way.'

* ★ ★

One of the first Chinese restaurants to appear in that district, *The Golden Lily* was usually crowded. This evening, however, it was very quiet.

Peter didn't even look at the menu. Without asking Delia what she wanted, he merely asked the waiter to bring a meal for two. 'Oh — would you like a drink?' he asked, almost as an afterthought, as the waiter went away.

That evening, Delia ate ravenously. Peter, however, merely played with his food, idly turning over noodles and pushing prawns and vegetables around his plate. Soon, he gave up even pretending to eat. Ordering coffee, he leaned back in his chair and watched Delia stuff herself.

Her appetite impressed him. 'So greedy,' he observed, shaking his head in disbelief. 'Yet you're so slim!'

'I work it all off. I worry the calories away.' Seeing the amusement in Peter's eyes, Delia blushed. 'Why don't you have some of that?' she suggested, pointing to a dish of mixed Chinese vegetables. 'It's really nice.'

'You eat it then.' Indulgently, Peter smiled at her. 'After all, you seem to need it.'

So, Peter drank his third cup of coffee, and Delia polished off the rest of the food. 'You'll have coffee now?' he asked.

'No, thanks.' Delia drank some water. 'I've had enough.'

'I should think you have. I don't know where you've put it all.'

A waiter walked past now, so Peter stopped him and asked for the bill. 'No,' he said firmly, as Delia opened her handbag. 'I asked you to come out for this meal, so I shall pay for it. That I insist.'

Once out in the street again, he turned up his coat collar and pushed his hands deep into his pockets. 'Come,' he said, sharply. 'It's cold.'

Delia came. Although her instinctive reaction to almost any order was to argue, to disobey — or do both — tonight, she did as she was told. She fell into step with him and together they arrived back at the car.

Their conversation during dinner had been general, and altogether non-committal. Peter said he'd been to a concert, which he'd hated, for the music had been new, modern stuff — full, as he put it, of jangles, thumps and bangs. Wondering whom he had been to the concert with, but not daring to ask, Delia told him about the film actor who was still suing the magazine for libel, but whose private life, it now transpired, was apparently even more of a midden than those few oblique remarks in *World Wide Magazine* had led its readers to believe.

But now, driving back to Delia's flat, they were silent. The car stopped outside the house. Should she ask him in? Delia wanted to. If Peter had been any other man, she would have done so without hesitation.

But, as she prevaricated, Peter spoke. 'Thank you for a very pleasant evening,' he said. Then, leaning towards her, he kissed her lightly on her cheek.

She turned her face to his. She smiled at him. 'Will you come up for a drink?' she asked.

'Thank you, no. I have to put a call through to Cologne. It's already very late, and I expect they've given me up, but there's something I must let my cousin know before morning.'

'*Must* you do it tonight?'

'I'm afraid so. But may I telephone you tomorrow?'

'Certainly.' Delia was an expert at hiding her feelings, and now she dared to hope that her disappointment did not show. 'Yes, please do.'

'Where will you be?'

'At the office until six. Then here.'

'I'll ring about half seven. Perhaps, this weekend, we might arrange to go out together? That is — unless you've already made plans?'

'I don't think I'm busy. I'd have to check my diary, but I — '

'I'll ring you, then. We'll work something out.' Peter kissed her again. 'Goodnight, Delia,' he said.

15

'What's the matter?' asked Peter kindly, as he and Delia walked past a stand of dripping conifers. 'Delia, what's wrong?'

'Nothing.' Bravely, Delia forced a smile. For, she had no idea at all why she felt so miserable. She was in the company of the one person with whom she wanted to be. She had him all to herself. So, shouldn't she be happy? Perhaps. But instead, she was desolate. Peter seemed almost as melancholy as she was.

But at least he was not quite so on edge. He no longer seemed determined to kill them both, for that Saturday morning he drove out to Hampton Court observing the Highway Code and the speed limits all the way. Braving the sleety drizzle, they walked all round the gardens.

Here, when they weren't silent, they made only the emptiest of tourists' remarks. Although they both longed to open their hearts, in fact they told each other nothing.

That evening, Peter took Delia to an expensive French restaurant in the West End. She ate everything that was put in front of her, while he pushed his food around his plate.

On Sunday, they walked in Hyde Park, where Peter stared in absolute astonishment at the hardy souls swimming and splashing in the icy, muddy Serpentine. 'I'll never understand the English,' he muttered, shaking his head in disbelief. 'God, I hate January! I wish it were summer. Summer in the mountains, at home.'

Later, he wasted more money, in an even more expensive restaurant. It wasn't the kind of place where the head waiter would even dream of asking a diner why he'd left his greens — but Delia, child of austerity that she was, looked on appalled to see so much food go to waste.

'Won't you come in?' she asked, as Peter pulled up outside her house. 'Just for five minutes? Have a glass of wine with me.'

'No, thank you.' Peter would not even meet her eyes. 'I must get back.'

'When shall I see you again?'

'I'll meet you for lunch, on Wednesday.' Now, he turned to look at her. 'Could you have the afternoon off?'

Delia swallowed hard. 'Yes, I expect so,' she replied.

But Wednesday was the magazine's busiest day! Wednesday afternoon was when the final copy was fitted, when the departmental editors had their weekly attacks of nervous hysteria, when the juniors ran panicking all round the office, invariably close to tears. 'That won't be a problem,' she said, firmly.

She could always go sick.

★   ★   ★

Delia spent the next two days in torment. Frustration and anxiety made her sleepless. Lying awake, she could think of nothing but Peter, and how much she wanted him.

Wednesday lunchtime finally arrived. 'I think I'll have to go home,' she told Jeremy, who glared at her — but who could see she looked far from well. 'I reckon I'm coming down with that 'flu.'

'Yeah. Perhaps.' Studying Delia's ashen complexion and observing the smudges of fatigue under her eyes, Jeremy stubbed out his cigarette. 'Subbing all done, is it?'

'Of course.'

'Copy fitted?'

'Julie's finishing it now. Helen can check it through. Her proof-reading's spot on, you know that.' Wearily, Delia rubbed her aching eyes. 'Look, Jeremy — they don't need me to nanny them.'

'I suppose not. Off you go, then.' Jeremy pursed his lips. 'Sweat it out over the weekend, eh? Back on Monday, fit as the proverbial flea.'

'I'll do my best.'

'See to it.' Jeremy sniffed. 'You can't afford to be ill, Delia. No way.'

★   ★   ★

Delia saw Peter cross the road, then merge with the crowd on the pavement. Now he was a mere twenty yards from the tube station entrance, where she was waiting for him.

As he walked towards her, she saw him push his hands into his pockets and hunch his shoulders against the London rain. This gesture pierced her to the heart, for it was so child-like, so sweet — and so pointless. He had no hat, nor umbrella, so the rain would still be running down his neck, still soaking into his shirt. He'd be bound to catch cold.

Now, Delia was running. Edging bystanders aside, she hurried along the pavement, splashing her stockings while the dirty London rain pattered against her face. 'Peter!' Breathless, but beaming with pleasure, she stood in front of him. 'Oh, Peter!'

'Delia.' He took his hands out of his pockets. Reaching out to her, he took her by the shoulders. He kissed her cheek. Only an inch or so taller than she was, his eyes were almost level with hers, and now they looked into her own, blue-grey meeting grey-blue.

'Where shall we go?' she asked, longing to hug him, but not daring even to touch him. Not in public. 'Peter, where — '

'I think to my flat. We'll eat there. Then, perhaps, a film? Is that okay?'

'Fine.'

So Peter flagged down a cab. Now, as the rain began to come down in torrents, he grimaced. '*Du lieber*,' he muttered, shaking his head. 'Always raining! Always *Mistwetter* here!'

'Oh, Peter!' As they hurried towards the taxi, Delia frowned in reproach. 'Germans *are* disgusting!'

'Are we? I don't think so.' Peter jerked open the door of the cab. Bundling Delia inside, he scrambled in after her. Unbuttoning his sodden raincoat, he grinned. 'That's something you imagine,' he said.

'Where to then, mate?' asked the driver, accelerating down Kingsway.

'Oh — Elbury Gardens. St John's Wood.' Peter shook his wet hair out of his eyes. 'Anyway,' he declared, 'if we're disgusting, the English are equally as bad. Or worse. In the office today, the girl who helps my secretary keeps jamming the keys on her typewriter. 'Shit, shit, shit,' she says, over and over again. I tell you, Delia, she makes me blush. The English swear far more than the Germans do. Always they're saying 'bloody hell', or 'bleeding' this and that.'

'Maybe.' Delia didn't want to argue. Instead, she looked intently at him, searching his face. She saw that although he was obviously very tired, he wasn't at all jittery today. In fact, he was as relaxed as he'd been that first time they met.

The desire to kiss him now became so great that she turned to look out of the window. When she glanced back at him, she saw his eyes were closed. Breathing regularly, he appeared to be fast asleep.

'Here, is it?' The driver had pulled up at a junction. 'This block here? Hey! You awake, or what?'

'Sorry.' Coming to, Peter shook himself. 'Yes, that's correct,' he said. 'Just here on the left. How much is that?'

★ ★ ★

Peter's flat was in a small, modern block. Built around a pretty courtyard, in which a fountain played, the main windows of each apartment looked down on to a communal garden, which was well-tended and probably very pleasant in summer time.

'This is nice.' Looking round the small sitting room, which was furnished with what she could see were probably rather valuable antiques, Delia smiled. Observing the comfortable disorder of books, magazines, discarded pullovers and squashed cushions — all the clutter and mess of a man living on his own — she smiled again. 'But I always thought Germans were so tidy!'

'Did you?' Peter shook his head. 'Delia, you have very strange ideas about Germans. I don't know how to start correcting you.'

'Germans *are* tidy!' Delia would not let him get away with that. 'When I went to Frankfurt, for my paper, I was invited into at least a dozen homes. There wasn't a thing out of place, in any of them.'

'No?' Removing a pile of books, Peter cleared a space on the sofa. 'Well, I'm not tidy at all. I like a room to look as if someone lives in it.'

'This one certainly does. But you've made it very nice, all the same.' Looking at the pretty Impressionist print which hung over the fireplace, Delia nodded her approval. 'It's very nice indeed.'

'Nice. Still the favourite English word.'

'What?'

'Nothing.' Shrugging off his wet mackintosh, Peter held out his hand for her coat. 'Look,' he said, 'I must go and light the oven. It's a casserole. Will you like that?'

'So you can cook?'

'Oh, no. Not very well, anyway. I wouldn't know how to make a casserole.'

'Then who did?'

'The lady who cleans for me. She thinks I need building up, so she makes this for me, every week. I'm sure you'll find it very — ah — nice!'

He disappeared into the kitchen. Two minutes later he returned, with a glass in each hand. 'Will you have a drink?' he asked. 'While we wait?'

'Thank you,' said Delia. 'That would be lovely.'

'Gin and tonic?'

'Please.'

'Sit down, then.' Taking a bottle from a tray on the bookcase, Peter splashed a generous measure of spirit into each glass. He opened some tonic water. Walking over to the sofa, he held out a drink for Delia to take.

As she accepted it, his eyes met hers. 'I want to sleep with you,' they told her. 'I want you in my bed.'

Now Delia made room for him on the sofa. But, instead of sitting down beside her, Peter took the armchair opposite. 'Why are you not married?' he asked.

'I'm sorry?' Delia stared at him. Invariably so extremely polite, Germans were sometimes unnervingly direct. 'What did you say?'

'Why have you no husband? No children?'

'I never told you I had no husband or children.'

'But it's obvious.' Dismissively, Peter shrugged. 'You did not need to say this much. So?'

Well.' Delia grimaced. 'If you must know, my best friend stole my lover.'

'I don't believe you.' Peter's eyes met Delia's. 'What really happened?'

'Exactly what I said.' Steadily, Delia looked back at him. She took a deep, deep breath. 'What about you?' she asked. 'Are you a married man?'

'Oh yes, I'm married.'

'Ah.' Delia's heart sank like a stone in water.

Of course, she had suspected. She'd tried to fool herself, but all along she had known. Trying to convince herself that here, at long last, was the kind, sensible, intelligent man she had been looking for all her life — the man who might even fall in love with her — she had wandered along the primrose path to ruin without even thinking about the ravines and chasms of heartbreak and despair which gaped on either side.

She took another deep breath. 'Why isn't your wife in England, then?' she enquired. 'Why isn't she here, with you?'

'It's not possible,' Peter replied.

'Why is that?'

'My wife and I are separated.'

'I see.' Delia looked down into her drink. She didn't know if she was relieved, delighted or appalled. 'I'm sorry to hear that,' she said.

'It's no matter.' Peter swirled his gin and tonic round and round the glass. 'We've been apart for years.'

'Have you?' Now, steeling herself for what he might say to her, Delia looked into Peter's eyes. 'Will you tell me about it?' she asked.

'Tell you what?'

'Well — what happened? Why did you break up?' Delia didn't want to upset him, but she needed to know. 'What's your wife like?' she asked. 'What — '

'She's just a woman, that's all.' Peter shrugged. 'She was a widow, five years older than me. We knew each other since one month. We fell in love. So we became husband and wife.'

'After just a month?'

'Yes. Thirty-six days, to be exact.' Peter stared down into his glass. 'Oh, I agree it was very sudden. But you see, in those awful days just after the war, people clung to each other. Marriages were very quickly made.'

'Even so — '

'You've been to West Germany.' Now, Peter was almost talking to himself. 'You've seen what it's like. There's still much to do, of course — it will be years before Cologne looks anything like what it was before the war. But all the same, it's clean, decent and tidy. The people are well-fed, well-housed and prosperous. Looking at Germany today, one can't imagine how it was in those earlier years. At zero hour.

'In Cologne, you know, we had nothing. No fuel, no clean water, no proper food. The people were starving. During that first winter of defeat, many of them just sat down in the streets and died of starvation or despair. Others died of cold. They had no fires to warm themselves, so they simply froze to death.

'Those who were determined to survive stuck it out in the cellars of their homes, or in squalid wooden huts. The city was in ruins, you see. Wet black ashes, gutted buildings and broken glass — that's all your bombers had left for us. Everything except the cathedral was smashed and destroyed.'

'Peter,' interrupted Delia gently, 'you don't have to tell me all this.'

'I want you to know.' Now Peter looked at her, blue eyes intent. 'Where was I? Oh, yes. Reni was living with her mother, in their bombed-out house near the *Domplatz*. Her husband had been in the east, a prisoner of the Russians. He came back in 1947, just half a man. Less than half a man.'

'What do you mean by that?'

'What I say!' Peter's eyes blazed. 'Delia, you must know this. The Russians are the children of Satan! The Nazis were wicked, I make no excuses for them. But the Russians had nothing to learn from the Germans.

'Reni's husband had been in a Soviet labour camp. There he had seen and suffered things of which, even today, I cannot bring myself to speak. Things one would not imagine human beings could think of. Let alone bear to do, or to endure.

'He would tell her. Every night he would sit beside her and take her hand, he would weep and he would speak of it. He was mad, I think, driven mad by what he had witnessed being done to others. Also by what had been done to him.

'Reni wept with him. In the end she became a little mad herself. He could see this, perhaps, but still he made her listen, night after night after night. But, try as he might, he could not burn the memories out of his heart.'

'What happened to him?'

'He died. Six months after he returned to Cologne, he went out alone for the first time, to take an evening walk. The following morning his body was taken out of the Rhine, near the *Mülheimer-hafen*. Oh, he may have intended to die, he may not. Who can say?

'I met Reni at the funeral. Her parents were friends of my father, and I'd known of her since childhood. We talked a little, standing together in the rain. The next day I met her in the *Domplatz*. We went and heard Mass, then we walked for a while amid the ruins. We talked more. I began to think she needed someone to look after her, and this was something I could do.

'But then one day I looked at her, I saw the sun shining on her face, and I understood that I loved her. So, Reni and I were married.'

'Were you happy?'

'Happy enough.' Peter shrugged. 'Of course, I had to work most of the time, I was in a gang clearing rubble. Often we spent whole days taking decayed bodies out of the ruins. Not a pleasant task.

'Reni and her mother came to live with us at our house — or what was left of it. She helped my mother with the cooking and so on. But she couldn't do much. She wasn't very strong.

'Then, however, that little seed of madness, which her first husband had planted, began to grow. Very soon, it flowered. She became stranger and stranger. She forgot to wash, she muttered to herself, she stopped people in the street and shouted at them, or begged them to help her.

'Finally she decided I was a Russian soldier, who had killed her husband. She threw knives and dishes at me. Once, she attacked me with a meat cleaver. I have scars on my arms still.

'She didn't want me anywhere near her. She hated everyone. She even pushed her own mother away. She hoarded food in an old rusty tin, and it went bad and made her ill.

'Sometimes she was almost sane. Sometimes she even knew me — she smiled at me, and kissed me, and wanted me to kiss her. But most of the time she was hostile and just sat in a corner, talking to herself.

'In the end, we had to accept that she needed treatment. Now she's in a nursing home. She seems fairly happy there — but she has no idea who I am. When I visit her she lets me hold her hand, she smiles, she tells me it's kind of me to come. She thinks I'm a doctor or social worker, I suppose.'

Bitterly, Peter laughed. 'The last time I saw her, she told me she'd written a letter to Dietrich, which she asked me to post.'

'Who is Dietrich?'

'Her first husband.'

'I see.' Sympathetically, Delia sighed. 'Why aren't you divorced?' she asked.

'Divorced?' Peter looked shocked. 'That would be impossible.'

'Why?'

'I'm a Catholic.'

'Catholics can be divorced, can't they? Or have annulments, or something?'

'Now and again they can. In very special circumstances. But — '

'But it's not an option for you.' Understanding now, Delia met his eyes. 'You believe that marriage is for life. You meant what you said in church.

You're one of the faithful.'

'I try to be.' Peter looked down at his hands. 'I try to believe, although sometimes it's hard.'

'You go to Mass, then? You go to confession and tell the priest you've sinned?'

'I have not made my confession for many years now.' Looking up again, Peter met Delia's gaze. 'But I don't think that's so important. Because in my heart, I still believe.'

'Yes.' Now Delia took a great risk, leaping headlong into the darkness of unknowing. 'So, Peter,' she began, 'if you were to go to bed with me, would you be risking your chances of eternal life?'

'Ah.' Peter considered it. 'I don't think so,' he replied, at last. 'I think that to go to bed with you would be just a little sin. God would not really mind it.'

'Is that what a priest would say?'

'It's some time since I spoke of such things with a priest. But yes, given these particular circumstances, I think a priest might well say that. A modern priest, that is.'

'So I would be your little sin.'

'If that's how you want to put it.'

A little sin. Delia had been called many things, but never anything quite so cruelly dismissive, so callous, so unfeeling, as that. Hurt, she bit her lip. She knew she ought to leave, and now. So, she got up from the sofa, and walked towards the door.

But, as she passed Peter's chair, he caught her hand in his. 'Don't go,' he said.

'I think I should.'

'Nonsense. You don't think that at all.'

'Don't I?' Delia was almost in tears. 'You do make this hard for me!' she cried. 'You know I — '

'Yes, I know. I want so much to kiss you, too.' Peter stood up now. 'Please — let's not deny each other that.'

Delia looked into his eyes. She knew she was beaten. 'As if I could deny you anything,' she said.

So Peter kissed her.

What did he taste of? Gin and tonic, certainly. But now Delia detected something unfamiliar, too. Some foreign toothpaste, or mouthwash. Not mint, but aniseed. Or caraway, or fennel. Whatever it was, this strangeness excited her. Soon, she was kissing him back with enthusiasm.

Encouraged, he undid the top buttons on her blouse. He kissed her neck. Then he was stroking her breasts.

Now she wanted his hands on her flesh. Undoing the rest of the buttons, she slipped off her blouse and let it fall to the floor. Closing her eyes, she let him take over.

Ten minutes later, Delia lay naked on the hearthrug, in her lover's arms.

He kissed her nose.

She licked his ear. Then she bit it.

He kissed her again. 'You hurt me then,' he whispered. 'Don't be so wicked.'

'But I'm your little sin.' Now, Delia narrowed her eyes at him. 'What else can you expect, from a little sin?'

Peter laughed. 'Beautiful little sin,' he said. Raising himself on one elbow, he looked down at her. With his index finger, he traced a line from her throat to her chest, then circled her breasts. 'Little sin, I'm sorry I couldn't wait for you.'

'Why were you in such a hurry?' Delia grimaced. 'Men,' she muttered. 'You're all the same. You hug and kiss a little, but then that's it. You think you've done your duty. The rest of the time, you think only of yourselves.'

'Nonsense,' said Peter. 'I like to please a woman. I think it's better for both if she has some excitement, too. But with you, today, it was impossible to hold back. Delia?'

'What?'

'I want to make you happy now.' Taking a cushion from the sofa, Peter slid it under Delia's hips. He spread her legs wide.

★ ★ ★

'That was lovely.' Stretching luxuriously, a quarter of an hour later Delia was completely satisfied. More than satisfied. In fact, she thought she would never be hungry again. 'Peter, you're a genius,' she said.

'Am I?' Peter ruffled her hair. 'Well — no one's ever told me that before. Thank you.'

'Thank *you*.' Delia sat up. She looked deep into his eyes. 'I love you,' she said.

'I love you, too. More than I can say.'

'More than you love Reni?'

'More than anyone I've ever known.'

'I see.' Delia looked deep into his eyes. 'Have there been many women in your life?' she asked. 'Apart from Reni, that is?'

'Hardly any.' Peter shrugged. 'Before Reni, there was one other girl. For a little while, I thought I loved her. But it was just — what's your word — an infatuation? Yes, that's it. In the end, it meant nothing at all.

'I loved Reni, very much. But after her, there was nobody. Until I met you.'

'Oh.' Delia kissed him. 'I'm so glad you met me!'

'So am I.' But now, Peter frowned. 'What about you, though?' he enquired. 'I can't believe there is no one special to you. So — is he away, perhaps? Or treating you unkindly just now? Delia, I should have asked you this long before. But I was so afraid — '

'There's no one. No one at all.' Delia hugged him. 'You've made me so happy today,' she said. 'But — '

'But what?'

'Did you mean what you said? Do you really love me best?'

'More than anyone or anything. More even than I loved my teddy bear. Or my old nurse's apple cake, eaten warm with cream.'

'I'm honoured.' Gaily, Delia laughed. 'Talking of food, I'm starving. Shall we eat something?'

'Oh, good God — the casserole.' Peter groaned. 'I'd forgotten all about that. It'll be dried out.'

'It doesn't matter. We'll eat it anyway.'

★ ★ ★

Peter went into the kitchen and turned off the oven. Then, taking Delia into the bathroom, he washed her, spraying her with the shower rose, soaping her and making her squeal.

They put on bathrobes and ate their lunch. Delia glanced at the kitchen clock. Half past six. *Half past six?* Where had the time gone?

'You don't have to go, you know.' Seeing her check her wristwatch, then shake it in disbelief, Peter reached for Delia's hand. 'But of course, if you wish to leave, I'll drive you home.'

Delia shook her head. 'I don't want to *leave!*' she cried. 'I know. Let's go to bed.'

In Peter's untidy bedroom a fat, down-filled quilt in a plain cotton cover lay on a beautiful, old-fashioned, three quarter sized bed. 'Big enough for us both, I hope,' said Peter, sitting down on it. 'Very comfortable,' he added, bouncing up and down like a child.

Delia sat down beside him. She undid the belt on his bathrobe. She kissed his neck. 'Your cleaning lady is right,' she said, looking at him. 'You do need fattening up.'

'Cheek!' Peter pushed Delia's wrap back from her shoulders. Rolling it down to her waist, he brushed it aside. Then they lay down together and began the afternoon's business all over again.

'Don't leave me,' he said afterwards, looking down at her.

'I shan't,' she replied, hugging him.

'You might. I think you could be cruel.' He looked into her eyes. 'You might cut out my heart. Throw it aside. Then you'd laugh. You'd wipe your blood-stained hands upon my shirt and walk away, looking for someone else to destroy.'

'Don't be so gruesome. As if I'd do anything of the kind.' Delia kissed his shoulder. 'Peter, for someone of your size, you're surprisingly heavy.'

He rolled away from her. Taking her in his arms, he pulled the quilt over their faces.

Delia sighed, then relaxed completely. Contentedly, she fell asleep.

Part Two

1964–1984

16

One of six successful applicants for secretarial posts with Eisenstadt UK, Jenny Hughes was informed that her own basic training would take place at the company's Acton office. So it was that, one cold wet Sunday afternoon in the autumn of 1964, she finally arrived at Mrs Berners' large Edwardian villa in the bleak suburbs of West London.

Getting off the train at Paddington, she'd lugged her cases across the litter-strewn concourse and fought her way on to the Underground. As she'd stood in the crowded, swaying carriage, she almost wished she had let Gareth bring her down, after all. He had suggested several times that he should drive her to London. Shirley had seconded that. But Jenny had been determined to go alone. 'I'm a big girl now, Dad,' she'd told him, looking up from her half-packed suitcase. 'I can manage all by myself.'

Back in Evesbridge, these had seemed fine, brave words. Now, with a man's wet mackintosh pressed clammily against the back of her head, and a fat woman breathing garlic fumes in her face, Jenny could see that independence and going it alone were perhaps not always so desirable, after all.

★ ★ ★

'Come in, come in. Let's have you in the kitchen. Warm yourself, yes? Poor child, you're frozen.' A large, motherly lady with a beaming smile, Mrs Berners always spoke in short, breathless sentences. Now, she ushered her new lodger into the kitchen and over to a glowing stove.

While Jenny stood there thawing, and drinking a most welcome cup of tea, Mrs Berners fussed around her like an old hen with one chick. Dabbing at her damp hair with a towel, she told her to take off those wet shoes. Otherwise, catch cold she would. Only when she was satisfied that Jenny was completely defrosted and relatively dry did she take her to see her room.

'You like it, yes?' she demanded, still smiling. 'Leon did it up specially. It was old-fashioned before. Heavy furniture, we had. Black oak stuff. 'Young girls don't like that rubbish,' says Leon. So he makes it a bit modern. Nice, eh?'

'Yes, very.' Jenny looked around her. She saw a white-walled room, a brand new Habitat chest of drawers and wardrobe, and a bright Indian rug. Sitting down on the bed, she found it was soft and comfortable.

At once, she felt at home. As Mrs Berners' husband came in with her suitcases, she opened her overnight bag and took out her hairbrush.

'That's right. Get yourself straight.' Mrs Berners drew the patterned orange curtains, then switched on the bedside lamp, which bathed the room in a warm, golden light. 'Come down to the kitchen when you're ready,' she added. 'It's tea time soon. We'll wait for you.'

That evening, Mrs Berners ran Jenny a bath, and when she returned to her bedroom she found two hot water bottles in her bed. She slid between the sheets, intending to read for a while. But ten minutes later she put down her book, and very soon she was fast asleep.

On Monday morning she was up early, trying to decide what to wear. In the end she chose a plain black straight skirt which just touched her knees, and topped this with a lavender-coloured jumper.

She polished her best black courts with a Kleenex, then slipped them on. Brushing her hair, she tucked it behind her ears, then put on just a little pink lipstick. She wondered about eye shadow, but then decided against it. She didn't want to look like a tart.

With a good breakfast lying queasily against her ribcage, she set off for her first day at the office. She reached the main road just in time to see her bus pull away from the stop. Opening her A to Z, she tried to find her way to the Underground on foot, but when she reached the tube station, she found it was on the wrong line for Acton.

She finally arrived at the office hot, breathless and panicking, with just half a minute to spare. It was only a week later that she realised she could in fact walk to work, taking a series of short cuts through some back alleys, then strolling through a park and a street market on the way.

The office in Acton was responsible for the routine, day to day administration of Eisenstadt UK, and took up half a floor in a large, modern block. Greeted by an immaculate receptionist, who looked as if she'd been freshly lacquered from head to foot that very morning, the newcomer was taken up to the third floor, then handed over to an equally smart secretary.

Allocated her own locker and told to hang up her coat on the hanger provided, Jenny's name was then formally entered in the Elevenses Book. 'Don't you like coffee?' enquired the secretary. For Jenny had ticked only the column for tea.

Jenny blushed. 'Not really,' she replied.

'Very English. But we'll convert you. Come along.' The secretary opened a door. Now, she led Jenny down the corridor to the general office, a large, noisy, open-plan place lit by huge picture windows and glaring neon lights. 'This way,' she continued, raising her voice above the clatter of typewriters, the hum of a dozen conversations and the insistent ringing of telephone bells.

'Where are we going?' asked Jenny.

'To see Mr Dierken,' replied the secretary. 'He's the training officer.'

'Is he German?'

'Yes.'

'Is he nice?'

'He's okay.' The secretary knocked on Mr Dierken's door. 'Do as you're told. Always be on time. Then, you should have no problems with him.'

★　★　★

'Miss Hughes? Do come in.' Firmly shaking Jenny's hand, Mr Dierken smiled in welcome. 'Now then, let me see — where's your file? Right. I think we'll get you started. Yes?'

Now Jenny found that, as the first of half a dozen

new recruits due to start work over the course of the next couple of months, her own personal training programme had already been prepared. Every working day for the next six weeks was accounted for in advance.

There was so much to learn! Apart from shorthand, typing and general office practice, she had to get to grips with the way in which this huge international organisation actually worked. Junior management staff from Sales, Accounts, Exports and Marketing took her on guided tours around their own departments, where she was expected to listen, learn, make notes, and ask intelligent questions. Then Mr Dierken would quiz *her*.

She found that, at the end of each day, she was so tired that all she wanted to do was go to bed. Plans for sight-seeing trips fell by the wayside, and telephone calls to schoolfriends who'd also come to live in the Big Smoke were not made.

'So, how you get on with this job of yours?' enquired Mrs Berners, one chilly evening a fortnight after Jenny had first arrived. 'Sit down, sit down. Have a cup of tea. Biscuit? So now I tell you. Those Germans work you too hard. Always exhausted you look.'

'It *is* tiring.' Gratefully, Jenny drank her tea. 'There's an awful lot to learn,' she admitted. 'But I expect I'll get there. In the end.'

'In your coffin you'll be, if you carry on at this rate.' Mrs Berners sat down herself. 'So when they make you managing director, then?'

'Not just yet. There's a six week probationary period to get through first. If I make the grade, I'll start my training proper.'

'So what you do then?'

'Spend a few weeks in each department, probably as a clerk. I'll also be going to day release classes at the local Tech, to do a course in Commerce. I don't know what that will involve, but there's an exam at the end, which I've been told I have to pass.' Ruefully, Jenny grinned. 'In the meantime, I'm an *Azubi*. Lowest of the low. A humble, ignorant trainee.'

'Not for ever. Soon you'll be the boss's secretary. Big shot you are then.' Smiling encouragement, Mrs Berners placed Jenny's dinner before her. 'Chicken stew,' she said. 'My own recipe, it is. Eat. Listen, a girl phoned you today. I took her number. Jess somebody, she was.'

'Jess Hallet?'

'That's it. Says she's your friend from school.'

'She's my best friend.' Jenny began to eat her dinner. 'I'll ring her tomorrow,' she said.

★ ★ ★

Now at London University, where she was taking a degree in English Literature, Jess Hallet found London every bit as overwhelming as Jenny did. She was lonely, too — for university was nothing like school. There was no sense of belonging, no idea of community at all.

First year undergraduates were left very much to their own devices. If Jess missed a lecture, if she skipped a seminar, no one seemed to notice. Let alone care. Even her own tutor, whom she'd imagined would take at least a nominal interest in her personal welfare, had failed to turn up for three out of the four weekly tutorials she should have had so far.

The college building itself was depressing in the extreme. A foetid 1930s pile in the East End of London, it had a cemetery on one side and a brewery on the other. The block which housed the Faculty of Arts looked like a cross between a church institute down on its luck, and a Victorian workhouse. It smelled of damp, dust and decay. On the whole, Jess was bitterly disappointed in Queen Alexandra College.

To add to her misery, her digs were cold and her landlady most unfriendly. Poor Jess had no hot water bottles in her bed, nor any special chicken dinners. Instead, she'd been given a key to her bedsitter and told be quiet at all times, especially after nine o'clock at night.

'So if I wish to die at all noisily,' she grumbled, as she and Jenny sat in a snack bar together sharing a banana milkshake, 'I may do so only between breakfast time and eight fifty-nine in the evening. Otherwise, I have to expire in silence.'

'Poor old you.' Jenny sighed in sympathy. 'I could ask my landlady if she wants another lodger, maybe?'

'There's no way I could live that far out. For one thing, I couldn't afford the tube fares to college.' Miserably, Jess sniffed. 'Oh — I expect I'll get a flat soon, with a couple of others. In Bethnal Green, or Stepney. Somewhere like that.'

'Where you can be noisy.'

'Yeah.' At the prospect of this, Jess cheered up a little. 'We'll have a bit of fun, then,' she declared. 'Play some decent music. Have all-night parties. You can come.'

'Thank you.'

'Don't mention it. Speaking of music, there's a rock concert in college this Friday. Some people from my year are going. Do you fancy it?'

★ ★ ★

Constantly on the move and permanently chasing their increasingly hectic schedules, for weeks on end Delia and Peter didn't set eyes on one another. If Peter was in Germany, as he often had to be for months at a time, they were obliged to be content to exchange letters and phone calls — as they did when Delia, now senior features editor on *World Wide Magazine*, was abroad.

In four years, they had perhaps spent a full six months in each others' company. In spite of that, however, Delia had imagined she knew all Peter's likes, dislikes, loves and hates. So she was surprised when, one day, he asked if she would like to go to Covent Garden.

'To see an opera?' she enquired. 'Or a ballet?'

'An opera.' Now he produced two tickets, for the coming Friday evening. 'Don't you like this idea?'

'Well, since you ask, not really.' This was an understatement. In fact, Delia hated it. Once taken to a Press preview of *Billy Budd*, she had almost died of irritation, aggravation and sheer boredom. She had come out into the sunlight vowing on her mother's grave never to go near an opera house again. 'Do you have to go?' she complained.

'Well, I should like to.'

'Oh.' Delia had planned to spend Friday evening at Peter's flat, preferably in Peter's bed. 'Well — which opera is it?'

'*Die Zauberflöte. The Magic Flute.* That's not the heavyweight stuff, you know. It's a sort of pantomime. Like the English Christmas treat.' Peter shrugged. 'But there's no need for you to suffer. I'll take Miss Heligmann, instead.'

'Miss Heligmann?' Delia stared at him. 'You'd take your secretary to Covent Garden?'

'Yes, why not? She's very fond of the opera. Her favourite of all is *Der Rosenkavalier*. But Mozart also will do.'

'I see.' Delia grimaced. 'Do you often take Miss Heligmann out?'

'Not often. I suppose about four or five times a year. On evenings when you are otherwise engaged.'

'Indeed.' Delia hadn't seen Peter for six weeks. The idea of letting him spend three or four precious hours sitting next to another woman — even a plain, middle-aged, opera-loving woman — was not to be entertained. 'Friday, is it?' she enquired.

'Yes. The fifteenth.'

'All right, then. I'll come.'

'Ah.' Now, Peter pulled a face. 'Poor Miss Heligmann,' he teased. 'She's been looking at me so expectantly this week. She knows it's about the time, you see.'

'Does she? Well then — if you'd rather take her?'

'I'd rather take you. But look, if you hate it, if it

hurts your ears to listen, you must tell me. Give it half an hour. Then, if you can't bear it, we'll go.'

'Oh, we couldn't do that. Look at the price of these tickets! It would be such a waste.'

★　★　★

'So, you managed to sit through it.' In the Garden's gilded foyer, Peter helped Delia on with her coat. 'Now I'm owing a favour to you.'

'Oh, but I enjoyed it.' Shouldering her bag, Delia beamed at him. 'Honestly, I loved it all. Every single minute. I'm converted.'

'You are?' Sceptically, Peter laughed. 'Well, that's splendid.'

As they came out of the theatre, Peter took Delia's hand. 'Are you hungry?' he asked, considerate as always. 'Shall we go and have something to eat?'

'No. I want to go home. Let's get a taxi.'

Back at the flat, Delia made some coffee and carried it through to the sitting room. Now, she noticed several letters to Germany, lying on the low table by the fire. Sealed and ready to be posted, they lacked only stamps. 'Shall I see to those for you?' she asked, as she cleared a space for the tray.

'What? Oh — the letters.' Peter looked up from the *Evening Standard*'s business pages. 'No, that's all right. My cleaning lady will post them on her way home tomorrow.'

'Okay.' As Delia poured coffee, she noticed the top letter on the pile was addressed to a Dr G R Heller. Peter had mentioned Dr Heller before, for she was a specialist at the clinic where Reni was currently undergoing a course of some revolutionary new treatment.

Delia shuddered. What if Reni's condition improved? What if she made a complete recovery? Might Peter want her back again? The very idea made Delia sick with dread.

'Did Reni like music?' she asked now, her tone deliberately light.

'I'm sorry?' Peter stirred sugar into his coffee. 'No, she didn't,' he muttered. 'In fact, she hated it.'

'Why was that?'

'It made her cry.'

'Why did it make her cry?'

'It made bad memories, I suppose.' Peter shrugged. 'That happens, you know. Personally, I can't bear to hear Wagner. Such terrible things are connected there, you see.'

'What things?'

'Just — things.' Peter frowned now. 'Don't cross-examine me,' he said. 'I don't wish to speak of Reni. At any rate, not tonight.'

★ ★ ★

But it was only natural that Delia should wonder about Reni, and be curious to know what she was really like. Peter, however, remained unwilling to discuss her — or at least, at any length. 'I don't ask *you* about *your* previous lovers,' he objected, when pressed. 'Don't expect to know every detail of my earlier life.'

Delia decided to let the matter rest. But then one

215

day, searching through his desk for some writing paper, Delia came across a photograph of her lover's wife.

A pretty blonde, she had large, light eyes and a round, rather childish face. Her smile was bright and artificial. Obviously put on for the photographer, it gave away nothing about the personality it concealed. But now, once again, Delia tried to imagine what Reni could be like.

She's just a woman, Peter had said. Only a woman, that's all. So, was she a nice person? Gentle, pleasant, and harmless? Or was she cruel, maybe? Bitter, vindictive, and unkind?

'Renate Maria Eisenstadt.' Delia said the names aloud. Now, she reminded herself that Reni was a madwoman. An apparently incurable lunatic, she posed hardly any threat to Delia herself. For, only yesterday, Peter had heard that even Dr Heller's expensive treatment had effected no noticeable improvement in her condition.

But, madwoman or not, Reni was a wife. Like a latter-day Mrs Rochester, she was locked away in some expensive private sanatorium in the Black Forest, but she was still Peter's lawful wedded wife, and the only one he was allowed to have. Or ever would have, unless she'd oblige Delia by dropping dead, so the widower could marry again.

'Do you love me?' Delia asked, that evening. Tonight, she needed to hear him say it, over and over again. 'Peter, tell me you love me.'

'I love you,' he said — but mechanically, as if it were the automatic response to a familiar catechism. 'Of course I love you.'

'Even though to love me is to imperil your immortal soul?'

'What *are* you talking about?' Looking up from a file, Peter stared at her in astonishment. 'Darling, I have an important meeting first thing tomorrow. I really haven't time for silly questions.'

'Peter, I am not asking silly questions!'

'No?' Carefully, Peter put his pen down on the coffee table. He placed his file beside it. 'Very well, then. What are you trying to say to me?'

'Just this. I've a good friend on the magazine who happens to be a Catholic. A few days ago, we had lunch together.'

'How nice for you.'

'Peter!'

'I'm sorry. Go on.'

'I asked her to explain about mortal and venial sin. Or little sin, as you like to call it. I told her it was for a feature, and I — '

'So what did she tell you?'

'She made everything crystal clear. Peter, if you die, you'll go straight to hell. You're in a state of mortal sin, and you — '

'What utter nonsense!' Laughing, Peter shook his head. 'Oh, darling! You heretics always get — what do you say — the wrong end of the stick, is it? You think that just because — '

'Geraldine's *not* a heretic!' Now, Delia was angry. 'You haven't heard a single word I've said! Listen, my friend is a practising Catholic. She goes to confession every week. She says adultery is a mortal sin!'

'Silly woman.' Peter rubbed his tired eyes. 'Well,

217

she's certainly put the fear of God into you! Look, darling — please don't worry about this. I don't.'

'Perhaps you should.'

'I don't think so.'

'But what if we were married?' Earnestly, Delia looked at him. 'If your first marriage could be annulled, then if I converted to Catholicism, we could — '

'That's not possible. You don't understand what you're asking me to do.' Peter took Delia's hands in his. 'I didn't think you wanted marriage, anyway?'

'I didn't think so, either. But — '

'There you are, then. Please — may we leave this for today?'

'If you won't discuss it, we'll have to.'

'Good girl.' Peter smiled. 'Thank you.'

'Don't mention it.' Any minute now, thought Delia sourly, he'll pat my head.

But he didn't. 'Actually,' he went on, 'I have something to tell you. I'd forgotten about it until just now. Today, I saw a report on Miss Hughes.'

'Miss Hughes? Do you mean Jenny?'

'I mean your friend's daughter. That *is* her name, isn't it? The girl you mentioned to me?'

'Yes, that's right. So? How's she getting on?'

'Quite well. She's passed her probation. Her training officer says she's one of the best of this year's lot.'

'Well, she's always been quick on the uptake. Prepared to work hard for what she wants, as well.'

'So it would seem.' Peter grimaced now. 'Does she know you're my mistress?' he asked.

'Of course not!' Delia was shocked. 'No one does.

You're my most closely guarded secret.'

'So how did she learn about the job?'

'You left an old staff magazine at my flat, so I glanced through it. There was an article saying Eisenstadt would soon be recruiting school leavers. Then I saw an ad for bilingual secretaries, in the *Daily Telegraph*. So I suggested to Jenny that she should apply.'

'I see.' Peter's relief was obvious. Now, he looked crafty. 'Her mother — was she perhaps the one who stole your fiancé away?'

'Gareth was never my fiancé.'

'But you did love him?'

'No, not really.'

'A little, perhaps?'

'No.' Delia shook her head. 'I'd never loved any man before I met you.'

'That's not true, I'm sure. But I'd like to believe it, all the same.' Coming to sit beside her, Peter ruffled Delia's hair. 'Shall we have a drink?'

'Yes, okay. I'll get it. What would you like?'

'Some tea, I think. But I'll make it.'

'Stay there.' Delia got up. 'Finish reading your report. Then you'll have some time for me.'

★   ★   ★

As she waited for the water to boil, Delia thought of Shirley. She thought of Gareth, too. She wondered about inviting them to London for a few days.

They could stay at her flat, couldn't they? Shirley and she could do some shopping. They could all take in a couple of shows. Perhaps they could even meet Peter. If only he wasn't Jenny's employer! That made it a bit awkward, somehow.

All the same, Delia did want Shirley to meet him. But then again — perhaps she didn't.

She could hear Shirley now. 'Oh, Delia!' she would cry. 'He's very nice, I agree. He's very good-looking, too. But — '

'I know.' Delia would be obliged to admit it. 'He's another married man.'

It wasn't that Shirley would disapprove — not exactly. But Shirley would certainly pity her. 'Poor Delia,' she would think, 'stuck in another dead-end relationship with a man who won't or can't do the decent thing.' When Delia had told her friend about Jack Kingston, they had cried in each others' arms. But, in the end, Shirley's sympathy had been almost as hard to bear as Jack's deceit.

Delia poured hot water on to the leaves. 'Poor Delia,' she could hear Shirley say, as she and Gareth drove back to Evesbridge. 'Poor old Delia, on the road to nowhere yet again.'

17

Delia's week had been even more hectic than usual. But, that fine Saturday morning, Peter was up early. He brewed fresh coffee, buttered a few rolls, then opened a pot of jam. He took a tray to Delia, who still lay in bed.

'Breakfast,' he announced. 'Delia? Wake up.'

'What?' Delia rubbed her eyes. 'It's too early,' she complained. 'Oh, Peter — I've been working my socks off this week! Let me have a rest.'

'Get up.' Having spent the past three days masterminding a deal which would effectively make his company's products the brand leaders through-out the Midlands and South East, Peter was still high on the adrenalin of success. He grinned. 'Working your socks off, indeed! You English don't know anything about really hard work.'

'Oh, shut up.' Delia yawned. 'Pour me some coffee, please. Black.'

So Peter poured. 'Shall we go to the seaside today?' he suggested. 'Blow away the cobwebs — is that what you say? We could drive down to Brighton, perhaps.'

'Well — '

'Or, if you don't fancy Brighton, we could go and have another look round that street market. The one where you bought all that awful junk jewellery. The stuff the trader swore was genuine art nouveau.'

'But I didn't believe him.' Delia sipped her coffee.

'It was very pretty junk. You must admit that.'

'It was rubbish.' Peter laughed. 'I've never in my life seen less convincing fakes than those horrible tin bracelets. So — shall we go and find you some more bargains?'

'I'd love to, but I can't. I must go home and finish my article on the spring collections.' Delia finished her coffee. 'Darling, I hate to leave you — but I must get it done today.'

'Must you?' Peter sniffed. 'I don't see why you have to write articles at all,' he complained. 'I'd have thought you could leave that sort of drudgery to your editorial staff.'

'I enjoy writing.' Delia got out of bed. 'I'll meet you for lunch, shall I?'

'If you can spare the time.'

'We'll go to the seaside tomorrow.'

'Perhaps.'

'Oh, Peter! Don't look at me like that.'

'Like what?'

'As if I'd kicked you!' Delia gave him a rather jammy kiss. 'This bedroom is an absolute tip,' she observed. 'The sitting room's a rubbish dump, too. If you're at a loose end, why don't you do some tidying up?'

Half an hour later, Delia had gone. Peter wandered into the sitting room. Disconsolately, he eyed the ubiquitous heaps of papers, old files and ancient magazines, which he supposed he ought to carry down to the dustbins. One fine day.

He went into the bathroom. Here, Delia's presence was almost tangible, for here he could smell her soap, talc and shampoo. Taking her warm, damp bathrobe in his arms, he hugged it. Burying his face in it, he inhaled.

Then, he went to his study. Getting out a block of white paper, he sat down to write his monthly letter to his wife.

★　★　★

Although Delia feared that he must, in fact Peter no longer loved Reni at all. But he still thought of her. He still felt that tenderness which he remembered from their first meetings. Now, even though love had quietly died, memories of shared happiness tied her to him, and always would.

Poor Reni, he thought. She didn't deserve to be forgotten and abandoned, for she'd hardly brought her misfortunes on herself.

He unscrewed his fountain pen. As usual, this would be a short letter, the sort one might write to a backward six year old. Now, while he considered what to say, he rummaged around for a sheet of scrap paper on which to try his pen. Despising biros and felt-tips, he always wrote in ink, and sometimes the nib got clogged.

Then, in large, clear handwriting, he told Reni what he'd been doing since he had written last. Or at any rate, he told her about some of the things he'd done. He wrote about a visit to a new factory in South Wales, and he described the scenery through which he'd driven. Then he gave her an account of an outing which the firm had arranged for the children of employees. He told her how much they had enjoyed going round Windsor Safari

Park and then seeing the castle and the guardsmen, in their red coats and big, black hats.

Running out of inspiration, he sighed. He knew he was talking to a wall. He ought just to accept it. This was all a complete waste of time.

★ ★ ★

In a small private nursing home near the little market town of Remersdorf, Reni Eisenstadt woke to a bright, clear morning. Lying in her comfortable bed, she watched the sunbeams darting through the half-closed curtains.

A small, blonde woman whose large blue eyes and little snub nose suggested a Disney fawn or rabbit, suddenly she started in alarm. Fearfully, she looked towards the opening door.

'Good morning!' The young, pretty nurse smiled at her. Placing the breakfast tray on the table beside Reni's bed, she fished in the pocket of her long, blue robe. 'A letter for you today,' she said, brightly.

'It's from England, isn't it?' Taking the envelope and squinting at it, for she was very short-sighted, Reni Eisenstadt returned the nurse's smile. 'Who can it be from?'

'Open it and see.' The nurse poured coffee. 'Perhaps it's good news.'

So, while the nurse buttered a roll for her, Reni did just that. She drew out two sheets of paper, smoothed them out and then, putting on her glasses, she read the letter through.

It was a nice letter, she thought, short but interesting. It was signed by someone called Peter.

Peter? Reni frowned. She must reply, of course. She'd do that today, before she forgot. But what could she say?

'I must go and see Frau Sommer now,' the nurse was telling her. 'Have you everything you need?'

'Yes, indeed.' Reni nodded her gratitude. 'Thank you, Sister. Everything.'

She looked at her letter again. Peter, Peter — who was Peter? Reni frowned hard, concentrating. But it was no good, she couldn't remember. Oh, it didn't matter, she'd ask the nurse later. Sister Mary Josef would be sure to know.

As Reni drank her coffee, she planned her day. She'd have a shower, then ask that nice Herr Altmann to drive her into town. She'd have her hair shampooed and set, then she'd perhaps go round the shops and look for a new dress. She'd get something blue, she decided. Dietrich always liked her in blue. Then she'd meet her friend Marta Hoffmann for lunch, at the *Dom* Hotel.

Just then, a sudden shriek made Reni spill her coffee. Now, her eyes widened in alarm. But then she realised what must be happening. It was only Greta Seligmann, being troublesome again. Poor Frau Seligmann, she suffered from the most awful delusions, which made her run down the corridors and barricade herself in a bathroom or the sluice, for she was convinced she was going to be raped. Now, she crashed into one of the bathrooms. The door slammed shut.

Poor Greta Seligmann, thought Reni. Poor thing, it wasn't her fault. In 1945, she'd been living in Berlin. When the Russians came, she was eleven years old. But that hadn't saved her.

Hearing Frau Seligmann begging the soldiers to leave her alone, repeating over and over that she was only a child, Reni shook herself. She was forgetful, she knew that. But, unlike poor Greta Seligmann, she wasn't mad. She thanked God she wasn't mad.

Reni finished her breakfast. Taking out a small hand mirror, she examined her face and smiled at herself, pleased with what she saw. It was nice to be pretty. Nice to look beautiful for when Dietrich came. He liked her to look her best, to be wearing a flowery dress with box pleats all around the skirt, and neat patent leather shoes.

'Peter?' she asked the nurse who came to remove the breakfast tray. Urgently, she shook the nun's arm. 'Sister, who's Peter?'

'Your husband.' Gently, Sister Frederika disengaged Reni's grasp on her wrist. 'Herr Eisenstadt,' she explained. 'Your husband.'

'Sister?' Reni was puzzled now. 'My husband's name is Dietrich,' she said. 'Paul Dietrich Kirchner. He's in Russia, you know. But he'll be home again soon.'

'Oh. I see.' Observing that Reni's colour was high and her breathing harsh, the nurse pressed a bell by her bed. 'Well then, let's hope — '

'He will come, won't he?' Reni was trembling now. 'On Friday — he's coming to see me on Friday. He promised he'd come!'

The doctor came into the little room. 'She's very bad this morning,' whispered the nurse. 'Very confused, poor soul.'

'Ah.' The doctor sat down on Reni's bed and felt

226

her pulse. 'We'll give her some Antrolon,' she told the nurse, *sotto voce*. 'Just five mls in some orange juice. It'll relax her. Frau Eisenstadt?' she began, softly. 'Frau Eisenstadt, why don't you slip on your dressing gown and come with me to the dayroom? The magazines have just arrived, all your favourites are there — so why don't we go and look at them, while Frau Steiner makes your bed?'

So Reni allowed herself to be ushered into the dayroom and be settled in a chair near the window with her pile of magazines, her embroidery wools, and the piece of canvas upon which she was working a spring bouquet.

When would Dietrich come? She looked out of the window, hoping to see him walking up the drive. But there was no one there.

Well, she reasoned, it was early yet, perhaps he'd come after lunch. He'd be in his lieutenant's uniform of course, and that would be nice because he looked so handsome in it, in the tight-fitting jacket and trousers and highly-polished boots. All the girls were crazy about him, and no wonder.

Reni threaded some yellow wool. As she sucked then knotted the end, she wondered again who this Peter was. Who was this person who seemed to think she wanted to know about Windsor Safari Park?

She began to sew. A novice brought her a glass of orange juice, which she drank. Some time later she glanced at the clock. Eleven thirty. Time for a snack, some biscuits perhaps and some coffee. Soon they'd be bringing it. Contentedly, Reni stitched on.

18

Completing her training programme and passing her exams in shorthand and typing with flying colours, Jenny was summoned to Mr Dierken's office to be informed she was now on the permanent staff. 'I'm sure you would like to use your languages,' he observed, as he glanced through her personal file. He smiled at her. 'Well, you *must* use them. It would be criminal to let these excellent A levels in French and German go to waste. I see your future in Exports, I think.'

The export manager's secretary was leaving soon, to have a baby. Jenny found she was to take her place. This suited her very well, for the export department was the liveliest and most hectic in the whole office.

It was becoming busier by the day. A range of instant coffees, which the company manufactured in England and had originally intended for the English market alone, was now being sold all over the world, particularly in France, Spain and Japan. In recent years, the Japanese had taken to instant coffee in a big way. They drank it iced, though, with grated chocolate sprinkled on top.

★ ★ ★

Although Jenny enjoyed her new job and got on well with her boss, she soon decided she wasn't cut out to be a secretary after all. While she'd been on probation, getting distinctions in her City and Guilds had seemed a worthwhile objective. But now she was safely on the corporate ship, she wanted to have her hand on the company tiller. So, as a first step towards attaining this, she decided to find out exactly how the international coffee trade worked.

At first, she found the sheer scale of it all absolutely bewildering. After oil, apparently, coffee was the most important commodity on the world market. More than twenty million people were involved in the coffee business, most of them living in South America, but an ever-growing number were involved in the expanding African trade as well. Whereas the international centre for trading in South American coffees was New York, the hub of business for most African coffees was right here, in London itself.

Taking books out of the staff library, photocopying articles to study at her leisure, and poring over the driest and dullest of company reports, eventually Jenny understood that the coffee business was a game of chance. Trading conditions depended on an almost impossibly complicated set of factors, most of these outside human control. For, a few nights' frost in — say — Pernambuco could cause production to fall drastically. This in turn would throw world prices completely out of line. Then, buyers worldwide would be on the verge of slitting their collective wrists.

Weighing up the options, Jenny decided she would never become a buyer of green coffee, for this was the person everyone blamed when things went wrong. A career in Sales, however, seemed very attractive. Daydreaming, now she saw herself as a high-powered international rep, jetting all over the world.

Looking at lists of statistics, she realised now that falling consumption in the USA meant the biggest potential crisis for the coffee trade was not failure of production — but a sudden dramatic fall in retail demand. On the other hand, the Communist Chinese didn't drink coffee at all. Yet. Peking, she thought, here I come.

When office staff were invited to put their names down for a tour of the new factory at Edgware, Jenny's name was first on the list. Now, she learned how raw green coffee imported from Latin America and Africa was processed. How a bean growing on a bush in Kenya or Brazil could end up in a London kitchen. This would usually be in a jar of Goldbrand Premium Instant. For the lazy English drank more soluble coffee than the rest of Europe put together.

★   ★   ★

As a multilingual secretary to a departmental head, Jenny had a certain status, and she now found herself a member of an exclusive little club, with distinctions of rank to preserve. She also came into close contact with the most flamboyant character in the whole office.

Tall, thin and fantastically clad in gaudy Indian prints, which swirled and shimmered and flapped against the furniture as she walked by, Maggie Clifford was the sales manager's personal assistant and — so office gossip went — much more besides. Summarily thrown out of London University after only half a term, it was something of a mystery that such a strange, exotic creature had found her niche in a staid, conventional company like Eisenstadt UK.

One Friday, over lunch in the staff canteen, Maggie invited Jenny to the party she was giving that weekend. 'Do come,' she encouraged. 'It'll be wild.'

Jenny wasn't especially keen. Jess Hallet had wild parties, at her near-derelict flat in Bow. There, enormous numbers of undergraduates crammed themselves into the most minute of spaces, had sex on the stairs or under heaps of coats, and drank huge quantities of vile, emetic punch. It was not Jenny's scene at all.

'I'm not sure what I'm doing tomorrow,' she said, carefully. She didn't want to give offence. 'But where's the party to be?'

'Kilburn.' Ignoring the No Smoking sign prominent on their table, Maggie lit a very skinny cigarette. 'But a mate of mine lives in Acton, and he's giving people lifts. He could pick you up. If you like.'

'Okay.' Now, Jenny smiled. Well, she thought — it might be fun. 'What time shall I be ready?'

'Eightish.' Fiddling with one of her long, dangly earrings, Maggie flicked ash on to her plate. 'Bring a friend, if you like. Don't worry about missing the last train — you can crash with us. Do you turn on?'

'I'm sorry?'

Maggie laughed. 'You don't,' she grinned. Now

she rolled, then lit, another cigarette. The smoke spiralled into the air, then wafted gently towards the table on the left.

'Oh, Christ. She's at it again.' Now, Robert Graham from Accounts turned to see the sales manager's secretary nonchalantly smoking her roll-up, and vigorously scratching her right armpit. 'Put that out,' he hissed. 'You've been warned once. Maggie, they'll sack you if they catch you again.'

'It's Miss Clifford to you, Mr Graham,' replied Maggie. Serenely, she smoked on.

Jenny went to Maggie's party. Told she could bring a mate, she had dragged Jess Hallet along, too. These days, Jess herself was a devotee of the ethnic look, and she also rolled her own. She and Maggie hit it off at once.

Soon, the pair of them were deep in conversation with another couple of girls, who were equally interested in acquiring illegal substances at bargain rates. Jess apparently had access to some really good shit . . .

Hearing there was to be a Founders' Day ball at QAC, Maggie told Jess she would rather like to go. There might be some good grass around, and when people were pissed they were more likely to share both sources and substances, too. 'I'll fix you up with a partner,' promised Jess.

'But I'm going to ask Herr Schretzmaier to take me,' Maggie told Jenny the following Monday morning, staring across the general office at a newcomer from the Bremen branch of the firm, who was by far the most correct and conventional of the German management team. 'It'll be an education for him. He's always saying he doesn't understand English youth.'

Jenny laughed. 'So you're going to enlighten him, are you?' she enquired.

'Yeah.' Maggie grinned. 'He's not as holy as he looks, believe you me. He might come on all prim and proper — but yesterday, when he asked if he could borrow me to take some dictation, he was watching my chest like he'd never even seen a pair of tits before.'

'Don't tell me. You weren't wearing a bra, so — '

'But I don't any more! I told you.' Pouting, Maggie smoothed the sheer cheesecloth of her smock over her generous breasts. 'So anyway, whenever I scratched my ear or shook my hair out of my eyes, I'd look up to find him staring at me. He was bright red in the face. I tell you — by the time I'd finished his letters, he looked fit to burst.'

'Poor man. Rob said his wife's still in Bremen. He's probably missing her.'

'I'd give him a good time, if he asked me nicely.' Maggie adjusted an earring. 'I quite fancy him, in a way. There's something about that icy blond don't-touch-me look that's a real turn on.'

'Leave him alone. He's a respectable family man.'

'Yeah, maybe,' Maggie agreed. 'But aren't they all? Well, he's away from tomorrow, anyway — he's going on some jolly little excursion to Holland, with the boss.'

'Which boss is that?'

'Herr Eisenstadt. The managing director himself. He hangs out in some luxurious office in Southampton Row.'

'Oh.' Jenny looked down at her finger nails. 'Have you ever seen him?' she enquired.

'Who, Herr Eisenstadt? No. He never comes here. If he wants to see somebody, they have to go to him.' Maggie grinned. 'I bet he's fat. Big and fat, with a spiky blond crew cut — and has this dead sexy PA, with blue eyes and yellow ringlets. He screws her on the shag pile, then she helps him take his Deutschmarks to the bank.'

★ ★ ★

The weekly office circular for the junior managers always went round the secretaries too, each of whom glanced at it, scribbled her initials on it, then threw it across to someone else.

'Here.' Maggie tossed Jenny the latest edition. 'Sensations. Revelations. Schretzmaier's been convicted of outraging public decency. He was picked up in Piccadilly Circus, naked except for a pair of green socks.'

'Do shut up.' Reading through the closely-typed pages, Jenny saw there was soon to be a vacancy for a section supervisor, in the sales office.

Section supervisors were the lowest form of management life, responsible at most for four clerks and two typists. But this job was also the first rung on the ladder to the top, for if a section manager made a success of running his own group, this almost inevitably led to promotion. To short postings overseas, expense account lunches, a company car — in fact, to a whole package of highly desirable things.

Jenny copied out the details. Then she typed an application for the job.

'You'll never get it. Never in a million years.' Flicking ash from her cigarette, Maggie dropped it in Jenny's tea. 'They'll appoint a man,' she predicted. 'They always do. It'll be a German. Some blue-eyed bastard from Bremen or Cologne.'

'Really?' Calmly, Jenny carried on typing.

'A dozen staff are already coming over from Bremen. Early next month. It's a fact — I read the confidential report on Dierken's desk.' Maggie shrugged. 'One of that lot will get the super's job. You've got as much hope as a snowball in a hot chimney.'

'Thanks for the vote of confidence, friend.' Pulling out her application, Jenny scrolled more paper into her machine. 'Look — I'm perfectly qualified for that job. I could do it just as well as anyone else.'

'Yeah, but you're a woman and you're English. Two big black marks there.'

'Three of the other section supervisors are English.'

'But they're all blokes.' Maggie grinned. 'Here, do you know who's on that particular section?'

'No. Who?'

'Dora Turner and Beryl Matthews. Christ, what a pair of harpies!' Unkindly, Maggie laughed. 'They'd crucify little old you. They caused Gustav Keller's burst ulcer. Did you know that?'

'I heard he'd been ill for years.'

'Garbage. He was as fit as a flea before they let those two old bags loose on the poor sod.'

Soon, everyone knew Jenny Hughes had applied for the vacant job. No one thought she'd get it. All the section managers were men, most of them German men at that. So there was general amazement when the English girl was among those shortlisted for interview.

The interview was conducted in German. Smart in Maggie's best black shoes and a neat dark suit, Jenny was bombarded with questions.

The sales manager gave her a thorough grilling. Then the export manager, Jenny's own boss, smiled at her. 'If you were offered this job,' he said, 'you would be required to travel. So, you'd be willing to go abroad?'

'Yes, of course.'

'Would you be happy to spend a few years in Germany? In Cologne, or at the new offices in Bremen, maybe?'

'Yes, I'd be quite happy to do that.'

'Excellent. Well, Miss Hughes, thank you for coming to talk to us. We'll let you know about the job in due course.'

★   ★   ★

'I got it!' Jubilant, Jenny waved the official confirmation in Maggie's face. 'I got it, Clifford, I got it.'

'You're welcome to it.' Maggie grinned. 'Dora and Beryl know already. They're planning to make your life *hell*.'

For Jenny's first couple of weeks as their section supervisor, Dora and Beryl did exactly that. Two middle-aged spinsters who disapproved of short skirts, long hair and female drivers, they thought the idea of working for a young woman as ridiculous as being subject to the whims of a performing seal. They tried to drive their new supervisor to distraction.

The other two clerks, a morose Rhinelander by the name of Karl Freihoff and a Miss — no one had ever discovered her Christian name — Hartmann, worked diligently but without enthusiasm. They had liked Gustav Keller, their former supervisor. Their sense of what was correct was mortally offended by the appointment of a mini-skirted English girl younger than any of them.

Eventually, by dint of sheer hard work and good example, Jenny won Karl Freihoff and Miss Hartmann round. Karl Freihoff dominated the other three clerks as autocratically as a rooster dominates his hens — so, after a good deal of clucking and squawking, Beryl and Dora also began to settle down. Jenny finally won them over for good when, one Thursday morning, Miss Hartmann had toothache and Jenny sent her home early. Then sat down and dealt with some of her outstanding files herself.

But this was evidently a mistake. 'You shouldn't have done that,' muttered Kurt Andersch, a section manager long overdue for promotion, and sour with it. 'When one of my clerks is absent, I divide his work between the other three. It is not correct for a manager to perform a clerk's duties.'

'We did the files between us,' retorted Jenny. 'The clerks saw me taking on more work, so they didn't mind when I asked them to do a bit extra too. That's teamwork, isn't it?'

'It's not management, though.' Kurt Andersch frowned. 'Miss Hughes, the mine owner does not roll up his sleeves and dig for coal in the pit.'

'Perhaps, if he did, the miners might work harder and complain less?' But Jenny knew he was right. The clerks would have her doing it all if she didn't watch out.

★　★　★

'Seen that new fellow in Accounts?' asked Maggie, as she and Jenny sat in the park one lunch time, feeding the ducks.

'No.' Jenny opened her bag and got out a packet of biscuits. Breaking them up, she offered them to the birds. 'Is he English? Or a German?'

'A Hun.' Maggie Clifford grinned. 'A great, big, blond, handsome Hun. Herr Michael Kaufmann.' Taking one of Jenny's broken biscuits, she ate it. 'Next time you're passing Accounts, have a look. See if you think I'm in with a chance.'

'Okay.' Jenny laughed. 'Maggie, it's not like you to be backward in coming forward. What's so special about this guy?'

'Go and give him the once over. You'll see.' Maggie sighed. 'He's a twenty four carat knock-out. I haven't seen anything that dishy for years.'

So, later that afternoon, Jenny strolled past the sales manager's office and went on down the corridor to Accounts. She saw the newcomer. Walking out of the chief accountant's office he passed her in the corridor, frowning in concentration.

He was all right, she supposed. Not really her type, though. On the whole, she preferred dark men.

★ ★ ★

A bright Saturday morning some weeks later found Jenny with nothing much to do and no one to do it with. Jess was on vacation, Maggie was visiting her parents in their old ancestral bung-hole, as she called it, and there didn't seem to be anyone else around either.

'You must go and have a poke round Royton Street Market sometime,' Maggie had told her. 'It's only a couple of tube stops from where you live. You were saying you wanted some mugs and stuff, for your room.'

So, that Saturday, Jenny took a tote bag and went to the market. Carefully, she picked her way between the stalls, wading through a litter of newspaper, squashed fruit and discarded plastic packaging. Royton Street Market was just about on the tourist trail, so here and there one heard a foreign voice trying to negotiate a deal, or a delighted squeak of pleasure from an American tourist who thought she'd got a bargain. But the market's main merchandise appeared to be filthy old clothes, tarnished metal goods, chipped china, wartime utility furniture and dubious-looking old engines. Plus the odd fruit barrow selling definitely sub-standard produce.

Jenny was unimpressed. She realised she should

have had Maggie with her, for Maggie loved places like this. She bought masses of twenties or thirties dresses and shoes, shawls and even underclothes, which she cleaned up and wore to parties.

Jenny was reluctant even to touch such stuff. But she enjoyed the good weather, she liked listening to the hawkers, and she watched the people go by. Coming to a stall stacked with glass and china, she found her way forward blocked by a fishmonger's van. So she stopped to look.

Jenny had always liked china ornaments. Back in Evesbridge she had quite a large collection of what she knew was largely tat, but of which she was very fond anyway. A childhood passion for white china horses had now given way to a general liking for blue and white china of all kinds.

She picked up a small blue and white vase. 'How much is this?' she asked.

'Sorry?' The dark-haired young man running the stall grinned at her. 'Oh, that. Five quid. Genuine Ming, that is.'

'Genuine Woolworths, more like.' Jenny put the vase back. Now she picked up a large dish patterned with vine leaves which would, she thought, make a nice fruit bowl. 'Genuine Sévres?' she enquired.

'You what?'

'Sévres? Late nineteenth century?' Encouragingly, Jenny smiled. 'Italian? French?'

'French!' The man's grin broadened. 'Bit of reject Staffordshire, that. Half a dollar to you.' Reaching towards a pile of newspapers, he snatched some up. 'Want me to wrap it for you?'

'I haven't said I'll buy it yet.'

'Two bob and it's yours.' Retrieving his dish, the trader wrapped it and held it out to her.

To her surprise, Jenny found two shillings were now charmed out of her pocket. She handed them over.

'Thanks, princess.' Jingling the coins, the man laughed at her. 'You want to smile like that more often. It suits you.'

19

'Are you doing anything Thursday evening?' Maggie asked one rainy lunchtime, as she and Jenny hung up their wet mackintoshes in the staff cloakroom and began to repair the damage to their make-up. 'Because if you're not, we're going to see some racing. Do you fancy that?'

'*We're* going, you say.' Jenny put her lipstick back in her bag. 'Who's *we*?'

'Me and Terry Bellman. He's dead interested in grotty old cars.'

'While you're dead interested in Terry?'

'You could say that. But I don't want to make it too obvious. Not yet, anyway.' Maggie grinned. 'Go on, be a sport. We'll fetch you and take you home.'

'We being you and Terry, in Terry's purple passion wagon. No thanks. I'd rather get the train.'

'Suit yourself. We'll see you there, then?'

'You might,' Jenny replied.

'I'll buy you a drink,' said Maggie, wheedling now. 'A hot dog, too. If you're lucky.'

'Big spender.' Jenny laughed. 'Okay, I'll come. It had better be good.'

★ ★ ★

A big field near one of the tube stations at the eastern end of the Central Line was the venue for the stock car racing. But, as Jenny walked on to the muddy concourse, all she could see were endless rows of traders' stalls selling what looked like ton lots of broken engine and old iron.

Men in jeans and leather jackets were eagerly sorting through it, and Jenny watched in astonishment as they exclaimed and argued, then exchanged wads of pound notes for lumps of what looked like rusting scrap metal. She didn't think this evening was going to be her sort of thing at all. Realising she should have worn her wellingtons, she ploughed on.

In the centre of the field a circuit was laid out, roped off with metal hawsers and buttressed with bales of dampened hay. Various old bangers were beetling up and down a practice track, while on the sidelines grimy men tinkered with the insides of battered little cars.

Here, the atmosphere was one of bustle and carnival. Small children sat on their fathers' shoulders, sucking lollies or ice creams, while the adults chatted to each other and discussed form. Then someone switched on the floodlights. To a chorus of boos, howls and sarcastic cheers, a dozen or so reinforced Hillmans and Morris Minors drove on to the circuit. The racing began.

For a while, Jenny watched the cars zooming round and round the track, bashing into one another and creating some nasty-looking pile ups. No one seemed to get hurt, however, and the St John Ambulance teams stationed round the perimeter of the track appeared to have nothing to do except lay bets.

To her surprise, she now found she was beginning to enjoy herself. The petrol fumes made her pleasantly light-headed, the smell of the oil was subtly intoxicating — but, more than that, the pervasive air of good humour made Jenny herself feel happy and relaxed.

Terry Bellman's purple Mini Minor had been in the car park, and Jenny had found a note addressed to herself taped to the windscreen. Eventually, she tracked Terry and Maggie down. Together they watched several races. But then, after some furtive whispering and even more furtive groping, Maggie and Terry disappeared. 'So much for not wanting Terry to think she was keen,' thought Jenny, as she walked over to a hot dog van. She would have a drink, she decided, then go home.

By the van, a tall, dark-haired young man in black cord jeans and a creased denim bomber jacket was busy talking the proprietor's ear off. Obviously, they were doing some complicated deal, and Jenny wondered if they would even notice her.

Eventually, however, the trader did. 'Yes, love?' he began. Telling the man in black cords to hang about, he grinned. 'What can I get you? Mark, old son — move out of this lady's way!'

'Sorry, sweetheart.' The man shrugged his apology — but then, glancing at Jenny, he grinned too. 'Well, stone me,' he exclaimed. 'It *is* you, isn't it? The lady as wouldn't buy the Ming?'

'Ming!' Still high on petrol fumes, Jenny laughed at him. 'Goodness. Fancy you remembering that.'

'I'd never forget a lovely face like yours.' The young man put two half crowns on the counter. 'Here, Denny. I'll get that.'

'Oh — thank you.' Blushing now, Jenny put

mustard on her roll. 'So you're involved in racing, too?' she asked, feeling she had to say something. He'd just bought her supper, after all.

'Racing? Not really.' The man shrugged. 'But I knows Mike Holt. He's the organiser. We go back a long way, Mike and me. You on your own?'

'I came with a friend. But she's disappeared.'

'Gone off with some fella, has she? Never mind.' The young man pocketed his change. 'Want to go for a walk?' he enquired, an attractive sparkle kindling his bright, brown eyes.

So Jenny went for a walk. 'Do you have that stall in the market every day?' she asked now.

'Nah. I only does the stall on Saturdays. Rest of the week, I'm a dealer.' The man shrugged. 'I'm out on the road, mostly. Gettin' old ladies to part with their valuable family heirlooms, so's I can flog 'em to the antique centres up West an' in the King's Road.'

'So the stall's not your livelihood?'

'God, no. Pocket money, that is. It's a nice little fiddle though, Saturday mornings in the summer specially.' The man laughed. 'Then, there's all these tourists, see. All 'avin' a poke round, lookin' for bargains. Pay anything, them daft buggers. You can fleece 'em rotten. They still love you.'

'Oh.' Torn between amusement and disgust, Jenny looked up at him. 'You're a villain then, are you?'

'What's that supposed to mean?'

'Well — you swindle tourists. You rob old age pensioners. You're a crook.'

'No, I'm not!' The man looked offended now. 'The tourists don't *have* to give me what I asks. As

245

for the old ducks — well, I pays 'em the goin' rate. Give or take. I shifts their old junk, an' they replace it with a nice bit of chipboard from the Co-op down town, don't need no polishin' nor nothing. Everyone's happy.'

'I see.'

'Do you?' The man shook his head at her. 'You're a cheeky little madam, ain't you?'

'Am I?'

'Yeah, you are! Well — it ain't every girl who goes around telling people she hardly knows as they're crooks and swindlers, and what not.'

'Sorry.' Chastened, Jenny blushed. 'I suppose you have a living to make.'

'Right, I have.'

'You don't actually cosh people or turn out their pockets.'

'Ain't done that yet.' The man laughed. 'But I might, if I reckoned it was worth it. How much you got in your dolly bag tonight?'

'I'm sorry?'

'Nothing.' The young man's expression became solemn now. 'I ain't a crook,' he insisted. 'I don't do old ladies, honest. Look — I never done you.'

'You tried to.'

'Nah.' The young man lit a cigarette. 'Could see you was a country bumpkin, wouldn've been fair. Well now — I'm Mark Strafford. Who are you?'

'Jenny Hughes,' Jenny replied, before she could stop herself.

'Have a drink, Jenny Hughes?'

'Are you paying?'

'Yeah, suppose so.' They stopped by a van selling

soft drinks. 'Coke for the lady, Emilio,' said Mark. 'One of them 'orrible ginger beers of yours for me.'

★   ★   ★

For the rest of that evening, Jenny walked round the field with Mark. She betted on a few of the races, and won a whole six shillings — although she lost nine.

Mark stayed close by her side. Eventually, he contrived to take her hand. For some reason, Jenny let him hang on to it. When at last she looked at her watch, she was amazed to see how late it was. 'I must go now,' she said, her voice tinged with something like regret. 'I have to catch the last train, you see.'

'I could run you home,' offered Mark.

'There's no need.' Rummaging through her pockets, at last Jenny found her ticket. 'Look, I'll have to run.'

'Give you a bell sometime, then?'

'I beg your pardon?'

'Phone you.'

'Oh — all right.' Now, Jenny found Mrs Berners' telephone number being simply charmed out of her. As easily as that two shillings had once been charmed out of her bag.

★   ★   ★

Two days later, Mark Strafford called her. He suggested they meet that Sunday lunchtime, in Trafalgar Square — by the entrance to the National

247

Gallery, to be precise. 'Why the National Gallery?' demanded Jenny.

'Why not?' countered Mark. 'Got something against the National Gallery, then?'

'No, but I — '

'See you, sweetheart. Take care.'

Coming out of the tube station in Trafalgar Square, Jenny saw Mark straight away. Sitting astride one of the lions on Nelson's monument, he was scattering broken crisps for the pigeons. 'Good afternoon,' she said, blinking into the sun.

'Hello, princess.' He held out his hand. 'Coming up?'

'I don't think so.' Jenny narrowed her eyes. 'Not in this skirt.'

'Go on!' Mark grinned. 'Give all them Jap tourists a thrill.'

'Certainly not!'

'Spoilsport.'

Mark jumped down. Today, he was dressed in clean blue jeans, a blue denim shirt and a black suéde jacket. His dark hair, blown back from his face by the dirty wind, curled against his collar. His face was tanned. His bright brown eyes shone, and the freckles dusting his nose made Jenny think of a smooth, new-laid egg.

She wondered how old he was. About twenty, she supposed. But he was much older in experience. His manner assured her of that.

Now, he stuffed his crisp packet into an already overflowing litter bin. He took Jenny's hand in his. 'Coming?' he asked.

So, together, they made their way out of the

square. Dodging camera-laden tourists looking for Swinging London, now they had to evade a great flock of sooty pigeons, who had evidently decided Mark was a good thing. 'Tell us all about about yourself, then,' he invited, as they walked along the Strand. 'Come on. Give us your life 'istry.'

'My life history?' Jenny laughed. 'Well — as you've already observed, I'm a country bumpkin. I came to London to get a job.'

'What sort of job?'

'I work in an office, for a coffee company.'

'Which one?'

'Eisenstadt UK.'

'Oh yeah, heard of them. Swiss, ain't they?'

'German, actually.'

'Same difference.' Mark offered Jenny some chewing gum. 'Tell us about your family. Got a Mum and Dad, have you?'

'Yes. No brothers or sisters, though.'

'You're lucky there.' Mark grimaced. 'I got one of each. Right little pains in the arse, the pair of 'em.'

'Oh? Why is that?'

'Well, my sister's a — oh, what's the words you use when you wants to be polite? A single parent, I suppose. Been on the Social since she was sixteen, has Lisa.' Mark shrugged his disgust. 'She's got two kids already. Both by different fathers. She'll prob'ly have half a dozen more by the time she's thirty.'

'Well — your brother can't be an unmarried mother.'

'True. But it might be better if he *could* get hisself pregnant. Help keep him out of stir, maybe.'

'I'm sorry?'

'He's inside. Doing six months in this poxy open prison for young offenders, somewhere up north. Been in and out since he was a kid, little tea leaf. Never done an honest day's graft in his life.' Mark found his cigarettes and a lighter. 'Smoke?'

'No, thanks. I don't.'

'Wish I didn't, costs me a bleeding fortune.' Mark blew smoke into the air. 'Where you from, then?' he asked.

'Evesbridge,' Jenny replied.

'Never heard of it.'

'No, you wouldn't have.' Jenny sidestepped a black plastic rubbish bag, inappropriately dumped right outside the Savoy Hotel. 'It's a little town in the Midlands.'

'Sounds boring.'

'Oh, believe you me, it is,' Jenny agreed. 'But it's full of old houses, all absolutely stuffed with antiques. You get up there with your van — '

'To rob old ladies?'

'You said it.'

'Told you before, I'm not a thief.'

'Thieving's the quickest way to riches and success,' Jenny teased. 'Or don't you want to be rich?'

'I'm gonna be rich, all right.' Mark grinned now. 'But I'm doin' things the hard way. Not like our Tony. Mug's game, his is. Come on.'

So now, turning off the Strand, they made their way towards the river. 'I want to show you this pub,' said Mark. 'Marquis of something it's called. It's down by the old Stairs here.'

Mark bought himself a pint of bitter and a packet of cigarettes. For Jenny, he ordered a glass of white wine, which he said was a lady's drink. He also ordered some sandwiches for their lunch.

While they waited for these to arrive, he drew her attention to the beauties of the pub. Indeed, it was charming. A half timbered, mediaeval inn, it had miraculously survived both the Great Fire and the Blitz. More to the point, it had so far survived the redevelopers, who swarmed like blow-flies throughout the early Sixties, for it was hidden away and well off the tourist track.

'Look over there now,' Mark said, pointing to the elaborate wall panelling. 'What do you make of that?'

'That old panelling, you mean?' Jenny peered into the gloom. 'I can't see it very well,' she admitted. 'Is it very special?'

'It's special, all right.' Mark grinned. 'It's your basic sixteenth century linenfold — but with flowers and shells and other bits and pieces thrown in. Unique, it is. Worth a bloody fortune.

'Now, find some old geezer with a country house needs doin' up — he'd have that panellin' like a shot. Pay you an arm and a leg for it too, no question.'

'I see.' The sandwiches arrived now, so Jenny took one. 'Tell me,' she said equably, 'do you see everything with an eye to taking it apart and flogging it to the highest bidder?'

'No, not at all.' Mark had continued to stare at

the woodwork — but now he turned to Jenny. 'I just like beautiful things,' he said, simply. 'That's why I like you.'

Jenny blushed scarlet. 'If you think I'm beautiful,' she muttered, 'you need glasses.'

'No, I don't.' Putting down his sandwich, Mark looked into Jenny's eyes. 'There's all sorts of beauty,' he began. 'There's the obvious sort — like a film star's, maybe. There's the clever sort — you look at something and you think, blimey, that's fantastic! However did they do that? But then there's the special kind. The sort of thing that starts from nothing, and grows on you. You got that.'

'Go on with you.' Jenny laughed at him. 'You mean, I have this mysterious, inner glow?'

'Yeah, that's right.' Reaching out to her, Mark stroked Jenny's face. 'There's something amazin' about you,' he murmured. 'You don't really notice it at first. But then, suddenly, it hits you.'

'How very painful.'

'I'm paying you a compliment, you cheeky little cow!' Mark scowled — but then, he pulled Jenny towards him. He kissed her, full on the lips. 'I know a winner when I see one,' he said, softly. 'You take my word for it.'

'Here,' said the barman, who had come over to remove their empty glasses, 'do you think you two could do your snoggin' in somebody else's pub?'

* * *

'I'm away all next week,' Mark told her as they walked from the tube station, for he'd insisted on

252

seeing her to her door. 'But tell you what. Come down the stall on Saturday and give us a hand. I'll pack up early and take you to the flicks.'

'Okay.' Jenny got out her latchkey. 'Look, you don't want to miss your train. You'll have to run as it is.'

Mark looked at his watch. 'Couple of minutes yet,' he said. He took Jenny in his arms. He kissed her.

Soon, she was kissing him back with enthusiasm. But then she pulled away. 'Mark,' she began, 'the train — '

'Stuff the train.' Mark made himself comfortable against Mrs Berners' front door. 'I'll get a taxi instead.'

* * *

Jenny could hardly wait for Saturday. All that week she had fits of the jitters and lapses of concentration, which were most unusual for her. 'Are you feeling all right, Miss Hughes?' asked Dora, for that morning Jenny had signed a letter without even looking at it. 'Or are you coming down with that 'flu?'

'I think I'm in love.' She didn't say it out loud, of course. 'That's it. I must be in love!'

The stall was already half set up when Jenny arrived, at ten past seven on Saturday morning. As she emerged from between the fish van and the second-hand furniture stall, Mark finished unwrapping a large ewer and matching dish, which he placed in the dead centre of the table. 'Hello,

253

sweetheart,' he said, beaming in welcome. He kissed her on the cheek. 'You okay, then?'

'Fine.' Jenny looked over the stuff he'd already set out. She picked up the ewer. 'This is nice,' she said. 'What is it?'

'Bit of Worcester.' Mark unwrapped a dish. 'Picked this lot up in Droitwich,' he explained. 'Dead cheap it was, an' all. This old junk shop was closing down, see — they're going to build a ring road or something across the site. Poor old geezer in there almost give it all away.'

'I see.' Jenny wiped the dust from the ewer's rim. 'There's some writing here,' she observed.

'Let's see.' Mark rubbed away the rest of the grime. '*Permitte divis cetera*. Leave everythin' else to the gods. Very nice, too.'

'How did you know that?' asked Jenny, impressed.

'I done Latin at school.' Mark grinned. 'I may look thick, but I ain't completely stupid, you know.'

'Evidently not.' Jenny blew on her cold fingers. 'Chilly, isn't it?'

'Yeah, told you to bring some gloves. Ain't you got none? Here, have my mittens. No, don't worry about me, I'm used to it.'

'Well, if you're sure.'

'Just put 'em on, right?' Mark ripped open a plastic bag and tipped change into his cashbox. 'Now look, if anyone asks you the price of anything, you weighs 'em up and tries to calculate the most they'll cough up. If they're foreign, make it double and fiddle the change.'

'But how should I know what to charge? I haven't a clue what anything's worth.'

'All this stuff on the left's up to a dollar. You should get five bob off your average punter, no trouble, but you can ask a bit less if they buy a couple of things. Or it's a kid wants something for his Mum's birthday.

'Stuff on the right's up to a fiver. More if you can manage it, but no less than two quid. See what you can get, that's the idea. Ain't you ever helped at a jumble sale nor nothing?'

'Not since the Brownies.' Jenny looked down at the stall. 'These bits and pieces on the left are worth next to nothing, so I charge five shillings for each of them, okay? This stuff on the right is worth a bit more, so I ask what I think the customer might pay, but don't accept less than two pounds?'

'You got it.' Mark grinned. 'Hey, meant to tell you, I sold that old pot you wouldn't buy. Got eight quid for it, from some fat Yank in a sealskin coat.'

'May you be forgiven.'

Jenny's first customer wanted a badly chipped Coalport dish. To her great surprise, he paid two pounds without quibbling. She then sold a mass-produced Staffordshire ornament for five pounds, which she blushed as she accepted — but the customer himself grinned at her in delight, evidently convinced he'd got a bargain.

Now, she could hear Mark earnestly telling a French tourist that something from the five shilling part of the stall was genuine Lalique, no question — and was astonished to see the man hand over three pounds.

'You're a daylight robber, you are,' she murmured, as Mark pushed the notes into the cashbox under the table.

'Go on, I done him a favour.' Mark grinned. 'You should've seen his wallet. Stuffed full of fivers, splitting at the seams it was. Now, think how nice that little bit of blue glass is going to look, in an apartment by the Seine.'

The morning brightened. The sun came out and the crowds grew. Glancing up from counting out some change, Jenny happened to look over towards the second hand jewellery stall, and there she saw someone she recognised. Or thought she did. Then the woman walked away from her, towards the antiquarian bookseller in the next row of stalls. But now, Jenny was almost certain she had seen Delia Shenstone. Delia and a small, dark-haired man . . .

'What you gawking at, then?' asked Mark, handing her the bar of chocolate he'd just been to get.

'Nothing.' Jenny accepted the chocolate. 'I thought I saw somebody I know, that's all. Over by the jewellery man.'

'Hope she ain't bought nothing.' Grinning, Mark bit into his own sausage roll. 'That Morry Foreman, he's a *real* crook. All his stuff's fake. He don't half stick it on, too.'

At four o'clock, Jenny helped Mark pack up. They stowed the unsold stock in his battered old van, then parked it in a friend's garage yard. They locked up the takings in his safe, then caught the bus into the West End.

'You went to grammar school, then?' asked Jenny,

as they bounced along on the top of a red London double decker, heading for Oxford Circus and Marble Arch.

'Yeah.' Mark lit a cigarette. 'Queen Mary High, Walthamstow.'

'Did you get expelled?'

'No, course not! Why do you ask that?' Mark was offended now. 'I left at sixteen, all nice and regular.'

'You'd had enough of school, I suppose?'

'Yeah, I'd done me O levels, and that.' Forgiving her, Mark grinned. 'The headmaster wanted me to stay on for As. Go to college. He nearly done his nut when I said I was leaving. But like I told 'im — I 'ad to go.'

'Why?'

'To get started, of course. To make a bit of money — I was sick of havin' no money.' Mark inhaled. 'See, me Dad ain't been in regular work since I was about ten. Dunno when he last brought so much as a brass farthing into our 'ouse, so I — '

'What's wrong with your father?' Remembering how often Gareth was ill, Jenny was sympathetic now. 'Was he hurt in the war, or something?'

'The war? He skived out of the whole of the bloody war!' Sourly, Mark grinned. 'He says he's got this weak chest. But since he smokes going on forty a day, I reckon if that's the case he ought to be six feet under by now.'

'Does your mother work?'

'Nah. Spends most of her time in the boozer, she does. Or down the Bingo, fiddling the score cards.' Mark shrugged. 'We're what the Social calls a problem family. That's what we are.'

'I see,' said Jenny. 'Where does this problem family live?'

'Leyton. Rainbow Road. Very appropriate that, what with all them blackies and Pakis round the place.' Mark looked at her. 'Now, don't get me wrong. I got nothing against any of them, I don't care who lives next door to me. Look, we got Catholics on the left, couple of old Jews on the right, Bengalis over the way, Sikhs two doors down from them — you name it.

'Me best friend's an Asian. His name's Jehangir, and he's one of the nicest blokes you could ever meet. Right sort to have on your side in a knife fight, an' all.'

'You don't really get into knife fights, do you?'

'Now and then, you have to.' Mark shrugged. 'It's the way things are, that's all. Look — if the Asians didn't stick up for theirselves, the villains would have it *all* their own way.'

'What do you mean?'

'Well — couple of months back, we had these sods pour petrol through this Paki woman's letter box, set fire to the place. Luckily, she and her kids got out, but the house was a write-off.

'Well, Jehangir knew who done it, so me and some of our mates, we got the buggers. They never done nothing similar again.'

'What did you do to them?'

'Put our initials on their balls.'

'*What?*'

'You heard.' Mark laughed. 'Have to watch meself down dark alleys these days.'

They'd reached Oxford Circus, so now Mark got

up to press the bell. 'Come on, then,' he said. 'Let's go an' see the new Chabrol. Have a bit of culture tonight.'

★　★　★

Even after she'd known him for the best part of a month, Jenny still couldn't decide whether Mark Strafford was a cocky little part-time criminal from the wrong side of the tracks — or a basically nice man whose rough edges needed just a tiny bit of smoothing. Then, he'd be perfect.

She wondered about asking Maggie's opinion. But then, she decided against it. As for Jess — well, Jess would say Mark was a yob. So Jenny kept him, and her indecision, to herself.

She was even more perplexed when she met Mark's best mate. Turning up at the stall one Saturday afternoon, Jehangir got stuck in, doing deals with a flair, determination and sheer Cockney cheek at least equal to Mark's own. But Jenny could hardly believe her ears when she heard how these allegedly dear friends spoke to one another.

'I saw that, you black bastard,' growled Mark as Jehangir, having sold a couple of candlesticks to a tourist, proceeded to stuff the two fivers into the pockets of his leather jacket. 'Look, you know the way we does things 'ere. Put the cash in the box.'

'Hang about.' Wrapping a china bowl for an old age pensioner, Jehangir beamed at her, then pocketed a few small coins. 'Right then,' he declared, 'that's my commission for today. Okay?'

'Thievin' Paki,' muttered Mark.

'Racist git.' Jehangir, a tall, handsome boy with skin the colour of milk chocolate and the most meltingly beautiful brown eyes, turned to Jenny and smiled. 'Why don't you and I call it a day?' he whispered. 'Come on, let's go to the pub. This fascist bastard can manage okay by himself.'

'Leave my bird alone, too!' Now, Mark elbowed Jehangir aside. 'Or do you want a fist in your face?'

'Mark!' Jenny was horrified. 'How can you — '

'Oh, he doesn't mean it. All mouth and trousers, aren't you?' Jehangir cuffed Mark about the head.

'Piss off.' But now, Mark grinned.

'You're worse than a couple of children,' said Jenny, shaking her head at them both.

20

Jenny knew she would meet Peter Eisenstadt some day. All the junior managers did. Only last week, Rob Graham had been summoned to Southampton Row.

But a phone call from the managing director's secretary, received one busy Tuesday morning, was something Jenny was definitely not expecting. Nor was it a particularly nice surprise. 'So, Miss Hughes,' said Miss Heligmann, 'I shall make an appointment for two thirty on Friday. Please don't keep Mr Eisenstadt waiting.'

'I shan't,' said Jenny. As if I'd dare, she thought.

'Don't be so bloody daft,' said Maggie Clifford, when Jenny confessed that the mere idea of meeting the boss scared her half to death. 'Listen, he only wants to look you over. Have a bit of a chat. Rob Graham says he's a really nice bloke.'

'Rob Graham says everyone's a really nice bloke.'

'Oh, come on. It's nothing heavy.' Maggie grinned. 'He won't eat you! God — anyone who can face Beryl and Dora first thing on a Monday morning could take on Napoleon himself — and win.'

But it was with a sinking heart that Jenny took the Central Line to Holborn and walked up Southampton Row. It was with deep misgivings that she introduced herself to Miss Heligmann, then followed her along the close-carpeted corridor to the office of the managing director himself.

Miss Heligmann tapped lightly on her boss's door and then, without waiting for a summons, stalked into the room. The man at the desk glanced up. 'Just one moment,' he said, to the person with whom he was talking on the phone. 'Yes, Miss Heligmann?'

'Miss Hughes, Mr Eisenstadt.'

'Of course. Please, Miss Hughes, do sit down. I shan't keep you a moment.'

Peter Eisenstadt went on with his call. But he was as good as his word and very soon he rang off, telling the caller he'd phone him back in ten minutes' time. Standing up now, he shook Jenny by the hand. 'Well, Miss Hughes,' he began, 'it's very nice to meet you. I hope you didn't have any trouble getting here?'

'No, none. I came by tube.'

'You don't mind that?' Peter Eisenstadt sat down again. 'Personally, I hate the Underground. So noisy and dirty.'

'Oh, it doesn't bother me.' Jenny shrugged. It's all very well for those who can afford taxis, she thought.

Now, the boss was opening his desk drawer. He took out a folder, which he opened and glanced through. Soon he looked up again, and met Jenny's eyes. 'This is all very good, Miss Hughes,' he said. 'Very good indeed.'

'Thank you.'

'We should thank *you*.' Putting down the statistical returns on Jenny's section, Peter Eisenstadt smiled at her. 'We're very pleased with you, and with your work.'

Nervously, Jenny smiled back at him. Was she expected to say something now, or should she wait for him to speak to her? Suddenly, she could bear the tension no longer. She felt she just had to get away. 'Is that it?' she demanded, abruptly. Far too abruptly, she realised now. 'I mean, is — '

'No, not quite.' Again, Peter met Jenny's eyes. Again, he smiled — but more kindly this time. 'Please try to relax,' he said. 'I didn't invite you here in order to tell you anything unpleasant. Far from it, in fact.'

He reached for another folder, which had been lying ready on his desk. 'At your interview for your present job,' he continued, 'you said you would be prepared to travel. This is still the case?'

'Certainly.' Jenny nodded. 'I'd like that very much.'

'Good. So, you would be willing to go abroad?'

It wasn't really a question. His tone implied she hadn't any choice. But Jenny decided to assume she had the option, and was simply agreeing to co-operate. 'Yes, of course,' she replied, airily. 'Where had you in mind?'

'Germany. Head Office, in Cologne.' Peter took the top off his fountain pen. 'You will be there for about three weeks. You'll visit the laboratories, see round one or two of the factories. Learn about production methods, look at current research and development, new styles of marketing — all that sort of thing. Then, you'll spend some time in the office. Perhaps they'll let you deal with some customer accounts.'

'I see. Well, that sounds very interesting.'

'You will not be travelling alone.' Now Peter Eisenstadt scribbled something on a piece of paper. 'Mr Kaufmann from Accounts will be going with you. You've met him, I believe?'

'Yes. He's a youngish man, isn't he? Tall, and fair-haired.'

'Is he? I don't actually know him myself.' Peter Eisenstadt flicked open the folder next to Jenny's own. 'Oh, yes,' he agreed, 'that's right. There's a photograph in his personal file here.'

Now, he handed Jenny the paper on which he'd written the names of the people she was to see in Cologne. 'Can you read my handwriting?' he asked.

'Yes, of course.'

'Good. So you and Mr Kaufmann put your heads together, and work out your itinerary. Well, I think that's all.' Rising to his feet, Peter held out his hand.

Jenny took it.

Warmly, Peter smiled at her. 'So, Miss Hughes,' he concluded, 'it's been a great pleasure to talk to you. Thank you for coming in. Keep up the good work, yes?'

'I'll try.'

'I'm sure you will.'

Standing in the corridor outside, Jenny found she could hardly breathe. Forcing herself to be calm, she took one, two, three slow, measured gulps of air. She wondered if there were a ladies' cloakroom near. For she was afraid she might be sick.

★ ★ ★

Maggie Clifford would go mad. As Jenny sat on the train back to Acton, she wondered if Maggie would ever speak to her again.

Over the past few months, Maggie had taken every opportunity to vamp Michael Kaufmann. He, however, had taken very little notice of her. He'd smiled politely when she'd offered to type some letters for him, he'd accepted numerous cups of coffee from her own fair hands — but that was as far as it went. Germans did not usually fraternise with working colleagues out of office hours, and Michael Kaufmann ran true to form.

'What's he like, then?' demanded Maggie, as she and Jenny ate lunch in their favourite café, the following Monday. 'Herr Oberführer, I mean. What does he look like, for a start?'

'He's short. Dark. Actually, he looks more Italian than German, except that his eyes are blue.' Absent-mindedly, Jenny stirred her lemon tea. Quickly, she drank it down. 'I must go, Maggie,' she said. 'I've a meeting with those people from regional sales at one.'

As she walked along the corridor to her meeting, Jenny thought about Peter Eisenstadt. She'd been thinking about him all weekend, too — in fact, she had been so preoccupied that Mark had asked her several times what he'd done. Why wasn't she speaking to *him*?

Peter had not been at all what she'd expected. For some reason, she'd always pictured him as a tall, broad-shouldered man. Blue-eyed, certainly — but heavily made and robust, not slight and small. Not somebody who looked like a teenage boy, in spite of being nearly forty years old.

He must have had an easy life, she thought. Cushioned by inherited wealth, he'd obviously never had even a day of worry, an hour of unease. Or, if he had, it didn't show on his face.

How alike they were! Looking at his hands, Jenny had seen her own long, slender fingers. Glancing at his face, she'd observed her own large, blue-grey eyes. His fine features had been passed on to his daughter so faithfully that Jenny wondered how anybody seeing them together could fail to notice the resemblance. For Peter's face was the same shape as Jenny's. His wide forehead, his high cheekbones and his small, rather narrow nose were exactly like her own.

He'd seemed such a nice, kind man. But, if he was nice, why had he abandoned her mother? Only a heartless, unprincipled wretch could have behaved like that.

But Peter *had* let Shirley down — there was no doubt of it. Therefore, he deserved no further consideration. 'Gareth's my Dad,' thought Jenny, as she checked her bag for the documents she would need at the meeting. Now, she felt guilty and disloyal for even thinking about Peter. 'Gareth's my real father — my only father,' she decided, as she opened the sales manager's door.

★　★　★

'So, there you are — I'm going to Cologne, and I'm travelling with Michael Kaufmann.' Jenny grinned. 'Well, Clifford? Aren't you livid? Aren't you green?'

'You jammy beggar. You lucky, lucky sod.' Maggie Clifford shook her head. She glowered — but then she grinned, too. 'You can seduce him in a couchette,' she said, 'then tell me all about it.'

'We're going by air.' Jenny glanced at her finger nails. 'I've told you before — he's not my type.'

'Go on with you. The answer to a maiden's prayer, that's what he is! *I* wouldn't mind getting my hand down his trousers, and if he — '

'Maggie, you're disgusting.'

'I know. I can't help it. I was born that way.' Maggie yawned widely. 'Hi, David!' she cried then, smirking at one of the clerks from the marketing department, who happened to be walking by. As the boy blushed, she giggled. 'Doing anything tonight?'

'Leave David Rogers alone,' said Jenny sternly, but so only they could hear. 'He's only sixteen.'

'Yeah, but he's got definite possibilities, wouldn't you say? Wonder if he's busy this weekend?' Maggie laughed. 'Oh, it's all right for some,' she muttered. 'Going on a romantic holiday for two with the Hunk of the Month, *somebody* will soon be having a damned good time.'

Jenny had spoken to Michael Kaufmann several times, but she didn't know him very well. He was in Accounts, she was in Sales, so they'd had very little direct contact. Now, however, five days before they were due to leave for Cologne, the two of them sat down to discuss their trip.

They glanced over some customer accounts which they'd been told to look at, and they studied some statistical returns. Happening to look up at the same time, they met each others' eyes. Michael grinned.

'It *must* be coffee time by now,' he said, stifling a yawn.

'Yes, it must be,' Jenny agreed.

Michael went off to fetch coffee for himself and tea for Jenny. Sitting down again, he pushed the bundle of files to one side. He rubbed his eyes. 'Not very interesting, I think,' he observed. 'All routine stuff.'

'Well, it would be.' Jenny shrugged. 'They'd hardly trust us with the important accounts, would they? For example, they wouldn't let us louse up the current negotiations with Sainsbury's or Marks and Spencer's.'

'I suppose not.' Michael laughed. 'This . . . louse up. You mean spoil?'

'That's right.'

'This word is not correct. You would not use it when talking to Mr Schretzmaier.' Michael shook his head. 'You teach me bad habits, I think.'

'Do I?' Well, thought Jenny, and Maggie Clifford would love to teach you a few more. Sweetly, she smiled. 'I'll try to be correct in future,' she said.

'Good.' Either not noticing or deciding to ignore her sarcasm, Michael smiled too. 'Will you like to go to Cologne?' he asked.

'Yes, I'm looking forward to it. What about you?'

'I shall be delighted. I shall see my fiancée again. She lives near Düsseldorf.'

'But you come from Cologne?'

'That's right.'

'I see.' Now, Jenny decided this might be a good opportunity to dig a little. 'How well do you know Mr Eisenstadt?' she asked, artlessly.

'Not at all. I've never met him.'

'I suppose you will, in due course?'

'It's possible, I imagine.' Michael shrugged. 'My mother knows the whole family,' he volunteered. 'She once worked for them, you see. But many years ago.'

'What did she do?'

'She was a secretary. She worked in the old offices, in the centre of the town. They're all gone now, of course. But she still sees Mr Eisenstadt's younger sister now and then.'

'Oh. So you got into the firm through the back door?'

'I'm sorry?'

'Just another incorrect expression.' Jenny opened a new folder. 'Were you at school with Mr Eisenstadt's children, perhaps?'

'Oh, no. He hasn't any.'

'Isn't he married, then?'

'He's married, but separated. He has been for years, in fact. His wife's ill. She's in a sanatorium somewhere in the Black Forest.' With the point of his biro, Michael stabbed at a corner of a file. 'She's a bit — what's your word? Crazy. *Verrückt*.'

'Is she?' Her heart starting to thud dangerously, Jenny rolled her own biro to and fro. 'How do you know all this?' she enquired.

'Office gossip. Old women's chat.' Michael grinned. 'Oh, don't look so sorry for him. He isn't lonely, you know. He has a very good friend.'

'You mean a mistress?'

'I suppose so.'

'Who is she?'

'A journalist. She works on that weekly magazine.' Michael frowned. '*World News*, is it?'

'You don't mean *World Wide Magazine?*'

'That's it. Delia somebody. That's her name.'

Jenny stared at him. 'You did say Delia?'

'That's right.'

'Delia Shenstone?'

'Yes. That's the one.' Opening his briefcase, Michael took out another bundle of files. 'The Friedmann account,' he said. Heavily, he sighed. 'Herr Friedmann needs a kick up the backside, is that what you say? It appears you and I are going to give it to him.'

'We are?' Jenny thought she was going to faint. Her eyes would hardly focus, and she could not have made any sense of the Friedmann file if she had tried. So now, her mind busy with a thousand speculations and confused ideas, she let Michael talk on.

★　★　★

'Cologne, eh?' muttered Mark. Strolling round Regent's Park, he and Jenny were enjoying some early evening sunshine. 'So what's this in aid of, then?'

'I'm going to the firm's Head Office,' Jenny replied. 'To see what goes on.'

'Do you want to go?'

'Yes. It will be good experience for me.' Jenny narrowed her eyes against the sun. 'It might be fun, too.'

'I'll miss you.'

'I'll miss you, too. But it's only for three weeks. Mark, why are you looking at me like that?'

'Like what?'

'As if you've lost a thousand pounds and found a ten bob note.'

'I don't want you to go, I suppose.'

'Oh.' Jenny shrugged. 'You go off in your van.'

'Yeah, well.' Mark lit a cigarette. 'It's different, me going off in the van. I'm a bloke. It's my job.'

'This is my job.'

'Not the same.' Mark blew out smoke. 'I'm a dealer, right? I got ideas, plans for the future. I got long term prospects to think about.'

'So have I!' Jenny took his hand. 'Oh, Mark — do cheer up. Look, I'll send you a postcard.'

'Thanks a bunch.' Mark sniffed. 'I have to be in Bristol on Sunday night,' he said, 'so I won't be able to drive you to Heathrow.'

'That's all right, I'll catch the bus.'

*　*　*

That following Monday morning, Michael and Jenny were to catch the seven o'clock plane from Heathrow. Since Mark was going off to Bristol, Jenny decided to spend the weekend before her trip in Evesbridge.

'Did I tell you I'm going to Germany?' she asked, as they all sat down to breakfast on Saturday morning.

'No, you didn't.' Putting down his copy of the *Daily Express*, Gareth looked at her. 'When's this coming off, then?'

271

'Monday. I'm going to Cologne. For three weeks.'
'What for?'

'Oh, just to look around, really.' Jenny smiled at him. 'I'm supposed to do a bit of work, but I don't imagine they'll expect me to get stuck in. I'll be able to do some sight-seeing. Take a boat trip up the Rhine, maybe.'

'Oh. Well, love — that all sounds very interesting.' Gareth stood up. 'Shirley, I told Tony Forrest I'd take him some of our spare runner bean plants. I'll do that now. Be back about ten, I expect. Shall we all go over to Worcester for lunch?'

'That's a good idea,' Shirely replied. 'We don't have to go too early, though. If you and Tony want a natter, or if you feel like a quick half at the Falconers' Arms — '

'That okay with you?' Gareth shrugged on his old tweed jacket. 'Right, then. I might do that. See you about half twelve.'

They heard the front door slam. The car engine spluttered, died, spluttered again, started. 'Well,' said Shirley, pouring herself a second cup of tea, 'so you're doing all right?'

'I think so.' Jenny buttered more toast. 'They seem quite pleased with me, in fact.'

'You'll be on the Board in five years' time.'

'I doubt that.' Jenny grinned. 'They're not very progressive. I'm the only female section supervisor, and I don't think there's a woman anywhere in higher management.'

'Well, somebody's got to be first.' Shirley put down her teacup. 'Have you seen him?' she asked.

'Him?'

'Yes. Don't mess me about, Jenny. You know very well whom I mean.'

'Well, as it happens, I have.' Jenny looked down at her plate. 'I've talked to him, too.'

'Oh.' Now Shirley played with the fringe on the edge of the tablecloth. 'What did you think?'

'He's very nice.'

'Ah. How's he looking?'

'Fine.' Jenny shrugged. 'He's very well preserved. For his age.'

'Which is? I mean, how old would you reckon he'd be?'

'Early forties, I'd guess.' Jenny drew a deep breath. She crossed her fingers under the table. 'He's getting a bit heavy now,' she went on. 'But he must have been really something in his youth.'

'Oh?'

'Yes. With those big shoulders and that square jaw. Those green eyes are fantastic. I don't wonder you fell for him.'

'Peter's eyes were blue.' Shirley was breathing harshly now. 'He was a small man, no taller than I am. He had delicate features, almost like a girl's.'

'Really?' Jenny met her mother's gaze. 'Well, this Peter Eisenstadt is tall, and quite big. His hair's grey now, but you can see it must once have been red. Oh, and he has lots of freckles. Those blobby ones which run into each other. But as I said, he's still a handsome man. He — '

'Jenny, is Eisenstadt a common name?'

'In Germany, you mean?' Jenny pretended to think about it. 'Well, not particularly. It's not like Smith or Jones. I suppose it might be as common

273

as — oh — Carpenter, maybe. Or Langford. Something like that.'

'It's not the same man. It can't be.' With trembling fingers, Shirley groped for her cigarettes. 'Jenny, your father was small. Pale skinned. His hair was dark, very dark. He was nothing like your boss.'

'Oh.' Jenny smiled. 'Well, there you are then. I told you all along that it might not be the same person.'

'Yes, you did.'

'You've been worrying about nothing.'

'Have I?' After a long, hard look at her daughter, Shirley got up. 'I've been silly, really,' she said.

'Yes.'

As her mother went through into the scullery, Jenny sighed with relief. It was just as well she'd left yesterday's *Guardian* on the train, for on one of the business pages there'd been a big photograph of Josef and Peter Eisenstadt.

There was speculation that soon the United Kingdom division of the company would be floated on the Stock Exchange. For the firm was expanding by leaps and bounds, seriously threatening the home markets of all the longer established brands.

21

Jenny found she liked Michael Kaufmann. He was, as Mark would have put it, a decent sort of bloke. That first evening he'd seen her safely to her hotel, and later telephoned to ask if she were comfortable, was her room all right? Then he told her that while they were in Cologne he'd have the use of his stepfather's car, so the following morning he'd pick her up and drive her to Head Office.

There, he introduced her to his own colleagues, and always kept a place for her in the canteen. 'I'll tell Sabine about this new English girlfriend,' chaffed one of the reps.

'You tell her,' said Michael calmly. 'Then Miss Hughes can explain that it's otherwise.'

Miss Hughes. Even in the course of casual lunchtime chat, everyone was still Herr This and Frau or Fräulein That. At the London office, the use of given names was becoming general among equals — one had to be senior in rank to be known by one's title and surname — but here in Germany, formality still prevailed.

All the same, everyone was very friendly, both in the office and out of it. Now, with typical German efficiency, Michael and his colleagues worked out a timetable for their English visitor, leaving very few hours of work or leisure unaccounted for.

Busy in the office, and after work taken ten pin bowling, to the cinema, or invited to *Abendbrot* at someone's home, Jenny found the time flew by. She almost forgot about Mark. But then he wrote to her, and she was surprised how delighted she was to receive his letter. Stuffing it into her handbag, she decided to read it as she and Michael sat in Cologne's usual early morning traffic jam.

Mark began by telling her he missed her and couldn't wait to see her again. He'd had a good week in Bristol, finding some nice spindleback chairs, a Georgian knife box and a Queen Anne tea caddy, all at good prices.

'You'll be relieved to know,' he wrote, 'that I didn't rob the old girls who sold them to me. In fact, I paid them a bit over the current wholesale rate.

'But I've also got some bad news. Jan is in hospital. A few nights ago he was walking home from his mate's house, and he was attacked. I know who did it, and when I get some people together we'll go after the bastards. They'll wish they hadn't bothered, I can tell you that.

'All the same, knowing the sods will get their faces rearranged doesn't help poor Jan. He's got a broken nose, three cracked ribs and some very nasty bruising. Of course, the police don't want to know anything about it. I imagine the villains who gave Jan a going over were counting on that.

'I've been to see him every day, and I think he's getting better. There shouldn't be any permanent scarring, so he'll still be able to get all the girls. He sends you his love and hopes you'll visit him when you come home.

'It's the fourteenth, isn't it? Ring me as soon as

you get back, and I'll pick you up. Look after yourself, sweetheart. All my love, Mark.'

All his love. Just a formality, surely? Still, Jenny was gratified. Pushing the letter back into her bag, she stared thoughtfully through the windscreen.

'Not bad news, I hope?' asked Michael, politely.

'No. Well, yes. In a way. One of my friends has had an accident. He's in hospital.'

'I'm sorry.' Michael changed gear. Now, smiling with satisfaction, he overtook a big blue BMW. 'Your friend, has he many hurts?'

'A broken nose and ribs. Bit of bruising.'

'That's bad.' Michael looked concerned. 'He's your boyfriend, yes?'

'My boyfriend's friend. But I like him a lot.'

'I see.' Michael turned into the office car park. 'I have a letter from Sabi this morning,' he said. 'She's coming to stay with me this weekend, and she suggests perhaps you might like to look round the city with us. On Saturday morning, if you're not so busy.'

'That's nice of her. I'd love to.' Jenny smiled her thanks.

But on Friday morning, as Jenny was working out some figures and plotting them on one of the enormous graphs which adorned the Sales office, she got a telephone call from the main switchboard.

'Ah, Fräulein Hughes,' said the telephonist tartly, 'I've found you at last. There is a message from Reception. Someone wishes to see you there.'

'Oh? Are you sure it's me they want?'

'There's no one else with your name here.' The telephonist sounded very frosty now. 'I'll tell them you'll be down in five minutes.'

Jenny was mystified. 'Someone wants to see me,' she told Michael. 'But I was supposed to meet Franz Hoffmann in Accounts at eleven. Could you perhaps go along in my place?'

'Certainly.' Michael picked up the files on Jenny's desk. 'I'll go now, and tell him you'll be along shortly.'

'Thanks. You're a mate.' Jenny grinned at him. 'I owe you one.'

The lift was somewhere at the top of the building, so now Jenny ran along the corridor and clattered down the stairs. Soon she arrived in the entrance hall, an imposing place full of vivid greenery and hi-tech photo-montages, presided over by two immensely tall, terminally smart receptionists whose immaculate *maquillages*, perfect scarlet finger nails and inch-long false eyelashes made Jenny feel a messy little scruff.

This pair of scornful beauties put the fear of God into most visitors to Eisenstadt GmbH. But they evidently hadn't overwhelmed this present one. Lounging against a potted palm and staring with undisguised disdain at everything and everyone around him, Mark was clearly not impressed.

'Good God.' Her high heels clicking noisily on the lacquered wooden floor, Jenny walked up to him. 'Whatever are you doing here?' she demanded, amazed.

'Thought I'd take a little holiday. Have a butcher's round this part of the Rhineland. Any objections?' Observing Jenny's frown, Mark scowled back at her. 'Thought I'd look up an old mate. If I'd known she'd be so bloody pleased to see me, I'd have got here a whole lot earlier than this.'

'Sorry. It's very nice to see you. Really it is.' Jenny ushered him towards a huge overstuffed sofa, of the type found only in reception halls. 'Sit down,' she invited.

'Thanks a million.'

'Now — what's the matter?' she asked. For he still looked very put out. 'Mark?'

'It's them Krauts.' Mark glowered. 'That painted cow in the 'orrible orange dress looked at me as if I was somethin' the cat dragged in. *You're* all done up like a dog's dinner, too. Where you off to today?'

'Don't be silly, Mark. These are my ordinary working clothes. I can't come to the office in jeans.'

'Pardon me, I'm sure.' Offended, Mark sniffed. 'Well anyway, you got too much make up on. All that mascara and eyeshadow, it don't suit you. Makes you look ill. When're you free?'

'At lunchtime.' Jenny glanced at her watch. 'Two hours from now.'

'Couldn't you get off a bit earlier?'

'No, not really. But you could find something to do, couldn't you? While you wait for me?'

'Like what?'

'Go for a walk? Go round the shops?'

'Oh, great.'

'Mark, I can't just drop everything and rush out with you!'

'Okay, okay, keep your hair on. Look, I can't go shopping here, everything's too bloody expensive.'

'Go and look at the cathedral, then. That's free.

Go round an art gallery. Do you speak any German?'

'*Ja, ein bißchen. Ich habe seit zwei Jahren in der Schule Deutsch gelernt.*'

'Near enough.' Jenny grinned. 'Right then, I'll see you in the *Domplatz* about one thirty. I'll treat you to lunch.'

'Right.' But still Mark scowled. 'Did you get my letter?' he enquired.

'Yes, I did. I was going to reply this weekend. How's Jehangir?'

'Getting better. Nice of you to ask.'

'Mark!'

'See you about half one, then.' Getting to his feet, Mark glanced towards the whispering receptionists. 'Don't let me hold you up any longer.'

★   ★   ★

By the time Jenny met him for lunch, Mark was in a slightly better temper. But, in his faded jeans and well-worn navy jumper, with his battered leather jacket slung over his shoulder and his hair curling round his collar, he looked like a gipsy down on his luck. She could see why the receptionists at Eisenstadt GmbH had been so curt with him.

As they ate their lunch, Jenny was treated to a detailed account of Jehangir's accident. Then, over coffee and cakes, she was told what Mark and his mates were planning for those responsible. She hoped no one English was listening. 'Give him my love,' she said, when she could get a word in edgeways. 'When you write to him, that is.'

'Will do.' Cheering up, Mark grinned. 'Write to him yourself, eh? Jan likes you.'

'Go on. He thinks all English girls are sluts.'

'He don't think that of you. I've put him straight there.'

'Oh you have, have you?'

'Yup.'

'I see.' Thoughtfully, Jenny cut into her slice of cake. She stirred her lemon tea. 'How long are you staying here?' she asked.

'Week or so.'

'Where will you sleep?'

'Oh, I've got it all sorted, don't you worry about that.' Picking up the sugar shaker, Mark almost emptied it into his coffee. 'I'm going to kip on this mate's sofa.'

'Which mate is this?'

'Fella called Anton. Met him at an auction in Ipswich once, done him a few favours since. He said if I was ever passing — '

'Where does he live?'

'Kielstraße. It's in a district called Ehrenfeld.' Mark pushed his hands into his pockets. 'Got a street map somewhere.'

'Is this Anton expecting you?'

'Yeah, sure he is.' Mark grinned. 'I phoned him from the station here, he said to come right over, I can stay as long as I like. So what we doin' tonight then, eh?'

Jenny arrived back from lunch rather late. She found Michael and everyone else gossiping about the long-haired hippy who had called to see Miss Hughes. 'Yes, I'm afraid something's come up,' she said. 'I'm sorry, Michael, but I shan't be able to meet you and your fiancée tomorrow after all.'

On Saturday morning, Jenny and Mark walked round the inner city, did some window shopping, then went into a small but very smart art gallery — where Mark distinguished himself by loudly declaring all the paintings to be rubbish.

'Well, it was you who wanted to come in here,' muttered Jenny, embarrassed. Now Mark was telling her and everyone else that a canvas full of dots and lines was a load of pretentious crap. 'If you hate everything, why don't we leave?'

'Got to get my money's worth, doll.' Mark grinned at her. 'Don't *you* think it's tripe?' he asked, as he eyed the picture in question once again.

'I don't like it, certainly.'

'There you are then.' Mark folded his arms. 'You think it's bloody awful, right?'

'Yes. But I'm not an expert, am I?'

'You don't need to be. You just got to be honest, that's all. Trust your own judgement.'

'"I don't know much about art, but I know what I like." Is that what you mean?'

'No, don't mean that at all.' Mark turned to look at her. 'You got a guide inside yourself, ain't you? Tells you right from wrong, good from bad? Use it now. Look, it's like the emperor's new clothes, sort of thing. You got to have a feeling for the genuine article. You don't let yourself be taken in by conmen, see?

'Right, I know I'm putting this very badly. But — well, that bugger there, he wants three thousand quid for chucking a pot of paint in your face. Some stupid git'll pay it. 'Cos it's Art. Art! Looks as if a monkey done it.'

'Maybe.'

'Definitely! Right then, what's this bastard's name? Haldemann. Remember that, okay? If you ever see a painting of his up for auction in Christie's or Sotheby's or anywhere else, and you see proper dealers payin' out real money for it, I will personally eat my leather jacket here.'

'Come on, let's go.' Jenny tugged at his sleeve. 'Before we're asked to leave.'

★ ★ ★

'Up the steeple then, eh?' Laughing at Jenny's frown, Mark gazed at the cathedral's twin towers. Two huge, blackened spires, they pierced the bright blue Westphalian sky. 'Look, you can't come to Cologne and not go to the top of the *Kölner Dom*.'

'Can't I?' Jenny bit her lower lip. 'Oh, I might as well admit it. I don't like heights.'

'I'll hold on to you.' Mark took Jenny's hand. 'You can't fall, I won't let you.'

'But it's so *huge*!' Jenny stared at the mountain of stone in front of her. 'I wonder if it's all original?' she asked. 'Did it survive the bombing intact?'

'Think it did,' replied Mark. 'Well, Anton says it was knocked about a bit. Had a few windows blown in, and the odd wall came down. But right after the war, they got working on it. Looks in fairly good nick now.'

'I wonder why it was left alone? The rest of the place was flattened.'

'It's a landmark, of course. Like our St Paul's. When there was gonna be an air-raid, see, the pathfinders dropped red flares all around it. Then the bombers knew exactly where they were. Once you knew where the cathedral was, you could work out the position of everything else, right?'

'So Anton says?'

'You got it.' Mark grinned. 'Coming up, then?'

'Oh, if you insist. But look, if I need to come down again, you'll let me. Won't you?'

'Yeah, sure.' Reassuringly, Mark smiled. 'Don't worry. You'll be safe with me.'

They went into the tower. They climbed up the narrow staircase, step after step after weary step. Finally, they came out into the sunshine again.

The view across the Rhineland was breathtaking. Leaning against the railings of the viewing platform, Mark held Jenny round the waist. He kissed her ear. 'Can you see the sea?' he murmured.

'No.' She buried her face against his chest. 'But I feel seasick!'

'Take a few deep breaths.' Mark hugged her. 'Look down there,' he said, marvelling. 'Look at the people, just like little ants.'

But Jenny was too afraid of vertigo to let herself to look down. Daring to glance around her, she kept her eyes firmly on the middle distance. 'I can't look down there,' she whispered. 'I'll be ill.'

'Come on, then. I'll take you back now.'

When they were back on ground level, Mark announced that he had an appointment. He had to see a dealer. 'Come an' meet him, eh?' he suggested. 'He's a nice bloke. Good mate, too. You'd like him.'

'I'm sure I would. But I don't think I can spare the time.' Jenny had some reports to write, and now she used this as an excuse to avoid meeting Mark's friend.

Being seen around the town with a gipsy was one thing, but hob-nobbing with elements from Cologne's criminal underworld was quite another. If she were spotted, that would do her career prospects no good at all. 'You go and meet this dealer,' she said. 'I'll do my reports, and see you this evening.'

'I might be a bit late.'

'Phone me tomorrow, then. At the hotel.'

'Okay.'

By the time Jenny saw him again, Mark had done some very good deals. With his friend Anton's connivance, he had also arranged to ship over some goods without paying excise duty on them — a dubious scheme which he assured Jenny was a hundred per cent foolproof, nevertheless. 'If I pays tax,' he objected, 'I'll lose half my profit. Bad business that would be.'

'You'll be joining your brother if you don't watch it,' said Jenny. 'You'll end up inside with Tony, you'll see.'

'No, I won't. He's thick. I'm clever.' Mark grinned. 'Don't you worry, sweetheart. They won't catch me.'

'No?' Jenny wasn't so sure. Mark seemed to court disaster. No, it was worse than that. He ran up and smacked it rudely in the face. She couldn't believe Fate would be kind to him indefinitely. 'But if you are caught — '

'Shan't be, stop worrying.' Mark grinned. 'You're

too bloody straight, that's your trouble. You don't have no fun.'

'I'm not sure that the guests of Her Majesty in Pentonville do, either.'

'Wouldn't know.' Mark laughed at her. 'I'm not gonna find out, neither.'

'No?'

'No.' As they strolled down a narrow alley, Mark hugged her. 'I really like you,' he said. 'Dunno why, but I do.'

'I like you, too,' Jenny said. 'I like you a lot.'

'Yeah?' Mark shrugged. 'You're ashamed of me, though.'

'I'm not!'

'You are, a bit.' He let her go. But then, he took her hand. 'Come on, princess,' he said. 'Better get you safe home to bed.'

22

Jenny's time in Cologne was drawing to a close. That Saturday morning, she would fly back to England. She had enjoyed her time in Germany, but she would be glad to go home.

Thursday evening was fine, so she and Mark joined the evening strollers on the riverside walk. 'But I have to work on Friday,' she told him, when he asked why she couldn't go home with him, on the ferry. 'I have things to finish. I've already explained that.'

'Yeah, but couldn't you get off just a little bit early? I want you to come on the boat, with me.'

'I have an air ticket.'

'Have you?' Gloomily, Mark pushed his hands into his pockets. 'Oh, well. That's that, then.'

'Come on, Mark. Cheer up.' Slipping her arm through his, Jenny hugged him. 'Is he scared, then?' she teased. 'Doesn't he want to be on a great big boat, all by himself?'

'I'd like to be with you. Dunno why, cheeky little cow you are.'

'You do express yourself so well,' observed Jenny, shaking her head. 'Well, then — I tell you what. I'll ask Michael if it's possible to change my ticket.'

'Who's Michael?'

'The man from the London office, who came over here with me. He's very nice. There's a girl in Personnel who fancies him rotten: so, if he'll talk to her for me, she might agree to swap my air ticket for one on the boat train tomorrow.'

'What about that stuff you got to finish?'

'I'll stay up late tonight.'

★   ★   ★

'That shouldn't be a problem,' said Michael. 'I'll speak to Hilde Biermann, in Personnel. If you let her have your air ticket, I'm sure she'll be allowed to give you cash in exchange. Are you looking forward to going back?'

'Yes, as a matter of fact I am,' Jenny replied. 'What about you?'

'I'm staying here.' Michael dialled Hilde Biermann's extension. 'No offence, but I've had enough of England and the English. I miss Sabi, too. So I asked my boss if I could come back here for good, and he said okay.'

Michael grinned. 'But don't think you have to take all those files back,' he went on. 'I'll send them by courier, instead. Ah, hello. Is that Fräulein Biermann? It's Kaufmann from Accounts here. I wonder if you could help me?'

Jenny arrived at the railway station with only minutes to spare. Soon, the train was speeding through the Rhineland. As Jenny watched the scenery flash by, Mark struck up a muttered conversation with a middle-aged Dutchman, who was sitting in a corner of their compartment. She hoped he wasn't doing any more shady deals.

At the Hook of Holland, they boarded the ferry. Overhead, seagulls wheeled and cried, mournfully calling each to the other. With this doleful music ringing in their ears, Mark and Jenny watched the Netherlands recede.

The wind was getting up now. Spray from the cold North Sea hit their faces, and all along the coastline they could see harbour lights beginning to glow. Soon, it would be evening. Tomorrow morning they'd be in England again.

'Tired, sweetheart?' asked Mark.

'A bit.' Jenny stifled a yawn. 'Can we go back to the lounge? All my luggage is there, and it's so cold and wet up here.'

'Right.' Mark got up. 'We could go to the bar, if you like,' he suggested. 'Or to my cabin. I got plenty of duty free.'

'You have a cabin?' Jenny was astonished. 'One of your own?'

'Yes. Well, I had to have somewhere to put all my stuff. Why — haven't you got one?'

'No. There weren't any left.' Jenny yawned again. 'Lucky thing,' she murmured, enviously. 'You'll be able to go to bed tonight. I'll have to sit in one of those nasty plastic chairs.'

'Oh, you can have my cabin. I'll stay in the bar.'

'I couldn't possibly let you do that.'

'Couldn't you? Well, I wouldn't leave you on your own in the lounge all night. Never know who might bother you.' Mark looked down at his feet. 'Or if you like,' he muttered, 'you could come and share my cabin with me.'

'Oh?' Jenny blushed. 'What's that supposed to mean?'

'Don't mess me about.' Mark frowned at her.

289

'Look, I never planned it like this. I never even give it a thought. But the thing is — well, I really fancy you. I'd like you to spend the night with me. But if you don't want to, we'll both sit up in the bar. Okay?'

'I see.' Jenny's blush deepened. 'You do have a roundabout way of putting things,' she said.

'Do I? Right, then — you'd rather I said, 'okay sweetheart, I've been dying to get your knickers off for months now. So here we are, an' how about it?''

'There's no need to be quite so crude!'

'Good grief, what *do* you want?' Exasperated, Mark glared at her. 'First time I set eyes on you I thought, yeah. Trouble for some poor bloke there, no mistake. There's a tease if ever I saw one.'

'I'm not a tease!' Jenny's eyes flashed. 'When have I ever — '

'There's all different ways of teasing. You don't even know you're doing it.' Mark scowled. 'That way you look at me, for instance. All big blue eyes an' innocence, as if you're darin' me to bite you or something — but you know damned well I won't.'

'Mark, I — '

'Oh, forget it. We going to the bar, or what?'

Jenny looked at him. Cross and tired, he was rubbing his eyes and glowering, as if he were trying not to cry. He looked exactly like a child who'd been promised a treat, but had it snatched away. Now, he was pretending he'd never wanted the treat anyway.

Pitying him, Jenny touched his sleeve. 'I think we'd better go to your cabin,' she said.

'Right.' Mark searched his pockets. 'Here's the key,' he said. 'Go down the stairs here, an' it's third or fourth on your left. Got your own toothpaste, or do you want to borrow mine? It's in the blue holdall. Good night, then.'

'Mark, you must come too.'

'What?'

'You heard,' said Jenny. 'Come with me.'

'Straight up?' Mark stared at her.

'Yes. Straight up.' But now, Jenny could not look at him. 'Mark, there's just one thing — '

'What?'

'You said I was a tease. Now you'll think I'm an easy lay. But actually, I'm a virgin.' Jenny was almost whispering now. 'I'm not on the pill,' she continued. 'I don't have a diaphragm in my handbag. So, if we *do* go to bed together, I hope you have some means of ensuring we don't have an accident tonight?'

'What?' Mark gaped at her. 'Jenny, sweetheart, you mustn't think — what I mean is, don't you trust me?'

'Of course I don't trust you!' Now, Jenny glared at him. 'Good God, I may be innocent — but I'm not stupid! If you want to go to bed with me, you must first make sure there'll be no after-effects. You must get some — some things.'

'Must I? May I ask where from, at this time of the bleedin' night?'

'*I* don't know!' Jenny's cheeks flushed scarlet. 'Don't they have machines? In men's lavatories, don't they have dispensers, or something?'

'I suppose they do.' Mark shrugged. 'Yeah, come to think of it, I saw one in the bogs near the duty free shop.'

'Go and use it, then. I'll wait in the lounge.'

'Okay. But look, Jenny — are you sure?'

'I shan't move, I promise.'

'You know I don't mean that. Sweetheart, are you sure you want to do this? With me, tonight?'

'At this moment, I'm sure.' Jenny narrowed her eyes at him. 'But don't mess me about. I might change my mind.'

'Woman's privilege, that,' said Mark, grinning.

'Don't be funny. Go and do your shopping.'

★ ★ ★

They walked down the steps to the cabins. The sea was not rough, but a soft swell was keeping plenty of passengers in their private quarters. Now and then a steward came down the passage with a covered bucket in his hand. 'Do you feel seasick?' asked Mark, as he unlocked the cabin door.

'No, I'm fine. What about you?'

'Me?' He grinned. 'I don't get travel sickness. I'm never ill at all.' He stood aside to let Jenny enter. Then he locked the door behind them.

The double cabin, the top bunk of which was covered with a litter of Mark's personal belongings, carrier bags of duty free cigarettes, and some bulky parcels presumably full of contraband, was very cramped. 'God,' Jenny muttered, as she trod on his foot, 'how they expect two people to share this poky little pit, I can't imagine. I didn't hurt you, did I?'

'No.' Mark turned on the radio. No sound came out. 'Damn,' he muttered, shaking it. 'The bloody batteries are flat.'

'It's not that,' said Jenny. 'We're right in the middle of the ship. There's metal all around us. That's why it won't work.'

'What a little smartarse.' Mark threw his transistor on to the top bunk. 'So we do without music,' he said. Then he kissed her.

'Is this a perk of all your little trips?' asked Jenny, a few minutes later. Taking off her wet coat, she draped it over a rail. 'Is this the way things always end up?'

'What?' Mark pulled off his jumper. He began to undo the buttons on his shirt. 'Oh, I get it. You mean, when I goes robbin' old ladies, do I try an' screw their granddaughters, too?'

'Well . . . do you?'

'No, I bloody don't.' Mark sniffed. 'I told you before — I ain't a crook. I ain't a bleedin' tomcat, neither.' Naked to the waist now, he took Jenny by the shoulders. 'Look, sweetheart,' he murmured, 'that's enough backchat for one day. This is serious, right? So if you've changed your mind, and you want me to go, tell me now.'

'I don't want you to go.'

'That's good. Sit down, then.'

They sat on the bottom bunk. Mark kissed her again, then slid his hands beneath her bulky sweater. 'Take this off,' he whispered.

Jenny did so. But now, clad only in a thin cotton top, she shivered. Not with cold, but with dread.

'Chilly?' asked Mark, puzzled.

'N-no.' Jenny's teeth were actually chattering now. 'I'm f-fine.'

Mark stroked her shoulders. Then, his hands were

293

on her breasts. 'Don't you never wear a bra?' he asked.

'N-not very often,' Jenny replied. She shrugged. 'Doesn't that make things simpler for you?'

'I suppose so.' He laughed. 'Although I must admit, gettin' a bra off is reckoned to be one of the best bits.'

'Well, you should know.'

'I told you.' Serious now, Mark looked into Jenny's eyes. 'Please, sweetheart — no more lip, okay?'

'Okay.'

'Shall we go for it?'

'Yes.' Jenny stood up. 'Show me what to do.'

★   ★   ★

It wasn't until they were both naked that Jenny finally relaxed. For then, instead of feeling shy, embarrassed and foolish, for some reason she now felt warm, sexy and infinitely desirable. Now, she wanted Mark to look at her. She wanted him to touch her. To kiss her. Anywhere. Everywhere.

How could people do this in the dark? She couldn't understand it. All she wanted to do was gaze and gaze, and let her lover gaze at her. But then, suddenly, she felt a nudge of fear. 'Mark?' she whispered.

'Yes?'

'Hadn't you better, well, do something? You *did* get some of those things, didn't you?'

'What? Oh, yes. Of course I did.' Reaching across the cabin, Mark pulled his jacket off the top bunk.

He took something out of the pocket.

Turning away, he opened the little cardboard box, then shook out something wrapped in foil. He tore the envelope across and took out the object inside.

'Don't look.' Sensing her at his side, he elbowed her away. 'Shut your eyes for a moment.'

'Why?'

'Because I bleedin' told you to, that's why!' Managing at last to get himself properly organised, Mark turned back to her. 'Lie down,' he said. His voice was curt with panic. 'God's sake, Jen! Please — lie down!'

When Jenny hesitated, he pushed her on to her back. Cursing the safety rail which was in his way, he climbed awkwardly on top of her. Muttering and swearing under his breath, eventually he manoueuvred them both into what was approximately the right position.

★　★　★

Several minutes went by but the lovers lost all sense of time. Finally, with a satisfied sigh, Mark relaxed. He closed his eyes. 'Oh, Jenny,' he murmured holding her close. 'Jenny, sweetheart — I do love you!'

'I love you, too.' Jenny kissed him. 'I love you very much. Don't let me go.'

'I can't.' Mark laughed. 'I'll fall out of the bloody bunk if I do.'

For a few moments more they hugged each other. Then Mark cleared his throat. 'Jenny?' he began.

'What?'

'Did I hurt you just now?'

'Not really.'

'Oh.' Mark frowned. 'But I thought it was supposed to hurt the girl. Her first time, an' that.'

'Ah, well — I did a lot of riding when I was younger. That's supposed to help when you — you know.'

'Oh. Right.' Mark kissed her shoulder. 'I think you ought to marry me,' he said.

'Oh?' Jenny smiled up at him. 'Why's that, then?'

'You and your mouth.' Mark shook her. 'You just said you loved me!'

'I do.'

'Right.' Mark looked into her eyes. 'Listen,' he said. 'I was nervous just now. Scared I'd make a mess of things — know what I mean?'

'Yes, I know,' Jenny replied. 'It was your first time, too. Wasn't it?'

'Yeah. No. Well, sort of.' Embarrassed, Mark looked away. 'Put it like this — it was the first time it really mattered. So I was scared I'd make a mess of it.'

'You didn't, though. I loved what you did.'

'Maybe. But now I want to love you properly. I want to get it right, for both of us.'

'I see.'

'Good.' Reaching for a box of tissues, Mark took a handful. He cleaned himself up. 'Now,' he said, 'no bits of rubber this time. If I make you pregnant, it won't matter. We're gettin' married anyway.'

'Are we?'

'Yes.' He took her face between his hands. 'Don't argue with me. It's what you want, too.'

'It is?' Mesmerised, Jenny blinked at him.

'You *are* going to marry me?'

'Well, I expect so.' Considering, Jenny chewed her lower lip. 'If I get pregnant today, that'll be all right?'

'It'll be fantastic.'

'Maybe it will,' Jenny agreed. 'So what do you want? A boy or a girl?'

'Our kid, sweetheart. Your child and mine.'

★ ★ ★

'Don't sit up.' It was half an hour later. Sticky, sweating, bruised, but filled with a warm, incandescent glow which made her eyes shine, Jenny held Mark close. 'Darling, you mustn't sit up!'

'Why not?' He kissed her. 'Ain't I heavy?'

'Yes. But if you sit up, you'll bang your head. Just sort of roll on to the carpet, then you won't get hurt.'

'Oh. Right.' Mark did as he was told. Standing by the washbasin, he turned on the hot tap. 'Come over here,' he said. 'I'll wash you.'

Jenny got out of bed. Standing up, she stretched. She licked her lips. 'I can taste you and me,' she said. 'Don't wash it away.'

'God's sake, woman! Do as you're told!'

So she let him wash her. Soaping her, he made rivulets of foamy bubbles along her shoulders and down her back. Rinsing her with his flannel, he splashed water all over the floor. He reached for a towel.

'I'll do this,' she said. 'You wash yourself.'

'Okay.' Next to her in that horribly cramped

space, he looked at her reflection in the mirror. 'You've nice little mole on your shoulder,' he said. Darting towards her, he kissed it. 'Tastes of you.'

'Well, it would. Mark?'

'Yeah?'

'You know all that stuff you told me about your family? About your thieving brother, and your sister and her illegitimate babies? Was it all true?'

'Afraid so.' Pulling on his jeans, Mark shrugged. 'Yeah, your parents'll double-take when they see my lot at the wedding. Better keep 'em apart until the big day.'

'Oh, my relations aren't so perfect themselves.' Jenny began to dress. 'At any rate, my mother isn't. She has what you might call a past.'

'How do you mean?'

'I suppose I ought to tell you.'

'That's up to you. But if it's something I need to know?'

'It's something I'd like you to know.'

'Fire away, then.'

So Jenny explained all about Peter and Shirley. Then she told Mark how Delia was involved, both as Peter's mistress and Shirley's friend.

'*I* think the three of them ought to meet,' she said. 'Someone should arrange it, and that someone could be me. But the thing is, I don't want anyone to be embarrassed. I've thought and thought — I've racked my brains, in fact — but I still can't see how to go about it.'

'It's simple.' Mark grinned. 'They can all come to our wedding,' he said.

23

When Jenny walked into her office on Monday morning, she was told her boss wanted to see her straight away. 'Ah, Miss Hughes,' said Mr Altdorf, as she entered his inner sanctum. 'How nice to see you again! Do sit down. Did you enjoy your time in Germany?'

'Yes, thank you.' Jenny smiled. 'I learned a lot.'

'I'm sure you did.' Kurt Altdorf was searching through a pile of papers on his desk. 'Here it is,' he said, at last. 'My dear Jenny — I have to tell you that you won't be with us for much longer. Don't look so worried,' he added hastily, for now Jenny was staring at him in alarm. 'It's promotion!'

'Really?'

'Oh, yes.' Jenny's boss grinned at her. 'I don't know what we'll say you are,' he began. 'A liaison officer, perhaps? Anyway — you'll be a sort of go-between, for both the English and German branches of the firm. You won't be attached to any one department. Instead, you'll be a mixture of PR lady and something else for which I don't know the correct English words.'

'A troubleshooter?' asked Jenny, beginning to catch his drift.

'Yes, that's it. You'll be answerable to Mr Eisenstadt himself.' Mr Altdorf shrugged. 'So naturally, you will be at Southampton Row from now on. But you will be missed here. I'm quite sure of that.'

★ ★ ★

'Is it true, then?' Judy Lacey, one of Jenny's typists, came scuttling over. 'We've heard you're going to Head Office. Is that right?'

'It seems to be.' Sitting down at her desk, Jenny scanned the mountainous backlog of work with distaste. 'So how long have you known about it?'

'I didn't *know* anything. There's been a rumour, that's all.'

'I see.' Jenny picked up a big, fat folder. 'Well, Judy? I'm sure you've lots of work to do?'

Dora and Beryl glanced at each other. One shrugged, and the other sighed. They didn't like change, and they'd assumed Jenny would be their supervisor for the next ten years at least. But now they'd have to get used to somebody new.

Jenny's section saw her off in style, with a surprise party and a present. As she looked at the pretty silver chain, her eyes filled.

'We'll miss you,' said Dora, sniffing.

'Yes, we will,' Beryl agreed. 'You've been the best supervisor we ever had.'

The best supervisor they'd ever had burst into tears.

★ ★ ★

The following week, Jenny moved to Southampton Row. There, she discovered she was to have her own

300

secretary, and a couple of clerical assistants, too — her own little kingdom, in fact.

Her job was to let people know what was going on. Simply that. Bilingual staff circulars, formal and informal company newsletters, and general directives — all these now came under the aegis of one particular person, and once the Bremen and Cologne offices had the number of Jenny's telephone extension, her phone hardly ever stopped ringing.

Jenny had imagined her promotion would push her into daily contact with Peter Eisenstadt, but her fears proved to be unfounded. He was hardly ever there. Then, a few weeks after Jenny had started her new job, Paul Mayer arrived from Bremen. A tall, fair, middle-aged North German, he now took over from Peter Eisenstadt almost completely.

Paul Mayer soon decided that, in Jenny, he'd found his ideal second in command, general factotum and right hand honorary man. He took her on visits to factories, and sent her to deliver his mandates to managers and staff alike. 'But you make them understand so well,' he said, when Jenny tentatively suggested he ought perhaps to see more of people himself. He grinned at her. 'I think sometimes you ought to be in the diplomatic service. Yes?'

Jenny agreed. She thought she'd put in for a pay rise soon.

★   ★   ★

Anton in Cologne was as good as his word. Although he and Jehangir's brothers had to drive up to Newcastle to collect it, Mark got his contraband in through the back door, found buyers prepared to deal in hard cash, and made a huge profit on the deal.

When Jenny saw him again, his ego was swollen to twice its normal size. 'I'm gettin' a place of me own next week,' he went on, after he'd spent at least ten minutes bragging about how brilliantly he'd cheated the Excise. 'Yeah, things is definitely on the up. I gotta have me own base now.'

'So you can party all night, and seduce your women in the comfort of your own home?'

'So I can seduce one woman, certainly.' Mark grinned. 'One at a time with birds. That's my motto. Nobody gets confused, then.'

'I see.' Jenny laughed, too. 'I've got some leave coming up,' she told him. 'Since you're so rich, why don't we go and have a little holiday somewhere? I quite fancy a dirty weekend.'

'Weekend?' Mark frowned. 'Can't. Got the stall.'

'Of course. The stall.' Jenny grimaced. 'You can't possibly miss a week on the stall. My God, Mark! You must be the most mercenary person I've ever met. You never stop thinking about money.'

'I ain't hardly ever got any, that's why.'

'You've got some now.'

'Yeah, well. I needs to buy in more stock with that.'

On their way to visit Jehangir, Mark was leading Jenny through a maze of scruffy East London streets. 'Are you sure you know where you're going?'

she asked him now, for she was certain they'd passed that particular betting shop five minutes ago.

'Of course I'm sure,' replied Mark. He took Jenny's hand. 'It's up here now. Listen, I don't *always* think of money. These days, I mostly thinks of you.'

'I bet.'

'It's true!' Mark hugged her. 'Can we tell old Jan?' he asked, as they walked up the hospital steps.

'No. Not just yet.'

'Oh.' Mark's face fell. 'You've changed your mind, then?'

'No, of course I haven't. But you must let me have a little more time.'

'But I love you! I thought you loved me.' Theatrically, Mark sighed. 'What do you need time for?'

'I just do. Look — you say you want me to marry you. But I hardly know anything about you.'

'Don't be daft.'

'It's true. When's your birthday? How old are you? What's your middle name? Have you had chicken pox?'

'My birthday's June the seventeenth. I'll be twenty. My middle name's Stephen, after me Uncle Steve, who runs the bookie's down Edmonton High Street. I dunno about the chicken pox.' Mark glared at her. 'So now will you make up your bloody mind?'

'Soon, I promise you.' Standing on tiptoe, Jenny kissed him. 'Come on,' she added. 'Jan will think we've forgotten him.'

★ ★ ★

'What are you doing with your little self nowadays?' demanded Maggie Clifford. It was the first time in weeks that she and Jenny had met. 'Got a secret affair going, have you?'

'No.' Jenny still wasn't ready to discuss Mark with Maggie. 'I'm just very busy, that's all.'

'We know! You're spending your entire life running after Mr Mayer. Or that's what we hear.' Maggie tapped Jenny on the lapel. 'You're getting yourself talked about. Know what I'm saying?'

'Oh, come on.' Jenny laughed. 'Mr Mayer's old enough to be my father. He's fat and fifty — hardly love's young dream.'

'I don't know about that.'

'What do you mean?'

'Think about it. He's well-heeled. Well-preserved. He's got a nice big shiny BMW, and an expense account to match. An attractive older man — that's what I'd call him.' Complacently, Maggie finished her sandwich. 'Well, then. If you're not having it away with Herr Mayer, you'll be interested to know that Terry and Les are having a party soon. They need to get some good shit in — but when they've sorted that out, they'll be ready to go. So, are you coming?'

'Perhaps. Will it be at the usual place?'

'Yes. They've taken over that whole house now, so it'll be really wild.' Maggie grinned. 'I've asked Jess, and that weirdo she hangs out with. They'll bring some decent stuff.'

'I don't doubt it.'

304

'So you'll come?'

'I might.'

★   ★   ★

Holding hands, stopping every few hundred yards to kiss and hug, Mark and Jenny walked from the tube station to Mark's new flat. 'It's just a room, really,' he admitted. 'But it's okay. Much better than Rainbow Road, anyhow.'

'It sounds great.' Jenny kissed him. 'Have you got some food in?'

'Yup. So we'll 'ave a bit of tea together, eh?'

'Lovely.' Jenny hugged him. 'Shall I cook? You could lay the table. If you've got a table.'

'I could open the plonk, too.' Mark grinned. 'I hate cooking,' he confessed. 'But I reckon it's a woman's job, anyway.'

'Oh, you do, do you?'

'Yeah, I do.' Grabbing her, Mark kissed Jenny full on the mouth. 'Tell you what. You make my dinner, then I'll give you a good time.'

Mark's new home was in Kilburn, in a decaying Victorian house which smelled of curry, cats and mould. As Jenny climbed the endless steps to the top floor, she feared the worst.

But Mark's own little flat was a revelation, an oasis of order and beauty amid the dirt and squalor of NW6. White-painted walls and window sills, along with a couple of cheap Indian rugs, some mismatched but well-chosen bits and pieces of furniture, and rows of well-stocked bookshelves, gave it the air of an unnaturally tidy college bedsit.

'What do you think?' he asked, as Jenny gazed in amazement.

'It's really nice!' She beamed at him. 'You're far better organised than I am. There's not a thing out of place!'

'I don't like mess. Grew up in a mess. Hated it.' Mark took Jenny in his arms. 'I do love you,' he said. 'I think of you all the time. I wonder about the other blokes you meet, and I worry you might get fond of somebody else.'

'I shan't.'

'Promise?'

'I promise. Mark, I have to go on a business trip next week.'

'Oh?' Mark scowled. 'Where you off to this time?'

'South Wales. There's a new factory opening in some valley or other, and my boss is going to give it the once over.'

'So why you gotta go?'

'He needs an assistant.' Jenny laughed. 'A nurse-maid, I ought to say. Mark, you don't mind?'

'Yeah, I do.' Mark kissed her. 'Be away all week, will you?'

'Monday to Friday, certainly.'

'Right, I'll go and 'ave a rummage round the North East. Hull, Newcastle and places like that. Don't look so worried,' he added. 'I don't really mind you going gallivanting. Just so long as you always come back.'

★ ★ ★

Jenny knew Mark hoped she'd come back from Wales having decided to marry him, but she returned to London still unsure. All the same, she was looking forward to seeing him again.

Mark was extremely pleased to see *her*. He'd found plenty of bargains in Newcastle and was anxious to boast about how astute he'd been. In the corner of his room were several large, bulky parcels, which he said contained some good stuff. 'Have a nice time on your business trip?' he asked, after they'd rolled around in bed together and got to know each other once more.

'Not very.' Jenny rubbed her eyes. 'It was too much like hard work.'

'Get over to see your Mum and Dad?'

'You must be joking. I had to work Saturday, and half of Sunday too.'

'You poor little bleeder.' Mark got out of bed. He made her some tea, then brought a mugful over. 'So you never got the chance to tell them you're going to marry a barrow boy.'

'No.' Taking her tea, Jenny looked up at him. 'I was thinking — perhaps I should take you to meet them, but as a friend. Then, after a couple of weeks, I could tell them they're going to have a son-in-law.'

'So you *have* decided, then?'

'Yes. I've decided.' Jenny glanced at Mark's bedside clock. 'It's time I was going,' she said.

'Oh?' Mark looked at her hopefully. 'You could stay here, if you like.'

'No, I can't do that. Mrs Berners will worry about me.' Swinging her legs out of bed, Jenny reached for her clothes.

Mark found his shirt. 'Shall we go to Evesbridge on Friday?' he suggested.

'What about the stall?'

'Stuff the stall. So, what about it? Do I get to meet your Mum and Dad?'

Jenny smiled at him. 'Well, if you're willing to let the stall go for a day, we could have that dirty weekend.'

'That's a thought.' Mark grinned back. 'What do you fancy doing?'

'I'd like to go to the seaside. To a small, cosy hotel. We'll have breakfast in bed, go for long, romantic walks, and you can ask me to marry you. Properly, this time.'

'On my bended knees, eh?'

'Yes. Then we'll come back to London and tell all the world.'

'Right.' Mark grinned. 'Come on, then. It's late.'

'You don't have to see me to Mrs Berners' door, you know,' said Jenny, as they sat on the train together.

'Of course I do.' Mark hugged her. 'Can't have you wandering about London all on your own. Someone might steal you away. Here, I was thinkin' — it's about time I met some of your mates.'

'Yes, it is.' Jenny laid her head on his shoulder. 'One of them is having a party next week, so we'll go together. Mark, this girl who's having the party — '

'What about her?'

'She's a terrible flirt. She's bound to fancy you.'

'Oh yeah?' Mark grinned. 'What does she look like?'

'She's tall and thin, with long black hair. She's got

fantastic legs and big boobs, and she thinks she's it.'

'Pretty, is she?'

'Yes, very.'

'I reckon I might fancy her back, then.' Mark laughed. 'Yeah, I think I just might.'

'What?'

'Only joking.' Mark stroked Jenny's hair. 'Oh, sweetheart — don't look like that! This girl, she could be Marilyn Monroe herself, an' I wouldn't care. I don't want anyone but you.'

★ ★ ★

They chose a little seaside resort in Dorset for their romantic weekend. 'It's perfect,' breathed Jenny, as she gazed at the view from their hotel window. 'It's absolutely perfect. Mark, did you say we were Mr and Mrs Strafford?'

'Yes, I did.' Mark shrugged. 'We are. More or less.'

They walked on the beach, the wind tugging at their hair. They ran across the sand and shingle, threw pebbles out to sea, and chased each other along the shore line. Then, exhausted, they fell laughing against the sea wall.

When he'd got his breath back, Mark picked Jenny up and swung her round and round. He loved the way she fitted against him, loved the way she smiled at him, and when he kissed her it was because he couldn't help it.

He put her down again. 'Look,' she said now, 'look at the village. How the street curves down to meet the sea. Isn't it lovely?'

'Is it?' Mark kissed her again. Then, glancing briefly at the pretty Dorset village behind him, he shrugged. 'It's okay,' he said.

'It's beautiful!'

'Do you think so?' Turning round, Mark studied the rows of pastel-washed cottages with a critical eye. Squat, square, stone-built, and all painted either pink or white or palest blue, they looked as if they'd grown right out of the landscape.

His gaze followed the road to some lightly-wooded hills, which rose behind the little town, enfolding it in a bower of green. 'It's too pretty-pretty,' he said. 'But then, I'm a Londoner. So of course I prefers buses and bricks.'

'Noise and dirt, too. But Mark, I thought you liked beautiful things?'

'I do. But this isn't beautiful. It's too chocolate-boxy. It's birthday card stuff.'

'Maybe.' Jenny smiled at him. 'Well, *I* think this place is lovely.'

'It is today.'

'Why today?'

'You're here.' Mark kissed her nose. 'The inside of Battersea Power Station itself would be lovely, if you were there.'

★ ★ ★

'You don't reckon you're pregnant, then?' asked Mark, as they lay in bed that evening, entangled in a lover's embrace.

'No, I'm sure I'm not.' Unbeknown to Mark, Jenny had now got herself fixed up with effective

310

contraception. She kissed him. 'Just as well, really.'

'Why do you say that?'

'Well, I don't think the firm would be very keen on having an unmarried mother walking around. It would make the place untidy.'

'You'll be married soon.' Mark kissed Jenny's shoulder, then stroked one breast. 'You know something?'

'What?'

'I've been thinking about you and that job of yours. I reckon you ought to give it up. Pack it in.'

'Oh, yes? What would I live on, then?'

'I'd see you right.' Now, Mark propped himself up on one elbow. 'I don't think married women ought to have jobs. Not really. Women with kids should definitely stay at home.' Looking at Jenny, he grinned. 'But if *you* wanted something to do, you might give me a hand. I could use a bit of help.'

Jenny laughed. 'So what would I do, exactly? Stand at your stall all day long, flogging tat to foreign tourists? Thanks, but no thanks.'

'I wasn't even thinkin' of the stall.' Mark grew serious now. 'In fact, I'm gonna give that up. Be a full time dealer. Get a proper business going, all legit.'

'So I could be an extra pair of hands?'

'Yeah, if you like. Look, I could do with somebody to come in with me. When I buy a big load, from a shop or house clearance, say, I always need a hand sorting the good stuff from the crap.

'Then there's the buyin'. You could maybe do some of that. I could teach you a lot about china and things. I really know what's what there.'

'So it would be a life on the open road, eh? In your van?'

'There'd be some of that. Yeah, some variety, like.'

'God.' Jenny tried to imagine herself as a glorified rag and bone merchant. She failed. 'Well, thanks for the offer,' she said. 'But I think I'll stay with Eisenstadt, if it's all the same to you.'

'It isn't, though.' Mark sat up. 'I want us to get married, right? I want to get settled down, have kids, get a proper home together. I got this plan — '

'Oh, I *see*. This plan is, I leave my job to help you heave old furniture about. Then, when I'm eight months pregnant, I go and live in some grotty little flat in the East End, while you wheel and deal all over the country. Is that it?'

'Yeah, sort of. Well, no. Not exactly. I'd get you a decent place. Look, I've got these deals on at the moment. If they go all right — '

'But what if they don't?'

'They *will!*' Mark scowled at her. 'Have a bit of faith in me, eh?'

'I do have faith in you. But honestly, this is daft. You live from hand to mouth as it is. I've got a decent job with good prospects. It would be crazy to give it up now.'

'You don't want to work for those Jerries all your life. Look, you don't know nothing about antiques, but you could still be very useful to me. You know about book-keeping, for a start. You could do all my paperwork. I could pay you a bit — '

'Eisenstadt pays me more than you ever could.'

'At the moment, maybe.' Reaching for his packet of cigarettes, Mark took one out. He lit it. 'All right,' he said, 'let's look at it your way. So you go on working for Eisenstadt. When the babies come, what then?'

'Oh, I'll have a nanny.' Airily, Jenny waved the problem away. 'A nanny or an au-pair. Anyway, I haven't decided if I really want children. Perhaps I'll find I don't.'

'Don't want children?'

'Maybe not.' Jenny shrugged. 'I haven't really thought about it.'

'Oh. But when we were on the boat together, you told me — '

'That was in the heat of passion.' Jenny laughed. 'I'd have said anything then.'

'Would you?' Mark got out of bed. He walked into the bathroom, and Jenny heard him cleaning his teeth. When he came back into the bedroom, he put on his jeans and sat down on the bed. 'I want children,' he said, firmly. 'Any woman I marry must be willing to have kids.'

'Oh? What if she can't?'

'Then I'd find out about adoption. But my wife must be a mother too.'

'Do you really mean that?' Jenny stared at him. 'Mark, my dearest, what if she doesn't want — '

'I'm telling you what I want!' He banged his fist down on the eiderdown, making the dust fly. 'I want a home!' he cried. 'I want a family! I want a wife who's where she should be, someone I can come home to in the evenings. What I don't want is somebody like my Mum, who's either in the pub or down the bingo — or at any rate, never bleeding there! Do you understand me, Jen? I want a proper home, with a wife and children in it!'

'Do you, indeed?' Derisively, Jenny sniffed. 'You want your dinner in the oven, slippers warming by the fire, children playing — and joyful cries of 'Daddy, Daddy' whenever you come home?'

'Yes.' Relieved that she understood, he smiled at her. 'Yeah, you got it exactly.'

'Oh.' Jenny scowled at him. 'Then I don't think I want to marry you, after all.'

'What? But, Jenny — '

'Let me get this straight,' said Jenny. 'You want me to marry you. Give up my job and work for you. Have your children, and look after your home.' Jenny looked at him. 'Is that the deal?'

'Yes, that's it,' Mark replied.

'Well, I don't think I'm hearing this.' Jenny sat up now. 'Mark, think about what you're offering me. A stake in a vaguely criminal enterprise. The chance of a basement flat in some deadbeat area of London. Half a dozen screaming brats — '

'Don't put it like that.'

'*Is* that what you're offering me?'

'I'll be a success one day. I tell you, Jen, I will! As I go up in the world, you'll go with me. I'm nothing at the moment, I admit. But if you help me now — '

'By darning your socks and having your kids. No thanks, Mark. That's not — '

'All right, all right, forget it.' Reaching for an armful of clothes, Mark jumped off the bed. He stalked into the bathroom, slamming the door behind him. Coming out again, he grabbed his coat, marched out of the bedroom and went down the stairs. Jenny heard him let the hotel's front door bang behind him.

He returned at two the following morning, slid into bed and turned his back on her.

At breakfast he would not speak to her, and they drove back to London in silence. 'Shall I see you tomorrow?' she asked, as he drew up outside Mrs Berners' front door.

'I'll phone.' Mark would not look at her. 'When I want to talk to you, I'll ring.'

'We'll sort something out.' Jenny touched his hand. 'Look, love — aren't you making a bit of a drama out of all this?'

'I don't think so.' Now, he turned to look at her. 'Are you still determined to stay at Eisenstadt?' he asked.

'Yes, certainly. For the time being.'

'When you marry, it'll be up to you whether or not you have kids?'

'Yes, but — '

'So basically, you'll do as you like? If I want something an' you want something different, we'll have to negotiate a deal?'

'Yes.'

'Then find a man who'll put up with that!' Mark glared at her. 'Go on! Find yourself some spineless little berk who'll let his wife have all her own way, and make him a joke to his mates!'

'Because it won't be you?'

'Right. Because it won't be me.'

'I see.' Jenny folded her arms. 'Well, I hadn't exactly planned to marry into the criminal classes, anyway.'

'I hadn't exactly planned to marry a bastard German.'

'How dare you!' Jenny jerked open the door of the van. 'You're a yob,' she spat. 'You're nothing but an ignorant, bigoted yob, and I hate you!'

Mark merely shrugged. So, grabbing her bag, Jenny jumped out of the van, then slammed the passenger door with such violence that a wing mirror fell off. 'Stuff you too, you grotty little rust heap,' she muttered, as she strode briskly away.

24

Delia was experiencing a mid-life crisis. At any rate, that was what she supposed it must be, for she certainly had no other reason to feel so insecure, so empty and so ill at ease with herself and life in general.

She ought really to be very happy. Peter had been away from England for almost the whole of that previous year, but now he was back in London for at least three months. Or at least, he said he was. Delia had walked into the flat in St John's Wood one evening to find him apparently settled in for a good, long stay. The unnatural tidiness which characterised his frequent absences had been replaced by a mess of books, papers, minutes of meetings and foreign magazines, which now littered every flat surface.

'Darling!' she'd cried, surprised but delighted to see him, for she had only come in to check over the flat, and he hadn't rung to say he was coming home.

'Hello.' He hadn't even looked up. Instead, he'd continued to stare at the chess board in front of him, on which there were seven remaining pieces. 'There must be some way out,' he muttered. 'I can't let Andreas get away with this.'

'When are you seeing him?' asked Delia.

'Tuesday,' replied Peter, his eyes still on the board.

'Oh. Well, now — shall we have a drink?'

'Gin and tonic, please. Ah, that's it.' Peter moved a bishop. 'Now if I let him take this rook — '

'Oh, for God's sake!' Delia wanted to hit him. 'Peter, I haven't seen you for five weeks! But all you can think of is your bloody bishop!'

'What?' Startled, Peter glanced up. 'I'm sorry, darling. I missed that. Did you say something important?'

'Oh, no. Of course I didn't.'

Delia went into the kitchen, and sulked. She hated Andreas Hartmann, an Austrian merchant banker and chess fanatic, who was currently based in London. These days, in fact, she hated all Peter's friends. Or rather, she hated the fact that he had interests and affections which were nothing to do with her.

She really must make her own life, she told herself sternly, as she stared out of the window down to the courtyard below, and watched the fountain play. The next time John Harrison, the dishy new sports editor at *World Wide*, suggested a game of squash, she would take him up on it. She'd go for a drink with him afterwards, too.

But now, Peter came into the kitchen. 'I'm sorry,' he said. 'Don't be angry with me.'

'Don't take me for granted, then.'

'I shall never do that.' Peter wrapped his arms around Delia's waist. 'I'm getting old and foolish,' he whispered, into her hair. 'You should pity me.'

'Manipulator.' Delia was not appeased. 'There aren't any lemons, you know. Nor bottles of tonic. You'll have to have your gin neat.'

Jenny did not hear from Mark for a week. Then it was two weeks. At first, she thought it would be better to let him have his sulk. But, by the time three weeks had crawled slowly by, she found she could bear it no longer. She telephoned a pub in Walthamstow, where she knew Mark and some of his mates regularly met to do deals. The barman promised faithfully to pass on her message, asking Mark to call.

Staring out of the window, she watched the traffic crawl along Southampton Row. She could easily write to him! She reached for some paper. But then her pride got the better of her. 'Let him stew a bit longer,' she thought. 'Let him simmer in his own bad temper.'

But then, when she still did not hear from him, when he did not even telephone, she realised she had to forget him. 'Let him go to hell,' she thought. 'Let him rot!'

Picturing to herself what life with Mark would actually have been like, now she imagined herself with two toddlers grizzling round her knees, and another baby on the way. She could see Mark and his numerous cronies permanently ensconced in her home. Doing their dubious deals, downing pints, they'd demand endless sandwiches and meals, and expect her to provide them. Mark didn't want a wife. He wanted a slave.

So did Paul Mayer. But, generous enough to appreciate that Jenny had helped him through a difficult patch, he now decided to do something for her. He recommended her for a temporary but reviewable posting to Germany, and six weeks later she was offered a well paid, interesting job in Sales at the Bremen office, with a company car and a fat package of extremely lucrative incentives thrown in.

She turned the offer down. So he secured her a pay rise. Then, over elevenses one morning, he told Jenny something about his time as a coffee buyer in the field, which was a job he had loved, for it had taken him all over the world.

Did Jenny see herself as a buyer? Mayer asked. There weren't many women in that area, but the opportunities were there, and Eisenstadt was a progressive company. Would Jenny like to spend a few months in South America or Kenya as a buyer's assistant, and see how she got on?

Jenny said she would think about it.

'You do that.' Paul Mayer smiled his encouragement. 'I think perhaps a break from office routine might be exactly what you need just now.'

'Is my work not satisfactory, then?'

'Your work is fine. But I feel you might benefit from a change. Call it career development, if you like.'

Later that day, Jenny's boss went to check out her personal file. Glancing at her leave chart, he decided it was high time she took some holiday. She looked so tired and drawn these days — quite obviously, she'd been overdoing things.

'You need a break, I think,' he told her, as he handed back the draft of a staff directive she had just prepared in both English and German, for general circulation. 'Take a week off. There's nothing much happening at present, so you can well be spared.'

'I intend to rough out that history of the company next week.' Wishing he'd stop being so kind and concerned, Jenny blinked back the tears which still threatened to flow, at any time. 'You must remember,' she muttered. 'Mr Eisenstadt commissioned it himself. He wants a five thousand word booklet. With lots of charts, diagrams and photographs. To explain how the company came into being and operates now. To be — '

'Sent out to universities, colleges, careers offices and so on,' interrupted Paul Mayer. 'Yes, yes. I know all about that.'

'Well, I've a photographer coming to see me on Tuesday. A girl who's doing some of the artwork is bringing her stuff in on Wednesday afternoon. Then I need to talk to the printers.'

'I can deal with that.' Mr Mayer folded his arms, a gesture which always meant he intended to have his own way. 'Have a week's holiday. That's an order.'

So Jenny spent three days idling about London, walking around the places where she and Mark had been together, and trying not to cry.

Then she went home, to Evesbridge. It would be for the last time, for Gareth had recently been offered a better job, in the offices of a Worcester hospital. So he and Shirley were moving out to a new bungalow, in the suburbs of the cathedral city.

Jenny helped them with the last of their packing, then climbed up into the loft and cleared that out, too. Strenuous physical labour exhausted her body, and for the first time in weeks she managed to get a few good nights' sleep.

But the days were still awful. Still the tears lurked behind her eyes, ever ready to flow. 'Oh, Jenny love! Don't cry!' Coming upon her daughter sobbing over a collection of teddies, dolls and soft toys, all bagged up for the move, Shirley sat down on Jenny's bed.

'I know how you feel,' she soothed, patting Jenny's shoulder. 'This house is part of you, isn't it?'

Jenny gulped, and nodded. There was no need to explain about Mark. It would only make her mother sad.

★　★　★

'Oh, come on!' Sitting in a crowded coffee shop on a dull Saturday morning, Maggie Clifford touched Jenny's sleeve. 'Don't give me all that garbage about being too busy to go out, I know it's not that. Jenny, you can tell me. I'm your mate!'

'What do you want me to tell you?'

'What's upsetting you? You look so bloody miserable lately. There must be something wrong.'

'There isn't.' Jenny manufactured a yawn. 'Mr Mayer's wearing me out, that's all.'

'Oh, I see!' Maggie grinned. 'That's the way the land lies, is it? Well, well, well!'

'What do you mean, well, well, well?'

'I mean, Miss Innocence, that the rumours which are flying all around the Acton office — and, I might add, sticking like chewing gum to cinema seats — are evidently not without some foundation in fact. Your secret is out. You're having a passionate affair with a married man. You're spending nights and days in Mr Eisenstadt's cosy little office, rolling around on the nice thick Persian carpets there.'

'I'm doing nothing of the sort!' Angry now, Jenny glared. 'God, Maggie! I've never even — '

'Well, come to Sheila's party then.'

'I don't want to come to Sheila's rotten party.'

'It'll be good.' Invitingly, Maggie leered, 'I'm getting in some seriously dishy men, and that's just what the doctor ordered. You need to be fixed up with a dishy man.'

'No, I don't.'

'Yes, you *do*! Now, listen to Auntie Maggie. You've got the hots for someone, haven't you? Someone who's not interested.'

'Have I? How can you tell?'

'It's obvious.' Maggie shrugged. 'You're thin and pale and listless. You're working all hours — you have to, because you're miserable when you're away from the office. You're pining away for that fat blond Hun.'

'You do talk nonsense!'

'Do I?' Maggie looked wise. 'A classic case of virgin's itch, that's what you've got. You need a nice man to sort you out. How old are you now? Old enough to know better, anyway. More than old enough to mope around the place mooning after Herr Mayer.'

'I am not mooning after Mr Mayer!'

'No? Well then, you want to get stuck into the twentieth century. Live a little! Take the padlock off your knickers — that'll be a start.'

'You're revolting.'

'I'll pick you up about eight. Be ready.'

Jenny sighed. 'Okay.'

* * *

Sheila Gregory was the wife of a history don at Queen Alexandra College, and had met Maggie Clifford when she was an undergraduate. After Maggie had been sent down, she and Sheila had remained good friends.

Sheila was famous for her parties, at which the in crowd smoked pot, snorted cocaine, and tripped on acid. Sometimes, rumour had it, they also got busted by the police — which always added to the fun.

Arriving rather late — for when Maggie called for her, Jenny had still been in her slip, muttering she had nothing suitable to wear — the two girls walked into a crowded, smoke-filled drawing room, in which people were dragging on joints, gulping down drinks and talking at the tops of their voices.

Soon, Maggie sloped off with some man. Jenny looked round the room, saw there was no one there she knew or wanted to know, and decided to leave. But, as she turned to go, her hostess came flapping over and cornered her.

'Maggie's little friend, isn't it?' Tipsily, Sheila Gregory beamed. 'Super to meet you at last. Now, to whom can I introduce you? Ah, yes. I know.'

She grabbed a man who had just walked in. 'This is Robin Langley,' she announced. 'He's a research student at Alex's. He's frightfully clever — aren't you, my lamb?'

'Am I?'

'Of course you are! Modest, too.' Grotesque in a tent dress made of black muslin, purple cheesecloth and assorted bits of rusty lace, Sheila Gregory grinned in Jenny's general direction. She gave Robin a pat on the bottom. 'Robin's doing some ghastly research into mediaeval English texts,' she went on. 'I really can't think why. Perhaps he'll tell you.' She drifted away.

'Stupid old bitch.' Or that was what Jenny thought Robin Langley said. But now, catching her eye, he smiled at her. 'Hello,' he said, pleasantly. 'Am I supposed to know you?'

'I don't think so.' Uncomfortably aware of his critical scrutiny, Jenny blushed. 'I'm one of Maggie Clifford's friends.'

'I see. Have you a name?'

'Jenny. Jenny Hughes.'

'Jenny. That's rather sweet. It suits you.' Again, Robin smiled.

Tall, dark and twenty or thereabouts, Jenny saw he was rather attractive. Brown eyes were set wide in an open, humorous face, black hair grew back from a high, intelligent forehead, and now she noticed how regular and white his teeth were. Altogether, he was what Maggie would call a dishy man.

'Well, what are you drinking?' he asked now. 'That disgusting punch? Shall I get you a refill?'

'No, I don't think so.'

'You're very wise.' Robin drained his own glass. 'There's some real wine somewhere,' he said. 'It's in the kitchen, I expect. Let's go and see if we can find it.'

So they went into the kitchen and there, as Robin had predicted, they discovered a crate of claret. 'Is this stuff intended for the party?' asked Jenny, as Robin opened a bottle. 'It was tucked away behind all those coats, so perhaps — '

'It's Hal Gregory's secret supply. But he won't mind us having some. He likes me.' Robin poured himself some wine. Now he made a great performance of examining it, sniffing it, then tasting it. Rolling it all around his mouth, he chewed at it, grimacing hard — and then, finally, he swallowed it.

'So what's the verdict?' asked Jenny, laughing.

'It needs time to breathe. But it's not bad, and you can't have everything.' Robin poured some into Jenny's glass. 'What do you think?' he asked.

Jenny tried it. 'It's very nice,' she said. 'A bit cold, though.'

'Warm it between your hands.' Robin downed his own glassful. 'Well, cold or not — it's a vast improvement on that meths they're serving in the *salon*.'

'Yes, I agree.' Cheeks flushed by the wine, Jenny smiled at him. 'I could definitely get used to this.'

So Jenny and Robin sat together on the draining board, drinking Hal Gregory's expensive wine. 'Did Sheila say you were at Alex's?' Jenny asked.

'Yes.' Robin poured himself another glassful of claret. 'Did she say you were the famous Maggie Clifford's friend?'

'Yes. Do you know Maggie, too?'

'That lady's praise is writ on flying banners, which carry all before her.' Robin's dark eyes sparkled. 'If I remember rightly, she lasted a whole term at QAC. I met her at a party there, I think. I still exchange the time of day with her. But I haven't ever had my leg over, as they say.'

'That's a disgusting expression.'

'Sorry.' Robin shrugged. 'I didn't mean to offend you.'

'You didn't offend me. But you don't have to talk about Maggie like that.'

'I've said I'm sorry.' But now, Robin grinned. 'I like Maggie a lot,' he said. 'She's a great girl. But she does have a somewhat tarnished reputation.'

Jenny decided to change the subject. 'Are you doing a doctorate?' she asked.

'Yes. But don't ask me what it's about. You wouldn't listen if I told you.'

'No,' Jenny agreed. 'I'm not very interested in the Middle Ages.'

'Neither am I. I'm an eighteenth century man.'

'But I thought Mrs Gregory said — '

'Mrs Gregory? Oh, you mean old Sheila. She's always getting the wrong end of the stick. I never bother to correct her.'

Robin poured the last of the wine into Jenny's glass. 'This isn't much of a party, is it?' he demanded. 'There's nothing to eat. Only poison to drink. I suppose those noisy buggers in the drawing room are all getting high. But I don't go in for any of that.'

'Nor do I.'

'Don't you?' Robin slid off the draining board. 'Shall we clear off, then? We could go and have something to eat, perhaps. Make ourselves scarce, before the fuzz arrives.'

'That's the most brilliant idea!' With half a bottle of Haut Médoc gurgling around inside her, Jenny felt more cheerful than she had for a a very long time. Now, she let Robin jump her down. 'I'll get my coat,' she said.

They walked out into the cool night air. A short tube ride took them to a little Greek restaurant, which Robin recommended.

Although the place was crowded and busy, a fat, sweating waiter bustled up immediately, flicking the checked table-cloths en route. Beaming extravagantly, he ushered them to a tiny corner table, then produced two huge, greasy menus.

Robin waved them away. 'Today's special, please,' he said. 'Twice.'

'But what will it be?' whispered Jenny.

'Minced donkey, I expect.' Seeing her look of horror, Robin grinned. 'Don't worry. You'll love it.'

★　★　★

'I've never had Greek food before.' Finishing her kebab and salad, Jenny licked her fingers. 'But I really enjoyed that.'

'Good. So did I.' Robin smiled at her. 'Would you like coffee now? Or something stronger?'

'Such as?'

'Brandy? Retsina?'

'What's Retsina?'

'Wine, with pine resin. You'd enjoy that, too.'

'I'll try some. But if I don't like it, you can have mine.'

'Okay.'

So they ordered retsina. As he cleared the table, the waiter presented Jenny with a red carnation, taken from the vase on the little bar. 'He fancies you,' whispered Robin, laughing as she blushed.

'Rubbish.' The wine making her light-headed, Jenny laughed too. 'He just wants a big tip.'

'No, honestly. He thinks you're a bit of all right.'

'Go on. Why should he?'

'Because you're so pretty, of course. Because you're incredibly sexy. Because you have eyes the colour of a summer sky, and the best legs this side of Hammersmith Broadway.' Taking Jenny's hands, Robin held them in his. 'What shall we do now?'

'I ought to go home.'

'Please don't.' Leaning across the narrow table, Robin kissed her on the lips. 'Come back with me, instead.'

'Where to?'

'To the house, or rather the slum, which I share with two other slobs. They're both away this weekend.'

Jenny shook her head. 'I don't think so,' she said.

'Please.' Robin's dark eyes glittered. 'I'll show you my Tibetan wall hangings.'

'Which you wouldn't show to just anybody, I'm sure.'

'No, indeed.'

Jenny looked at him. Tonight, it was true, too much alcohol had seriously warped her powers of judgement. But, even stone cold sober, she'd have been attracted to Robin.

Broad shouldered, he was nevertheless slim and athletic. In a blue cotton shirt and denim jeans, he looked cool and sexy. He radiated all the self confidence of a man who knows he's attractive — and that was an attraction in itself.

So now, she was seriously tempted. Missing Mark, she was also missing all the things he'd taught her to need. She glanced down at Robin's hands, which still held hers. Long fingered, well shaped, their nails were clean and neatly trimmed.

Mark had had nice hands, too. Hands very like these.

She looked up, to meet Robin's eyes. 'Let's go,' she said.

25

Peter Eisenstadt finished reading the draft of the company's annual report, and closed the folder. Glancing at his watch, he saw it was very late. Now, should he make a pot of strong coffee and go over the figures in more detail, or should he go to bed? Perhaps not. He wouldn't sleep, if he did.

That afternoon, he'd arrived back from a trip to Germany. He had seen his family and even squashed in a visit to Reni. But that had been a complete waste of time. She'd had no idea who he was. Preoccupied by the loss of some special yellow embroidery thread, she had had him searching through her workbox and looking all round the day room, before finally sending him off to borrow some more, from another creative needlewoman immured in the secure wing.

His sisters had been nagging yet again. The elder was already trying to persuade him to come back for Christmas this year. 'I hate to think of you all alone in London,' she had said. 'Dear Peter, promise me you'll come.'

As he made himself some coffee, Peter wondered what his sisters would say if he *did* go to Cologne that Christmas. If he took Delia with him, and made it clear she'd be sharing his bed.

His elder sister would probably be horrified. Adultery, under her roof! *Du lieber Gott!* His younger sister, on the other hand, might not object at all. But the whole family would stare and comment, the children would be as fascinated as the adults were astonished or shocked, and he couldn't subject Delia to all that.

She was in Amsterdam at present, but she'd be back tomorrow. He'd meet her at the airport, he decided. He was longing to see her again.

★   ★   ★

He arrived at the airport just in time to hear her flight arrival announced. Ten minutes later he spotted Delia herself, coming across the concourse. Ten seconds later, she was in his arms.

'Peter?' Surprised to see him, for a long moment Delia simply stared — but then she smiled. 'Hello, sweetheart,' she said. She hugged him. 'So how are you?'

'In very bad shape.' Melodramatically, Peter sighed. 'God, I've missed you!'

'I've missed you, too.' Delia kissed him. 'I must say, I'm very flattered that you've skived off work, just to fetch me.'

'What is this . . . skived?'

'You're playing truant.'

'Ah.' Peter grinned. 'But I'm the boss. I do as I please.'

Back at the flat, Peter took Delia's coat, drew her chair up to the fire, then fixed her a drink. 'Would you like a sandwich?' he asked.

'No, thanks. I had some on the plane.'

'Right.' Peter sat down on the arm of her chair. 'How was Holland?' he asked.

'Flat. How are all the Eisenstadts?'

'Fine.'

'Good.' Delia screwed her courage to the sticking point. 'What about Reni?' she enquired.

'She's no better.' Peter sighed. 'I went to the nursing home. It was a lovely day, so I asked if I could take her out for a drive. The doctor said no, it might frighten her. So I just sat with her for a while.'

'Did she know who you were?'

'No. I suspect she thought I was the occupational therapist. Or a new doctor. She told me she was being treated for depression. She didn't like her new drugs at all, she said. They were making her confused.'

'Why did she think you were a doctor?'

'God knows. But the doctors don't wear white coats any more. It's a new policy, you see. It's supposed to make the patients feel less institution-alised. I think it just confuses them.

'I was speaking to one of the nuns about it, and she agreed with me. But, she said, some of the poor souls are so confused anyway that perhaps it makes no difference in the end. The nuns are very kind.'

Peter put his glass down on the coffee table. 'That's enough about Reni,' he said. 'Let's talk about you.'

'There's nothing much to say. Except that I've had an offer.'

'That sounds exciting.'

'It is!' Delia grinned. 'I sat next to David Lascelles on the plane. He's the proprietor of the revamped *News Digest* magazine. He asked how things were going on *World Wide*. Then he asked me if I'd like to be an editor one day. One day soon, that is.'

'Did he indeed? So?'

'Well, I shan't leave *World Wide*. But I can maybe use David's interest as some sort of leverage. On the other hand, if I were an editor — '

'Decisions, decisions.' Peter kissed her. 'I've missed you.'

'You told me.'

'Come to bed.'

'Don't you want some lunch? You ought to eat.'

'There's only cheese, or eggs. I'll eat later. When you're hungry again.'

★　★　★

'I've met a man.' Black hair wild, dress more eccentric than ever, Maggie Clifford looked totally manic. 'Did you hear me, Jen?' she demanded. 'I said I've met a man!'

'You're always meeting men.' Visiting the Acton office, Jenny had stopped by Maggie's desk. Now she affected an exaggerated yawn. 'What's so special about this one, then?'

'He's lovely.' Flopping into her chair, Maggie sighed. 'I'm going to marry him. We'll have a great big house in the country, cats and dogs and hamsters, lots and lots of babies — '

'Good grief.' Jenny stared. 'Whatever have you been taking?'

'Nothing. I'm just high on happiness. That's all.'

'I see. In other words, this is your actual, genuine madness.'

'Oh, don't be like that.' Maggie grinned. 'By the

way, have you moved yet?'

'Yes. Last Saturday.'

'Why didn't you ring me? I'd have helped.'

'I had plenty of help,' said Jenny. 'Robin and a friend of his — Simon somebody, a big strong bloke — they borrowed a van. Then I got Jess to round up a few students.'

'What's it like, your new place?'

'It's okay. Expensive, but convenient. You'll have to come over to dinner some time.' Jenny flicked open her diary. 'What about next Tuesday?'

'Great.' Maggie beamed. 'What about my new man? Can I bring him, too?'

'Yes, of course you can,' replied Jenny, warmly. 'I'd like to meet him. So come on — spill the beans. What does he look like? What is he called?'

'His name's Chris Allingham. He's short, dark, and Welsh. Well, half Welsh. He's a biochemist, at Imperial.'

'Did you meet him at Sheila's party?'

'Yes. He arrived just after you sloped off with your new conquest. Now, what else can I say?'

'Is he nice?'

'Oh, yes. Very nice. A perfect gentleman.' Maggie thought for a moment. 'He doesn't look like one, though. He's built like a stevedore. Or one of the Pontypool front row. He's got hands like bunches of bananas. His manual dexterity, however, is second to none. He can bring a girl to — '

'Yes, okay.' Jenny laughed. 'Keep the details of your sex life to yourself.'

'Be like that.' Maggie shrugged. 'How's Bobbin?'

'Robin's very well.'

'*He's* very experienced, too.' Maggie grinned. 'Clever, good-looking. Just the sort of guy you need, in fact.'

'Yes, I'm sure.' Jenny blushed. 'I must go now, Maggie. I have a lot of work to do.'

★   ★   ★

Finding she was spending a fortune on tube fares into central London, Jenny had given up her digs in Acton and moved into a small rented flat off Holborn. Too expensive, too small, it was, however, very convenient for work and Jenny had plans to paint and decorate, to make it really hers.

Robin promised to help, in fact he'd been lavish with suggestions for improvements — but so far he hadn't actually done anything.

Maggie and her new man came to dinner. Introductions were made. Robin kissed Maggie full on the mouth, but Chris appeared not to notice. So Robin gave her bottom a squeeze, and Chris couldn't avoid hearing her squeal.

Soon, it was obvious to Jenny that Robin thought Chris a bore. It was equally clear that Chris didn't think much of Robin's brilliant conversation, or his psychedelic tie. But Maggie, still high as a kite and chattering like a starling, appeared not to notice the tension at all, so Jenny told herself she was imagining things.

Jenny had cooked a safe, easy casserole and the meal itself was a success. Prompted by Maggie, Chris washed up. He made a good job of it, scouring the pans to shining perfection, getting all the brown marks off the casserole dish, and washing every last trace of lipstick from the glasses and cups.

'He has a lot of practice,' explained Maggie, as she watched him. 'Scrubbing out test-tubes, and all that.'

'Come on, slacker. Do your bit.' Chris tossed her a dry tea-towel. 'Jenny,' he went on, 'that was a splendid dinner. Perhaps you could lend Maggie here some of your recipes.'

'I can read *Honey* magazine too, you know.' Maggie flicked him with her tea-towel. 'Look, I'm learning.'

'Got a long way to go though, haven't you?' Chris grinned. 'Omelettes we had last night, Jenny. Chamois leather's more tasty. Easier on the jaws, too.'

'Pig.' Maggie hit him. 'Just you wait.'

★   ★   ★

'She tells me they're getting married,' said Jenny, who was emptying ash-trays and plumping up cushions before going to bed. She sat down beside her lover. 'I thought he was rather nice, actually.'

'Did you?' Robin reached for his cigarettes. 'I thought he was rather boring. A typical physicist, or whatever he is. But I saw you eyeing him up. Did you fancy him?'

'Chris?' Jenny shook her head. 'No. Not in the least.'

'That's a relief. You do have some taste, after all.' Putting down his cigarette, Robin reached out to stroke Jenny's hair. 'Darling, why don't we do it, too?'

'Do what?'

'Get married, of course.'

'Are you serious?'

'Yes, I am.' Robin took her in his arms. 'Well?'

Jenny looked at him. She realised he wasn't teasing. She considered for a moment. Then she thought, why not? Well, there were plenty of reasons why not. For a start, she wasn't in love with him.

But, on the other hand, she certainly liked him. He was clever, he was kind, he was entertaining, and he was amazingly enterprising in bed. 'Is that an actual proposal?' she enquired.

'Yes, it is.' Robin hugged her. 'I do love you,' he whispered.

'Do you?'

'Of course I do.'

'Oh.' Drawing back, Jenny met his bright, brown eyes. 'But *what* do you love, exactly?'

'Well, there's your neat little bum. Your sweet little ears. The mind in between them, of course. But most of all, I love you for your feet.'

'My feet?'

'Yes.' Robin kissed her. 'They're absolutely beautiful. Tiny, pink and perfect. I'd like to eat them, especially the toes.'

'You're a pervert. That's what you are.'

'I know.' Robin hugged her. 'So — what about it?'

'I don't know.' Flattered, Jenny smiled. She ruffled Robin's black hair, making it stand up like feathers. 'What's in it for me?'

'You'll be the wife of a rising star, that's what.

Look, I'll be a lecturer at twenty three. A reader at twenty eight. Full professor by thirty, vice chancellor by forty five, and you'll be Lady Langley.'

'I'm dazzled.' Jenny laughed. 'Is all that really on the cards?'

'I'm sure it is.' Robin laughed, too. 'Then again, I'm handsome, intelligent and good in bed.'

'True.'

'You're madly in love with me, too.'

'Am I?'

'Certainly.' Slipping his hand inside Jenny's blouse, Robin stroked a breast. He grinned. 'There,' he said. 'Proof. You adore me.'

'If you say so.' Jenny sighed. Wrapping her arms around Robin's neck, she let her body take over. 'Oh, darling,' she murmured, 'I'm so tired. Let's go to bed.'

26

'Going to have a long white dress? Half a dozen sweet little bridesmaids? All the trimmings?'

'I don't think so.' Although her body was satisfied, her heart and mind were desolate, and all Jenny wanted now was to go to sleep. Robin, however, lay wide awake and talkative, right in the middle of her bed. 'Could you move over a bit?' she asked, as he rattled on. 'I'm going to fall out otherwise.'

Obligingly, Robin rolled over. Reaching for his cigarettes, he lit one. 'A register office do, then?' he enquired.

'If you like.'

'Don't you care?'

'Not particularly.' Lying on her back now, Jenny stared up at the ceiling. 'What about you? What do you want?'

'Darling heart, I honestly don't mind. But I thought all women had special dreams and schemes about their big day?'

'Oh.' Jenny shrugged. 'Well, then — shall we have a register office wedding in Worcester? Followed by a reception at a nice hotel, for a dozen or so friends?'

'That's okay by me. But won't your mother complain?'

'She might.' Again, Jenny shrugged. 'Yes, I expect she'll grumble a bit. But she'll come round in the end.'

When she realised her only child's wedding was to be such a small affair, Shirley put up more than a token resistance, practically insisting on Blackstone church and the village institute afterwards — for the sake of the grandparents, if nothing else. But, in the end, she gave in gracefully. Then, she and Gareth spent more than they could afford on a very smart reception at one of Worcester's most expensive hotels.

Robin's parents, well-established solicitors in partnership in a small Surrey town, were extremely gracious towards Shirley and Gareth. Mrs Langley observed that the flowers were lovely, that Jenny looked very pretty in that peach two-piece, and that personally, she always thought a good sparkling wine preferable to a cheap champagne. How wise Shirley was to have decided on Kriter, rather than some inferior vintage of Veuve Clicquot.

'I wish you joy of her ladyship,' murmured Shirley, as she and Jenny watched Mrs Langley sail away to patronise somebody else. Resplendent in navy and white spotted silk, soon she could be heard remarking that although they were rather cramped for this kind of function, these old inns nevertheless had a certain charm, so rare in this day and age.

Shirley shook her head. 'Will they be over to see you often, do you think?' she enquired.

'I doubt it,' Jenny replied. 'They're too busy.'

'Doing what?'

'Conveyancing. Helping people get divorced. All that sort of thing.' Jenny shrugged. 'It's a living, I suppose. Did Delia write?'

'Yes, in the end. She said she was definitely coming. Looking forward to meeting Robin, too. But it appears she found better things to do, after all.' Shirley sighed. 'She hasn't been to see me for two years or more now. She hardly ever writes. I suppose these days I'm not good enough for *her*, either.'

'I'm sure it's not that. She must have a lot — '

Just then, a sudden movement — the sound of a door opening, and a blast of fresh air rushing into the room — made Shirley glance round. Her features broke into a great, beaming smile. 'Well, talk of the devil!' she cried.

'Delia!' Jenny beamed, too. 'Oh, Delia! You made it, after all!'

'Better late than never, I suppose.' Now, Shirley hugged her friend. 'Hello, stranger. Well — you missed the most important bit.'

'I know.' Delia shrugged her apology. 'The train broke down at Charlbury,' she explained, 'so I hired a taxi. But it took *ages* to get here. I began to think it would be quicker to get out and walk!'

She gave Jenny a long, appraising stare. 'You look absolutely lovely,' she declared.

'Thank you.'

'Don't look at me like that! It's true.' Now, Delia bit her lip. 'Is there anything left to eat?' she asked, humility itself. 'There was no buffet car on the train, and I'm starving.'

'We'll find you something.' Glancing round, Jenny

342

spotted Gareth, being talked at by Mrs Langley. 'We'll feed you,' she said, 'and rescue Dad on the way.'

Robin came up now, kissed his wife, then looked pointedly at his watch. 'Time to be making a move, I think,' he said.

'Already?' Jenny wanted to talk to Delia. For, when she had written out Delia's wedding invitation, she had added, 'do bring a friend.' Then she had signed, sealed and posted the envelope, before she could change her mind.

But had she seriously wanted Delia to bring Peter Eisenstadt to the wedding? What would she have done if he *had* turned up? Now, thinking about it, Jenny realised she had been very, very stupid. If Peter had come, it would have been horrible and embarrassing, for everyone concerned.

Now, Robin was hugging her. 'Wake up, darling,' he said. 'Come back to Planet Earth!'

'I'm sorry?' Jenny blinked. 'What do you mean?'

'You've been in a world of your own most of the afternoon. I'm not sure if you're really here, even now.'

'Don't be silly.' Jenny smiled at him. 'I'm just happy, that's all.'

'Good. So am I.' Robin nodded towards Delia and Gareth. 'Who's your mother's sexy friend?'

'Delia Shenstone. She's a journalist on a magazine.' Jenny frowned. 'Do you really think she's sexy?'

'Not half as sexy as you. But for an older woman, she's quite something. It's the expensive clothes and designer jewellery, I expect.' Unkindly, Robin laughed. 'Look at my mother. She's gone bright green.'

★ ★ ★

Delia arrived back in London very late that same evening. Pressed by Shirley to stay, she had pleaded a backlog of work, but actually she was anxious to see Peter again. He had been on a business trip to the USA, but was due back in London that Saturday afternoon.

She put her latchkey into the lock just as he came up the stairs himself, so they met on the landing. Delighted to see her, he beamed. 'Well — you look very smart! But where on earth have you been, at this late hour?'

'To Jenny's wedding. I told you I was going.' Delia kissed him. 'I thought you were coming back on the earlier flight?'

'We had to change planes. There was engine trouble.' Peter yawned. 'Oh, God — I'm so tired!'

'Come in and sit down, then. Don't hang about here all night.'

Following his usual homecoming ritual, now Peter unzipped holdalls and cases and upended carrier bags, scattering his belongings all around the flat. While he made a mess, Delia made some coffee.

'So, did you enjoy this wedding?' he enquired, coming into the kitchen to find some biscuits and cheese, and to give his mistress a hug.

'It was all right.' Delia shrugged. 'But I'm not a great one for weddings, myself.'

'Nor am I.' Peter found a packet of cream

344

crackers. 'Where did you have to go?'

'All the way to Worcester. It's a cathedral city, in the Midlands. I don't suppose you've even heard of it.'

'Well, as it happens, I have.' Peter grinned. 'I was driven through it in a truck, back in 1945. On my way to the internment camp.'

'Really? Where was the camp?'

'Oh, I forget. Near a village called Bradstock — or maybe it was Bradbrook — Latimer.' Trying to remember, Peter frowned. 'I think that was the name, anyway.'

'If you'd come back from America in time, you could have gone there today. On a sentimental journey.'

'What a terrible idea!'

'You could have come to the wedding, too.'

'I don't think so.' Peter loosened his tie. 'Poor girl! There she is, getting married. It's the happiest day of her life. Then, in walks her employer, with her mother's best friend. How embarrassing for her.'

'But you know Jenny. You — '

'I've met her once or twice, that's all. Darling, that's quite enough about weddings. Come and see what I've brought back from New York, for you.'

'Is it something nice?'

'Well, I hope you'll think so. I saw it in a shop in Fifth Avenue. I don't usually like modern jewellery, but this necklace is quite pretty. Come and try it on.'

★　★　★

Robin completed his thesis on some obscure aspect of the life and works of Henry Fielding and then, as a timely wedding present, he was offered a junior lecturership at his own college. A three year contract, it would probably lead to permanent tenure, and Robin was delighted. He was on his way.

His parents were delighted, too. Having a real, live university lecturer in the family was a tremendous bragging point at dinner parties. Now they presented him with a large cheque, to be used as a deposit on a house.

Property was cheaper south of the river, so Jenny and Robin decided they'd concentrate their searches there, eventually fixing on a large but dilapidated house in Greenwich.

Miles from any tube station, in the middle of a terrace of similarly decaying liabilities, it was the kind of property which estate agents always say has great potential — but, three weeks after they'd moved in, Jenny wondered what on earth had possessed her when she'd agreed to sling this great millstone round her neck.

True, Robin had promised that the long vacations would be devoted to renovation, but somehow Jenny couldn't quite believe this, for Robin was the sort of man who couldn't so much as change a plug. The use of a hammer and chisel was beyond him, he thought Black and Decker were obscure Elizabethan playwrights, and, as far as Robin was concerned, plumbing was a closed book likely to remain so.

Jenny's worst fears proved to be well founded. The summer vacation came round, but Robin did not even lift a paintbrush. He liked the house as it was, he said. No, he didn't want to redecorate the sitting room. It was a pity to spoil the smoky patina of years, and the yellowing plaster ceiling had a certain period charm, didn't Jenny agree? He did help tile the bathroom, and eventually he put up some ready-made bookshelves. After all, one had to have bookshelves. But that was as far as it went.

Autumn arrived, and Robin went back to college. Looking round her hell-hole of a kitchen, Jenny sighed. 'Don't worry,' said Robin, when she told him the window-panes were loose, and that the roof leaked, too. 'I'll get some buckets. They'll catch the drips.'

They had to. The Langleys couldn't afford the necessary repairs. These would have to wait either for the mortgage interest rates to go down, or for the spring, when Jenny would get a pay rise. She hoped she would, anyway.

One fine Saturday morning in March, they were eating a leisurely breakfast in bed. From their window, they could see a pair of house martins flying to and fro, taking little bits of straw and twig into some hidey-hole they'd just discovered, constructing a nest in the eaves.

'Look at those birds.' Sticky with marmalade, Robin gazed at the house martins. 'How do they know what to do?'

'It's called instinct,' said Jenny. 'Robin, we must get a lawn mower, and some decent garden shears.'

'Can't I just go to the barber, like everyone else?'

'Do please be serious, just for once! Now — shall

we go to Sheargold's, in Blackheath? Or Turner's? That's nearer.'

'Either. You choose.' Robin kissed her on the mouth. He unfastened the buttons on her nightdress. 'Take this off,' he said.

★　★　★

A year went by. Two years. On balance, Jenny supposed she was happy. She knew in her heart that she was not in love with her husband, but she certainly liked him. He was her lover, and he was her friend. He made her laugh, too. Surely that was enough for any woman? In any case, being in love was horrible. It clouded your judgement, ruined your digestion, and made you thin and ill.

A cold, wet January brought with it a rather unpleasant strain of 'flu, and Robin caught it. During convalescence he was fretful and complaining. 'Come to bed,' he implored. 'Keep me warm.' When Jenny did so, he fell upon her greedily, breathing his germs all over her face.

By the end of the month, Jenny herself was feeling not exactly ill, but certainly a bit odd. Then she missed a period. Then, one lunchtime, she was sick, and the feeling of nausea persisted for the rest of the day.

'I'm pregnant.' Unpacking her third carrier bag, she dumped the last of the weekend's groceries on the kitchen table. 'Robin? Did you hear me? I said, I'm expecting a baby.'

'Are you?' Looking up from the marking he had spread all over the work surfaces, Robin reached across to grab an apple. 'Jolly good show.'

'I'm sorry?'

'Well done you.' Robin grinned. 'So soon we'll be into nappies, bottles, and too many sleepless nights.'

'I suppose so.'

'Goodbye career woman, hello mummy. Looking forward to chucking in the daily grind?'

'I shan't give up work. I can't.' Jenny shoved the last bag of vegetables into the cupboard under the sink. 'What do you think we'd live on?'

'Dunno.' Robin shrugged. 'We could sponge off Dad, I suppose.'

'I don't think so.' Sitting down, Jenny poured herself a cup of tea. 'I'll be getting a pay rise next month,' she said. 'I'm in the running for promotion to sales manager, too. It would be great if I could swing that.'

Robin ruffled her hair. 'That's my girl,' he said.

* * *

'He's you all over again.' Stroking his soft, black hair, and admiring his long-lashed, deep blue eyes, Shirley held her grandson in her arms. 'What are you going to call him?'

'Adam,' Jenny replied. 'Do you like that?'

'Adam Langley. Yes, that's very nice.' Shirley handed the baby back to his father. 'Adam Robin?'

'No, just Adam.' Robin put the child in his cot. 'Jenny, my love, I must go. I've a lecture at ten. I'll see you this afternoon.'

'Busy lad, isn't he?' Shirley watched Robin walk down the ward, then bang through the double doors. 'Has he done up a room for the nursery yet?'

'No. But he says he will.' Jenny shrugged. 'Mum, we're both busy. Things like decorating aren't really important, so they have to wait.'

'Your Dad and I will do it. Over the weekend. I'm going to clean up your kitchen, too.'

'You don't have to, you know.'

'I do! God knows what's lurking behind that sink of yours.' Shirley pursed her lips. 'Then your Dad's going to make a start on that forest you call your garden. He says he'll put spuds in for you next spring, to break the soil up a bit.'

'That's kind of him. Tell him I said so.'

'Tell him yourself! Now, have you given up this nonsense about going back to work?'

'I'm afraid not. I'm having eight weeks off, then I'm going back.' Jenny shrugged. 'Mum, I have to. We'll all starve if I don't.'

'I don't like the idea at all. In my day, husbands provided for their families. Wives did housework.'

'Well, wives are expected to work outside the home today.'

'So it would seem. Jenny, I meant to ask you — how's your friend Maggie? Did she and Chris get married after all?'

'It's funny you should ask that. She rang me up yesterday.'

★   ★   ★

After living together for three years, Maggie and Chris finally got round to making themselves legal.

The day after Jenny gave birth to Adam, Maggie phoned the hospital to tell her the wedding had at last been arranged.

'You *are* coming, aren't you?' she asked, anxiously. 'You will be there? To leaven all the maiden aunts?'

'Maiden aunts? What sort of affair is it going to be?'

'Oh, the works!' Maggie groaned. 'Mum's booked the church and paid the vicar. We're having bells, the full choir, the village organist — the lot. You'll have to sit through hours and hours of all that 'I, Magdalen Elizabeth, take thee, Christian David,' crap. God, I shall *die*.'

'So shall I,' said Jenny, laughing. 'Are you honestly Magdalen and Christian?'

'For our sins, dear heart, we are.' Maggie laughed too. 'Listen now, here's the lowdown. The reception's at the Court Hotel, Mortimer's Bridge. The men must wear morning dress — '

'Okay, okay.' Jenny scribbled down the address of the hotel. 'Morning dress for his lordship, something smart for me. What are you wearing?'

'I shall be a vision in white tulle.'

'Good heavens above.'

'Shut up. If you so much as snigger, I'll murder you. Actually, now my father's realised how much it's all going to cost, he's trying to talk Ma out of some of the expense. It's too late, of course. He keeps telling *me* about some woman who stood before the fire in her bridal gown, and set herself alight on her wedding morn. She died, of course.'

'Oh, charming.'

351

'Quite. Chris says we should pre-empt all this by sneaking off to a register office.'

'Why don't you, then?'

'Oh, Ma would kill me. Chris's old Mam would have a heart attack. She's Welsh, you know, very Valleys, very pious. *Bread of Heaven*, and all that stuff. So look — are you and Bobbin coming, or not?'

'Could we bring Adam?'

'Sure. How is he?'

'Fine. Maggie, what do you want for a wedding present?'

'No glasses. No cutlery. Nothing trendy from Habitat. What about a kilo of dope, for me to smoke when I'm on my own?'

'Haven't you given that up yet?'

'Trying to.' Maggie giggled. 'Right, then. I'll see you tomorrow, if I may presume to drop in for ten minutes?'

'Of course you may. But you'll have to fight your way through the doting grandparents.'

'All billing and cooing and saying Adam looks just like his Daddy?'

'No, they all say he looks like me.'

'So he's the milkman's, eh? Thought as much. Well, I must dash. Got a hundred letters to do. Hey, we're all going electric next week. That'll be fun. The old bags are panicking — clutching their manual typewriters to their withered bosoms, and threatening to resign.'

★ ★ ★

Maggie's wedding was a riotously joyful affair, with Magdalen and Christian playing their parts to perfection. They spoke up well in church, she looked beautiful and he, while not exactly handsome, looked dignified and deserving of the lovely woman who stood at his side.

Afterwards Maggie let her hair down, Chris took off his jacket and they turned their reception into a party. Maggie danced with all the old men, Chris kissed all the old ladies, and the wine flowed like water, for there were no tiresome economies like a paying bar.

All Chris's maternal relations took full advantage of Mr Clifford's largesse, and by the time the bride went to change, a dozen of the bridegroom's cousins had formed themselves into a choir and were singing Welsh rugby songs, surprisingly melodiously for men who could no longer stand without support.

Jenny and Robin had booked a room in the hotel. 'How are your stitches these days?' enquired Robin, as he sat down on the edge of their bed.

'I think they must have dissolved. I can't feel them, anyway.' Having given Adam a feed which was probably two thirds alcohol, Jenny was not surprised to observe that the baby had fallen into a deep slumber. 'Robin?' she whispered.

'Yes, darling?'

'I think I must have had too much champagne.' Blushing, Jenny avoided his gaze. 'They say to leave it for at least six weeks. But I feel ever so randy.'

'So do I.' Robin kissed her. Lightly, he stroked one breast. 'Does it hurt if I touch you there?'

'No, not at all. In fact, it's very nice.'

'I do love you.'

'I love you, too.'

There. She'd said it. Today, she almost meant it. Now, while little Adam slept, Robin and Jenny made love. They also started another baby.

* * *

'It wasn't my fault you forgot your thing!' grumbled Robin, when he heard the shocking news.

'I didn't think I needed it!' Jenny glared at him. 'The books reckon you *can't* conceive when you're breast feeding.'

'Well, the books are bloody wrong, aren't they?' Robin glared back. 'Now we're in the shit!'

'Not necessarily.'

'You can't go out to work and look after two kids.'

'I don't think I'm going to have any choice.' Jenny shrugged. 'Other people manage it. Why shouldn't I?'

It was a girl this time. Now Beth Porter, the most blessedly reliable child-minder in all Blackheath, had two little Langleys on her baby farm.

But then Beth herself became pregnant again, and she told Jenny she really didn't see how she was going to carry on minding now — 'not with your two, and three of my own, and another on the way, and my ankles the way they are. The doctor says I ought to be in bed, really.'

This was a disaster. Child-minders — good, capable child-minders, that is — were as rare as rubies. 'You look after them,' said Robin. 'Stay at home for a few years, eh?'

'But what will we live on?'

'We'll cope.'

'How?'

'Dad will help us out.' Robin grinned. 'You could take in washing. I can just see you out in t'scullery. In your mob cap and pinny. Dashing away with a smoothing iron.'

'Oh, shut up.' Jenny thought for a moment. 'I could take in book-keeping, I suppose.'

'There you are, then. Look, we've got a little bit in the bank. We shan't actually starve.'

27

'I've become a non-person,' thought Jenny, as a dreary round of playgroups, coffee mornings and charity bazaars literally took over her life. 'I am Robin's wife, I am Adam's and Jane's mother — but I'm not *me* any more.'

'Well, gang? What are you doing today?' Spooning soggy rusk into Jane, Robin was trying to read the *Guardian* as well, so most of his daughter's breakfast was ending up on the kitchen floor.

'We're all going to a new mother and toddler group at St Paul's. Then we're going to the Waterbabies' Club down at the baths.' Taking the spoon, Jenny continued to feed Jane herself. 'What about you?'

'Lectures, seminars, tutorials — the usual daily grind.' Robin grinned. 'It's all right for some.'

Quite, thought his wife. Envy threatened to choke her.

★   ★   ★

Putting the brake on the double buggy, Jenny took her children out of their harnesses. Together, they went into the church hall.

A dismal Victorian Gothic monstrosity, this smelled strongly of dust and even more unpleasantly of lavatories. 'Excuse me,' Jenny began, addressing a fat young woman in unsuitably tight jeans, 'do you know — '

'Ah!' The playgroup leader smiled brightly. 'A new Mum! Now, was it you I spoke to on the phone yesterday?'

'Yes. You must be Helen.'

'That's right. Helen Dyer.'

'Jenny Langley.'

But the playgroup leader wasn't interested in Jenny Langley. Instead, she beamed down at Adam and Jane. 'So! These two little charmers are?'

'Jane and Adam.'

'Lovely!' Helen Dyer took a chubby little hand in each of hers. 'Linda?' she called, towards the malodorous kitchen. 'Come out here for a moment, and talk to a new Mummy! Then show her how to use the urn. The two of you can make us all some tea.'

Linda eyed Jenny up and down. 'Right,' she said, briskly. 'You can wash them cups up, if you like. The Men's Club has left 'em all dirty again.'

★ ★ ★

Jenny adored her children. In fact, she loved them to bits. For they were so beautiful. Their skins were soft and unblemished, their eyes clear and bright. She loved to play with them, to watch them grow, to watch them learn.

Small children, however, have no real conversation. While it is delightful to have a soft little hand in one's own, or feel the warm weight of a roly-poly little body on one's lap, it is tedious to answer the same questions over and over again. After a hundred readings, even the most fascinating Ladybird book begins to pall.

Robin took little interest in Adam and Jane. Indulgent and tolerant, he let them crawl all over him, invade his bed and pull his hair — but he never actually played with them. In truth, they bored him.

When Adam started at infants' school and Jane joined a local nursery group, Jenny decided to take in book-keeping, doing the accounts for three or four small businesses. This kept her brain functioning, but it also increased her desire to be in the company of intelligent, grown-up people again.

She was soon to have the chance. That following month, Robin's teaching contract was favourably reviewed: but he found that because of spending cuts, he was not to be given permanent tenure. He was secure only for a further three years.

Jenny decided she must go back to work.

'Why?' demanded Robin.

'Because we'll be living on baked beans forever if I don't!' she replied.

'Oh.' Picking up a book, Robin hid behind it for the rest of the evening.

Scanning the *Evening Standard* daily, Jenny eventually noticed an advertisement for a job which appeared to be tailor-made for someone like her. The work sounded interesting, the hours were flexible, and the pay wasn't bad, either.

She wrote off for an application form. She was invited for interview, then told she'd been shortlisted. Two weeks later, she heard she'd got the job.

'I'll be working for this agency,' she explained. 'I'll be finding houses, staff, schools and all that sort of thing, mainly for foreign businessmen.'

'Really? What fun.' Robin picked up a copy of the *Guardian*.

'It pays well, and I can arrange my own schedule. Darling, it's ideal!'

'Is it?' Robin shrugged. 'Can you have the school holidays off?'

'No. But then you'll be here.'

'Don't bank on it. I've a conference in Liverpool this Easter. There's a summer school in Cambridge in August, and I must prepare — '

'Don't make difficulties, Robin! We'll manage.' Encouragingly, Jenny smiled at him. 'We'll cope, you'll see.'

'Well, don't come moaning to me when you get stuck. You don't *have* to take this job.'

'I do if we want to keep this house. Do you know how much the mortgage is these days?'

'We could move.'

'To what? A maisonette in Battersea? A caravan on the Isle of Dogs?'

'You have to rub it in, don't you?'

'What do you mean?'

'I wish you'd come right out and say it.' Robin grimaced. 'I know I'm not a good provider,' he muttered. 'I'm not keeping you in the style to which you'd like to be accustomed. But all the same — '

'Don't be so silly. I'm not doing this to spite you!'

'No?' Robin would not look at her. 'All right,' he muttered, 'go out to work. But get this clear from the start. If you insist on having a job, then it's up to you to make arrangements for the kids. I'm not cut out to be a nanny, so if you're not able to look after the children yourself, you'll have to find someone who can.'

'I will!' Now, visions of unreliable child-minders, unqualified nannies, and hopeless, feckless au-pairs who'd neglect her children and burn her saucepans, rose like so many horrid spectres before Jenny's eyes.

She bit her lower lip. But then she squared her shoulders. Other people managed. Why shouldn't she?

★　★　★

Adam and Jane adapted well to the new regime. Robin, on the other hand, didn't. Accustomed to good home cooking, he complained bitterly if dinner were fish and chips from the takeaway. Unable to find a clean shirt one morning, he flew into a rage and refused to speak to Jenny for three whole days.

During the long vacations, during which Jenny had assumed he would at least help to look after his children, he did nothing of the sort. Taking them swimming or on outings proved beyond him. Adam and Jane asked why Jenny couldn't have more time off, at least during their holidays. It was so boring, being stuck at home with Dad.

'I'll take you out on Saturday,' promised Jenny, seeing her longed-for lie-in disappear into Never Never Land, for the fourth week running. 'We'll go to the fair on the Heath, shall we? We'll have candy floss and hot dogs.'

'Great! Can we take Julian and Sarah, too?'

★ ★ ★

'I still reckon this new job's a bit of a comedown,' observed Robin, one Thursday evening, as he lolled on the sofa drinking the Scotch which he could now afford again, and watching his wife catch up on her housework. 'I mean — I can see it's all very glamorous, meeting oil sheikhs and Texan millionaires. But surely it's rather demeaning for a high-flyer from top management to be reduced to clerking, for a glorified estate agent?'

Jenny looked up from the ironing. 'I'm not a clerk, and I don't work for an estate agent,' she said.

'What are you, then?' Robin grinned. 'A Girl Friday? A high-class procureuse, maybe? I meant to ask you, actually — do those clients of yours ever make improper suggestions, or ask you to find them a good time?'

'No, they don't. People hire me to find houses, not to provide personal services of that kind.'

'Ah! So you do work for an estate agent, after all!'

Jenny threw a sock at him. Then she put the ironing board away, leaving all Robin's stuff still in the basket. 'If you want your shirts pressed,' she said sweetly, 'you can do them yourself.'

★ ★ ★

361

'I'm going to advertise for an au-pair, I think,' she told him, later that evening. 'Hilda Taylor's a good minder, but her house is filthy and her kids always have colds, so Jane will be going down with everything under the sun when the winter comes.

'But if we have an au-pair, she and you can divide some child-minding between you.'

'Yeah, okay,' said Robin. With half a bottle of whisky inside him, he was inclined to be slightly more co-operative than usual. 'But for God's sake, don't get a Frog.'

'Why ever not?'

'They don't wash. It's a fact! A French girl will stink the place out.'

So Jenny hired Lisette, an irreproachably hygienic Swiss girl. She was the first of many freebooters who shared the Langleys' home, whose boyfriends dossed down in their spare bedroom, and who sometimes fell in love with the young, handsome master of the house.

But Robin never gave them even the time of day. Fiercely xenophobic, he grumbled constantly about the presence of foreign tarts, and asked why Jenny couldn't hire an English nanny, instead?

'*You* hire an English nanny,' Jenny replied. 'You find the forty quid a week for her wages, you buy her a car of her own. You go to Harrods and order her uniforms, two for summer, two for winter and a special one for Sundays.'

★ ★ ★

Jenny liked her job, she loved her children, but combining work with childcare wore her out. Waking bright and fresh in the mornings, she rushed about all day, and by evening she was too exhausted to do more than lie on the sofa and yawn. Frequently, the children lay and yawned with her, staying up later than was good for them. But Jenny hadn't the heart to pack them off to bed. They saw far too little of their mother anyway. Perhaps, she thought guiltily, she ought to give up work. At least for a year or two?

But then the mortgage rate went up. A massive rates rise nearly gave Robin heart failure, and for days he muttered about the bloody robbers on the Greater London Council who ran their Jags and slags at his expense. Then Robin himself was told that if he wanted a readership, he ought to consider applying to other universities, because London's teaching quota had been cut back yet again.

Jenny always put the children to bed. She found the night-time ritual very comforting, and thoroughly enjoyed the baths, the hair-washing, the story, hugs, kisses, I love you Mummy, and lights out. Then, with the children all tucked up and dozing off, she usually went to bed herself, too tired even to skim a few pages of the overdue library book on her bedside table.

She never wanted sex. If Robin even touched her, she pushed him away. 'I'm tired,' she would mumble, into her pillow. 'Leave me alone.'

'You're always tired. Too tired to go out, too tired to cook a decent meal, too tired to do shit bugger all.' Tonight, Robin became angry. Earlier, he had given the children their tea, helped them with their homework, and now he expected a reward. Not a rebuff.

He pulled Jenny round to face him. 'You're too tired even to look at your own fucking husband,' he cried. 'Or rather, *non*-fucking husband these days!'

'There's no need to swear.' Jenny turned over again. 'Put the light out. It's hurting my eyes.'

Robin clicked off the lamp. Then he got out of bed.

'Where are you going?' asked Jenny, for now he was putting on his clothes.

'Out.' Robin tucked his shirt into the waistband of his jeans. 'Oh, and by the way — I think Jane's coming down with something. She's been looking peaky all day, and at teatime she was scratching.'

'Has she any spots?'

'Some little red ones, on her chest.' Robin leaned across the bed. Spitefully, he pinched Jenny's cheek. 'It's measles, I expect. Adam's got it, too.'

28

Forrester, Lane and Hendry might have been glorified estate agents, but they were much more beside. The three partners — together with their staff of highly-trained, multilingual assistants — found homes, staff, nannies, workmen and schools for an international clientèle of corporate business-men and women.

Over ten years or so, they had built up a worldwide reputation for efficiency, reliability and speed. They could take on the most complex of commissions, arranging the purchase or leasing of one or several dozen homes, and drawing on a veritable army of plumbers, painters, decorators, tilers, builders, caterers, nursing staff, domestics and teachers of English as a foreign language. Although they did not, as Robin had supposed, supply call girls.

The work was very involved and extremely demanding, but Jenny loved it. When everything dovetailed and a job was finally completed, she felt she'd achieved something special. When the final bill was despatched and the client paid by return, enclosing a letter of commendation, she felt a warm glow of satisfaction.

A team of seven — the three partners, Jenny and her colleague Dot Farley, together with two super-efficient secretaries — ran the whole show. Dot, an energetic, happily-unmarried twenty-five year old, hired and fired maids, cooks, nannies and chauffeurs. But both she and Jenny could cover for one another, and together they made a good team.

Although she enjoyed working for FLH Associates, Jenny hadn't been there long before she realised she could run an agency like this herself, maybe from home. 'Perhaps when the children are older,' she thought, as she leafed through that day's post. 'When they're half way through secondary school, and out all the time anyway.'

How quickly the years had slipped by! Adam was twelve now, and even little Jane was a responsible, mature eleven year old, already as tall as her mother. Soon they'd be teenagers, leading their own private lives.

★　★　★

One busy Wednesday morning, Jenny was researching a project, making notes and jotting down possible contacts, when one of the secretaries came in to place a slim file on her desk. 'Thanks, Connie,' she murmured, without even looking up. It wasn't until lunch-time that she picked up this file and opened it.

On the first page was a letter from a Spanish company, asking for a quote on a relocation deal. On the second was a list of individual clients, all wanting to be found houses or flats in central London.

Idly, Jenny glanced down the column of names. Suddenly, she started. She blinked, refocused, then looked again. But she hadn't been mistaken. The name was still there, still burning off the page.

Strafford, she read. Mr Mark S.

Jenny's heart bumped against her ribcage. Her throat tightened. With shaking fingers, she turned up the rest of this client's details, and there, on expensive headed paper, was the name of the company for which Mark Strafford worked. 'Strafford, Clarke and Viner,' she read now. 'Specialists in Eighteenth Century English Furniture.' At the bottom of the sheet were the names of the directors of the firm. They were M S Strafford, M Viner and J G Clarke.

Jenny thought she was going to be sick. Hurrying to the cloakroom, she bathed her face in cold water. For the rest of the day she worked mechanically, in a daze.

★ ★ ★

'Look, Dot,' she began, a week later, 'I know you don't usually show clients round houses, but I'm going to be a bit pushed for time this morning. Could you possibly slip out and take a Mr Strafford over a place? His appointment's for ten thirty. It would only take you half an hour, at most.'

'No problem.' Dot leaned back in her chair. 'Actually, I was wondering what to do with myself this morning. So what's the big rush for you today?'

'I'm sorting out this United Electronics package.' Jenny sighed with relief. 'I've got to get the costings done by lunchtime, and they're more complicated than they look. I think I'm going to have to bump up this initial estimate by at least two thousand pounds.'

'Oh, United Electronics counts in round billions. They won't care if we stick on an extra couple of grand.' Dot slipped on her shoes. 'Right. If I go now, I can nip into Sainsbury's on the way, and get in my week's supplies. Chuck us the keys.'

'Do you want the Renault? Or the new Ford?'

'I'll take the Ford today.' Dot reached for her jacket. 'So now you owe me one, okay?'

'Okay.' Jenny punched some figures into her calculator. 'I'll ring round the domestic agencies for you. Then I'll sort out that stupid woman at Adbrook Helps, who does nothing of the sort.'

'It's a deal.' Dot slipped the car keys into her pocket. 'See you. Don't work too hard.'

★   ★   ★

'So how did you get on with Mr Strafford?' It was lunchtime now, and Jenny was picking at her cheese and chutney roll. 'Was everything okay?'

'Yeah, fine.' Dot grinned. 'No hassle at all. He was an easy one. Well, it makes a change.'

'Young or old?'

'Late thirties, I'd guess. Much too old for me, but rather tasty all the same.' Dot opened her packet of sandwiches. 'He's been in the States for several years, but he's back in England permanently now, and he needs a central London base. He's single. Well, divorced, at any rate.'

'He actually told you he was divorced? Just came

368

right out and said it?'

'Well — no.' Dot laughed. 'He didn't actually say. But it was written all over him.'

'How do you mean?'

'Well, he definitely wasn't gay. But he didn't mention a family, and that house isn't big enough for more than one person. Or two extremely close friends. So — he must be divorced or single. I'd go for divorced.'

'Did he like the house?'

'He absolutely loved it. God, I wish they were all as easy to please.'

★ ★ ★

'Mr Forrester was dropping hints about one of us starting to learn Arabic,' observed Jenny, as she and Dot studied a new commission from a company in Kuwait, later that same week.

'Oh, God.' Dot pulled a face. 'He can hint on.'

'That's what I thought at first.' Jenny opened another folder. 'But for an extra couple of thousand a year, I might consider it. So when are you seeing that Mr Strafford again?'

'Next Tuesday, I think. At two.' Dot flicked open her diary. 'Yeah, that's right. He only wants another quick look round, to do some measuring or something. He said once he'd done that, he'd give us a decision one way or the other.'

'I wonder what he wants to measure?'

'Jesus, I don't know. He wants to see if all his valuable antiques will fit in, I suppose. Oh — didn't I tell you? He's a dealer. Now, those three Yanks from Aston, Vesey Inc, who wanted a house south of the river — what do you reckon to this place?'

★ ★ ★

Jenny spent a week in torment. Running on auto-pilot at work, at home she was irritable and moody, snapping at the children and more or less ignoring Robin.

She could think of nothing but Mark Strafford. Wanting desperately to see him again, she didn't think she dared. For that way, madness lay.

'Sickening for something, are we?' asked Robin that Tuesday breakfast time, as she swore at him for dropping some toast, marmalade side down — of course — on the clean kitchen floor. 'Or is it just executive stress?'

'What?'

'Is your estate agent working you too hard?' Robin grinned. 'Or do you need a course of something? Some nice, soothing tranquillisers, maybe? A little Valium, perhaps?'

'I don't think so.'

'I reckon it might be the change of life. Do you get hot flushes? Panic attacks? Soon, you'll be having violent mood swings — well, you get those already. You — '

'Have you been reading *Woman's World* again?'

'Yeah, the one in the downstairs loo. There was a special supplement on the menopause. Very fascinating it was, as well.'

'I see.' Jenny grimaced. 'I think *you'd* better get off to school,' she told Adam, who was listening to

370

all this with the greatest interest. 'Jane, have you picked up your ballet shoes? Okay then, remember you're going to tea with Alice Parker tonight.'

'I know, I know.' Jane grinned. 'Can I have some money for the bus?'

'Here. Forty pence — that's all the change I have.' Jenny finished her cup of tea. She picked up her handbag. 'See you all this evening,' she said.

★　★　★

'I'll go and meet Mr Strafford today, shall I?' asked Jenny, offhandedly. 'You'll be rather busy, what with all that National Steel Industries paperwork to get through by five o'clock.'

'Yeah, I was just thinking that.' Dot opened a filing cabinet. She passed Jenny a folder. 'Don't try to rush him,' she advised. 'He was very nice — but he looked a touchy sort of chap, all the same. You know your high-powered executive.'

'Yes. I'll be careful.'

Jenny parked the company's Renault in the cobbled forecourt, then let herself into the house. She saw at once that it must be for someone without children. For one thing, it was very luxurious, and for another it was very small: hardly big enough for even two people to share.

A mews cottage of the kind originally designed for a groom and his wife, but now priced out of the range of anyone not seriously rich, it had been extensively remodelled. Downstairs, there was an elaborately-decorated sitting room, and a small but expensively fitted kitchen. Upstairs, a truly luxurious gold and marble bathroom had an equally opulent, galleried bedroom alongside. 'Just the place for assignations,' thought Jenny. 'Tailor-made for candlelit seductions, or secret affairs.'

Leaning over the balustrade, she looked down from the bedroom to the sitting room below. She smiled to herself. It was all so vulgar! Gilded and panelled and furbished to a ridiculous degree, this was exactly the sort of place one would expect to appeal to an East End barrow boy made good.

She wondered if Mark were renting or buying. Opening the folder, she looked to see how much this little bit of Hollywood set down in SW1 might cost. Seeing all the noughts, she almost choked.

The door bell rang. Jenny checked her watch. He was right on the dot, naturally. Being a turbo-powered wheeler dealer, whose time was money, he wouldn't be late.

She went down the stairs.

She opened the front door.

Hands in his trouser pockets, Mark stood on the doorstep. 'Mrs Langley?' he enquired, not really looking at her.

'Yes,' replied Jenny. 'Please come in.'

'Thank you.' He walked into the hallway.

Jenny went into the sunlit sitting room. As Mark followed her, she turned to look at him. He saw the sunshine light up her face. He saw her eyes sparkle. He saw her smile at him.

'My God.' He sat down on the window seat. He stared at her. 'Christ all bloody mighty,' he muttered, 'what the hell are you doing here?'

'I work for the company selling this house. It's as

simple as that.' Jenny looked at him. 'Well, now — is there anything else you need to know? Or shall I just leave you to get on?'

'Yes! No! Hang on a moment!' Mark rubbed his face. 'I'm not dreaming, am I?'

'I'm afraid not.' Jenny met his eyes. So, was he pleased to see her? Or was he upset? Annoyed? To her dismay, she honestly could not tell. 'I-I'll be on my way, then,' she began, her voice a little unsteady in spite of herself. 'Look — I — I'll call you — '

'No. Stay here.' Mark stood up. 'You can make yourself useful. Hold the other end of the tape.'

Mark did his measuring. Then he made a great thing of examining each window frame, lock, wall-socket and light switch. He studied the kitchen units in minute detail, and he tested all the taps. He walked back into the sitting room and leaned against the door frame. 'It's all got to come out,' he said.

'I'm sorry?'

'Everything has to go.' He gazed around him in distaste. 'All the light fittings, the panels, the cabinets — they're all horrible, and they've all got to go. The sooner the better, if you ask me.'

'I see.' Jenny made a note in her file. 'So you'll definitely be buying?'

'Yes. Then I want the place gutted. Can your firm see to that?'

'Certainly. But won't you — '

'Right. My solicitor will be in touch.' Mark opened the sitting room door. Two seconds later, he was gone.

29

Peter Eisenstadt looked through the window. Now the rainswept tarmac came rushing up to meet him. The wheels of the Lufthansa jet bumped on the runway. Contentedly, he sighed.

It was good to be back in London. For, ugly, dirty London, where the weather was still as dreadful as ever, where the dustmen were on strike yet again, where the litter blew about everywhere, escaping from the bursting black sacks which seemed to ornament every doorway and lean against every lamp post, was now his home.

He collected his hand baggage and walked into the airport bookshop, where he saw that this week a popular women's magazine was giving away two sachets of Goldbrand Decaffeinated Instant.

He shook his head. The company had tried so hard to persuade the English to buy good filter coffee — but, on the whole, they'd failed. It was that horrible instant stuff, which Peter would never even dream of drinking himself, that had made him rich.

Goldbrand had by far the largest share of the market now. Shares in the company had rocketed. As he waited for the rest of his luggage to appear on the carousel, Peter reflected that he should be grateful to England, for England had made him the success he was today.

Then, of course, Delia was in London. She had

never succumbed to David Lascelles's blandishments, and her tenacity had paid off, for now she was deputy and often acting editor of *World Wide Magazine*.

But she was also a busy investigative journalist, travelling all over the globe. She was in New York today. Tomorrow, however, she'd be back. He'd fetch her from the airport himself.

★   ★   ★

Peter felt in his pocket, checking that the rolls of jewellery he'd brought from home were still there. They were. These beautiful old-fashioned necklaces, rings and bracelets, which had been his mother's but which his sisters had declared they wouldn't be seen dead in, would now belong to Delia.

Diamonds and amethysts, all set in palest gold, they would suit her fair colouring — and she'd always had a passion for art nouveau.

He parked the big, black Mercedes and looked at his watch. There was plenty of time yet. He untied one of the bundles, took out a ring, and studied it. He thought it would fit. If Delia liked this one, he'd buy her others like it. A ring for every finger. He knew a dealer who could find him exactly the right sort of thing.

Heathrow Airport was as chaotic as ever. Looking this way and that, Peter pushed his way through the crowds. Now, he saw her. He ran towards her and took her in his arms.

'Hello, darling.' Delia looked at him. She shook her head. 'So you're playing truant again?'

'Yes.' He beamed at her. 'I'm skiving off the whole day. Wicked, yes?'

'Very.' But now Delia frowned. 'You look absolutely dreadful,' she scolded. 'You've lost an awful lot of weight. No — don't argue with me. I know how it's been.

'You haven't bothered to eat. You've had no exercise or fresh air. You've been burning up and down the M4, into the factories, back to Head Office — '

'Indeed? So how do you know all this?'

'I know *you*!' Delia sighed. 'You ought to slow down, you know. You're making yourself ill.'

'I feel fine.'

'You don't look it. You need someone to take you in hand.'

'Well, here you are.' Affectionately, he hugged her. 'Where's your luggage?'

'It's coming through now. Look, that Pan Am stuff over there is ours. Will you go and find a taxi?'

'I brought the car.' Picking up her overnight case, Peter led her towards the carousel. 'So how was America?' he asked.

'Hot. Tiring.' Ruefully, Delia shook her head. 'The coffee was absolutely vile.'

'Weak, bitter and tasteless?'

'Exactly.'

'It's always that way in the States.' Grabbing a trolley, Peter piled Delia's cases on to it. 'The USA imports all the cheap rubbish. It's no wonder the younger generation prefers Coke.'

★ ★ ★

376

'It's lovely. Absolutely gorgeous. Thank you!' Delighted with her presents, Delia beamed. 'But really, I ought to stick to junk. The genuine article is much too good for an old woman like me.'

'It's not nearly good enough.' Peter yawned. 'Oh, God — just look at this place. I'd meant to ask Mrs Harley to come round and tidy up, but I forgot.'

'Never mind.' Sitting down beside Peter, Delia kissed him. 'You're hopeless,' she said. 'What you need is a mother.'

'Or a wife.' He took her hands in his. 'I've been thinking about us,' he said. 'I've decided we ought to buy a house. A home, for the two of us.'

'Really?' Delia stared at him. 'But how — '

'Hear me out. Now, you're almost certain to get the editorship of *World Wide* — '

'Am I?'

'Well, I think so. Don't you?'

'Maybe.' Delia shrugged. 'Jeremy's definitely going to the *Sunday Chronicle*. I might get his job.'

'So soon you'll be much less of a wanderer. In fact, you'll be in London almost all the time.'

'But you won't.'

'Yes, I shall. From now on, I'm to be based in London permanently. I've arranged it.' Peter looked deep into Delia's eyes. 'Darling, I want so much to be with you! I've wanted it for years. But always one of us has been coming or going. Always you've been away, or I've been in Germany.

'Now, however, all that's changed. So, I want us to live as a married couple. I believe that, in your heart, you want it too.'

'Do I?' Still bemused, Delia considered it.

'Delia, don't you like this idea?'

'Well — yes. In a way.' Now, thinking about it, Delia smiled. Then she frowned. 'But consider the practicalities of it all,' she said. 'I haven't time to go house-hunting. Have you?'

'No, but I've thought of a way round that.' Triumphantly, Peter grinned. 'I know of a very good firm of agents, whose best speciality is finding homes for busy people like us. Apparently, their service is first rate. An acquaintance of mine has used them only recently, and he was most impressed by the way they managed everything for him.'

'Who is this acquaintance?'

'A certain Mr Strafford. He's a dealer in antiques. He found me those ladder-back chairs, and the little Georgian side table I have in my study. Come to think of it, he could furnish a house for us. He has very good taste. He's not a robber, either — unlike so many of his kind.'

'I see.' Delia sighed. 'Someone ought to take care of you,' she said. 'You're not at all well. Today, you look as if you're on drugs. Do you think you should see a doctor, perhaps?'

'Why?'

'Just for a check up. Go and see Dr Hirsch. Ask him to look you over.'

'I may do that.' Peter shrugged. 'When I have time.'

'I'll phone him tomorrow, and make an appointment.' Now, Delia bit her lip. 'Peter, what will your relations say if you set up home with me?'

'I don't care what they say. What I do is none of

their business, anyway.'

'They might make it their business.'

'It's possible, I suppose.' Peter shook his head. 'My sisters would certainly be curious. I expect Franzi would fly over specially, to give me her famous lecture on mortal sin.'

'What would she say to me?'

'God knows.' Now, Peter laughed. 'Poor Franzi. She must be the only person in the civilised world who still believes in hell.'

* * *

The anonymous letter, written in a childish, unformed hand, was brief and very much to the point. 'Dear Mrs Langley,' Jenny read, 'I thought you should know that Dr Langley is seeing a girl. She is in his third year tutorial group. They are always together, and yesterday they were in his room for almost an hour, with the door locked — '

Jenny read this nasty little missive through to the end, then screwed it up and threw it in the bin. Looking out of the window, she wondered if what it implied could be true. Then, if it was, why she didn't care.

She picked up the phone, and dialled. 'Is Maggie there?' she asked Chris.

'I'm afraid she's out gallivanting tonight.' Indulgently, Chris laughed. 'She's at her Ladies' Kung Fu. Or is it motor maintenance on Mondays? Anyway — can I help?'

'I don't think so. I'll ring back later, perhaps. Will she be in by ten?'

'Probably, unless she and her fellow self-improvers slope off to the pub. Poor Jenny — *you* sound rather low.'

'I am, a bit.'

'I'm sorry to hear that.' Chris cleared his throat. 'Look — ah — it's not Robin, is it?'

'How did you know?'

'I don't. I was guessing.'

'Oh. Chris, do you know something I don't?'

'What?'

'It doesn't matter. I think I know, anyway.' Jenny sighed. 'Tell Maggie I'll phone her tomorrow, would you?'

Jenny replaced the receiver in its cradle. So Robin *was* involved with another woman. How involved, she wondered. He'd had little flirtations before, she was almost sure of it. But how far had this present business gone?

30

Along with other members of his faculty, Robin liked a drink. He and a fellow English lecturer often went on a pub crawl together. Invariably, they ended up at this other man's house in Hackney, where they slept it off.

But getting drunk in front of his head of department, then telling Professor Harding that his recently-published study of the Brontës was a load of reactionary tripe, was a serious mistake. It was to cost Robin dear. For, despite having produced very well-received biographies of Oliver Goldsmith and Samuel Richardson, Robin was now passed over for the Readership in Comparative Literature which he'd been as good as promised. This went instead to an outsider from Manchester — a much younger man who, Robin declared, didn't know his arse from his elbow.

Although his own tenure was now confirmed for a further three years, Robin's disappointment had a profound effect on him. Always somewhat sarcastic, he now became downright abusive. Always outspoken, he was now aggressive in the extreme.

Now, he let his hair grow down over his collar, and wore the same scruffy denim jeans week in, week out — in open defiance of his head of department, who didn't care for long hair on men, and didn't like his members of staff to wear even clean, tidy jeans in college.

'Can't afford any,' he muttered, when Jenny pointed this out to him, and suggested he should at least buy himself a pair of Marks and Spencer's trousers. 'We're not all raking it in, like you.'

The children seemed to get on his nerves even more than Jenny did. As Adam came into the kitchen one evening, Robin got up and very pointedly left the room. Seconds later, the front door slammed behind him.

'A very good evening to you, too,' called Adam, after him. He sat down at the kitchen table. 'Where's the miserable sod gone now?' he enquired, geniality itself. 'Where — '

'I don't know.' Busy at the cooker, Jenny pushed a strand of hair away from her hot face. 'Don't call your father names.'

'Why not? He's a total pain in the backside these days. Don't you agree?'

'I don't wish to discuss your Dad's behaviour with you.' Intently, Jenny looked into her saucepan. 'Could you peel me some potatoes, please?'

'Yeah, sure.' Adam ran cold water into the sink. 'Look, Mum — if he's giving you a hard time, you don't have to grin and bear it. If I were you, I'd tell him he could just — '

'Adam, stop it!' Jenny sighed. 'You don't know what you're talking about, so shut up.'

'He's going through a mid-life crisis.' Unabashed, Adam tipped a bagful of King Edwards into the sink. 'He's re-evaluating his role in society. That's what the jeans and long hair are all about. See?'

★ ★ ★

Re-evaluating his role in society or not, Robin came back in time for dinner, so the family all sat down together. 'This is nice,' said Jane, cutting up her meat. 'I like roast pork, it's my favourite.'

'I thought this was rabbit.' Grinning, Robin met his daughter's startled gaze. 'Roast haunch of rabbit. I reckoned your Mum had taken her little hatchet to old Flopears, out there in the yard.'

'Mum!' Horrified, Jane dropped her greasy knife and fork on the carpet. 'Mum, how could you — '

'Don't be so silly! Of course I didn't!' But now, Jenny would have given almost anything to take a hatchet to Robin himself. How dared he sit there so smug and irritating, upsetting his daughter and annoying his wife? How could he be so rude and unpleasant to Adam? If he was indeed going through some sort of crisis, was there any need to take his frustrations out on his son?

Glancing at him, she was revolted. His long hair had dandruff in it, and his shirt collar was filthy. How could he think looking like an elderly hippie was either appropriate or attractive? He was simply a mess.

Suddenly, she thought of Mark. She saw his face, she heard his voice — and now a pang of lust gripped her so hard that she felt quite faint. Clutching her stomach, she moaned aloud.

'Whatever's the matter?' cried Adam, alarmed.

'Heartburn.' Jenny put down her fork. 'There are some powders in the medicine cabinet. Get me the packet, there's a love.'

★　★　★

Handing Jenny her drink, Maggie sat down. 'Seven year itch then, is it?' she demanded.

'It's nearer seventeen years now.' Jenny sighed. 'Maggie, could I ask you something? Do you ever wish you hadn't married Chris?'

'I don't, as it happens.' Downing her vodka and tonic, Maggie signalled to the barman for another. 'I know it must sound horribly naff to say this — but in fact, we're very happy together.'

'But surely even he has some irritating little habits? Some tiresome little quirks that nearly drive you out of your mind?'

'Of course he has. Dozens of them.' Maggie grinned. 'He's terminally untidy — he leaves computer print-out and litter everywhere. He doesn't change his socks until they're ready to walk towards him. When he throws them at the wall, they stick. He's always on the booze, and when he's pissed he sings all those horrible Welsh or Irish folk songs. All blood and guts and misery, and England's cruel red.

'Which brings me, of course, to the sodding rugby. When Wales loses at Twickenham — or wherever — he sulks for a fortnight. Flora and I creep about the place like little mice, almost afraid to breathe.'

'But on the plus side?'

'On the plus side, he does his share of the housework. Not that it's much, I grant you — I'm not houseproud. He looks after Flora. He goes to Tesco and the local market. He's a fantastic lover and he knows how to unblock a sink. In short, he's a girl's best mate.'

'A paragon, in fact.'

'Yeah. I'm afraid so.' Maggie shook her head. 'Jenny, what's the matter? You can tell me.'

'I can't, because I don't know myself.'

'I see. Well — if it gets really rough and Bobbin becomes totally unbearable, you and the kids can always doss down with us.'

'It won't come to that.' Jenny shrugged. 'Robin's not the problem. Not in that sense, anyway.'

'What is it, then? Have you found another bloke?'

'No.' Jenny got up. 'Same again, is it?'

For, she couldn't discuss Mark with Maggie. Having had her heart stolen, then cut up into little bleeding bits, it had taken her years to get over him. But now, it seemed, she was willing — indeed, she was anxious — to let him hurt her all over again. This must mean she was mad. Jenny didn't want her best friend to think she was completely insane.

★ ★ ★

Mark had read the look in Jenny's eyes. He also knew the value of biding his time. House purchase negotiations took nearly eight weeks but, the day after he'd finally signed the contract to buy the mews cottage in SW1, he was outside Jenny's office. His car parked half on and half off the pavement, he sat waiting patiently, smoking one cigarette after another.

Coming through the front door of the Georgian town house which was FLH Associates' central London premises, Jenny saw him at once. She froze. Trying to decide whether to make a run for it or dash back into the office, she found she was unable to do either. She simply couldn't move. Mark got out of the car.

'Hello, Jenny.' He smiled at her. His hand was on her sleeve. 'How are you today? Well, I hope?'

Jenny looked at his hand. Although the pressure on her arm was feather light, it seemed to burn right through the material of her jacket to scorch her skin. 'Yes,' she managed to articulate, in the end. 'I'm perfectly well, thank you. What about you?'

'I'm fine.' Eloquently, Mark shrugged. 'I thought I ought to see you,' he went on, easily. 'Just to explain.'

'To explain what?'

'This and that. What I'm doing here in London again, for one thing. How I came to be buying that house.'

'You have every right to buy a house.' Wishing he would take his hand away — desperately wanting him to leave it there — Jenny stood like a statue. 'You don't have to tell me anything.'

'I don't *have* to, I know. But I'd still like to talk to you, if I may.' He shook his head. 'It was such a shock, seeing you there that afternoon.'

'I expect it was,' Jenny agreed. 'Of course, I didn't expect it to be you. Strafford isn't a common name, I admit. But you can't be the only one in London.'

'No, I suppose not.' Mark stepped back a little. 'Come and sit in the car,' he invited. 'You'll catch cold, standing about in this wind.'

Sitting in the comfortable warmth of Mark's navy blue BMW, Jenny smiled. But it was a bright, brittle smile. It did not reach her eyes. 'Well?' she enquired.

'What do you want to talk about?'

'Anything you like.' Now Mark lit a cigarette. 'You don't smoke, do you?' he asked, frowning — as if he were trying to remember.

Jenny shook her head. 'No. I never did,' she replied.

'I'm on about sixty a day now.'

'More fool you.'

'Come on, sweetheart! Don't be mean to me.'

'I'm sorry.' Jenny would not look at him. 'I really ought to go,' she muttered. 'I've things to do.'

'Come and have a drink.'

'I don't think I should.'

'Why not? A drink in a public place, in the middle of the day — where's the harm in that?' Stubbing out his cigarette, Mark pushed his keys into the ignition. 'I'll take you to a pub for a sandwich, then bring you back here. How's that?'

'I don't usually bother with lunch.'

'No?' Critically, Mark looked her up and down. 'You are too thin,' he observed. 'You were always slim, of course — but you never used to be scrawny.'

'Well, thank you!' Jenny glared at him. 'You haven't lost your flair for a compliment, have you?'

'I say what I think. That's all.'

'Quite. You always did.' Now, Jenny stared at him. 'You've changed, too,' she observed. 'You're almost unrecognisable, in fact.'

'What's that supposed to mean?'

'Well, look at you! You don't wear jeans or tatty jumpers now. That suit didn't come off the peg, either.'

'Well, I'm sorry about that. If I — '

'You speak differently, as well. No taint of Walthamstow these days, is there?'

'I beg your pardon?'

'All your aitches are in the right places.' Sweetly, Jenny smiled. 'There are no bleedings, bloodies or bastards any more.'

'Finished, have you?'

'No, not quite.' Jenny gazed all about her. 'I love this car,' she said. 'Was it expensive? Yes, I can see it must have been. Even if you got it through a mate for cash, no questions asked, I doubt if there was much change from twenty grand. Well, Mark — you've definitely come up in the world. I'm very impressed.'

'Always were a sarcastic little cow, weren't you?' Mark lit another cigarette. 'Did you plan it?' he asked.

'Plan what?'

'Oh, come on. You gave me the shock of my life, you know you did. I thought I was seeing a ghost.'

'Yes, you did look a bit startled.'

'You enjoyed it, didn't you? Making me double-take like that. Okay, so now I've got a surprise for you. These days, I'm quite friendly with your old man.'

Jenny gaped at him. 'You're friendly with my *what*?'

'With Mr Eisenstadt. Your Daddy.' Observing Jenny's look of blank astonishment, Mark laughed. 'It's all above board,' he went on, 'so don't worry. He's just a customer, that's all. He came into our new shop one day, after a particular bit of Sheraton. We found it for him, and he's bought quite a lot of stuff from us since.'

'Oh.' Jenny felt sick.

'He's a nice bloke,' Mark continued. 'He looks like you. Yes — I'd say there was a definite family resemblance there.'

'You're making all this up.'

'I'm not!' Opening the glove compartment, Mark took out a bundle of cards. Riffling through them, he found the one he wanted. 'Here,' he said. 'Peter Eisenstadt. Eisenstadt UK, Halston House, Southampton Row.' He handed Jenny the card. 'See?'

Jenny took the card, and saw. Turning it over, she observed that Peter Eisenstadt had written his home address and telephone number on the back. 'Mark,' she began, 'you didn't ever mention — '

'No, of course not.' Mark retrieved his card. 'Do you ever run into him?' he asked.

'No, never.'

'Don't you think he ought to know about you? I mean, he's not married, is he? He hasn't any children, either. No other children, that is.'

'You don't know that.'

'Well, he's never mentioned any.'

'Why should he? Why would he think that might interest you?' Jenny chewed at her lower lip. 'Mark?'

'What?'

'I might get in touch with him one day. I don't know how, or when. But understand this. It's absolutely no business of yours. So, if you ever say anything, do anything to make him even suspect — '

'Don't worry, sweetheart. I shan't.' Mark grinned. 'I wouldn't want to upset a good customer, would I?

He was in the shop last week, actually. He had a lady with him.'

'How fascinating.'

'Yeah, isn't it?' Mark lit another cigarette. 'She was a classy piece of stuff. A bit past her best, but still a very attractive woman. Could she be the one who — '

'I really wouldn't know.'

'No. I don't suppose you would.' Mark started the car. 'We'll go to the Queen's Head, in Derwent Square.'

'No, we won't.' Jenny opened the car door. 'I told you, I've things to do. Adam needs new trainers, and — '

'Okay, forget it.' Mark shrugged. 'What about tomorrow, instead?'

'I'm tied up all day.'

'Look, do you want me on my bended knees, or what?'

'Oh, Mark! I'm sorry.'

This was it. Now, Jenny thought, I must tell him I never want to set eyes on him again. Never, for as long as I live. 'I could see you one evening after work, perhaps,' she began.

'Could you?' Mark brightened visibly. 'Where?'

'Let me think.' Jenny considered. 'Oh, I know. There's a wine bar in Alderson Road. That's quite pleasant. It's on my way home, too.'

'Right.' Now Mark looked as if he'd won both the Premium Bonds and the Irish Sweepstake combined. 'I'll meet you there about half six.'

'Fine. Do you have an A to Z?'

'I'll find it. Don't you worry. I'll be there.'

'What a bloody awful place.' Eyeing the bright green plastic palms, pseudo-rustic seating and ubiquitous fake bamboo which was admittedly rather tacky and ill-advised, Mark shook his head in derision. 'Are the wines as well-chosen as the interior decoration?' he muttered, grinning all over his face.

'The wines are perfectly okay.' Daring him to start rubbishing The Glasshouse out loud, Jenny narrowed her eyes. 'I'll have a spritzer, please.'

'No, you won't. We'll have a decent bottle of Meursault. If the pretentious bastards here have got such a thing.' Noticing an indoor waterfall complete with twinkling fairy lights, Mark muttered something inaudible but almost certainly obscene. 'Go and sit down over there.'

Mark ordered and paid for the wine, then joined Jenny at her table. A bare twenty seconds later the proprietor himself came scuttling over, bearing a bottle and two glasses, which he set before them with a flourish.

'Thank you.' As the man went away, Mark laughed, as if at some hilarious private joke. He smiled at Jenny. 'Well, how's your wine?'

Jenny tasted it. 'Actually, it's delicious,' she replied. 'Mark, where's Mrs Strafford today?'

'Down the boozer, I expect,' said Mark, lighting up. 'Gettin' them in, along with the old man.'

'Where's your *wife*?' Jenny glared at him. 'Is she here in London, with you? Or is she at home, on the country estate?'

'I haven't got a wife. I'm divorced.' Mark

shrugged. 'Next question?'

'Have you children?'

'Yes, two boys. Twins.'

'Oh.' Jenny stared down at her hands. Then she glanced at Mark's, which were mere inches from her own. Well-shaped and perfectly clean, with neat, straight-cut nails, the fingers on his left hand were bright yellow. 'How many cigarettes did you say you smoked?' she asked.

'Sixty odd a day. I don't actually count.' Again, Mark shrugged. 'I know — it's a dirty, filthy habit. It's taking years off my life, and all that.'

'It is, too. You're bound to get emphysema. Or even lung cancer. Doesn't that bother you?'

'I have to die of something.'

'Not necessarily in a hospital, coughing your heart up and fighting to breathe.'

'But that's not your problem, is it? Nor shall I be taking up a bed you'll need.' Mark stubbed out one cigarette, then lit another. 'Being a fully-paid-up capitalist swine, I shan't have to burden the NHS. Instead, I shall expire in some luxurious private clinic in the Cotswolds, at my own expense.'

Now Mark beckoned the barman, who came over right away. 'Is everything all right, sir?' he enquired, obsequiousness personified.

'Fine, thank you.' Graciously, Mark smiled. 'We'd like some sandwiches, please. What sort do you have?'

'Cheese, egg and cress, or ham. Or I could do you a special?'

'We'll have ham, please. On brown bread, with some decent French mustard.'

'You're a joke, you really are.' Jenny said as she watched the barman walk away. 'How much did you tip him?'

'Nothing, yet.' Mark drained his glass. 'But he's made a good few quid already. He charged me well over the odds for this plonk. Bastard thinks I don't realise.'

'You just let him screw you, did you?' Jenny laughed. 'That's not your style.'

'It's not, is it?' Mark opened a fresh packet of cigarettes. 'Drink up now, there's a good girl. Shall we have another bottle?'

'I have to go soon. It's the au-pair's night off.'

'Give her tomorrow night off, instead.'

Half an hour later the wine bar was filling up nicely, and Jenny had relaxed. Catching up on past history, she was pleased to hear that Jehangir had gone to college as mature student, qualified as a doctor, and was now a senior registrar at Guy's Hospital. Mark's sister Lisa had four children, but also a husband in the Merchant Navy, which suited Lisa just fine. His brother Tony was out of Parkhurst at present — but he still mixed with stupid villains, so there was no hope for him.

Then Mark told Jenny about a recent business trip to Italy — 'with Anton, you remember Anton? No, you never met him, did you?' — which had been a catalogue of disasters from beginning to end. Mark's take-off of a seriously bent customs official made her laugh, and she was still laughing when she looked up and saw him.

Robin.

Robin and a girl.

A young, scruffily dressed child-woman, Jenny supposed she must be an undergraduate. Or perhaps she was that postgraduate student who was writing a thesis on eighteenth century English dialects? Whoever she was, she knew Robin Langley well enough to be holding his hand.

Robin glanced in Jenny's direction. He saw his wife, and he saw Mark. For a long moment, he stared. But then, muttering something to his companion, he took her by the elbow and turned her back towards the door. They disappeared into the night.

'What is it?' asked Mark — for Jenny's laugh had frozen in mid air. 'Sweetheart, what — '

'Nothing.' Jenny jumped to her feet. 'I must go.'

'Why? Jenny, look — '

'Don't phone me.' Jenny grabbed her handbag. 'Don't get in touch. I don't — I mean, I can't see you again.'

'Why the hell not?' Gathering up her coat, holding it against him like a hostage, Mark stood up too. Leaving a full packet of cigarettes lying on the table, he followed Jenny out of the wine bar. They stood on the pavement, looking at one another.

'What's the matter?' demanded Mark. He shook her arm. 'You look as if you've just seen a ghost.'

'Give me my coat,' said Jenny.

'I'll drive you home.'

'Please, Mark! Give me my coat!'

Mark unlocked the car door. 'Get in,' he said.

Jenny snatched at her coat. She pulled it free. Running up the road, she hailed a providentially passing taxi.

By the time Mark had recovered from his surprise, chased and almost caught up with her, she was in the cab. The driver was pulling out into the heavy early evening traffic.

★　★　★

'You're home late,' said Robin.

'Sorry. I was held up.'

'Don't worry about it.' Genially, Robin grinned. 'Things come up. I know that.'

Robin was stretched out on the sofa, reading a paperback novel. Sitting at the dining table, the children crouched industriously over their home-work. The clock on the mantelpiece ticked reassuringly, the curtains were drawn against the darkness, and all was peace and harmony.

Jenny unbuttoned her coat. 'I had to meet a client,' she said. She met her husband's eyes. 'Has Maria gone out?'

'She's just tarting herself up to leave.' Swinging his legs off the sofa, Robin stood up. 'Your dinner's in the oven. Fancy a cup of tea first?'

'If you're going to make one.'

'What about you kids?'

'Coke please, Dad.'

'Fizzy orange for me.' Jane looked up from her maths investigation. 'A piece of that chocolate cake too, if Pigface here hasn't scoffed the lot.'

Adam thumped her.

Jenny followed Robin into the kitchen. As he filled the kettle, she reached for some mugs. 'What time did you get in?' she enquired.

'About ten minutes ago.' Robin looked straight at her. 'I was in a faculty meeting till seven, then I had to see a student.'

'I see.'

'What do you mean, you see?'

'Nothing.' Jenny took off her coat. She hung it up.

'I always think it's a shame to spoil things. Don't you?' Robin poured hot water into the teapot. 'I mean, what's said can't be unsaid. But if nothing's said at all, perhaps no damage is done.'

'What on earth are you talking about?'

'They're smashing kids.' Robin put the milk and sugar on the tray. 'Look — we may have messed things up for each other, but we've got something right. We've produced two really great kids. It would be a pity to spoil everything for them.'

'I suppose it would.' Jenny picked up the tray. 'Come on. Let's go and have our tea. You can tell me all about your day.'

31

Mr Lane and Mr Forrester were checking through Jenny's work on the United Electronics relocation package. They were pleased by what they saw. To FLH Associates, that particular deal was worth thousands. Tens of thousands, perhaps, in future contracts and goodwill.

The partners looked at each other. Mr Lane raised his eyebrows. 'Well?' he demanded. 'Shall we go ahead?'

'Yes, I think so,' Mr Forrester replied. 'Otherwise, we're going to lose her. Well — her children are growing up. She's very ambitious. I'll bet you anything you like she's going to want to set up on her own some day. Some day soon, in fact.'

The following morning, the three partners called Jenny in to a meeting. They told her they had plans. 'What sort of plans?' she enquired.

'Well,' replied Mr Lane, 'the business is expanding. We're growing fast. We've diversified a lot recently, but now we want to branch out even further. In fact, we were thinking of starting an employment agency. Initially, for office personnel. But later — well, we'll see.'

'So we're going to be recruiting more staff,' Mr Hendry went on. 'Another three or four at least.'

'Right.' Jenny met his eyes. 'So where does that leave me?'

'Well, these people will need to be trained. But

with the routine contract work, the design consultancies and the new public school advisory service, the three of us are already up to our eyes.' Philip Hendry smiled. 'So we were wondering if you'd like to become our training officer, and take over the domestic services side of the business, too? You could have your own office. One or two part time staff.'

'What about Dot?' asked Jenny. 'She's always dealt with that sort of thing.'

'We've plans for Dot. Don't worry about her. Now, what do you think of our offer?'

Jenny took a deep breath. 'If I accepted it, I should also want a partnership,' she replied. Sweetly, she smiled. 'Actually, Mr Forrester, your proposal comes at a critical time. I was thinking about setting up on my own, you see.'

'Were you?' Mr Forrester looked at Mr Lane. 'But then — '

'You wouldn't have to worry about losing business. I'd build up my own clientèle.' Jenny looked at him, blue eyes wide. 'There's plenty of work available. I wouldn't take any of your customers away.'

'You would. We've at least a dozen firms on the books who always demand that you handle their affairs. You'd naturally take their business with you.'

'Maybe.' Jenny shrugged. 'Of course, I wouldn't want to turn clients away.'

'Quite.' Mr Hendry stood up. 'I can see this is going to be rather a long session,' he said. 'I'll just ask Connie to make us all some tea.'

* * *

Jenny returned home that evening extremely pleased with herself. In a month's time, she would have a company car, a big increase in salary, and soon — if she played her cards right — a partnership in the firm.

Now she told Maria she'd be paying her an extra three pounds a week. Then she informed the children they could go to Corsica for their summer holidays after all.

'Corsica, eh? Brilliant!' Adam punched the air. 'Ace. Fantastic. Great.'

'Magic,' added Jane, grinning. 'Claire Reynolds will be green. She's only going to Butlins at Skegness. Hey, Ma — if you've struck it rich, could I have one of those new sweaters from Benetton? You said they were too expensive. But if you're in the money now, might you — '

'Could I get that denim jacket?' cut in Adam. 'Or a pair of loafers?'

'Well, I suppose so.' Jenny laughed at him. 'So who are *you* trying to impress?'

'Gill Nicholson in 2J.' Jane grinned. 'He thinks if he's all got up like the King of Cool, she won't be able to resist him. The fact that he's got a face like a monkey's bum won't — Ow! Ma! Stop him, can't you? He's killing me!'

'Adam, please don't murder your sister.'

'Hell, Mum! She's always taking the piss!'

'My God, I could never be a school teacher.' Jenny glared at him. 'Let her go, Adam! This minute!'

Adam thought about it. But then, after giving her French plait a final, vicious twist, he pushed his sister away.

Aiming a neat kick at his ankle, Jane edged round to the other side of the table. She sat down beside her mother. 'Have you got any brochures, then?' she asked.

'Yes. Dozens.' Jenny tipped them out of her bag. 'Now, I was wondering about this place here.'

Soon, the three of them were deep in discussion and debate.

★　★　★

Jenny's increased responsibilities meant longer working hours, and with them came the problem of organising adequate child care. 'Oh, plenty of other kids in my year go home to empty houses,' Adam assured her. 'We'll be okay. Anyway, Maria's here most days.'

'That's true.' Jenny looked up from her shopping list. 'Well, then — I'll tell Mrs Hammond next door when you'll be on your own. So if you ever have a problem, you can go round to her.'

'Fine.' Adam grinned. 'Don't fret, Mum. We won't invite any axe murderers or dope dealers in. There'll be no wild parties, promise.'

The children coped very well. When Jenny got back from work, Adam usually had a cup of tea ready, and for one glorious week, while she was doing her cook's badge at Guides, Jane even prepared the evening meal. But then, one Tuesday evening, Jenny walked in to find both her children in a terrible state.

The au-pair was at her language class, so they were alone. Jane had obviously been crying. In response to her mother's demand to know what was wrong, she began to cry again. 'It's Granny,' she choked out, at last. Clinging to Jenny, she sobbed her heart out. 'Oh Mummy! Poor Gran!'

Adam closed the front door. He took his mother's coat. 'It's your Mum and Dad,' he muttered.

'What about them?' Looking from one child to another, Jenny felt a horrible black terror, as if a thousand snakes were writhing in her stomach. 'Adam, tell me!'

'The policeman couldn't stop any longer.' Adam would not look at her. 'He offered to send a WPC round, but we said we'd be okay. He said you must ring this number — I wrote it down some-where — '

Jane was weeping hysterically now.

'*What's happened?*' Cursing the idiot of a copper who'd come round with bad news, then left two children alone to digest it, Jenny took her daughter in her arms. 'Oh, for God's sake — one of you tell me!'

'There's been an accident.' White-faced, Adam met his mother's eyes. 'They were coming back from town — I suppose they'd been shopping. This other car was on the wrong side of the road. Grandad braked or swerved or something. But he skidded, and there was a head-on collision. Grandad's in hospital with a broken arm and head injuries.'

'Oh, God.' Jenny sat down. 'What about my mother?'

'She was taken out unconscious. She died in hospital this afternoon.' Adam burst into tears. 'Oh, Mum!'

Jenny rummaged in her pocket, found a Kleenex, and handed it to him. Then she got up from her chair.

'Don't go out again!' Jane held on to her arm. 'Please don't go out!'

'Of course I shan't. But I must — '

'I hate it when you're not here!' Jane was shaking violently now. 'I hate it!' she wailed. 'I'm afraid!'

'I shan't leave you.' Jenny took Jane's hand. 'I must just phone Mr Forrester, that's all.' While I still can, she thought. Before I start to cry, too.

★　★　★

'Good grief. What a terrible thing to happen.' George Forrester clucked in sympathy. 'Jenny, my dear — I'm so sorry.'

'Thank you.'

'Is there anything we can do?'

'I don't think so. But if there is, I'll let you know.'

'Make sure you do.' Mr Forrester took a deep breath. 'I don't know what to say.'

'There isn't anything, really.'

'No. Oh, Jenny — before you ring off, there is something else. Just after you left today, a Mr Strafford phoned. He wanted to speak to you. It was urgent, he said.'

'Oh.' Too numb with shock to be interested in

anything Mark might have to say, Jenny shrugged. 'Well, he'll just have to talk to one of you.'

'Yes. Well, I imagine you'll need some time to sort things out. We'll see you next Monday, perhaps.'

'Yes.'

'If there's anything. Anything at all.'

'Thank you. I must go now.' Jenny hung up.

★　★　★

The evening dissolved into a blood red London twilight. Darkness fell at last. The children had a comfort meal of baked beans on toast and hot chocolate, then went to bed.

Jenny phoned the Worcester Royal Infirmary, where a ward sister told her that as yet there was no change in Gareth's condition. She was chatty, sympathetic and kind, and said that the prognosis was good. The patient had had a brain scan, which had revealed only minor contusions, so there was every possibility he would make a complete recovery. She promised to ring the moment he regained consciousness.

So Jenny stayed by the phone. With a bottle of whisky for company, she waited for Robin to come home.

At half past eleven, he did. Smelling strongly of patchouli or some similar ethnic scent, he flopped down on the sofa. Yawning, he stretched. 'Boozing all alone?' he enquired, genially. 'Solitary alcoholism — wouldn't have thought that was *your* scene?'

Robin himself was drunk. Or at least, half drunk. Overlying the patchouli, or whatever, was a strong reek of spirits. But competing with both was the smell of recent sex.

Jenny grimaced in distaste. Now, she decided she would go to bed, leaving Robin to sleep it off on the sitting room sofa. But then, she changed her mind. Having drunk far more whisky than was good for her, she felt more than equal to a battle of words with him. So, she would have one. 'Robin,' she began, 'I don't quite know how to tell you this. But something awful — '

'What is it?' Now, Robin stared at her in alarm. 'Jenny, are the kids — '

'They're both fine. It's my Mum and Dad.'

★   ★   ★

Robin didn't pretend to be heartbroken. But, all the same, he was sympathetic. He expressed his concern very properly, and even tried to take Jenny's hands in his. But she pushed him away. 'There's something else,' she said.

'What?' Having had his gesture of consolation summarily rejected, Robin scowled now. 'Well?' he demanded.

'I want a divorce.' Jenny kept her eyes on his face. 'I've wanted one for years now. I didn't ask you before, because I didn't want to upset my mother. But now there's no need to pretend, and I — '

'Pretend?' For a moment, Robin looked winded. But then, he rallied. 'You've no grounds for divorce,' he muttered. 'But even if you had, what would you do about the children? What would you say to them?'

'They'd understand.' Jenny shrugged. 'Half the kids in their school seem to come from single-parent families, anyway.'

'Who is it? That bloke in the wine bar?'

'He was a business client. Robin, there's no one else. I just want to be free of you.'

'Why?'

'Well, for a start, you've been seeing other women.'

'Have I?' Robin grimaced. 'How do you know? Come on, spit it out. What's that fat bitch been telling you now?'

'If you mean Sheila, I haven't spoken to her for months.'

'So it's feminine intuition, is it?'

'For God's sake, Robin! It's obvious!' Jenny's blue eyes flashed fire. 'The scarlet letter's there, for all to see!'

'Oh.' Robin poured himself some whisky. 'You don't want a divorce,' he muttered. 'You need me. What if your father were to die? You'd have nobody then, except the kids.'

'On the contrary, I have dozens of relations.'

'Have you?' Robin grinned. 'Who are they, then? A tribe of country cousins? Funny — I don't remember them at the wedding.'

Jenny took a deep breath. 'I have my father's family,' she said.

'Yeah. One old auntie, isn't it? In Leeds. Big deal. Jenny, if your father dies — '

'There's no reason why he should.'

Robin reached for the bottle of whisky. With a remarkably steady hand, he poured himself another

405

generous measure. 'Let me get this straight,' he said. 'Your Dad's been in a road accident. He's in hospital with head injuries. Right?'

'Yes. But — '

Robin took Jenny's glass. 'I think you've had enough for tonight,' he said. 'I'll go and put your blanket on. Then we'll get you to bed.'

'Robin, listen to me!'

'Well?'

Jenny looked at him. Now, she could have gone meekly to bed, and blamed her indiscretions so far on the whisky. But tonight, she had drunk too much even to consider the value of restraint. She told Robin everything. All about Peter and Shirley, all about Delia, all about Mark.

He heard her in silence. When she had finished, he scowled at her. 'It makes no difference,' he said. 'You're still my wife.'

'Robin, I don't want you! I don't love you, I don't need you, I — '

'You think I'll let you divorce me so you can marry some jumped-up Cockney barrow boy?' Robin's dark eyes were like flints. 'Don't even begin to try.'

'But, Robin — '

'Shut up.' Robin struggled to his feet. 'I'd fight you,' he hissed. 'I'd get the best lawyers there are, and they'd drag you through the dirt. You lying, deceitful bitch, I'd have your name — *and* your so-called father's name — in every newspaper in the land. I'd also make sure you never saw your children again!'

32

Shirley was buried next to her parents, in the quiet country churchyard near her childhood home. When Jenny arrived back from Worcester, tired and depressed after a horribly dreary weekend which had included the funeral and several long, distressing visits to the hospital where Gareth still lay unconscious, she collapsed into bed and fell fast asleep.

On Monday morning she phoned the office to tell them she'd be back at work the day after next. She ushered Robin off to college, sent the children to school, then sat down to sift through a great pile of her mother's letters, other papers, and personal effects.

At half past nine, she heard the postman's whistle. The letterbox rattled, so she went to pick up the mail. Among the circulars and bills, there was a letter for her.

The handwritten address looked like old fashioned German script, modified to take into account the limitations of English postmen. The envelope bore a London postmark.

Puzzled, Jenny slit it open. Reading the letter inside, she received the shock of her life. Only a few lines long, it was nevertheless clear and very much to the point. It was signed, Peter Eisenstadt.

Sitting down, Jenny read it again. Peter Eisenstadt informed her that, very recently, he had been told he had a daughter living, and that this daughter was Jenny herself.

He said he hoped shortly to be in touch again. If, in the meantime, Jenny wished to write to him, she should do so at the above address.

Jenny shivered. The very coldness of those few curt lines suggested he thought the whole thing must be a pack of malicious lies. So now, the spectre of ruinous litigation rose up before her, a horrid, threatening ghost. She looked again at the sheet of paper in her hand. Now, it struck her as odd that Peter Eisenstadt hadn't sent even this short letter through his solicitor.

For the first time in years, she actually wanted Robin to come home. Already, she was planning how to murder Mark Strafford — but she would need an accomplice, and Robin was the obvious person to press-gang into helping her.

It was well past three when she heard Robin's car draw up outside. Before he could even take off his jacket, she thrust the letter into his hands. She watched while he read. 'How could he?' she demanded, now in tears of terror, frustration and rage. 'Robin, how could he do this to me?'

'He didn't.' Smugly, Robin grinned. 'I wrote to him. I sent him a nice, long, interesting letter.'

'You did *what?*'

'You heard.' Robin laughed, and now Jenny could smell the alcohol on his breath. 'So, there you are. Do you still want to divorce me? Well, now you've somewhere to go. Back home to Daddy.'

Jenny wanted to kick him. Punch him. Hit him until he bled. 'But why did you do it?' she cried, uncomprehending. 'Why do something as stupid and pointless as that?'

'Because you hurt *me*.' Robin would not look at her. 'I loved you,' he muttered. 'I loved you so much! Once, I thought you loved me. But you've never even liked me, you — '

'Robin, that's not true. I — '

'Oh, forget it. I certainly have. Is there anything to drink in this house?'

But now the phone began to ring, so Jenny went into the hall to answer it. 'Who is it?' called Robin, coming out of the kitchen with a can of lager in his hand.

'Just a wrong number.' Jenny reached for her mackintosh. Picking up her handbag, she slung it over her shoulder. She left the house.

She went to a public call box and phoned Mark back. 'It's Mr Eisenstadt,' he told her, without preamble. 'He's ill. I thought you would wish to know.'

'Oh.' Blankly, for now she knew nothing could surprise her, Jenny stared at her reflection in the glass. 'H-how did you find out?' she stammered, at last.

'We had an appointment,' Mark replied. 'I was supposed to be showing him some jewellery I'd found. I don't often deal in rocks, but anyway — I'd heard of a bloke selling this little lot of art nouveau stuff, and I thought Mr Eisenstadt might be interested. He'd asked me before to look out for that sort of thing, you see.'

'Then?'

'Then I had a message to say he wouldn't be able

to meet me after all. I phoned his office and they told me he was ill. So I spoke to his secretary, and she gave me the name of the hospital he's in. I needed to know about this stuff, you see. There's some American after it, very keen I understand, so I couldn't keep the guy hanging about.'

'But is he very ill?' asked Jenny, woodenly. 'I mean — he's not dying or anything, is he?'

'No, I don't think so. He spoke to me, actually — said he was in for some tests. Jenny, I get the feeling you already know about this.'

'I don't know anything at all. But my husband wrote to him recently, so I was afraid — '

'Your *husband* wrote to him? Why?'

'It's too complicated to explain over the phone.'

'You can tell me about it later, then. But don't worry. Mr Eisenstadt told me he's been meaning to have these tests for some time. I don't suppose it's anything serious.'

'I do hope you're right.'

'So do I, sweetheart.' Mark laughed. 'I shan't get my commission otherwise. Look, why don't you ring his lady friend? Have you got her number?'

'Somewhere.' Jenny pushed another coin into the slot. 'I ought to call Delia anyway,' she went on, miserably. 'To tell her about my Mum and Dad.'

'What about them?'

Jenny told him.

'Oh, God. I'm so sorry.' Now, for the first time, Mark sounded genuinely distressed. 'Is your Dad badly hurt?'

'He's unconscious. But he might pull through.'

'Poor Jenny.' Mark drew a deep breath. 'Look,

sweetheart — we must meet.'

'What for?'

'To talk. Just to talk. I'll take you out to lunch.'

'I'm very busy at the moment. I can't — '

'But you must eat, so have some lunch with me. I'll pick you up from work on Wednesday, about one. There's a nice Italian place near your office. I'll book a table.'

'Okay.' Too tired, confused and upset to argue, Jenny rang off. Coming out of the call box, she saw Adam walking up the road towards her.

'Is the phone on the blink?' he enquired.

'Yes. But it was a fault on the line. The operator said it should be back to normal in ten minutes or so.'

'Good. Mum, have you heard any more about Grandad?'

'I rang the hospital earlier today. He's still in a coma.'

'Are we going to Worcester again this weekend?'

'I expect so. I want to get the rest of Mum's things tidied up.' Jenny sighed. 'Oh, Adam!' she wailed. 'What a mess it all is! What am I going to do now?'

'You'll get it sorted, Mum.' Adam hugged her. 'You always do.'

★ ★ ★

From her office window, Jenny watched as the navy blue BMW drove past, pulled in, then stopped on a double yellow line. Mark got out and locked the door.

Standing on the office steps, she shook her head. 'Oh, Mark,' she thought, 'why aren't you fat? Why aren't you greasy and bloated? Or toothless, or bald? It would make things so much easier for me!'

'Hello, sweetheart.' Mark kissed Jenny's cheek. 'The place is just along here,' he said.

It was a pleasant restaurant. Cool, green and quiet, it was the ideal place for a non-committal lunch date. 'This is really nice,' said Jenny, conversationally.

'It's okay, I suppose.' Mark shrugged. 'What would you like?'

'A salad, please,' Jenny replied.

'Is that all?'

'Some chicken, maybe.' Jenny glanced at the menu. 'I'll have that,' she said pointing at the menu's 'specials' column.

But when their order came, Jenny merely played with her mixed salad. Mark moved his pasta round and round the dish. 'Isn't that any good?' he asked, looking at Jenny's still-laden plate.

'It's fine.' Jenny sighed. 'I'm not very hungry, that's all.'

'Sweetheart, you must eat!' Mark's eyes met hers. 'Try to get something inside you.'

'You're a fine one to talk. You're never going to finish that.'

'I'm at least going to try.'

But it was Mark who gave up first. 'We ought to make some plans,' he said, pushing his plate aside. 'Decide what to do.'

'We're not going to do anything.'

'No?' Mark took Jenny's hand. 'I love you.'

'No, you don't. I'm a scrawny, sarcastic cow. How could anyone love me?'

'Here we go again.' Mark shook his head. 'Tell me about your husband.'

'I don't wish to discuss Robin.'

'Are you happy with him?'

'Mark, stop this!'

'I thought as much.' Complacently, Mark smiled. 'How soon could you leave him?'

'Oh, for God's sake!'

'I'm sorry.' Catching the waiter's eye, Mark requested the bill. 'It was fine,' he replied, when asked if anything was wrong with the food. 'We're in a bit of a hurry, that's all.'

They stood on the pavement outside. 'What shall we do this afternoon?' asked Mark.

'I'm going back to work,' replied Jenny, walking away now.

'Why don't you come home with me, instead?'

'To commit adultery? I don't think so.'

'Touché.' Mark sighed. 'Jenny, I'm very sorry about your parents. I hope your Dad makes it.'

'Thank you.' They had reached the office now. Jenny looked up at him. 'Actually, Mark — there *is* something I'd like to know. How did you get hold of my home phone number?'

'I looked you up, of course.' Mark grinned at her. 'I went through all the Langleys until I found you.'

'Honestly?'

'Yeah, straight up. It cost me a fortune, I expect.' Mark shook his head. 'I used my own phone, too. So I can't offset it against tax now.'

'That was an expensive mistake.'

'Right, it was.' Now, Mark laughed. 'But it's an expensive business, this being in love. Listen — I have to go now, but I'll be in touch.'

He found his car keys. A minute later, he was driving away, leaving Jenny deep in thought.

33

'You look much better today.' Newly promoted to managing editor of *World Wide Magazine*, Delia had been out of town for the past week, but now she was home again. 'How do you feel?' she enquired.

'I'm okay.' Peter shrugged. 'I don't have any pain. I'm just tired.'

'Well, you're in the right place to sleep.'

'Also to have a coronary, I think.' Peter grimaced. 'I had rather a shock last week,' he explained. Opening the drawer of his bedside table, he took out a letter. 'It seems my past is catching up with me.'

'How do you mean?' asked Delia.

'This was sent to the office. Fortunately, my secretary didn't open it.' Peter handed her the letter. 'Read that,' he said.

'But what — '

'Darling, just read.'

So Delia read. Then, she re-read. She looked at Peter. But then, she turned away. 'I don't believe a word of it,' she muttered, at last. 'It's absolute nonsense. It must be.'

'Must it?'

'Of course it must! Somebody is trying to blackmail you. Or play some kind of stupid joke.'

'I don't think so.' Peter retrieved his letter. 'Look at me.'

'What?'

'Look at me!'

So Delia looked. 'Well, maybe,' she conceded, at last. 'I suppose there's a very slight resemblance. Turn towards the light.'

Peter obliged. 'It's obvious, isn't it?' he demanded. 'It's as clear as day.'

'I don't know!' Still in shock, Delia stared at him. 'But — do the circumstances fit? Were you in Evesbridge, in 1945? Did you have an affair with Shirley Bell?'

'Yes.' Again, Peter shrugged. 'Then I went back to Germany. I fell in love with Reni, and married her instead.'

'But Shirley gave birth to your child.'

'So it would seem.' Peter rubbed his eyes. 'I know what you're thinking now,' he muttered. 'How could he have been so cruel? How could he have left the girl, and the unborn child? But, Delia — I didn't know she was pregnant.'

'Didn't you ever write to her?'

'No. I couldn't. But she had my address. She never wrote to me.'

'So?'

'So, I assumed she had forgotten me. Or changed her mind. After all, it would not have been an easy thing, in those days, for an English girl even to go to Germany. Let alone to marry a German.

'How could I have asked her to leave a comfortable home in England, to come to a city which was just a pile of rubble? Where there was nothing to eat, and where half the people were walking around in rags? I thought — '

'She would take one look and go straight home again?'

'Exactly.' Peter stared out of the window. 'It wouldn't have worked, anyway. Shirley was a nice girl — but she wasn't interested in literature, or music, or anything like that. She wasn't even a Catholic. So, I told myself she had considered all this, and decided to forget me.'

'I see.' Now, Delia recalled her own first meeting with Shirley Bell, and her own first sight of the pretty, dark-haired child. 'Do you remember Jenny?' she asked.

'I remember her. I have thought of no one else for the past three days.'

'Do you think she is your daughter?'

'I'm sure of it. I can see her now. She's mine.'

'Did you reply to this letter?'

'I wrote a short note. To Jenny. I told her I'd received a letter, and that I'd be in touch again later. I didn't know what else to say.'

'I don't suppose you did,' Delia agreed. 'Do you want to see her again?'

'Perhaps, when I'm better, we ought to meet.'

'Perhaps.' Now, Delia looked at him. 'But you must have heard me mention Shirley a hundred times,' she said. 'You knew she lived in Worcestershire. Did you never even wonder?'

'Wonder what? Shirley is not an unusual name.' Candidly, Peter looked back at her. 'Did you never tell her about me?'

'No, never. It would only have worried her, knowing I was involved with a man who couldn't — I mean, who would never — '

'Do the decent thing by you, either.' Peter bit his lower lip. 'You must hate me now,' he muttered. 'If not for hurting you, then for behaving so badly towards your friend.'

'Don't be ridiculous!' Delia took his hands in hers. 'Oh, darling — you never meant to hurt her! Or to hurt me!'

'No, but — '

'Don't upset yourself. We'll sort something out, don't worry.' Now, firmly, Delia changed the subject. 'That agency rang me this morning,' she said. 'They've found a house for us.'

'Oh?' Not really interested, Peter nevertheless tried to sound as if he was. 'What's it like?'

'It's lovely. It's a little Georgian villa, with three bedrooms, a sitting room with pretty french windows, and a garden. There's garaging, too.'

'Where is it?'

'Chelsea.'

'Is that okay?'

'It's ideal. When you're better, we'll go and take a closer look.'

'We? You still want to live with me?'

'Darling, of course I do!'

'Then buy this place. I'll arrange for the money to be released. Do everything in your name only — then, if anything happens to me, the house will be yours.'

'Peter, don't be so morbid. Nothing's going to happen to you.'

'I hope not. But do as I say, all the same. Delia?'

'Yes?'

'Does this business of Jenny make a very great difference to the way you feel about me?'

'Did you love Jenny's mother?'

'No. I don't think I ever did. I was infatuated, that's all.' Peter sighed. 'I was far from home, and lonely, and she was kind to me. I suppose that makes it even worse.'

'I don't think so.' Delia shook her head. 'Shirley spoke of you once,' she continued. 'She liked you, certainly. When you left, she was very upset. But I don't think you actually broke her heart. I know she loves her husband. *He* adores Jenny. All things considered, perhaps it's worked out for the best.'

'So, one day you may forgive me?'

'There's nothing to forgive.' Delia kissed him. 'Don't worry any more. Get well, instead.'

★ ★ ★

After an exhaustive battery of tests, Peter was finally diagnosed as having some peculiar bacterial infection which had weakened his lungs and damaged a kidney. There were appropriate drugs, however, so now he swallowed cocktails of antibiotics and waited patiently for his body to mend. While he remained in hospital, Delia arranged the purchase of the Chelsea house.

She now discovered that one of the partners in the firm of Forrester, Lane and Hendry was a certain Mrs Jenny Langley. After some thought, she decided not to mention this to Peter. He didn't need any more surprises. As for herself, she felt that these days nothing could astonish her any more.

Eventually, Peter began to recover. He put on a little weight, he lost the extreme pallor of sickness, so he was allowed home. Delia took three weeks' holiday leave and looked after him, making him eat properly and, although she had never been either a competent or confident driver, taking him out of London in the big, black Mercedes, to breathe fresher air.

★　★　★

'You've a much healthier colour this morning.' Drawing back the bedroom curtains to reveal a bright and beautiful Saturday, Delia was delighted to see the sunshine. 'How do you feel?' she asked.

'Better. Very much better.' Peter yawned, then stretched. 'I think I'll get up.'

'Stay there. I'll put some toast on.'

Delia made breakfast. As she and Peter ate, they listened to the morning news, but only half heard the details of that day's crop of horrors. Switching over to a local station, now they learned that several violent robberies had taken place in North London, carried out by a man equipped with an army revolver, whom members of the public should not approach. If he were spotted, however, they should ring this number. A three car pile-up in which two people had died had blocked the south-bound lanes of —

'Nothing but death and disaster.' Reaching across the bed, Delia turned off this catalogue of gloom. 'But at least you're fit and well again.'

'Yes. That's something.' Now, Peter kissed her. 'You're so beautiful,' he said. 'I do love you.'

'Yes, I know.'

'When I was ill, I was so frightened. I thought I

would die. Then I was afraid that even if I recovered, I might never make love with you again.'

'Silly.' Delia ruffled his hair. Today, Peter looked so handsome. One would never have guessed that, only a fortnight ago, he'd seemed half dead. What was more, he was one of those sickening people who definitely improved with age. Too slight and insubstantial in youth, he'd since broadened out a little, and middle age really suited him.

Delia gazed into his eyes. The irises clear and blue, the whites pure and unblemished, they were the eyes of a child. Again, she ran her fingers through his hair. 'You're going ever so grey,' she observed.

'I know.' Peter grimaced. 'It's horrible. I look so ugly and old.'

'No, you look distinguished.' Delia hugged him. 'I love you so much,' she said. 'I couldn't bear to lose you. Don't ever be ill again.'

After a fine weekend the weather changed, and Monday morning was dull, cold and rainsoaked. Promising to be home early, Delia went off to work, leaving Peter alone.

He finished his breakfast, then took the newspaper through to the sitting room. He glanced at the business news, but then he got up again and went into his study.

There, he found some writing paper. Pushing aside a mountain of files and reports, he wrote to his daughter. He suggested they meet for lunch later that week, at a small French restaurant near Leicester Square.

'By the way, I'll be having a longer lunch hour today,' said Jenny. 'I'm meeting a new client, and he's taking me out for a meal.'

'Oh. Right. I thought you were looking extra smart this morning.' Busy with a set of complicated costings, Dot hardly glanced up. 'Have fun,' she murmured. 'We'll see you when we do.'

That morning, Jenny had agonised for half an hour over what to wear. She was still not quite sure about the black straight skirt, cream silk blouse and a grey tailored jacket, finished off with gold jewellery and black patent high-heeled shoes. But now, these would have to do.

She had decided she would be cool with Peter. She owed him nothing. She wanted nothing from him. But all the same, by the time she reached Leicester Square, she found she was in a state of nervous terror. Her heart was hammering against her ribs, she was breathing harshly and her blouse was sticking to her shoulder blades.

Now, she practised the breathing exercises she'd learned in natural childbirth classes. Eventually, she felt just a little calmer. Taking a deep breath, she pushed the door of the restaurant open wide.

Inside, she found one of those cool, gloomy places where businessmen meet, to do deals over bottles of excellent claret and good French cooking. The *maître* came up at once, welcomed her effusively, then led her to an area in the darkest part of the restaurant, where the tables were spaced widely apart.

'Your guest, sir,' he murmured. 'Sir?'

'Yes?' Peter Eisenstadt looked up from his book. Seeing Jenny, he rose to his feet. He held out his hand. 'My dear Jenny,' he said, simply. 'It's so nice to see you again!'

★ ★ ★

The waiter handed them menus, then retired to a discreet distance. Jenny began to look through the courses on offer.

'You had no problems in finding this place?' asked Peter politely, as he read.

'None at all.' Jenny kept her eyes fixed firmly on the *carte du jour*. 'In fact, your directions were impeccable.'

'Good.' Putting down his own menu, Peter looked at his daughter. 'Jenny,' he said kindly, 'I can see you're nervous. But really, you don't need to be. I don't intend to embarrass or annoy you today.'

'Nor I you.' Glancing up, Jenny met his eyes. 'Will you order for me?' she asked. 'Something light will do. I'm not very hungry.'

So Peter spoke to the waiter, who went away and soon returned with a basket of warm rolls and a plateful of fat, shiny olives.

Peter broke up a roll. 'I don't know why your husband decided to write to me,' he began. 'But believe me when I say that I'm so pleased he did. Tell me — have you always known?'

'Yes. Well, since I was quite small, anyway. I didn't know all the details, of course.'

'Details?'

'My mother explained that my natural father had left us. But that was all she said.' Jenny shrugged. 'It never bothered me. As far as I was concerned, her husband was my Dad.'

'I see.' Peter nodded. 'Will you tell me a little about yourself?' he asked. 'Nothing especially personal. Just something about your childhood, perhaps. Something you might tell a friend.'

Jenny considered for a moment. But then, hesitantly, she began to talk. She described her first seaside holiday, at the age of four or five. Then she recalled her first day at school.

'I said I wasn't going back the next day, because I knew everything already.' Remembering, she smiled. 'I was a very self-important, bossy child. But then, only children often are.'

'You have no brothers or sisters, then?'

'No. None.'

Now, the first course arrived. So Jenny stopped talking, and began to eat. Peter fell silent, too.

Although both Peter and Jenny went through the motions of eating their lunch, neither actually consumed very much. The atmosphere between them was far too tense for comfort or good digestion, and it was only over coffee, with the prospect of escape imminent, that Jenny began to relax even a little.

She'd been dreading Peter asking after her mother. She knew for a fact that, if he did, she would burst into tears. But so far he hadn't mentioned Shirley at all, and now she dared to hope he wasn't going to.

'You haven't told me anything about yourself,' she

said, as she stirred in some more sugar, both to make the coffee palatable and because she was feeling a little faint now. 'I know almost nothing about you.'

'On the contrary, I expect you know rather more than I might wish.' A little colour crept into Peter's pale face. 'For instance — you know about Delia, I suppose?'

'Yes. But I learned of that by chance.'

'Chance. That's not quite the right word, I think.' Peter met Jenny's eyes. 'Jenny, tell me honestly — do you hate me for what I did?'

'No, of course I don't hate you. Why should I?' Jenny shrugged. 'I don't suppose you meant to hurt anyone. I accept that these things happen.'

'Indeed they do.' Peter stirred his coffee round and round and round. 'Do you have children yourself?' he enquired.

'Yes, two. A boy and a girl.'

'Have you a photograph of them?'

'I think so.' Opening her handbag, Jenny rummaged through it. Eventually she found a holiday snapshot, taken the previous summer. 'Adam and Jane,' she said, passing it across.

Peter studied the picture intently. Then he looked up and searched Jenny's own face, comparing the children's features with hers. 'The boy is very like you,' he observed, complacently. 'Doesn't everyone say so?'

'Yes, they do. But Jane is more like her father.'

'They're beautiful children.' Peter smiled. 'A great credit to you. May I perhaps meet them one day? Just as a friend, naturally.'

'Yes.' Jenny smiled too. 'Yes, of course you shall. You may keep the picture too, if you wish.'

'Thank you, that's very kind.' Peter put the photograph in his jacket pocket. 'I shall be moving house shortly,' he told her. 'I'll send you the address, shall I?'

'Yes, please do.' Relaxing almost completely now, Jenny put her coffee aside and sat back in her chair. 'Thank you for a delicious meal,' she said.

'My pleasure.' Peter summoned the waiter. 'I'm so glad we've been able to talk,' he said. 'I hope we'll be able to meet again soon.'

'That would be lovely.'

'I'm happy you should think so.' Peter took out his wallet. 'Well, now I shall be getting a taxi. May I take you anywhere?'

'No, thank you all the same. I have to do some shopping.'

'I see.' Peter stood up. 'Well then, I'll phone you. Thank you for coming today.'

They stood together on the pavement until a taxi stopped for Peter.

They shook hands again.

Then they said goodbye.

★ ★ ★

'Was it a success?' asked Dot, as Jenny came back from the cloakroom, humming to herself and looking happier than she had for days.

'I'm sorry?' Jenny frowned. 'Was what a success?'

'Your lunch date. With your new client.' Dot narrowed her eyes. 'I thought you said a customer

426

was taking you out to lunch?'

'Oh. Right. I did.'

'So how did you get on? Will you be seeing him again?'

'Yes. Definitely.' Jenny smiled. 'There are going to be a few slight problems. But nothing I can't sort out, I'm sure.'

34

'Did you ask her to come and see us?' asked Delia, when Peter told her whom he'd met for lunch that day.

'I said I'd be in touch.' It was evening now, and Peter looked drained and ill. 'I do feel rather faint,' he admitted, when Delia enquired. 'Perhaps I'll go to bed.'

'Maybe you should,' Delia agreed. 'I'm glad you've talked to Jenny,' she added. 'She's a nice girl, isn't she?'

'Very nice. In fact, she's charming. She was very kind to a wicked old man.'

'You're not wicked!'

'You don't think so?' Peter loosened his tie. 'Well, I'm not very virtuous. I don't repent, you see. There'll be no forgiveness for any of *my* sins.'

★   ★   ★

It had needed lots of redecoration and refurbishment, but at last the house in Chelsea was ready. Delia's own little flat was up for sale, the lease on Peter's had only six weeks to run, and finally the two of them spent their last night together at the flat in St John's Wood.

'Goodness, how tidy it looks!' exclaimed Delia. Shaking her head, she stared all around Peter's empty sitting room. 'With the clutter all packed and your old rubbish thrown away, it looks so neat!'

'As if a ghost lives here.' Peter shrugged. 'Won't you hate to live with such a messy person as me?'

'You put up with all my faults and failings, so it's only fair that I should put up with yours.' Delia kissed him. 'I don't mind a civilised mess.'

'But we'll have some terrible arguments, I think. You're so very tidy.'

'We shan't argue at all,' said Delia, firmly. 'We never have, and we won't begin now.'

The weather forecast had predicted a day of rain, but now the showers seemed to have gone over. The sun was shining on wet pavements, and there was a smell of greenery in the air, which contended with and almost overcame the usual smell of London dirt.

'Let's go out for lunch,' suggested Delia. 'Look, the removal men won't want us here. We'll only get in their way.'

'Where shall we go?'

'To that Italian place near Trafalgar Square. We'll go and feed the pigeons, have lunch, then go to the house and see how they're getting on. I'll come back later and check this place over.'

'Okay,' Peter agreed. 'God, what's that rumbling noise? It sounds like a Churchill tank.'

'The van's here.' Looking through the window, Delia saw the men getting out. 'Come on, darling. Let's get out of their way.'

The removal men came clumping up the stairs. Speaking to their foreman, Delia found they would indeed prefer to work unsupervised. Peter sat in the empty kitchen, staring vacantly out of the window.

But he let Delia fasten his coat, then wind a scarf around his neck.

'Will you be all right?' she asked anxiously, observing he was distant and preoccupied. 'Peter, what's the matter?'

'Nothing. I just feel a bit shaky, that's all.'

'Shall we stay here, then?'

'No. We'll go out. I expect some fresh air and exercise will do me good.'

'I'll find us a taxi.' Delia went to the front door. 'Turn the radio off,' she added, as she picked up her keys. 'Unless the men want it on, that is.'

The radio was an old one whose batteries were almost flat, and now it croaked and crackled. 'Yeah, leave it,' said the foreman, as the local news came on. 'Let's see if they've caught that fella with the shooter.'

They hadn't. Just before dawn, two men had broken into a North London jeweller's shop and stolen several thousand pounds' worth of Swiss watches. While one had been caught, the other had escaped in a white Ford Cortina, registration number something or other. He was armed, and members of the public were warned again not to approach him, but instead to ring this number or contact any police station.

'Stupid bastard,' observed one of the removal men. 'Playin' with shooters — mug's game that is. Don't you reckon, squire?'

Peter shrugged. Now, he heard Delia calling him. She'd found a taxi, so was he coming today or tomorrow?

Slowly, he went downstairs.

★　★　★

They took the taxi into the West End and, as Delia
had suggested, walked to Trafalgar Square. Much to
the disgust of the tourists with their ever ready
cameras, Nelson's Column was shrouded in
scaffolding and blue plastic sheets, but their children
played happily on the lions, shrieking and laughing
and sliding off the great beasts' slippery backs.

'Shall we go and eat now?' asked Delia. 'It's early,
so I expect there'll be a table free.'

'I don't want lunch just yet.' Peter had forgotten
his gloves, and now he pushed his cold hands deep
into his pockets. 'I'd like to see that new exhibition
at the National Portrait Gallery.'

'I think we should have lunch.' Delia took his
arm. 'Darling, you must eat! It was starving yourself
that made you so ill.'

'I don't starve myself.'

'You do!' Delia grimaced. 'Come along, Peter. It's
lunchtime.'

'All right. But could we go somewhere quiet? Like
the Almeida, in Tanner Street?'

'We don't *have* to go anywhere.' Now Delia was
worried. 'You don't look at all well,' she said. 'Shall
we just go home?'

'Not to that mess.' Peter squared his shoulders.
'There's nothing wrong with me,' he said. 'I've just
got a bit of a headache, that's all.'

'You're not going to faint, are you?'

'Of course not.'

They went up St Martin's Lane, then turned into
the narrow street leading to the restaurant. The sun

431

was shining very brightly now. The gratings, railings and windows sparkled, and Delia felt her spirits lift. She took Peter's hand.

He smiled at her. Then, most uncharacteristically — for he hardly ever touched her in public — he kissed her cheek. Then he spoke. 'I think I'll get a *Standard*,' he said, as they emerged into Terrace Walk. 'From the news stand across there.'

'Okay.' Delia was looking in a shop window. 'I'll wait here.'

But now, as Peter crossed the street, she heard the sirens wail. As he pushed his hand into his pocket, to find some small change, she heard a different but equally spine-chilling sound. This was a discordant electronic shrieking, and it came from the car which was hurtling the wrong way up the street.

As Delia jumped back, the white Ford Cortina mounted the pavement, careening along inches from the walls. Then it smashed straight into a bollard, coming to a standstill not ten yards away from her.

There was a blur of sight and sound. A police car, its lights flashing, drove up behind the Cortina and rammed it. Now there was a voice yelling, 'Get down, get down, get *DOWN*!'

A few seconds ago, the street had been almost empty. There'd been no traffic, and only a few quietly strolling pedestrians, thinking about their lunch. But now there was noise and movement. Now a woman's frightened shrieks and a child's terrified howling echoed all around, bouncing off the tall buildings. Wide-eyed, Delia stared at the confusion before her. She blinked in disbelief.

The street was full of vehicles now. Three, four

police cars had wedged themselves into the junction of Tanner Street and Terrace Walk, and Delia watched as men in uniforms tumbled out of them, taking up positions in doorways or behind parked cars. On the opposite side of the road from her, a couple of policemen armed with revolvers crouched beside a cluster of convenient dustbins which gave them some rudimentary cover.

The man in the white Cortina was trapped.

Shrinking back against the wall, then sliding into a sitting position and eventually lying prone on the pavement, Delia still thought she must be dreaming. That she was imagining a scene from an American gangster film. For this couldn't really be a Saturday lunchtime, in a quiet London street . . .

Peter paid for his newspaper, then turned to go back across the street. He'd heard the sirens, of course, and had vaguely understood what must be happening. But the sun was in his eyes, he felt light-headed — and now he hesitated, uncertain what to do.

The man in the Cortina levelled his revolver at the policemen by the bins. As if turned to stone, Peter stood motionless, the only civilian remaining on his feet. Half frozen with terror, Delia willed him to keep still. For there was a chance, a slim chance, that the gunman hadn't seen him.

'Don't anyone move!' The man in the Cortina glared all around him, then fixed his eyes on one of the policemen opposite Delia. 'If anyone comes near me, he gets it!'

'Hey you, get down!' Another policeman, glancing

sideways from a doorway, now noticed Peter. He tried to attract his attention. 'Get *down!*' he repeated, desperately, out of the corner of his mouth.

Peter did not seem to hear. So now the policeman broke his own cover and edged towards him, perhaps intending to push him on to the pavement, flat on his face, out of harm's way.

The man with the gun fired, shot after shot after shot, aiming at the policeman's chest. The bullets went wide, missing their target by at least three feet. But then, to her horror, Delia saw Peter stumble. Clumsily he toppled forwards. In slow motion, as if his bones had dissolved and his body turned to jelly, he slumped against the news stand, then rolled over on to his back and lay still.

'Peter!' Oblivious of danger, Delia jumped to her feet and ran to him. Pushing a policeman aside, she fell on her knees beside him. Taking his hand, she chafed it. Holding his wrist she felt for the pulse, which she feared would not be there.

Now she saw that the bullet had hit him in the head, just above his left eyebrow. Now, a thin but fast-flowing trickle of blood slid down his temples and into his hair, matting it with sticky red gore and making a scarlet pool on the dirty pavement where he lay.

His eyes were closed and his expression calm. But for that trickle of blood, one might have guessed he'd fainted. Taking him by the shoulders, Delia shook him, willing him to open his eyes.

In the confusion, the gunman had been overpowered. Now he was standing between two policemen. When Delia looked up at him, she saw a mere child, a boy of about sixteen, who seemed to be on the point of bursting into tears.

A skinny, urban scarecrow, the wretched creature stood abject, hangdog, looking uncomprehendingly at his victim. 'I never mean to do 'im,' he muttered, over and over. 'I never meant *him* no 'arm!'

'Are you his wife?' Now, a police inspector had appeared. He crouched beside the body. He touched Delia's arm. 'Madam? Are you this gentleman's wife?'

'No.' Delia wouldn't look at him. 'No, I'm not.'

'A friend, perhaps?'

'Yes. A friend.' Delia took Peter's hand in hers. Her vision blurring, she blinked away some tears. She looked at him for what she knew would be the last time.

The policeman was talking again, telling her an ambulance was on its way. She wondered if she ought to ask them to fetch a priest. Would Peter have wanted one? She turned to the inspector. 'Can somebody go and find a priest?' she said.

'I beg your pardon, madam?'

'I said, can someone find — ' But then, angrily, she dashed away her tears. 'It's nothing,' she muttered. 'I didn't say anything.'

'I'm sorry, madam. I thought you asked me to find a priest.' Again, the inspector touched Delia's sleeve. 'Was the gentleman a Catholic?'

'It's none of your business what he was.'

The inspector stood up now, and his place was taken by a young policewoman. 'Come on, love,' she said kindly, helping Delia to her feet. 'I'll come home with you, shall I? We'll make you a nice cup of tea.'

'No, we won't.' Delia shook off the comforting hand. 'You made a right mess of that,' she cried, glaring at the inspector. 'A proper bloody shambles, that was!'

She began to cry in earnest now. 'Leave me alone!' she sobbed, elbowing the policewoman aside. 'I'll get a taxi home.'

Home? Where was home? she wondered, as the WPC and another constable caught her, as she fainted against the inspector's chest.

35

Jenny laid her head against Mark Strafford's chest, and cried and cried and cried. She wept not only for Peter, for the father she'd hardly known, but also for Delia, deprived so violently of someone she had loved.

Mark took Jenny over. Every day he collected her from the office and took her to lunch, obliging her to eat. At half past five exactly he met her from work and took her home.

By the time a week had elapsed, Jenny was near breaking point. Realising this, the following lunchtime Mark drove past the restaurant and took her home with him. 'Go and have a nice hot bath,' he told her, closing the door behind them. 'Lock yourself in, then have a good long soak. You'll feel much better.'

'Shall I?'

'Of course you will.' He ushered her towards the stairs. 'You know the way.'

'May I use your bathrobe?'

'Sure.'

Mark went into the kitchen. He prepared lunch, and when Jenny emerged from the bathroom, he sat her down at the table and told her to eat. 'Did you make this?' she demanded, as she peered into the steaming casserole. 'All by yourself? From scratch?'

'Yes.' Wryly, Mark grinned. 'I've even learned to cook. So come on. Eat it while it's hot.'

'That was very nice.' Reaching for a paper napkin, Jenny dabbed at her mouth. 'Sorry to be so messy. But I never could eat pasta tidily.'

'Neither could I,' said Mark. 'Now — would you like some more?'

'No, I'm full. Honestly.' Warmed, fed, relaxed and actually feeling much happier now, Jenny smiled at him. 'But that was delicious. Thank you.'

'My pleasure.' Mark stood up. 'Will you have coffee?'

'No, thank you.'

'Oh, right — I remember now. Lemon tea, yes?'

'Please.' Warm and comfortable inside two luxurious bathrobes and several soft, fluffy towels, Jenny was reluctant to go and get dressed.

'Come and sit in a comfortable chair.'

'Okay.'

Mark went round the table to help Jenny up. As he did so, however, his hand brushed her shoulder. 'Calm down, sweetheart,' he murmured, for now she shrank from his touch. 'I wasn't going to grab you.'

'No?'

'As if I'd dare.' Mark grinned. 'Come here a minute. There's some sauce on your chin.'

'Don't!' Jenny backed away. 'Mark, I'm warning you! Lay one finger on me — '

'Christ, this is ridiculous.' Mark glared at her. 'I only want to help you!' he cried. 'To relax you. To comfort you. But if I even *look* at you for a moment, you get hysterical.'

'I don't! But you — '

'Stop it.' Cautiously, Mark reached out to stroke Jenny's face. 'You know you need me.'

'Do shut up!' Tears coming into her eyes, Jenny tried to blink them away. She failed. Soon, she was sobbing like a little child.

Mark let her cry. Taking her in his arms, he waited for her to relax. Eventually, she did. 'Come on,' he said, lifting her face to his. 'Let's stop messing each other about, and go to bed.'

'That's not a good idea.' Wanting him, longing for him, Jenny began to cry again. 'It would only lead to more aggravation.'

'Nonsense.' Mark kissed her cheek. '*I* think it would make everything right again.'

'Do you?' Dubiously, Jenny bit her lip. She thought about it. 'Okay, then,' she agreed. Too tired, miserable and confused to argue any more, she shrugged in exhausted resignation. 'Let's get it over with.'

'Well, I reckon that's about the most romantic thing anyone's ever said to me.'

'I'm sorry. But you might as well know now. You'll be the one doing the work.'

⋆   ⋆   ⋆

They went upstairs, to a bleached-out, almost empty bedroom. Here, thick white cotton curtains filtered the rapidly fading daylight, soft white rugs cushioned Jenny's bare feet, and a fat white duvet lay spotless and apparently untouched on large double bed. The cold, icy purity of it all made Jenny shiver. She thought, this is unreal. It's like a room in a dream.

Standing by the window, she turned to look at Mark. 'This isn't going to work,' she began. 'I'm sorry, but — '

Mark kissed her. Unfastening the bathrobes, he pushed them away from her body. He knelt down in front of her, and held her. 'Help me, sweetheart,' he whispered, his face against her heart. 'I can't do everything.'

So Jenny knelt, too. She unfastened his shirt, undid his belt, and eased him out of his clothes. 'You haven't changed a bit,' she observed, looking at him.

'I must have,' he said.

'No. Well — maybe just a little.' Jenny looked into his eyes. 'I was so afraid you'd be fat,' she whispered. 'Red-faced and bull-necked, with a beer belly hanging over your belt — '

'Oh, charming.' Mark wobbled Jenny's nose with his. 'I am a bit heavier,' he admitted. 'But I used to be much too skinny as a kid.'

'You were lovely.'

'Maybe.' Now, Mark studied Jenny. 'You need to get outside a few square meals,' he said. 'I know it's fashionable to be slim, but you're far too thin. How much do you weigh?'

'I don't know! About seven stone ten, I expect.'

'My God. That's practically anorexic.'

'Is it?' Jenny shrugged. 'So you don't want me now. Is that what you're saying?'

'Don't be silly. But look at you. You're like a

starving kitten. I'm twice your weight. I'd flatten you.'

'I don't care if you do.' Jenny kissed him. 'I want you,' she said, suddenly overpowered with emotion. 'I need you so much. Make love to me.'

★ ★ ★

'Did I hurt you?' he asked afterwards. For Jenny lay silent, staring up at the ceiling. 'Jenny?'

'Of course you didn't hurt me.' Stretching luxuriously, Jenny turned to smile at him. 'That was wonderful,' she said. 'Fantastic. Marvellous. In fact, it was all the things the songs say. It was making love.'

'I thought so.' Greatly relieved, Mark grinned back at her. He kissed her nose. 'I told you it would make you feel better,' he said.

'You were right. But — Mark? What's the matter?'

'Why did you let me go?' Grasping her shoulders, Mark shook her. 'Why didn't you come after me? Why didn't you kick me, hit me — make me see sense?'

'Because you didn't want me!'

'I did! You can't imagine how much I wanted you!' Now, Mark looked close to tears. 'It was the most stupid thing I ever did, leaving you.'

'No. You were right to break it off. I'd never have married you, not with all those conditions attached.' Jenny looked into his eyes. 'Mark?'

'What?'

'You've done very well for yourself. Did you have some lucky breaks? Or was it sheer hard slog that got you where you are today?'

'A mixture of the two.' Mark shrugged. 'Do you remember all that stuff I got from Germany?'

'You mean your contraband?'

'My illegal imports. Yeah.' Mark grinned. 'Well, I did a few good deals on them. Later on, I went to some country auctions in Sussex. I had a run of luck there, too. There was one Georgian table, I got it for a fiver. It turned out to be worth fifteen hundred quid. I met Mick — '

'Who?'

'Mick Viner, one of my partners. He was trying to set up an export business to the States. Well, we got together, raised a bit of capital, and made it all happen. We shipped over whole container-loads of stuff.

'The Yanks couldn't get enough — in fact, they fell over themselves to buy. Things just snowballed from there.'

'What about your private life? Did you ever find a little woman prepared to do exactly as you said?'

'Yes. Strangely enough, I did.'

'Who was she?'

'A secretary. She worked for a building society.' Mark shook his head. 'Her parents kicked up one hell of a fuss when she wanted to marry me. They had their eye on this bank manager up the road, you see. But all the same, she stuck to her guns.'

'So you married her. What went wrong?'

'It's hard to say, really.' Again, Mark shrugged. 'I liked Susie. I really did. She was a very nice girl.'

'But?'

'We had nothing in common. No shared interests

or hobbies. She wasn't bothered about the business, either. All she wanted was a nice home to impress her mates, a couple of kids, and a flash car to drive them about in. My job was to provide it all.

'Her parents made a lot of trouble for us. God — her father wouldn't give me the time of day unless I went down on my bended knees first. Her mother thought I was a yob.'

Mark sighed. 'We did try. But there wasn't enough time to be together, to do things as a couple. I was away so much.'

'Working too hard.'

'Perhaps.'

'She had too much leisure, and you had none.' Jenny stroked the fine dark hairs on Mark's wrist. 'What happened?' she asked. 'Did she find another man?'

'Yes. A civil servant from the tax office which was trying to sort out my financial affairs.' Mark grinned. 'As it happens, he's quite a decent bloke. The boys like him a lot. It's all worked out very well.'

'But didn't you think your marriage was worth fighting for?'

'No.'

'Why?'

'You know why,' Mark replied. 'I don't need to spell it out for you.'

'Maybe not. Well, I must go.' Jenny sat up. 'The children will be home from school soon. It's Maria's day off, and I — '

'I'll drive you.' Mark reached for his shirt. 'Shall I see you tomorrow?'

'Yes, if you like.' Light-headed with happiness now, Jenny laughed. 'I know! We could use the bed.'

'I didn't mean that. We have things to sort out.'

'Do you want me to leave my husband?'

'Yes.'

'Why is that?'

'You love me. You don't love him. Everything's quite simple, isn't it?'

★ ★ ★

In spite of her grief for her parents, concern for her failing marriage, guilt about her liaison with Mark and anxiety about her children, who would no doubt suffer most if there was a divorce, Jenny could not help being happy. She went about the house singing, and Robin glared at her, demanding to know what she had to be so sodding cheerful about.

At work, everything was running smoothly. The formalities had been settled, and she was now a partner in the firm. The other partners took her out for a celebratory dinner. 'Well,' said George Forrester, raising his glass, 'here's to the continued success and future expansion of Forrester, Lane, Hendry and Langley Associates.'

'It's a bit of a mouthful, that,' said Henry Lane.

'It is, rather.' George Forrester swallowed some more Chardonnay. 'I was wondering if we ought to change it. To something snappier.'

'Well, I'm sure Mrs Langley could come up with a few suggestions.'

'Jenny?' Philip Hendry topped up the new partner's glass. 'What do you think?'

'Come on, Jenny.' Henry Lane handed each partner a paper napkin, to scribble on. 'Something snappy,' he ruminated, taking out his biro. 'But what, exactly? What sounds right?'

★ ★ ★

The day after the dinner Mark phoned, to suggest a meeting. 'I only want to talk,' he said. 'I'll pick you up from work on Wednesday.'

'Thursday would be better.'

'Thursday, then. About six, okay?'

Sitting by the fire in Mark's cream and white sitting room, Jenny rested her knees on her chin. 'It's no good,' she repeated, for the tenth, for the twentieth time. 'He won't let me go. He says I may do as I please — I can sleep with every man in London, for all he cares. But he won't divorce me.'

'Spiteful git.' Mark looked at her. 'Or is it you? Don't you really want to leave?'

'Yes. But I have to be careful. The children — '

'You'll get custody, don't worry. Look, if he won't divorce you, you divorce *him*.'

'I can't.'

'Of course you can.'

'But I've no grounds. No real grounds, that is.'

'Find some.' Mark was pacing the floor now. 'Listen — if you loved him, I wouldn't be carrying on at you like this. I wouldn't ask you to choose. But you don't even like him!'

'I never said that.'

'You don't have to, it's obvious. Look, Jenny. He can't care for you. If he did, he'd have spent these

445

past few weeks helping you. Talking your problems through. Instead, he's just left you to get on with things, alone.

'So he's guilty of indifference, neglect, mental cruelty — you name it, he's done it. Listen, I know this bloke in chambers. He's helped me out before, and he's good. I'll take you to see him on Monday.'

'You'll do nothing of the sort!' Jenny glared at him. 'Stop pushing me around, do you hear?'

'I'm not pushing you! I'm trying to sort things out, that's all. To deal — '

'Well, I'm not a deal, am I?' Jenny's blue eyes flashed fire. 'I'm not a bit of Chinese Chippendale you're trying to flog! I'm a person, and I have a say.'

'Okay, okay. Don't lose your temper.' Mark stopped pacing. He sat down beside her. 'Don't look like that,' he said.

'Like what?'

'Hurt. Upset. Look, I'm sorry if I'm pushing you. I don't mean to.'

'All right.' Jenny shrugged. 'You can't help it, I suppose. Once a barrow boy — '

'Always a hustler. Yes, I expect you're right there.' Now, taking Jenny's hands in his, Mark looked into her eyes. 'You know I love you,' he said. 'I only want what's best for you. I'd do anything — '

'Would you? Even make me a cup of tea?'

'Even that.' Mark laughed. 'But I'd rather take you to bed.'

'Really?' Magically — for, a moment ago, she'd been so cross with him — Jenny felt the tension ebb away. It was replaced by a warm, creamy wave of desire. 'I'd like that,' she said.

'Let's go upstairs.'

'It's nice and warm in here.'

'We'll stay here, then.' Mark kissed her. 'We'll take our time today.' He loosened his tie.

Then the doorbell rang.

Mark swore. He jumped to his feet. 'If it's those bloody Mormons again,' he grumbled, 'I'll — '

'Don't answer it.' Jenny laughed at him. 'Just pretend you're out.'

'I can't do that. It might be important. A parcel or something.' Jerking open the sitting room door, Mark strode off down the hallway.

Jenny heard a muffled conversation and then, to her astonishment, the caller walked into the sitting room. He looked around him. 'Very nice,' he said, at last. 'A bit basic, but very smooth.'

Neither Mark nor Jenny spoke. Robin looked Mark up and down. 'Finished with her, have you?' he enquired. 'Had your six pennyworth for today?'

'Stop it, Robin.' Jenny stood up. 'What do you want?'

'I've come to take you home, of course. Back to where you belong.' Robin grinned. 'Madam, your carriage awaits. Or rather, my old Escort does. It's double parked, so we'll have to hurry.'

'Don't tell me what to do,' retorted Jenny. 'How did you find this house?'

'It was easy.' Rummaging in his pockets, eventually Robin produced Jenny's address book. 'M. Strafford,' he read. '24B Randall's Row, SW1.' He handed her the book. 'So — are you coming?'

'I suppose I must.' Jenny didn't want a scene

— or worse. 'Goodbye,' she said, looking up at Mark.

'Goodbye, sweetheart.' Ignoring Robin completely, Mark took Jenny by the shoulders, then kissed her on the mouth. 'I'll be in touch.'

★ ★ ★

'What were you going to do?' asked Jenny, as she and Robin drove away. 'Stick one on him?'

'Nah. Not really my style.' Robin grinned. 'He was a bit big for me to tackle.'

'So a knock-out contest between the Cockney Yobbo and the Gentleman Scholar isn't likely to be on the cards?'

'I'm afraid not.' Jerkily, Robin changed gear. 'Sorry to disappoint you. I'm well aware that seeing me get smashed to a pulp would give you the most enormous thrill.'

They turned into the main road. Now, Robin seemed determined to kill them both. Overtaking a lorry, he zigzagged down the highway, grinning as other drivers swerved out of his way and blared their horns at him.

Jenny hung on to her seat, and prayed.

They sent the children upstairs to bed and the au pair to her language class. As Jenny glanced through some letters on the hall table, Adam sidled half way downstairs again. 'Mum?' he whispered.

'What?'

'He's not very happy tonight, is he? Dad, I mean.'

'Is he ever happy?' Jenny opened a bill. 'Adam, go and do your homework. I'll be up myself soon.'

'After you've had a row, I suppose.' Adam sniffed. 'Look, Mum — you don't have to take any stick from him.'

'What do you mean?'

'Stand up for yourself.' Adam winked. 'I'll be rooting for you. Night.'

'I told you to go to bed,' growled Robin, who'd just wandered into the hall. But then, even as he spoke, a dark shape appeared against the window of the front door. The bell rang twice.

'God, we are busy tonight.' Now, Robin turned and ambled off towards the kitchen. 'You answer it,' he muttered. 'I expect it's your barrow boy, come to take you away.'

'I doubt it.' Jenny opened the front door. 'Good evening?' she began. 'What can I — '

'Mrs Langley?' demanded the girl on the step.

'Yes, that's right.'

'Dr Langley's wife?'

'Yes, but — '

'Thank God.'

The girl was distraught. Wild hair streaming, eyes flashing, her whole body was shaking. Whether she was enraged, distressed or in physical agony, however, was not at all plain. Now, as Jenny stood there bemused, she poured out such a stream of invective, complaint and abuse that her listener could only stare.

Then she began to sniff.

Then she started to cry.

'But who *are* you?' asked Jenny, trying in vain to understand. 'For a start, what's your name?'

The girl muttered something almost inaudible.

Jenny glanced behind her. 'It's a Miss Summerson, Robin,' she called. 'At least, I believe that's what she's called. She wants to see you, I think.'

'Georgina?' Robin slouched into the hallway. He stared, but then he frowned. 'Oh, Christ,' he muttered. 'That's all I need.'

'Is that Robin?' Craning her neck, the girl tried to see past Jenny and into darkness of the house. 'Dr Langley, I mean? Is he actually here?'

'Yes, he's here.' Jenny stood aside. 'You'd better come in.'

Taking the girl into the sitting room, Jenny motioned her towards the sofa. 'Well, Miss Summerson,' she began. 'I — '

'Call me Georgie. Everyone does.'

'Miss Summerson — if, as I suspect, you've come to tell me you want my husband, I don't think it's appropriate for me to call you any such thing. Do you?'

'Well, maybe not.' Fidgeting now, rather than shaking, Miss Summerson looked at Robin, who had now sloped in. 'You've told her, then?' she demanded, sharply.

'No, I haven't.' Now Robin reddened. Fascinated, Jenny watched him squirm. 'Look, Georgie. You know what I said — '

'You *said*, you'd tell her! You did! Last week, you promised — '

'It's not that simple.' Robin glared at the girl. 'Christ Almighty! Why did you come here?'

'Robin, don't be so horrible. I think it was very brave of Miss Summerson to call.' Pouring out three sherries, Jenny handed them round. 'Look, if you two want to get married — '

'Stop jumping to conclusions, Jen.' Gulping his sherry, Robin poured himself another, then tossed that back as well. 'We're going out,' he said.

'We?' asked Georgina Summerson.

'You and me.' Grabbing the girl's arm, he pulled her to her feet. 'By the way,' he muttered, as he brushed past his wife, '*don't* think of phoning that lout and asking him round.'

'Why not?'

'Because I'm going to get smashed, that's why not. When I come home, I shall be in a great grandfather of a temper. If that bastard's BMW is parked anywhere near my house, I shall slash the tyres and put a brick through the windscreen, I shall break the aerial in two and kick the paintwork to glory. Then I'll do some damage to him. Got it?'

'Yes, I think so.' Seeing that Georgina Summerson was impressed, Jenny didn't argue. Silly little twit, she thought, as the girl gazed at Robin with adoration beaming from her large brown eyes. Let her find out the hard way. I had to, after all.

36

The half term holiday came round. Bribed and cajoled by Nana Langley, who'd promised them all sorts of treats, the children went off to stay the week with Robin's parents.

While they were away, Jenny visited the Worcester Royal Infirmary, where Gareth had at last regained consciousness. 'You'll come and stay with me,' she told him firmly. 'No, Dad. Don't argue. You're to come and live with us. At least for the time being.'

Still too ill to quarrel with this determined, energetic little woman, and well aware that his discharge from hospital lay many weeks into the future, finally Gareth agreed. 'What will Robin say, though?' he enquired. For Gareth had never thought much of Robin, and the feeling was mutual. 'Won't he mind?'

'Don't you worry about Robin. He won't be around very much. He's otherwise engaged.' Delighted to see that although it would be a long-drawn-out business, Gareth's recovery was well under way, Jenny hugged him. 'Oh, Dad! I'm so glad you're getting better!' she cried.

As Jenny had promised Gareth, Robin would definitely not be around much. In fact, he left. Announcing that Jenny had become so intolerable that he couldn't stand her a moment longer, he said he was going to live with his research student, who had a flat in Sheila Gregory's house.

Theatrically, he packed a suitcase. He told Jenny he'd send for the rest of his things in due course. 'You can have a divorce,' he added, carelessly. 'I'd rather like to marry Georgie, and since I'm not a Muslim or a Latter Day Saint — '

'Is she pregnant?' interrupted Jenny.

'What if she is?'

'I just wondered, that's all.'

'Mind your own business.' Robin scowled. 'It's nothing to do with you.'

Jenny shrugged. Then, as the front door slammed behind Robin, she picked up the phone. 'That's right,' she said, 'Mr Strafford. My name is Mrs Langley. Yes, I'll hold on.'

Jenny spoke to Mark for five minutes or more. Then, glancing at her watch, she realised that if she didn't leave now, she was going to be late. 'I'll have to dash,' she said, apologetically. 'So, darling — seven o'clock tomorrow evening. Or thereabouts. Okay?'

'Okay,' Mark agreed.

★ ★ ★

Reaching the main road, Jenny flagged down a cruising taxi — which was a good omen indeed, for black cabs weren't so easy to find this far south of the river. She arrived at the house in Chelsea with time to spare. As she approached the front door, Delia opened it. 'I saw you paying off the taxi,' she explained. 'Well — don't just stand there. Come in.'

Jenny stood in the hallway. 'This is lovely,' she began, politely. Indeed, it was. Reflected from the river, the clear afternoon light made dancing patterns on the pale walls, and the whole area seemed to shimmer, as if it were under the sea.

For a few moments, Delia let her guest gaze. But then she opened a door. 'Come into the drawing room,' she invited. She led the way into a large, cream and white salon. Then, turning to Jenny, she held out her arms.

For a long, long minute, they simply held each other. Delia was an inch or two shorter than Jenny, and now, child-like, she laid her head on the younger woman's shoulder. As if Delia were in fact a child, Jenny hugged her. 'Do you want to cry?' she whispered.

'No.' Delia held Jenny tight. 'I've done all my crying. In fact, I've cried so much there are no tears left.'

'Shall we sit down?'

'If you like.' Delia let Jenny go. Then, taking her hand, she led her towards one of the large, cream-coloured sofas. 'I *would* have come to her funeral, you know,' she said. Only the faintest note of reproach was detectable in her voice. 'I would have made the effort to be there.'

'I know you would. I should have told you sooner, then asked you to come with me.' Jenny sighed. 'But there was so much to do! So much to organise. Gareth was ill, too. But — oh Delia! I'm so sorry.'

'Don't worry about it.' Delia shrugged. 'How is Gareth now?'

'Getting better. Delia?'

'Yes?'

'I'm sure he'd like a visitor from the old days.'

'Meaning me.' Glancing away, Delia bit her lip. 'I was never very nice to him, you know. I don't think — '

'He'd love to see you. I know he would.'

'Oh.' Looking up, Delia met Jenny's eyes. 'Then of course I'll go.'

The clock on the mantelpiece ticked. For a few moments, neither woman spoke. Then, Jenny broke the silence. 'Did you go to Cologne?' she enquired, but carefully. 'I mean, did you — '

'No, of course I didn't.' Delia sighed. 'Oh, darling — just imagine it! There they'd have been, all the Eisenstadts, all the respectable wives and mothers, his sisters and their husbands and children — and me. The scarlet woman. The spectre at the feast.'

'Oh, Delia! You mustn't call yourself that. You — '

'They had the works, you know. Solemn High Mass. All in Latin. In the Cathedral, of course — that would have been the only place big enough, and even then I expect half the congregation was related to him.' Delia was babbling now, almost talking to herself. 'One of his cousins is Archbishop of Cologne. Did you know that? Cardinal — oh, I can't remember the name just now, but he — '

'Delia, don't!' Jenny took her friend in her arms. She stroked her hair. 'How do you know all this?' she murmured.

'His cousin came to see me. Mr Josef Eisenstadt himself, the company chairman, he actually called on me.'

'How did he know where to find you?'

'I didn't ask. But he knew about me.' Delia shrugged. 'He was very kind, in fact. I must admit that. He wasn't at all snide, or patronising. You know, I rather liked him.'

'Oh. Well — that's good.'

'He didn't stay long. He had some tea with me, then he left. He said he'd be in touch. I don't know if he will. Jenny?'

'Yes?'

'Do you think they ought to know about you?'

'I'd wondered about that.' Jenny herself shrugged now. 'I don't think so,' she said, at last. 'Let his family remember him as they thought he was. After all, I don't need *them*. If I contact them, they might think I want — '

'Your children are his grandchildren. They have cousins whom they might like to meet.'

'I'll give it a bit more thought. I don't want to rush into anything, do I?'

'I suppose not.' Delia stood up. She squared her shoulders. 'Darling girl, I have to go to a meeting now. I'm late already. Can I drop you somewhere?'

'Aren't you having any time off work?'

'I decided not to.' Delia's smile was brave, but brittle. 'It's best to keep busy, don't you think? Where's my handbag?'

★ ★ ★

'That was very nice indeed,' said Mark, as he carried the dinner plates through to the kitchen. 'A bit of all right, in fact.'

'Thank you.' Jenny smiled at him. 'Would you like some coffee now?'

'No. Later.' Wickedly, Mark grinned. 'Now tell

me,' he whispered, 'from which catering firm was that little lot delivered? Or was it a Marks and Sparks special?'

'How dare you!' Mortally offended, Jenny stamped hard on his foot. 'My God, Mark! You're such a — '

'I was only joking!' Laughing now, Mark hugged her round the waist. 'Jenny — please! Not the other foot! I dropped a big glass paperweight on it last week, and it's still giving me hell.'

'I'll give you hell! I'll teach you to be funny with me!'

'I do love it when you're angry. Your eyes actually throw out sparks.' Mark kissed her. 'Right, then. Now I know you can cook, I have to marry you.'

'Get lost,' retorted Jenny, curtly. 'Why do I need to be married?' she demanded. 'What would I get out of it? I already have everything I want.'

'Everything?'

'Certainly. I'm a partner in an expanding business. I have my own home. I don't want to give all that up.'

'You don't have to.'

'In due course I'll have my own company, with my name on the letterhead. I'll be — '

'Didn't you hear what I said?' Mark sat down at the kitchen table. He pulled Jenny down beside him. 'You don't have to give anything up.'

'Not much. Mark, *I* don't want to be little Mrs Strafford. The famous Mark Strafford's other half.'

'You don't have to be. Keep your house. Keep your job, keep your name. You're known profession-ally as Mrs Langley, so stay Mrs Langley. Keep everything you already have. But marry me.'

'Keep everything I have, *and* marry you?'

'Yes. Listen, I've got it all worked out — '

'Oh, no. Not that again.'

'Listen, will you? You love me. So marry me. Then your children will have a man in the household, and that might be a good idea. Especially since they're at that difficult sort of age when they — '

'You could help me beat them into submission, you mean?'

'Stop interrupting. We could even have a kid of our own, perhaps. It's not too late.'

'It most certainly is!' Vehemently, Jenny shook her head. 'I'm well on my way to forty — I don't want to start all that cots, nappies and push-chair stuff again.'

'Okay. Scrap that.'

'Don't worry, I shall,' Jenny agreed. 'I saw Delia yesterday,' she went on, firmly changing the subject. 'I went to call on her. Just to have a chat.'

'Yes.' Now, Mark looked grave. 'How is she?' he asked.

'Fine.'

'Really?'

'Well — no, of course she's not fine. She's still missing Peter, naturally. But she looked well, and she's very busy, being editor of that magazine.

'She asked after my Dad. She told me she'd visit him. They were friends, you see, a long time ago. I'd like to think they could be friends again.'

'What is there to stop them?'

'Nothing, really.' Jenny sighed. 'She said she'd seen Peter's cousin. The family knew all about her, you know. They had done for years. She said Mr Eisenstadt was very kind. He told her that of course all Peter's personal things would be hers, and that the family would see she was well looked after.'

'Would she want to be looked after?'

'I don't know.' Glancing up, Jenny met Mark's eyes. 'It's odd, isn't it?'

'What is?'

'That in spite of all her successes, to be Mrs Peter Eisenstadt was all she really wanted in the end. Oh, she's done very well for herself. But I think she'd have sacrificed it all to have become Peter's wife.'

'All women want to be wives.'

'That's not true.' Jenny touched Mark's temples. 'You've gone white here,' she observed. 'Did you know?'

'I did, actually. It's stress does that. Having nobody to look after me.' Mark shrugged. 'But I'll be all right now. You're going to marry me, aren't you?'

'No.'

'I'll stop smoking.'

'It's not that.'

'What is it, then?' Taking a strand of Jenny's hair, Mark twisted it round his fingers. 'Aren't I rich enough?'

'You're a millionaire, aren't you? At any rate, you're much richer than I am.'

'I'm too stupid, then?'

'You're stupid sometimes, certainly. But that I can forgive, since I am, too.'

'Ah.' Mark sighed. 'Then it's something more basic, is it? I've grown too fat and too ugly.'

'Now don't fish for compliments.' Jenny laughed. 'You know perfectly well you're one of those tiresome men who grows even more attractive as they get older.'

'Is that right?' Now Mark beamed. 'So when I'm sixty I shall have all the rich old widows chasing me?'

'I shouldn't be at all surprised. You keep your hand in and you'll be good for another thirty years yet. Mark, I don't suppose you've lived like a monk since your divorce?'

'Who's fishing now?'

'Sorry.'

'That's okay.' Mark took her hands in his. 'So you could save me from a life of debauchery and fornication,' he whispered. 'Come on, Jen. Say you'll be my wife.'

'No.' Jenny shook her head. 'No, I shan't marry you. I shan't marry anyone.'

'You sound like your friend Delia. Just like her.'

'You've only met her once.'

'Once was enough. I've read her articles, too.' Mark kissed Jenny's fingers. 'I love you,' he said. 'I always did.'

'I love you. I never stopped loving you. I think that's enough for any man. Darling, do you think you could make us some decent coffee?'

'I didn't think you liked coffee.'

'I like that new variety they've just brought out, that expensive Colombian blend the Scandinavians buy. I've got a packet in. So will you make us a pot?'

'Certainly.' Mark stood up. 'You'll have to help

me, though. I don't know where all the stuff is.'
'Can't you find it?'
'No.' He smiled at her. 'Get up and help me look.'

THE END

We do hope that you have enjoyed reading this large print book.

Did you know that all of our titles are available for purchase?

We publish a wide range of high quality large print books including:
**Romances, Mysteries, Classics
General Fiction
Non Fiction and Westerns**

Special interest titles available in large print are:
**The Little Oxford Dictionary
Music Book
Song Book
Hymn Book
Service Book**

Also available from us courtesy of Oxford University Press:
**Young Readers' Dictionary
(large print edition)
Young Readers' Thesaurus
(large print edition)**

For further information or a free brochure, please contact us at:
**Ulverscroft Large Print Books Ltd.,
The Green, Bradgate Road, Anstey,
Leicester, LE7 7FU, England.
Tel:** (00 44) 0116 236 4325
Fax: (00 44) 0116 234 0205

Other titles in the
Ulverscroft Large Print Series:

PLAIN DEALER

William Ardin

Antique dealing has its own equivalent to 'insider trading', as Charles Ramsay finds out to his cost. Offered the purchase of a lifetime, he sees all his ambitions realised in an antique jade cup, known as the 'Loot'. But as soon as the deal is irrevocably struck he finds himself stuck with it like an albatross around his neck — unable to export it without a licence, unable to sell it at home, and in a paralysing no man's land where nobody has sufficient capital to take it off his hands . . .

NO TIME LIKE THE PRESENT

June Barraclough

Daphne Berridge, who has never married, has retired to the small Yorkshire village of Heckcliff where she grew up, intending to write the biography of an eighteenth-century woman poet. Two younger women are interested in her project: Cressida, Daphne's niece, who lives in London, and is uncertain about the direction of her life; and Judith, who keeps a shop in Heckcliff, and is a divorcee. When an old friend of Daphne falls in love with Judith, the question — as for Cressida — is marriage or independence. Then Daphne also receives a surprise proposal.